THE ANARCHISTS

▲▼▲

JOHN HENRY MACKAY

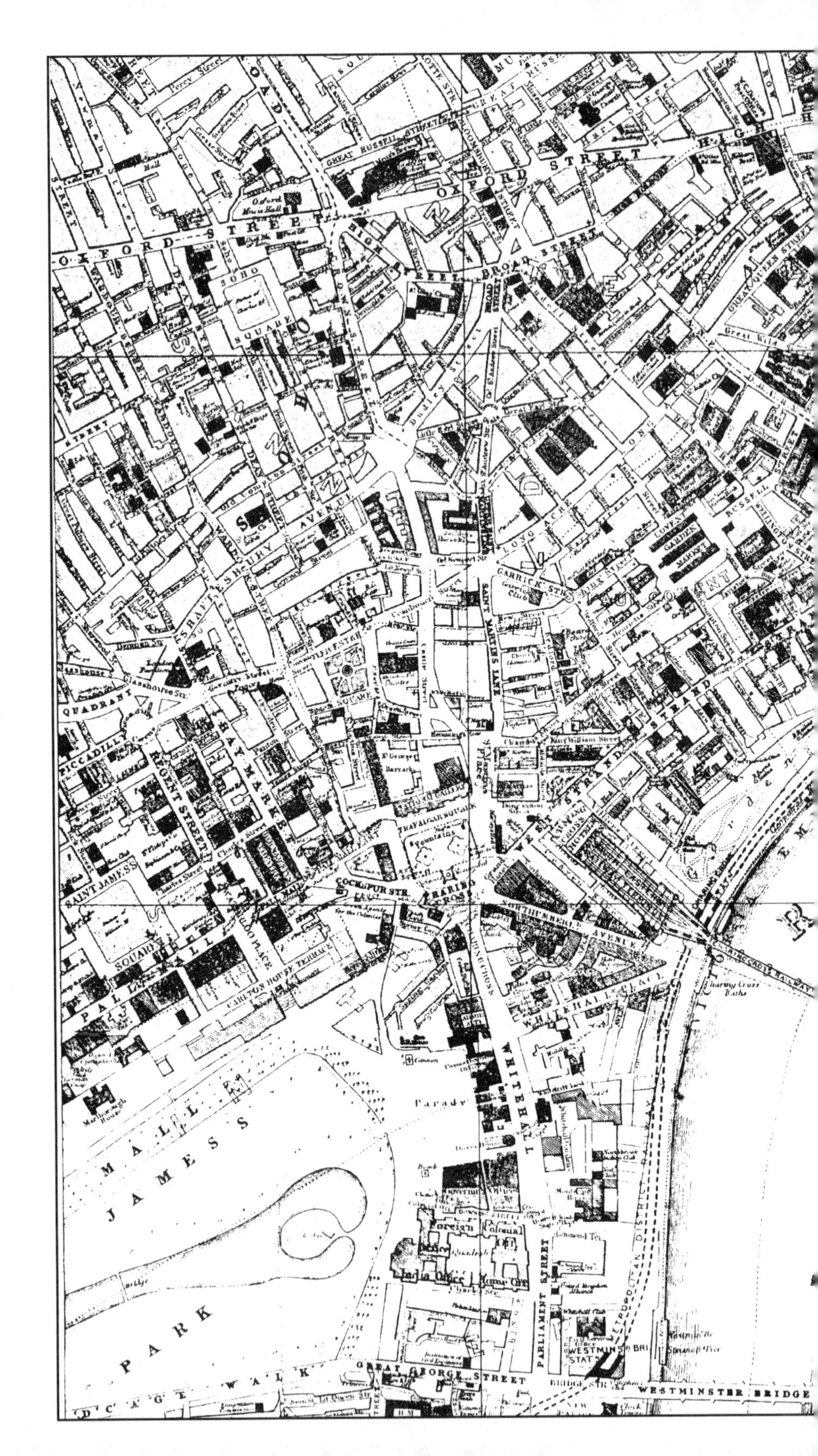

Percy Street
GREAT RUSSELL STREET
Oxford Music Hall
OXFORD STREET
HIGH STREET
BROAD STREET
SOHO
SQUARE
DEAN STREET
WARDOUR STREET
SHAFTESBURY AVENUE
LONG ACRE
GARRICK STR.
COVENT GARDEN MARKET
RUSSELL
Denman St.
Glasshouse Str.
QUADRANT
PICCADILLY
REGENT STREET
HAYMARKET
St George Barracks
TRAFALGAR SQUARE
Fountains
COCKSPUR STR.
CHARING CROSS
STRAND
CHARING CROSS HOTEL
NORTHUMBERLAND AVENUE
WHITEHALL PLACE
Charing Cross Baths
CHARING CROSS RAILWAY
SAINT JAMES'S
SQUARE
PALL MALL
WATERLOO PLACE
CARLTON HOUSE TERRACE
Marlborough House
Parade
WHITEHALL
MALL
JAMES'S
PARK
Foreign Colonial
Office
India Office
Home Office
PARLIAMENT STREET
METROPOLITAN DISTRICT RAILWAY
GREAT GEORGE STREET
BRIDGE STR.
WESTMINSTER BRIDGE
BIRDCAGE WALK

CENTRAL LONDON AT THE TIME OF *THE ANARCHISTS*

The Anarchists

A Picture of Civilization at the Close of the Nineteenth Century

by

John Henry Mackay

with a portrait of the author, and a study of his works

by Gabriele Reuter

translated from the German by George Schumm

▲▼▲▼▲▼▲▼▲▼▲

a post-centenary edition with essays by Hubert Kennedy, Edward Mornin, Sharon Presley, and Peter Lamborn Wilson

edited by Mark A. Sullivan

▲▼▲▼▲▼▲▼▲

Autonomedia Black Triangle

The Anarchists by John Henry Mackay

Autonomedia
P O Box 568
Williamsburgh Station
Brooklyn, New York 11211-0568
info@autonomedia.org
www.autonomedia.org

ISBN 1-57027-066-X

Autonomedia Black Triangle Antiauthoritarian Classics
is a publishing project of
Autonomedia, the Libertarian Book Club, and the Mackay Society.

▲▼▲▼▲▼▲▼▲

Other John Henry Mackay titles published in English

Dear Tucker (Edited & translated by Hubert Kennedy)
Fenny Skaller (Translated by Hubert Kennedy)
The Freedomseeker (Translated by Charles & Nora Alexander)
The Hustler (Translated by Hubert Kennedy)

Anarchist of Love: The Secret Life of John Henry Mackay by Hubert Kennedy
John Henry Mackay the Unique by K. H. Z. Solneman
The Storm! A Journal for Free Spirits: John Henry Mackay Festschrift Edition

Printed in the United States of America

CONTENTS

▼

John Henry Mackay's *The Anarchists*

An Introduction by Hubert Kennedy

A brilliantly accurate portrait of a particular time and place, John Henry Mackay's *The Anarchists* still moves us today with its timely message of freedom. On its publication in 1891 the book made Mackay, as he later recalled, "famous overnight"; for once in his life he was in the "right place at the right time."[1] Mackay attributed the success of *The Anarchists* to its subject matter, but it was rather the clarity of his presentation of social and philosophical views in a setting that lent immediate force to them. With regard to the chapter "Trafalgar Square," for example, it has been remarked, "There have been many accounts of 'Bloody Sunday' from that day to this, but none could be more graphic than the eyewitness account offered by Mackay."[2] Mackay was indeed an eyewitness to the events he described with such skill in *The Anarchists*. Although in fictional form—and Mackay's ability as a writer is abundantly evident—the book is not a novel. It is, if you will, a work of propaganda, but one that is a genre of its own. As such it continues to fascinate, as individuals in each new generation awaken to the perception that freedom does not come automatically in this world, indeed, is not readily at hand. Although a century old, *The Anarchists* continues to be a guide for freedomseekers. A true champion of liberty, Mackay impresses by the clarity of his insight into the human condition and inspires with his vision of individual sovereignty.

Born in Greenock, Scotland, on 6 February 1864, Mackay was only nineteen months old when his father died; his mother then returned with him to her native Germany. In his memoirs, Mackay recalled that after school and one year with a publishing house, he was an auditor at three universities, the last being in Berlin, where he "came into touch with 'literature,' the very latest, the most naturalistic, and with its more or less pure representatives." He added, with delicious sarcasm, "They were all geniuses. I felt that I did not belong and went to London."[3]

Mackay did not say why he chose London in the late spring or early summer of 1887, but the effect of his year there was indeed memorable:

> I went to London, and it was there, in London, where the great transformation in my seeing and thinking took place, which was to give my life direction and my work meaning: the immense movement, called the social, gripped me too and dragged me into its maelstrom. I began to realize that it was the question of all questions and experienced the highest that a young man in that age, which alone is able to think so feverishly and to sympathize with down to the last fiber, can experience—to be shaken to the depths under the iron grip of new perceptions.
>
> The social movement!
>
> Where to in it? To the right or to the left?
>
> There was no hesitation or wavering.
>
> I went to the left, always farther and farther to the left, until I landed there where it went no farther, and where I still stand today.
>
> The social movement!
>
> What, in contrast to it, was that other now, which likewise behaved so revolutionary, the literary one of naturalism?
>
> A tempest in a teapot!
>
> London—your unforgettable year, which gave me my book! More than that which gave me myself![4]

Mackay went to a London full of Germans, especially political refugees as a result of Bismark's Anti-Socialist Law of 1878. Mackay commented on this law in *The Anarchists*:

> He knew those multitudes whom not only the hope of better wages, but also the hope of a freer and truer life, compelled to leave their country; for how was it possible for them to live under the constant pressure of a mad law—the disgraceful law, as popular opinion named it—which presumed to murder thought, to stifle speech, and to keep watch over every movement?[5]

Mackay no doubt also came to know many from "those multitudes" individually, as he frequented their clubs and read their publications. In particular, he was familiar with the Club Autonomie, which was founded in 1885, with their first clubhouse at 32 Charlotte Street. A new clubhouse was soon needed as the membership grew rapidly; the club eventually moved to 6 Windmill Street. Mackay's characters Auban and Trupp go to the clubhouse at the end of Chapter I and again in Chapter VIII, where the new (and old) rooms are described (on page 144).[6] It was in the club's paper *Die Autonomie* that Mackay first published some of the revolutionary poems that were later collected in his *Sturm*.

Mackay likewise describes in Chapter VI a visit to "the club of the Jewish revolutionists of the East End" on Berner Street, E.C. Their Yiddish paper *Arbeter Fraint* (Mackay gives it the English name "The Worker's Friend") first appeared in 1885 and by the end of 1889 was "recognized by all Jewish unions in operation as their official organ."[7] The "Arbeter Fraint" press later published *The Anarchists* in Yiddish.[8]

"So as to come to an understanding" of the "tremendous impressions" of the year in London, Mackay "needed rest and quiet"; thus early in 1888 he "buried" himself for several months in the small town of Rorschach on the Swiss side of the Lake of Constance (Bodensee), moving in late summer to Zurich, a city he then returned to again and again.[9] *The Anarchists* was written in the years 1888 to 1891, during which Mackay was often traveling. He then took his work to his old friend J. Schabelitz in Zurich, who had already published Mackay's *Sturm* in 1888. In his memoirs Mackay tells an amusing anecdote about the completion of his work:

> In Zurich, while the messenger from the printing shop was waiting for the manuscript, in an attic room (which is not to say that I always lodged in attic rooms), a gust of wind pushed the window open and drove the pages out. With a clothesline around my body I climbed after them and fortunately fished them out of the gutter.
>
> Thus was *The Anarchists* finished.[10]

Mackay tells us in his introduction to *The Anarchists* that before completing it he had become acquainted with *Liberty* and its publisher in Boston, Benjamin R. Tucker, who was to publish the English translation of his work.[11] He also mentions there the major works of P.-J. Proudhon and Max Stirner. Proudhon had been a particular interest of Tucker, who had published his own translation of Proudhon's *What is Property?* already in 1878. Stirner had more recently become a special interest of Mackay, but he had already determined to write a biography of the philosopher of egoism. Mackay first read a mention of Stirner's *Der Einzige und sein Eigenthum* in the summer of 1887 in the British Museum during his study of the social movement, and he wished then to acquire a copy sometime. According to Mackay, "That happened, however, only a good year later. I had not again come across the name of its author."[12] The work made a "tremendous, unforgettable impression" on him. This impression may be first seen in the changes in *Sturm*. The first edition had been published in early 1888, before his reading of Stirner; the second edition of 1890 is not only dedicated to Stirner, with a dedicatory poem, but along with new poems showing the influence of Stirner, some of the older poems have been altered. *Die Autonomie* had praised the first edition of *Sturm* and also published several poems included in the later edition. According to Thomas A. Riley, "Not until February, 1890, did the paper break with Mackay definitely. Then, after a crushing review of the new individualistic edition of *Sturm*, *Die Autonomie* published nothing more of Mackay's."[13] Mackay may have regretted their lack of support, but by them he had found it in Benjamin R. Tucker and *Liberty*.

No doubt part of Mackay's pleasure in personally meeting Tucker in Europe in the summer of 1889 was the direct contact with someone who shared his appreciation of Stirner. If Mackay's American biographer, Thomas A. Riley, exaggerated the extent to which Tucker may have impressed Mackay with Stirner's ideas—as Mackay's German biographer, Kurt Zube, has pointed out[14]—Zube probably underestimated the extent of Tucker's acquaintance with Stirner. True, Tucker did not read

German, but his good friend James L. Walker did and had read Stirner's work already in the summer of 1872.[15] Thus, it is likely that Tucker and Walker discussed Stirner's ideas more than the exchange in *Liberty* in 1887 indicates. It is also possible that George Schumm, the translator of *The Anarchists* had discussed Stirner with Tucker.

At any rate, *The Anarchists* reflects the ideas of both Proudhon and Stirner. But while Proudhon is prominently mentioned in the book as an influence on the ideas of Mackay's central character Auban (page 68), Stirner is nowhere mentioned. This agrees with the Frenchman Auban's limited knowledge of German, "that language, which sounded odd and unfamiliar on his lips" (page 19); Stirner's work was not translated into French until 1900.

"London and the events of the fall of 1887 have served me as the background for my picture," Mackay tells us in his introduction, and indeed the dates are made quite precise. The story covers a period of five weeks, from 8 October to 13 November, with the final chapter perhaps a month later. Although not a novel, Mackay uses various fictional devices to heighten the reader's interest, some of which are not readily apparent to today's reader. The "action" of the story begins, for example, when the central character, Carrard Auban (representing Mackay), meets his friend Otto Trupp (modeled after Otto Rinke).[16] The latter soon begins to complain:

> "Fifteen years! And for nothing!" said the workingman, wrathful and indignant.
>
> "But why did he go so carelessly into the trap of his enemies? He must have known them."
>
> "He was betrayed!"

Contemporary readers would have known immediately that they were speaking of John Neve, who had just been sentenced by a court in Leipzig to fifteen years in prison.[17] This sets up a tension, like the structure of a German sentence, where the tension is resolved only by the final verb. Here the resolution of the tension calls for the appearance of Josef Peukert, who was widely believed to have been Neve's betrayer, and indeed Peukert does appear at the very end of the book.[18]

It is easy to read Mackay's book as fiction, yet part of its fascination is the realization of the historical exactness of Auban's observations as he walks through London. J. M. Ritchie states that "the book is really an extended walk through London's streets.... On the way Auban registers the things about the city which strike the stranger,"[19] and he mentions several, including "Charlie Coburn doing 'Two Lovely Black Eyes,'" a song that he introduced just the year before.[20] The protest meeting at South Place Institute, which is attended by Auban in Chapter II, "The Eleventh Hour," must also have been witnessed by Mackay, for it was a historic event. Hermia Oliver has confirmed Mackay's date of 14 October 1887 for it.[21]

Mackay was not an eyewitness to the Haymarket affair, but his chapter on "The Tragedy of Chicago" was carefully researched, as he indicates in his introduction. In fact, this was one of the earliest parts of the book to occupy him, for he wrote several articles on the subject, one of which was published already in 1888.[22]

The heart of the book, however, is not the moving description of these tragic events, but the discussions among Auban, Trupp, and others of the relative merits of the various directions within the socialist movement, especially the opposition of communistic and individualistic anarchism. Thus Chapter V, "The Champions of Liberty," has the central place in the book. Mackay later called attention to this in *The Freedomseeker*, his "sequel" to *The Anarchists*. There Auban again appears, this time as an older friend of that book's central character, Ernst Förster, and a brief review of his life includes:

> During the bloody days of the Chicago Haymarket affair he had lived in London, where his Sunday afternoon discussions with representatives of all shades of socialist opinion had earned him a certain fame.[23]

Indeed, those "Sunday afternoon discussions" found an immediate and repeated echo. Rudolf Rocker, who went to London in 1895 and was editor of *Arbeter Fraint* from 1898, recalled the effect of Mackay's book:

> Ninety-nine percent of the anarchists at that time in Germany had no idea at all of the original anarchist movement and its efforts.... Those comrades who were acquainted with the underground period of the movement in Germany were without exception followers of communistic anarchism. They previously knew nothing of another direction. Then in 1891 appeared in Zurich John Henry Mackay's novel *The Anarchists*, which caused a great sensation.... It came to group meetings and in the discussion evenings to endless debates over the question: Communistic or individualistic anarchism?—and not a few arrived at the view that individualism embodies the real train of ideas of anarchism.[24]

Mackay's book indeed caused quite a sensation in Germany. The Anti-Socialist Law of 1878 had been allowed to expire in 1890, so that the book could be openly distributed. (Mackay's *Sturm* had been banned under the law.) It was widely reviewed, especially by the socialist press—both in its original edition of 1891 and again in the People's Edition of 1893—and if the reviewers did not always agree with Mackay's conclusions, almost all found the work impressive and moving. As was his custom, Mackay did not respond directly to the criticism and misinterpretations of his work, but he did make a slight addition to the People's Edition, explaining in a new foreword.

> In one piece, however, I thought it my duty not to change it, but to so explain it by a few supplementary lines that it is no longer open to misunderstanding, as some have felt warranted in charging.[25]

In 1928 Mackay made an extensive revision of *The Anarchists*, but the changes were stylistic and would not essentially affect the present translation. Apropos, I think George Schumm's translation is excellent. I would have done some things differently; for example, on page 5 where Auban observes a "ten-year-old youngster who was seeking to beg a penny of the passers-by by turning wheels before them on the moist pavement." I confess that when I first read that I wondered what kind of "wheels" the boy was "turning." The German makes it clear that he was turning cartwheels. But this is a small matter, and Schumm's translation has the enormous advantage of preserving the flavor of the period.

If *The Anarchists* caused a sensation on its publication, this was not the case with the second of Mackay's "Books of Freedom", whose publication was delayed until after World War I. *The Freedomseeker* appeared in 1920 and he later wrote of it:

> Never has a book been more shamelessly passed over in silence than this book.
>
> What a contrast to the time when I was young and *The Anarchists* appeared!
>
> Then: uproar about the book and about me.
>
> Now: silence. Only silence.[26]

When Mackay died on 16 May 1933, the *New York Times* printed a report from Berlin:

> John Henry Mackay, author and poet, called in Germany an "anarchistic lyricist," is dead here at age 69. He became famous in the nineties as author of "Anarchists" and "Storm."[27]

By then all open discussion of such books had disappeared in the political upheaval of the time, and as he also had difficulty finding publishers for his purely literary works, Mackay had largely disappeared from public view. Of course there was no mention of him in the Nazi period. Nor were the immediate post-war years any kinder. It seemed that Mackay was indeed a forgotten figure.

There are several reasons for the neglect of Mackay's writings, but one of the most powerful was not just the revelation of his homosexuality, but the fact that he had unashamedly, if under a pseudonym, fought for the right of men and boys to love one another.[28] Instead of a taboo subject, Mackay saw this issue as a social question whose solution would come only with the solution of the social question in general, *i.e.*, along the individualist anarchist lines indicated by him. Mackay's views on this subject were elaborated only later and there is no direct indication of them in *The Anarchists*, but he drew the connection in *The Freedomseeker*:

> In how many ways did physical love, for example, manifest itself!—The monogamous man found protection from all the dangers of love in the haven of marriage and, instead of being grateful for his fortunate conformity, made a great fuss about the immorality of others; the man who ventured out onto the open sea captured what there was to capture and found the only real permanence in variety; a third, who loved not the opposite sex but his own sex, was persecuted and despised because he loved as *his* own nature dictated.[29]

If Mackay's engagement for the cause of homosexuals was a factor in his neglect, it was, ironically, precisely that effort which has given an impetus to the current revival of interest in him. As the modern gay liberation movement gained momentum on this side of the Atlantic and returned to Germany, where it originated, the republication of Mackay's writings on the subject sparked a revival of interest in his anarchist ideas, not only among those directly concerned in the gay cause, but also among those who, in the new climate of acceptance of homosexuality, could see without prejudice the universal application of Mackay's principle of "equal freedom for all."

In many respects, Mackay's early work *The Anarchists* remains his most compelling statement of this principle. This unique "picture" (Mackay coined the term *Kuturegemälde* for it) is both historically accurate and a guide for today; its power to move and inspire us remains undiminished by the century that separates us.

Notes:

1 John Henry Mackay, *Abrechnung: Randbemerkengen zu Leben und Arbeit* (Freiburg/Br.: Verlag der Mackay-Gesellschaft), pp. 72, 75. Unless otherwise noted, all translations from German are mine.

2 J. M. Ritchie, "John Henry Mackay's London," *New German Studies* 8 (1980), p. 215

3 Mackay, *Abrechnung,* p. 33. Mackay used the term *Literatur* in the disdainful sense of Paul Verlaine, whose expression he approvingly quoted and whom he referred to as "one of the greatest poets who ever lived." p. 18.

4 Mackay, *Abrechnung,* p. 34. Although Mackay claimed to have written one of the earliest examples in the direction of naturalism, he came to view the movement as having "stirred up so much dust in dried-up brains." p. 65.

5 John Henry Mackay, *The Anarchists: A Picture of Civilization at the Close of the Nineteenth Century,* trans. George Schumm (Boston: Benj. R. Tucker, Publisher, 1891), p. 65. [Page 41 in present edition. All other page references are to the present Autonomedia edition — Ed.]

6 The clubhouse addresses are in Andrew R. Carlson, *Anarchism in Germany, vol. 1, The Early Movement* (Metuchen, NJ: The Scarecrow Press, 1972), p. 336. Although the Windmill Street clubhouse is described in Chapter VIII of *The Anarchists* as if Auban were there for the first time, it seems likely that Mackay also had that address in mind for the end of Chapter I, since he also referred there (page 12) to a former meeting place and Windmill Street connected Charlotte Street with Tottenham Court Road. (It must be said, however, that the location described at the end of Chapter I is also consistent with the side entrace of a Charlotte Street address.)

7 William J. Fishman, *Jewish Radicals: From Czarist Stetl to London Ghetto* (New York: Pantheon Books, 1974), p. 182.

8 See "The Editions of *The Anarchists*" in this volume. Apparently Mackay did not recognize Yiddish as a separate language for he never listed this publication among the translations of his work.

9 Mackay, *Abrechnung,* pp. 35, 57.

10 *ibid.*, p. 73. Although Mackay dated his introduction to *The Anarchists* "Rome, in the Spring, 1891," he wrote to Tucker from Zurich on 19 January 1891 that the work "was placed in the hands of the printers today." See "Glad Tidings from Over Sea," *Liberty,* no. 178 (21 February 1891), p. 3.

11 Mackay inexactly states there that *Liberty* had been published "more than seven years," but in fact the paper was then in its tenth year. This was corrected in later German editions.

12 John Henry Mackay, *Max Stirner: Sein Leben und sein Werk* (Freiburg/Br.: Verlag der Mackay-Gesellschaft, 1977), p. 5. The title of Stirner's work may be translated "The Unique One and His Property," but when Benjamin Tucker published the book in 1907 in the brilliant translation of Steven T. Byington (1868-1957), it was Tucker himself who gave it the title *The Ego and His Own.*

13 Thomas A. Riley, *Germany's Post-Anarchist John Henry Mackay: A Contribution to the History of*

German Literature at the Turn of the Century, 1880-1920 (New York: The Revisionist Press, 1972), p. 53.

14 Kurt Zube [K. H. Z. Solneman], *Der Bahnbrecher John Henry Mackay: Sein Leben und sein Werk* (Freiburg/Br.: Verlag der Mackay-Gesellschaft, 1979), p. 52.

15 See James L. Walker, *The Philosophy of Egoism* (Colorado Springs, Colo.: Ralph Myles Publisher, 1972), p. 62.

16 See "Some Personalities in The Anarchists" in this volume for the identification of these and other unnamed characters in the book.

17 Mackay made a small chronological error here, for Neve's trial ended on 10 October 1887; thus Trupp could not have known the outcome two days earlier. Another small slip occurs on page 129, where Auban says "last Sunday" when he meant "Sunday before last" or "Sunday of last week."

18 In the case of Peukert, Mackay has deliberately changed the chronology, presumably to tighten the "action" of his story. Peukert left London at the end of 1887, to return briefly after over two years in Paris and Bilbao, Spain. He then left for New York. In the final chapter of *The Anarchists* these two departures from London have been compressed into one. Mackay actually met Peukert during his Parisian exile. (See Carlson, pp. 372, 391.)

19 Ritchie, p. 208.

20 Charlie Coburn was the stage name of Colin Whitton McCallum (1852-1945), a cockney comedian of Scottish descent. His song *The Man Who Broke the Bank at Monte Carlo* is perhaps better known, but was introduced only in 1890, after the period described by Mackay.

21 Hermia Oliver, *The International Anarchist Movement in Late Victorian London* (London: Croom Helm, 1983), p. 47. In addition to the speakers mentioned by Mackay, she also names Stepniak, George Standing, and G. B. Shaw. Later, on page 73 of *The Anarchists*, this meeting place is apparently referred to as Finsbury Hall.

22 John Henry Mackay, *Acht Opfer des Classenhasses* (Zürich: Mitgliedschaft deutscher Socialisten, 1888).

23 John Henry Mackay, *The Freedomseeker: The Psychology of a Development*, trans. Charles and Nora Alexander (Freiburg/Br.: Verlag der Mackay-Gesellschaft, 1983), p. 158.

24 Rudolf Rocker, *Johann Most: Das Leben eines Rebellen* (Berlin: Verlag "Der Syndikalist" Fritz Kater, 1924), p. 383.

25 From the preface to the People's Edition of *The Anarchists*, as given (presumably translated by George Schumm) in *Liberty*, no. 281 (24 February 1894):

> 11. Since the present edition is a translation of the original German edition, the changes may be noted here. There are two: 1) On page 84 Auban makes the statement: "Every other word you speak is abolition. That means forcible destruction." In later editions he adds: "It is also my word. Only I mean by it: dissolution." 2) On page 84 Auban asks the rhetorical question: "But what do you understand by free love?" In later editions his answer is preceded by: "What else can you understand by it, if you are consistent enough to apply the principle of brotherhood—as you represent it in the devotion to and renunciation of labor—also to that field, than:"

[These additions have been included in the present edition — Ed.]

26 Mackay, *Abrechnung*, pp. 93-94.

27 *New York Times*, 23 May 1933, p. 22:1.

28 Mackay's writings under the pseudonym Sagitta were all put on the Nazi list of forbidden books. But it should also be noted that the post-war Adenauer regime in West Germar.y was hardly more tolerant of homosexuals than the Nazis had been.

29 Mackay, *The Freedomseeker*, p. 143.

Return to the Nineteenth Century

Peter Lamborn Wilson

I ADMIRE JOHN HENRY MACKAY to the point of joining a Society dedicated to propagating his ideas and writings. The volume you hold in your hands is, in part, the result of that admiration, and the work of the John Henry Mackay Society, and its founder, Mark Sullivan. But whence this interest in the dusty old tomes of 19th century anarchism?

Mackay's real originality lies in his impeccable application of anarchist philosophy and psychology to the problem of sexuality. With the possible exception of Emma Goldman no other anarchist of the late 19th-early 20th century made the simple step of declaring that all non-coercive (*i.e.*, mutually consensual) forms of love belong essentially to the freedom of the individuals who define their happiness thereby. Mackay alone realized that no other view of the matter will stand against anarchism's critique of power as "morality." Unfortunately the other anarchists of his time were blinded by Consensus-trance, or else too timid to speak. They could accept "free love" for man and woman; their "sex radicalism" went no further.

By now, of course, we might logically expect that anarchists—at least!—have been able to understand Mackay and his plea on behalf of "other" sexualities. Despite the neo-puritanism and AIDS-panic of the 1980s and 90s (eerie replicas of the Victorian moralism and syphillis-panic of the 1880s and 90s), we might expect that the anarchists alone would resist all hysterical reaction and the culture of body-hatred that goes with it. Even if the rest of the Left capitulated (and the Left is nothing if not "moralistic"), anarchists alone would refuse to betray the ideals of the "Sexual Revolution." Anarchists would still defend...*love*. Right?

Wrong.

During a recent exchange of letters on the subject of "intergenerational sensuality" printed in several issues of *Anarchy: A Journal of Desire Armed*, it became obvious that more than half the correspondents had allowed their minds to be warped by Consensus Values—or unconscious dread of the Witchhunt—and were prepared to denounce all love between older and younger persons as "exploitation." Thus the only difference between Christian bigots and anarchist bigots is that the latter condemn love for being politically incorrect. Rational evidence and authentic testimony to the contrary will not "convert" such unthinking reactionaries—as Mackay also found, to his bitter sorrow. His fellow anarchists ignored or condemned him. His "Sagitta" project, a series of pamphlets on the "Nameless Love," sank without much trace. And since his apparent suicide in 1933—cheating the Nazis, who would have killed him—not much has changed. Victorian sex morality pervades the totality of our *fin-de-siecle* discourse; the 19th century refuses to die.

Mackay himself rediscovered and propagated the work and ideas of a still-earlier anarchist, Max Stirner—generally acknowledged as the key philosopher of Individualist Anarchism, the brand of anarchism adhered to by Mackay. At one time the anarchist movement included a great number of Stirnerites, from the rational and pacific Benj. Tucker to the crazy bandits of the Bonnot Gang. In the 1880s and 90s the main ideological split in anarchism divided anarcho-communists from anarcho-individualists. Mackay's *roman à clef*, herewith republished in a new, definitive edition, still steams and creaks with the intensity of the debate. Which was "absolute"? the self or the other? ego or group? And what were the implications for the Revolution in which all believed with millenarian faith, and longed to see? Organization? Direct Action? Propaganda of the deed? Attentat? Labor agitation?

We might expect that anarchism would eventually manage to isolate and overcome the false dichotomy in which this debate was rooted. Even at the time there were anarchists who were able to wrap their minds around both Stirner and Kropotkin, "anarchist-without-adjectives" like Voltairine de Cleyre, Emma Goldman, Errico Malatesta—or synthesizers like the "Great Pantarch" Stephen Pearl Andrews—or somewhat later, Gustav Landauer. In the 1950s the Lettrists and Situationists developed a synthesis of "Marx and Stirner" which sought to reconcile the individual's pleasure with the playful synergy of the group. A synthesis of Charles Fourier and Nietzsche would belong to the same category of "post-ideological" construction.

In such a context, absolute categories presented as dichotomies are considered semantic traps, camouflaged with bad consciousness. If Nietzsche's theory of the individual (the Free Spirit) and Fourier's theory of the group (the Passional Series) are read as complementary rather that as contradictory, certain dissonances resolve themselves into strange new harmonies. Self and Other, no longer domineering the cognitive horizon as absolute of categorical imperatives, are now seen as dyadic energies rather than opposing forces. We have here something like a Taoist dialectics, snakily sinuous and sportingly ambiguous rather than "scientific" and sober. Here there is room for Michel Serres's third speaker, the Hermetic "parasite," the *bothland*. Here language no longer nails us into boxes; nor has language lost its "meaning." Instead, we have arrived at a poetics of self and other in which each completes the other's meaning.

So—we might expect that *by now* anarchism would have resolved the fight between Individualism and Communism, and arrived at a viable synthesis, what Bob Black calls "Type 3 Anarchism." But...apparently not. A New York anarchist group recently held a debate on the subject—all the old shibboleths were dusted off and trotted out...someone whispered to me, "This is like 1971!"—but he should have said "like 1887!" The debate sounded like a scene out of Mackay's *The Anarchists*...ah, will the 19th Century go on for ever and ever?

Those who *do* know the Past are condemned to watch while other idiots repeat it over and over again.

And so, oddly enough, *The Anarchists* remains a book which needs to be re-read, even now in this enlightened age—which is not so very different from London, 1887 (air pollution, hideous poverty, police oppression, class hatred, racism...)—despite our pretentions to a post-Industrial "Information Economy"—and to CyberGnosis, the transcendence of the body through Virtual Reality. Factories are still belching out crap somewhere, and some anarchists still need to be told that "Work" is an illusion, that "Revolution" means *another turn of the screw*, that martyrdom is merely the revenge of the terminally resentful, that "freedom" is not an abstract noun.

To read Mackay's prose with enjoyment we must remind ourselves that *this is still the 19th century*—only TV and LSD have been added.

To read Benj. Tucker's original American edition helps us—typography is a kind of time machine—to drift back into the pre-electronic pacing and language of a writer whose lyrics were set to music as *leider* by Richard Strauss. Mackay constantly reveals the particular slant of a double-barrel writer. Interestingly, one might consider him as a kind of mirror-image of B.Traven, who lost German and adopted English. Like Traven, Mackay never intended his anarchist narratives to be read as novels, but rather as "bastard" or translational hybrid forms made of narrative and polemic—a balance later perfected in drama by Brecht. (One might mention Céline here—too bad he was a fascist.) Traven and Mackay wrote long *rants* in the form of stories, although Traven based himself on the structure of the adventure novel, while Mackay used more classical and "literary" models. And "Traven" of course was in reality the Stirnerite anarchist Ret Marut, who escaped certain death in the fall of the Munich Soviet of 1919 and created his new identity in Mexico. Ret Marut and Mackay probably knew each other; certainly they knew each other's work.

Finally, *The Anarchists* may be read as a fascinating glimpse behind the atmospheric facade created by Mackay's contemporaries, better-known writers like Arthur Conan Doyle and Joseph Conrad. Their fog-bound gas-lit London was haunted by the Evil Poor, and by the agents of Chaos, the criminal masterminds, the mad bombers and conspirators of the Social. Their view of the era has prevailed, Conan Doyle's in pop fiction and other media, Conrad's in the Temple of the Canon of EngLit. "Civilization" is represented by the values of the oppressor class (as Traven noted about Conrad), and by their champion, the Detective (the solar deity and folkloric hero of the 19th century). In Mackay's text however we suddenly find ourselves *inside* the menacing wall of fog and poverty which for Holmes and the Secret Agent represents the *other* London, the fearful erotic Jewish-cockney-immigrant-criminal realm of Fu Manchu's Limehouse. Now we see the same ancient city through a new perspective—no less romantic in its way, no less 19th Century—but inside-out and upside-down. The dark conspirators with their funny accents and shabby overcoats...where are they?

It is no longer the Other. It is I.

New York City
Vernal Equinox
1993

Some Personalities in *The Anarchists*

Hubert Kennedy

In his introduction to *The Anarchists* Mackay wrote: "The names of living people have been omitted by me in every case with deliberate intent; nevertheless the initiated will almost always recognize without difficulty the features that have served me as models." A century later it is not so easy to identify them, and I have been able to do so only in a few cases. I present them here in the order of their appearance in the book.

Page 3, "a woman who allows herself to be called": Queen Victoria (1819-1901) assumed the throne on the death of her father King William IV in 1837.

Page 3, "a man coming from the direction of Waterloo Station": Carrard Auban, the central character of the book, is the spokesman for Mackay and thus may be immediately identified with him.

Page 13, "a man of about forty years, in the not striking dress of a laborer": Otto Trupp, Auban's friend and opponent, has been identified as Mackay's acquaintance Otto Rinke (1853-1899) by both his German and American biographers.[1] "Rinke was born in Schmiegel in Posen, the son of a forest official. He was a huge man and was often referred to as Big Otto. By nature he was argumentative, gruff, and heavy fisted. Until 1890 he had the respect, but not always the love of those in the anarchist movement." Rinke helped form the German-speaking Anarchist Communist Party in Switzerland. He began publishing *Der Rebell* there, then moved to London, where the paper was superseded in 1886 by *Die Autonomie.* Hounded by the English police, Rinke moved to the United States and settled in St. Louis, Missouri, where he died in 1899 "at the age of 46, by choking to death on a piece of meat which he was eating in haste in order to get to an anarchist meeting."[2]

Page 15, "he mentioned a name": John Neve, a central figure in the German anarchist movement of the 1880s. On 10 October 1887 he was sentenced to fifteen years in prison (where he died on 8 October 1896).[3]

Page 25, "a woman in a simple, dark dress": This is Gertrud Guillaume-Schack (1845-1903). In 1880 she founded the *Kulturbund* that was to be the first German branch of the International Federation for the Abolition of State Regulation of

Prostitution, which was founded in England by the social reformer Josephine Butler. When in early 1885 a law was proposed in the Reichstag that was supposed to protect women workers, but would in fact have the effect of putting thousands out of work, Guillaume-Schack called a protest meeting and founded in Berlin a "Union for the Protection of the Interests of Women Workers." This was forbidden by the state, and when she founded a similar union in Hamburg in November, the state used the circumstance of her Swiss citizenship (a result of a four-month marriage to a Swiss artist) as an excuse to deport her in July 1886, when she went to England. There she frequented Friedrich Engels' house until she became aware how little he took seriously her engagement for the women's question and above all for the situation of prostitutes, and that he could not accept her sympathy for anarchism.[4]

Page 26, "a pale man in the dress of a High Church clergyman": This may have been Stewart D. Headlam (d. 1924), an active Christian socialist of the period. Mackay may have mistakenly thought he was deprived of his living.[5]

Page 26, "a little woman dressed in black": "This is clearly Charlotte Wilson, the first editor of the London anarchist-communist paper *Freedom*, which began publication in 1886. This is clinched by the lines at the bottom of page 32, 'She had probably asked for some names and notes for her little four-paged monthly paper,' which *Freedom* was at that time."[6] Born Charlotte Mary Martin in 1854, the daughter of a surgeon, she attended the institution at Cambridge which a few years later became Newnham College. After leaving university, she married Arthur Wilson, a stockbroker. She was the editor of *Freedom* from its first number in October 1886 until her retirement in 1895.[7]

Page 29, "a little man, in a long coat, with a long, heavy beard": This is, of course, Peter Kropotkin (1842-1921). He lived in England from 1886 until 1914. If Charlotte Wilson was the real organizing force of *Freedom*, "Kropotkin provided its ideological inspiration, as he continued to do until his break with the Freedom Group over his support for the Allies in the First World War."[8]

Page 31, "a man who was mentioned as one of the regenerators and most active promoters of industrial art": "This can only be William Morris."[9] Poet and artist, William Morris (1834-1896) also worked as architecture and studied the practical arts of dyeing and carpet weaving. He helped found the Socialist League in 1884 and edited its organ *The Commonweal* from 1885 until he was deposed in 1889. After leaving the League in 1890 his disillusionment became apparent, although he lectured to the Hammersmith Socialist Society until the year of his death.

Page 32, "a strange old man whose face certainly no one ever forgot after having once seen it": This is "the astonishing Dan Chatterton who published forty-two numbers of the wildly individual *Chatterton's Commune—the Atheist Communistic Scorcher* from 18 September 1884 until his death in 1895."[10] Chatterton was a well-known figure of the day and even became a main character in Richard Whiting's novel *No. 5 John Street*, where he has the name "Old 48."

Page 76, "a young student of social science, a German poet": It is possible that this is also Mackay.

Page 129, "the man in New York, who was incessantly clamoring for the head of some European prince": Johann Most (1846-1906) was a foremost exponent of "propaganda by deed." His journal *Freiheit* was first published in London in 1879 and then in New York from his arrival there in 1882.

Page 143, "in the person of one of its first and most active champions": Johann Most. (See the note to page 129.)

Page 174, "a man who had been one of the most feared and celebrated personalities in the revolutionary movement of Europe": Josef Peukert (1855-1910), one of the founders of the Club Autonomie in London in 1885, was suspected of having betrayed his comrade John Neve to the German police in early 1887. He left London in the late fall of 1887, going first to Paris, later to Spain, and in 1890 to the United States.[11]

Notes:

1. Thomas A. Riley, *Germany's Post-Anarchist John Henry Mackay: A Contribution to the History of German Literature at the Turn of the Century, 1880-1920* (New York: The Revisionist Press, 1972), p. 42; Kurt Zube [K. H. Z. Solneman], *Der Bahnbrecher John Henry Mackay: Sein Leben und sein Werk* (Freiburg/Br.: Verlag der Mackay-Gesellschaft, 1979), p. 41.

2. See Andrew R. Carlson, *Anarchism in Germany, vol. 1, The Early Movement* (Metuchen, NJ: The Scarecrow Press, 1972), pp. 78 and 97.

3. See Carlson, chapter XI, esp. p. 369.

4. See "Gertrud Guillaume-Schack," in *Hermes Handlexikon: Geschichte der Frauenemancipation* (Düsseldorf, 1983), pp. 121-123, and "Gertrud Guillaume-Schack," in *Grosse Frauen der Weltgeschichte* (Klagenfurt, 1987), p. 201. I am grateful to Claudia Schoppman for this identification and for copies of the references. The birth year, 1845, is given in Hermia Olivier, *The International Anarchist Movement in Late Victorian London* (London: Croom Helm, 1983).

5. I am grateful to S. E. Parker for this suggestion.

6. Personal communication from S. E. Parker, to whom I am very grateful for this identification.

7. See John Quail, *The Slow Burning Fuse: The Lost History of the British Anarchists* (London: Granada Publishing, 1978), esp. pp. 56 and 206.

8. George Woodcock, *Anarchism: A History of Libertarian Ideas and Movements*, 2nd ed. (New York: Viking Penguin, 1986), p. 375.

9. J. M. Ritchie, "John Henry Mackay's London," *New German Studies* 8, no. 3 (Autumn 1980), pp. 203-219, here p. 213.

10. Quail, p. 61. I am grateful to S. E. Parker for this identification.

11. This identification was made already by Zube, who wrote that Mackay had a passing acquaintance with Peukert (Zube, p. 41). See Carlson, Chapter XI, for a full exposition of the Neve-Peukert affair.

John Henry Mackay the Anarchist:
His Message to Libertarians Today

Sharon Presley

As I sat down to write this essay, I reflected upon the time I first discovered John Henry Mackay in a wonderful anthology called *Patterns of Anarchy* (Anchor Press, 1966. The editors called the excerpt from Mackay "...probably the handsomest piece in the collection," and they were right. I was enchanted by the excerpt and, when the 1972 library reprint of *The Anarchists* became available, I lost no time in buying it. Years later, when I had the opportunity to obtain a first edition of the 1891 paperback, I felt privileged and very lucky. Over the years, Mackay has continued to hold a high place in my esteem, sharing that special spot with only a handful of other anarchists—Lysander Spooner, Emma Goldman, and Voltairine de Cleyre.

The reasons for this esteem are many—Mackay's insight into the contradictions of state socialism and communist anarchism and his understanding of human nature, both of which give his thought continuing relevance today; the lush and moving eloquence of his writing style, which contributes to the pleasure of reading Mackay; his passionate but logical defense of individual sovereignty and individual liberty, which makes him an inspiration to read. Mackay possessed a rare balance of the rational and the emotional, logic and compassion—the mind of a philosopher, the heart of a sage, the soul of a poet. A combination no less rare among anarchists, alas, than any other group of people, but one exquisitely realized in John Henry Mackay.

Mackay's vision, as presented in *The Anarchists*, is strikingly prophetic. He foresaw the inevitability of state socialism leading to destructive terrorism, as recently uncovered information in the once Communist-bloc countries like Rumania have demonstrated even to the previously blind. He foresaw the negative consequences of concentrating power in one big monopoly—the State, as the wretched economic conditions of the former Soviet Union so painfully demonstrate. He foresaw the negative consequences of ideology that imposes what people *should* be instead of allowing people to be what they *choose* to be. Insistence on "morality" instead of choice leads to the imposition of force on people's private lives, as a galaxy of modern examples from the terrorism of communism and fascism to the urban orgy of violence resulting from anti-drug laws so pointedly demonstrate.

Mackay's penetrating insight even led him to an early anarchist-feminist critique of marriage. Like Emma Goldman and Voltairine de Cleyre, his contemporaries, he also saw legal marriage as a trap, both economic and psychological, a kind of mutual exploitation without love. Mackay's call for independence is entirely compatible with modern feminist analysis and, in fact, is ultimately even more radical because it dares question the role of the State in what is a private concern between two individuals.

The relevance of Mackay to issues *within* the modern anarchist movement, however, was what first struck me about Mackay's insight. My first encounter with Mackay, the excerpt in *Patterns of Anarchy,* addressed itself to his criticism of communist anarchism and its enamourment with its anti-property position. With piercing logic, Mackay went right to the heart of the matter—if you really are an anarchist, you must accept the right of individuals to make noncoercive choices even when the choices are distasteful or abhorrent to you. Having met my share of intolerant people who call themselves anarchists but seem to hate capitalism more than they hate the State, Mackay's argument struck an especially responsive chord. If an anarchist, by definition, believes in individual sovereignty and therefore, individual choice, then if individuals choose to own private property and want to engage in mutually agreed upon exchange of goods with each other, they have that right. Many so-called communist anarchists, like Mackay's character, Trupp, refuse to accept the idea that, "comes the millennium," someone *might* want to make what is to them such a distasteful choice. They adamantly insist that "everyone" would choose a communalist society. With unrelenting logic, Mackay's protagonist, Auban, forces Trupp to face the possibility that someone might make the choice to engage in private exchange. And then what? Your answer determines whether you're really an anarchist or not.

Unfortunately, Mackay's argument is still painfully relevant and very much needed today. The narrow ideologues and naively, rigidly intolerant fools are still around, as I found out at a 1989 West Coast Anarchist Conference in San Francisco. The handful of individualist anarchists like myself, as well as the IWW contingent (for whom I had great respect) banded together in self-defense against dozens of self-appointed anarchists who tried to write *us* (the individualists and syndicalists) out of the movement as if *they* owned it! All because we didn't conform to *their* idea of what *they* imagined anarchism to be...

But the anarchist philosophy will always survive the fools. There will always be a remnant who understand the true spirit and meaning of anarchism, who will passionately guard and cherish the ideals of individual sovereignty, as Mackay did. He understood that anarchism is not defined in terms of a particular economic system or a particular organization of society but only in terms of individual liberty and individual sovereignty. Mackay, who was a poet as well as a novelist, summed up the spirit of the anarchist philosophy eloquently in his poem:

"I am an Anarchist! Wherefore, I will
Not rule, and also ruled I will not be!"

This concept of individual choice is the leitmotif that suffuses Mackay's book like a brilliant white light, shining the beacon of love of liberty and passionate devotion to individual sovereignty into the dark corners of human misery and misbegotten ideologies of late 19th century London. With an elegant logic that foreshadows the great French existentialist and resister to authority, Albert Camus, Mackay asserts that the ultimate choice is to either accept or reject individual liberty. In his anti-war essay, *Neither Victims Nor Executioners* (Liberation Press, 1963), Camus posits an analogous existential choice: "All I ask is that, in the midst of a murderous world, we agree to reflect on murder and to make a choice. After that, we can distinguish those who accept the consequences of being murderers themselves or the accomplices of murderers, and those who refuse to do so with all their force and being. Since this terrible dividing line does actually exist it will be a gain if it is clearly marked." Mackay delineates a similar dividing line in the realm of political philosophy.

Mackay's insistence on the philosophy of individual choice demonstrates his remarkable insight into human nature. One of the most consistent patterns to emerge from the psychological research literature of the last several decades is the psychological importance to the individual of perception of choice and perception of control. Individuals are more psychologically healthy and productive, less destructive to themselves and others if they believe that they are in control of their lives and see themselves as having choices rather than being helpless pawns.[1] Mackay's belief that people must be free to make their own choices is also consistent with a large body of literature in counseling, clinical psychology and human growth therapy as is his insight into the consequences of poverty and violence on children. As his vignettes of the slums of London imply, children bred in violence and misery, children raised without love, turn into hateful, violent adults.[2]

Another recurring theme, one as relevant for libertarian and anarchist philosophy today as in Mackay's time, is the theme of egoism versus self-sacrifice. The denunciation of communism for championing self-sacrifice is a familiar theme in the literature of the current libertarian movement, and most especially, in the works of novelist/philosopher Ayn Rand. But Rand's "enlightened self-interest" and denunciation of "altruism" (as she defines the word) and indeed, the brisk "me-tooism" so prevalent in the libertarian movement, has a very different flavor than Mackay's egoism. What Mackay's examination embraces that is missing from Rand's expositions and from much (but not all) libertarian rhetoric is true, heart-felt compassion for the wretched, miserable, downtrodden victims of the coercion of the State. Though libertarians, Rand, and Mackay all believe in principle that liberty is the key to ending poverty and economic misery, the concern for victims of the State is more than just an abstraction for Mackay.

Page after page of heart-rending descriptions of the wretched, sub-human conditions of the poor in turn-of-the-century London and the devastating effects on the minds and souls of the poor are moving in a way Rand's prose never is. Though Mackay too denounces self-sacrifice, he clearly does not believe that an egoist position precludes the possibility of genuine compassion for others—the "children without parents, without hope" barely clothed in dirty rags, wallowing in "misery, hunger and depravity" (not unlike conditions today in many third world countries or even in our own ghettoes and slums), the young women who see no hope for survival except to sell their bodies (not unlike too many young women in our urban cities), the body of a homeless man who had starved to death, even the pain of seeing young children so psychologically and morally corrupted by their misery that they take pleasure in torturing a cat.

Not abstractions, not airy principles, but harsh, painful reality. A reality that Mackay sees clearly as caused by the State and its coercive stranglehold on the economy. Like Rand and the libertarians, Mackay understands that the solution to human economic misery is to reduce (Mackay would say "abolish") the authority (ability) of the State to grant special privileges to the powerful few. But, unlike Rand and so many libertarians, he does not distance himself from the consequences to individuals, does not deny the compassion and concern that any decent person should feel for one's fellow human beings damaged by coercion and corruption beyond their control. How different is Mackay's pain from the economic opportunism of a Walter Block, who blithely asserts in his book, *Defending the Undefendable* (Fleet Press Corp. 1976), that prostitutes choose to sell their bodies because it's their most "rational" economic alternative (so that makes it all OK). Yes, they certainly have the right to make that choice but does this abstract "right" in any way address the social reality of conditions that would make these poor women perceive themselves as having no other choice? This callous indifference to social psychological reality and personal emotional reality is unfortunately quite pervasive among libertarians today. And unless they stop playing their little intellectual games and start caring about the real plight of real people as Mackay did, libertarianism will go nowhere. Mind without heart is no more humane than heart without mind.

This split between thought and feeling, between reason and emotion, is one that continues to plague the modern libertarian movement, due, at least partly, to the influence of Rand. Though Rand asserts that reason and emotion are not contradictory, one senses in her writings a lurking suspicion of the compassionate, nurturing, kindly emotions. I personally have never imagined reason and logic to be "cold" as so many people do but if anyone's logic is "cold," it is certainly Rand's. Not because it is necessarily wrong but because it is so intellectually distanced from its companion—feeling and emotion—and from the real-life consequences of the principles.

It is Mackay, not Rand, who lives and breathes the true balance of reason and emotion. His logic tells him that misery and poverty are a result of the behemoth State, the special privileges of the greedy and powerful enacted through the vicious monopoly of the State. And co-existing with this reasoning, as a *logical* extension of this conclusion, are his feelings of compassion for the victims of the State.

In no way does Mackay's compassion compromise his egoism. Though compassion per se is not directly discussed, Mackay takes it for granted that such emotions are reasonable and appropriate.

A contemporary libertarian position that also reflects this balance of reason and emotion, of love of liberty and compassion, is Dr. Peter Breggin's work on conflict resolution. His Three-Dynamic theory proposes that there are three basic methods of resolving conflicts: coercion, liberty and love. The dynamic of coercion sees individuals as objects to be involuntarily subjected to arbitrary force. The dynamic of liberty sees individuals as agents or doers who engage in voluntary exchange. Value is *earned*: the emotions are esteem and respect. The dynamic of love sees individuals as having *inherent* value and worth. The emotions are sharing, nurturing, caring and compassion. Libertarians, as well as Rand, have incisive critiques of the dynamic of coercion and brilliant defenses of the dynamic of liberty but, as Dr. Breggin points out, they have given little or no attention to the dynamic of love. He proposes that reverence for self entails a reverence for others, that kindness, empathy, generosity and compassion are crucial ingredients in our personal, social and political lives.

Though Breggin's discussion of "love" or reverence for others is far more explicit than Mackay's, the spirit of Mackay's "love" permeates the book. By example, by what he chooses to describe, Mackay communicates his concern for humanity and reverence for life. Both Breggin and Mackay demonstrate that it is possible to have a consistent defense of individual sovereignty and liberty—to be consistent individualists without succumbing to the "looking out for number one" mentality that the Left accuses libertarians of having (unfortunately with justification in many cases). Both demonstrate that the either/or of individualism/altruism is a false dichotomy, that one can be compassionate and loving without compromising egoism and individualism.

The modern reader will thus find in *The Anarchists* pleasure, inspiration and challenge. You will delight in the literary feast that Mackay offers you—the beauty, poetry and elegance of his writing style. You will be intoxicated by the heady, exhilarating clarion call to the defense of individual sovereignty. And, if you, modern reader, are also willing to search your heart and mind, you may be called upon to expand your understanding of justice, rights, and individualism.

For those of you who are not anarchists or libertarians but who yearn for justice, Mackay asks you how justice is possible for individuals when using the coercion of the State.

For those of you who are socialists, marxists, or communist anarchists who confuse State corporate capitalism with true free enterprise and demand an end to *all* private property, Mackay asks you how you can reconcile your compassion for the poor and downtrodden with your denial of liberty and rights.

For those of you who are libertarians, who believe in theory that reason and emotions are not contradictory but who have little compassion, Mackay asks you implicitly how you can integrate your yearning for justice with feelings of caring.

Feast in the literary and philosophical delight that is *The Anarchists* and be the wiser for it.

NOTES

1. For discussion of the consequences of lack of perceived control, see H. Lefcourt, *Locus of Control,* Lawrence Erlbaum Publishers, 1976; R. deCharms, *Personal Causation,* Academic Press, 1968; M Seligman, *Helplessness,* Freeman, 1975. Also see any contemporary social psychology textbook.
2. The landmark study, *The Authoritarian Personality* by Adorno, Frenkel-Brunswick, Levinson, and Sanford is an early study (1950) demonstrating the warping effects of parental violence and rigid control on children. In recent decades, the studies of developmental psychologists, Diane Baumrind and Martin Hoffman, further support the idea that loving families where reason and autonomy are the preferred child-rearing method, as opposed to physical punishment, produce highly moral, psychologically healthy children. A vast literature on the devastating effects of childhood physical and sexual abuse also exists.

An Underground Classic Seen in a Different Light

An Exploration of *The Anarchists* by the Editor

Why republish a now obscure anarchist classic by a one-time celebrated but now almost forgotten anarchist author? This is a question I asked myself many times before deciding to seek a publisher for a centenary edition of the English translation of John Henry Mackay's *Die Anarchisten.* What value did I see in the book? In addition to its historic value, I answered myself, it is the enduring, almost archetypal, themes expressed in the work that make its republication worthwhile: the struggle of the oppressed against their oppressors, of the individual against the group, of society against the state, of the creative mind against the fixed ideas of organized tradition.

When it made its first appearance in 1891, the *New York Morning Herald* said "*The Anarchists* is one of the few books that have a right to live.... For insights into life and manners, for dramatic strength, for incisiveness of phrase, and for cold, pitiless logic, no book of this generation equals it." (As quoted in *Liberty*, December 12, 1891). That generation has long since departed the scene, yet it is my conviction that the book that made Mackay known then has the right to do so now.

Discovering The Anarchists

It was well over twenty years ago that I purchased a copy of the Revisionist Press 1972 reprint copy of *The Anarchists* from the new Laissez-Faire Books on Mercer Street in New York City. I took it with me on a sort of coming-of-age journey from small-town Connecticut to lush Hawaii and the deserts and mountains of the North American West—a far cry from the Victorian London of John Henry Mackay.

I had recently discovered the wonderful radical individualist anarchist tradition of which Mackay was a shining star, along with such other luminaries as Benjamin R. Tucker, Stephen Pearl Andrews, and Max Stirner. These were the heroes who accompanied me on my pilgrimage to discover the world—and myself. I could not help but identify with young Carrard Auban, Mackay's protagonist, whose vision of life felt very much like my own:

> The wanderer walks alone. But he does not feel lonely. The chaste freshness of nature communicates itself to him. He feels: it is the morning of a new day (p. 293; this edition, p. 180).

Shortly after my return to the mainland, I settled in the New York City area and made contact with Laurance Labadie, the son of Tucker's old comrade, the Detroit labor agitator and individualist anarchist, Jo Labadie. Laurance was living at what was originally the School of Living homestead in Suffern, northwest of the city. He befriended me and showed me his archival collection of anarchist literature dating back to the 1800s. Included were original copies of *The Anarchists*, and a few other works by or about Mackay. Laurance, himself the son of a radical author and publisher, impressed me with his admiration of Mackay's writing and, incidentally, Mackay's photograph. Indeed, by then, I was aware of my own strong attraction to Mackay and desire to share this attraction with others.

It is now, for my generation, like the noontime to which Nietzsche's Zarathustra responded by going down the mountain to the world of humanity to share the fruits of his wanderings. And so it is the task of this generation of anarchists to share its tradition—and it *is* a tradition—with the next generation. It is my hope that new readers of *The Anarchists* will discover something of the "freshness" I also experienced. Mackay's uniqueness is not so much the individualist anarchist vision he embraced, which he took with gratitude from Tucker and Stirner, but *the way* in which he transmitted it to others via the media of poetry and story, as well as the vast scope of this vision, which Peter Lamborn Wilson commends to us. And so it is *the spirit, the style and the scope* of this anarchism that, I trust, will delight and capture the heart of the new reader.

The Anarchists as Libertarian Socialists

> "In abolishing rent and interest, the last vestiges of old-time slavery, the Revolution abolishes at one stroke the sword of the executioner, the seal of the magistrate, the club of the policeman, the gauge of the exciseman, the erasing-knife of the department clerk, all those insignia of Politics, which young Liberty grinds beneath her heel." — Proudhon (from the masthead of Tucker's *Liberty*)

> "The differences between an individualst and a communalist radicalism are not absolute. The individual liberated from conformity and fighting the social wrongs enforced by that conformity is acting for the good of the community." — Kenneth C. Wenzer, *Anarchists Adrift: Emma Goldman and Alexander Berkman*, Brandywine Press, page 45

John Henry Mackay insisted that his two "Books of Freedom", *The Anarchists* and *The Freedomseeker* (*Der Freiheitsucher*, 1920), were works of propaganda, not art. They were written not as novels, but as communications of ideas in semi-fictional form. Among the ideas Mackay wished to communicate was the distinction he saw between anarchism and revolutionary communism on the one hand, and anarchy and the regime of monopoly-capital on the other. The central chapter of *The Anarchists*,

"The Champions of Liberty", features a debate between the two main characters of the book, the individualist anarchist Carrard Auban and the communist anarchist Otto Trupp. This chapter first came to my attention as part of the excellent anthology *Patterns of Anarchy* (edited by Leonard I. Krimerman and Lewis Perry, and published by Anchor Doubleday in 1966). The significance of this central chapter, for me, lies less in the differences it sees in the two anarchisms than in their common ground, which is also brought out, but less elaborately. Let me elaborate here.

Mackay's anarchism owed a lot to the writings of Benjamin R. Tucker, the American publisher of the journal *Liberty* (1881-1908). Tucker introduced English-speaking readers to the full spectrum of radical thought of the nineteenth century, often publishing the first English translations of important works such as Proudhon's *What is Property?*, Bakunin's *God and the State*, and Tchernychevsky's *What's To Be Done?* Other radical European writers published by Tucker included Kropotkin, Tolstoy, Olive Schreiner, George Bernard Shaw and Oscar Wilde (in addition to American antistatists such as Lysander Spooner and Voltairine de Cleyre). Tucker's Unique Book Shop in New York's Greenwich Village played a role in the education of writers such as Eugene O'Neill. Perhaps only Emma Goldman and her journal *Mother Earth* had more influence than Tucker and *Liberty* on the thinking of turn-of-the-century American anarchist intellectuals. And it may be a measure of Mackay's influence that Goldman, although Tucker's arch-rival (or, rather, *an*arch-rival), prefaced her brilliant essay, "Anarchism: What it Really Stands For", with the complete poem "Anarchy" by Mackay *(Anarchism and Other Essays*, 1917, Mother Earth Publishing Association, New York, p. 47), reprinted here on page L.

Tucker was a cosmopolitan radical, an internationalist and a socialist—as well as an individualist. Tucker hailed socialism as "war upon usury in all its forms, the great Anti-Theft Movement of the nineteenth century." (*Liberty*, May 17, 1884; *Instead of a Book*, Benj. R. Tucker, New York, pp. 361-3.) He distinguished between two socialisms, one authoritarian and one libertarian, quoting the French journalist and historian Ernest Lesigne, who declared the future of socialism belonged to the libertarian. Tucker's words on the subject are worth quoting here: "Liberty insists on Socialism...on true Socialism, Anarchistic Socialism: the prevalence on earth of Liberty, Equality, and Solidarity." (*Ibid.*) The young Mackay shared this same optimistic view.

Today, socialism has been tarred with the brush of statism so thoroughly that few seem to be aware that socialism once stood for the liberation of humanity from poverty and war, not its enslavement. As both Mackay and Tucker pointed out, both anarchism and state socialism called for the abolition of private economic monopoly (of land, money, exchange, and ideas). Anarchism went further and advocated the abolition of the *source* of all economic monopoly—the monopoly of law, the state. This is a point of distinction not only from state socialism but also from laissez-faire capitalism. It is, I think, a significant and sad fact that many libertarian individualists today seem to consider socialism, rather than statism, to be the number one problem. This is indicative of a conservative tendency to drift to the right and worship the idol of "privatization." As another of Tucker's rivals, the more moderate "single tax" reformer Henry George, pointed out, the privatization of what is by nature common property, land and legally-created monopolies, is just as much robbery as is the socialization of what is by nature individual property, the product of a person's labor. Like George, Tucker distinguished between individual and common property. Individuals are the owners of their labor and labor products, but occupant-users, not owners, of the land, natural resources, and ideas they produce with. "Property" is not the possession of one's labor product, but the privilege (the private law) of collecting an income for the *use* by others of what one did *not* produce. And so with Proudhon he proclaimed: "Property is theft."

We are now at the close of the twentieth century—a century has passed since Mackay penned, Schumm translated, and Tucker published *The Anarchists*. Having defeated state socialism, monopoly capital's *Pax Romana*, the counterfeit "New World Order" widens the gap between rich and poor once more, as well as devastates the earth on an unprecedented scale. While much of the anarchist heritage may seem quaint, naive, and outdated, nevertheless, by contrast if by nothing else, it reveals the bankruptcy and shallowness of much of the public "dialogue" between various forms of statist apologists, "left" and "right."

In *The Freedomseeker*, sequel to *The Anarchists*, Mackay wrote that he stood at the furthest point on the left. Originally, "left" meant opposition to the established order and implied change in a libertarian direction. Of course, "right" therefore meant a conservation of the established order and implied authoritarian control. The right is the defense of privilege, the left is the advocacy of freedom and equality. In fact, the anarchist socialist Proudhon *and* his critic, the laissez-faire individualist Bastiat, both sat on the left in the French Assembly, whence "left" and "right" acquired their political meaning. One of the legacies of the so-called Cold War is a heritage of misinformation, which includes the notion that "the left", along with "radicalism" and "socialism", stood by definition for statism and totalitarianism. With the defeat of state socialism in Russia and Eastern Europe comes the notion that "the left" is discredited—but in reality, state socialism was a right-wing phenomenon in Russia, as it remains in China—and as is the multistate corporate capitalism that is now riding roughshod over the earth. As China/U.S. relations indicate, state socialists and corporate capitalists do not make strange bedfellows: the wholesale violation of human freedom in pursuit of economic power remains business-as-usual for both parties.

When all is said and done, however, even when labels are used according to their original meaning, misunderstandings often follow. The various dialogues and debates recreated in *The Anarchists* challenge the readers to put aside labels, ideological prejudices and fixed ideas, and examine individuality and community—as presented here in Mackay's *Kulturgamälde* or "Picture of Civilization"—with fresh eyes and an open mind. Perhaps this "Picture" will offer some images useful to a creative synthesis of the vital and valid elements of individuality and community.

THE ANARCHISTS AS GNOSTICS: IN SEARCH OF THE FREE SPIRIT

> "And life itself told me this secret: "Behold," it said, "I am that *which must overcome itself again and again.*"—Friederich Nietzsche, *Thus Spoke Zarathustra*, Penguin Books, page 138.

> "If you meet the Buddha on the road, kill him."—Zen aphorism

> "People rely on causes because they haven't been able to make their own life a Cause sufficient unto itself. Through the Cause and the sacrifice it entails they stagger along, backwards, in search of their own will to live."—Raoul Vaneigem, *The Revolution of Everyday Life*, Left Bank Books & Rebel Press, page 187.

> "I will not be pushed, filed, stamped, indexed, briefed, debriefed or numbered. My life is my own."—Patrick McGoohan, a.k.a. Number Six, *The Prisoner* (1967 British television series)

IN ADDITION TO ANARCHISM, there are other turn-of-the-century trends of thought and culture that provide clues to the significance of John Henry Mackay and *The Anarchists.* One of these trends was the creative clash between Western rationalism and the irrational, or non-rational, subconscious realm lying in wait within the personality of the average Victorian. The writings of Nietzsche and Freud are best known for addressing this trend. Less known in this context are anarchist, feminist and free-love critics of Victorian culture such as Victoria Woodhull, Olive Schreiner, Voltairine de Cleyre, and of course Emma Goldman, who wrote:

> The explanation of the storm raging within the individual, and between him and his surroundings, is not far to seek. The primitive man, unable to understand his being, much less the unity of all life, felt himself absolutely dependent on blind, hidden forces ever ready to mock and taunt him. Out of that attitude grew the religious concepts of man as a mere speck of dust dependent on superior powers on high, who can only be appeased by complete surrender. All the early sagas rest on that idea, which continues to be the *Leitmotiv* of the biblical tales dealing with the relation of man to God, to the State, to society. Again and again the same motif, *man is nothing, the powers are everything.* Thus Jehovah would only endure man in condition of complete surrender. Man can have all the glories of the earth, but he must not become conscious of himself. The State, society, and moral laws all sing the same refrain: Man can have all the glories of the earth, but he must not become conscious of himself. ("Anarchism: What it Really Stands For", *Anarchism and Other Essays*, pp. 51-52)

In many ways, Mackay wrote out of similar insights. In his works of pure fiction, as Edward Morning writes, Mackay's characters reveal his love of human diversity and a non-judgmental appreciation of how each unique person struggles against "the powers" to "become conscious of himself." These powers include not only the state, society, and one's fellows, but also the internalized image of an authoritarian

God—Freud's "superego." Echoing Proudhon and Bakunin, whose portraits adorn his abode, Auban declares "God must fall in every shape." Mackay's critique led him to embrace a counter-spirituality found in the writing of Max Stirner:

> If religion has set up the proposition that we are sinners altogether, I set over against it the other; we are perfect altogether! For we are, every moment, all that we can be; and we never need be more. Since no defect cleaves to us, sin has no meaning either. Show me a sinner in the world still, if no one any longer needs to do what suits a superior! (*The Ego and His Own*, 1963 Libertarian Book Club edition, page 359).

Similarly, Mackay's friend Rudolf Steiner was influenced by Stirner and Nietzsche as well as by Madame Blavatsky's Theosophy, before going his own way in developing Anthroposophy. And it was in Mackay's London that The Hermetic Order of the Golden Dawn was attracting rebellious and *avante garde* writers, both men and women, including the poet William Butler Yeats, Constance Wilde (wife of the notorious Oscar), the soon-to-be-notorious Aleister Crowley, and Buddhist monk-to-be Allan Bennett. Buddhism, popularized by Theosophy, attracted political, as well as spiritual, rebels and libertarians, including Dyer Lum, the "Tuckerite" anarchist, lover of Voltairine de Cleyre, and close friend of the Chicago Haymarket martyr Albert Parsons whom he succeeded as editor of *The Alarm*. Likewise, non-violent Christian anarchism was developed by Tolstoy and adopted by anarchists across the individualist-communist spectrum, such as Emma Goldman's feminist ally and "Single Tax Anarchist" Bolton Hall, and the ex-Tuckerite and self-described "Free Socialist" J. William Lloyd.

In rejecting established religious authorities and embracing the sovereignty of direct individual experience in matters of the spirit, these and other anarchists may be considered among the heirs of medieval antinomians such as the Brethren of the Free Spirit, and the original heretics of Christendom, the ancient gnostics.

A diverse milieu of sects in the late Roman Empire, the gnostics were spiritual anarchists who opposed "the archons", "the powers" that "are everything"—the gods "in every shape." They sought "gnosis" or knowledge of the "unknown God" *within* themselves, *beyond* all shape and form—they dared to become conscious of themselves. Likewise, Mackay sought a kind of gnosis in the self-realization and apotheosis of the individual. Taking clues from Stirner more than from Nietzsche, he chose a path of radical self-acceptance rather than "self-overcoming." At bottom, however, these may turn out to be two aspects of the same process of spiritual development, as when one struggles to overcome self-hatred—the internalized condemnation of oneself, or an aspect of oneself, by others—as did Mackay in regard to his own homosexuality. Indeed, Stirner's manifesto of self-assertion, *Der Einzige und sein Eigenthum* (first published in English by Tucker in 1907 as *The Ego and His Own*) is an extended critique and overcoming of all "fixed ideas" or "spooks" of the mind —"archons" by another name. But unlike most ancient gnostics, Stirner—and Mackay—embraced the "corporeal self."

Mackay's personality, which he struggled to accept, included opposing tendencies, as he reveals in many of his writings. This is most clearly seen in the story of *Der Syberit*, where the narrator struggles between creative work and the pursuit of Epicurean happiness. It is Apollo versus Dionysus, and Nietzsche versus Stirner. The story ends with his resolution or synthesis of his life's riddle, paradox or "koan" (to borrow a term from Zen).

Opposing tendencies are also symbolized in the main characters of *The Anarchists*. Clearly, Carrard Auban represents the conscious side of John Henry Mackay, and Otto Trupp, Auban's comrade from his revolutionary youth, his unconscious, his "shadow"—the past he is leaving behind. And the character of Dr. Hurt is perhaps based on Dr. James L. Walker who introduced Tucker to Stirner in the pages of *Liberty*, and represents Mackay's new embrace of egoism, his imminent future at the time of the writing of *The Anarchists*. Walker's influence is also suggested in the book's final chapter by Auban's identification with "the early morning *walker* at the break of a new day." (Emphasis added.)

Mackay's antinomian gnostic spirituality is further expressed in this last chapter, entitled, simply, "Anarchy." In place of God "in every shape," he exalts both the self-realized individual, the "Wanderer" or "walker" and "the immortal name: Anarchy!" In this last chapter, Mackay also seems to echo the ancient gnostic and apocalyptic writings directed against the Roman Empire, wherein dire visions of war and judgment—the revenge of the oppressed—are followed by that of a victorious new society (new Jerusalem), and a new person (new Adam)—the true individual, self-realized (divine) and free, rising out of the ashes of revolutionary (religious) martyrdom. In the end, the dialectical tension of centuries—between self-sacrificing egalitarianism and self-realizing individualism—is portrayed by Mackay as playing a necessary role in the ultimate future victory over Leviathan. But like his gnostic ancestors (who eschewed unnecessary martyrdom), Mackay proclaims the here-and-now presence of ultimate victory within the enlightened mind of Carrard Auban. And so Auban assumes the mythic role or archetype of the Hero who overcomes all obstacles and realizes the Sangreal of his quest — self-ownership and liberation —Stirner's *Eigenkeit*.

Although John Henry Mackay credits Max Stirner's egoism of equals but not (unlike Emma Goldman) Friederich Nietzsche's aristocracy of "free spirits" — Carrard Auban is the image of both Stirner's "unique one" and Nietzsche's "superman." The climax of *The Anarchists* echoes both the lyric spirit and mythic style of the finale of the latter's *Thus Spoke Zarathustra* (pp. 333, 336):

> On the morning after this night, however, Zarathustra...emerged from his cave, glowing and strong, like a morning sun emerging from behind dark mountains.... "This is *my* morning, *my* day begins: *rise up now, rise up, great noontide!*"

Full Circle: The Once and Future Anarchists

From the west to the east, from the rich to poor, Victoria owned them all.
—The Kinks, *Victoria*

...Life
Cannot belong to us. We
Belong to life. Life
is King.
—Sangharakshita, *Complete Poems 1941-1994*, Windhorse Publications, page 285

In *The Anarchists*, we enter the world of young John Henry Mackay, the world of the Victorian Empire—a world very different yet very similar to our own world of the American Empire, as well as that of the Roman Empire. After all, the Empire is, in the end, the Empire. Leviathan has been around for millenia, and those who speak the truth against it, speak to, for, and in solidarity with generations that follow in the struggle. As this book reveals, Mackay understood this.

Indeed, if there is one quality that does make *The Anarchists* a great work, with "a right to live," it is the *compassion* that underlies the "insights...dramatic strength...incisiveness of phrase...and cold, pitiless logic...." But to be pitiless is not to be without compassion—for pity erects a barrier and a hierarchy between the fortunate and the unfortunate—while compassion destroys barriers and undermines hierarchies. Mackay was, if nothing else, an individualist who *consequently* felt compassion for and unity with the unemployed and working people he described and championed. As Sharon Presley elaborates in her own words, it is this compassion that separates genuine *anarchist* individualism from the other individualisms that, in the end, disarm people by advocating the greed-oriented values that keep the Empire going.

This compassionate or sympathetic aspect of anarchist individualism owes much to the radical spiritual movements of the West, going back through the likes of Blake and Godwin, Spence and Weddeburn, the Jubilee movement, the radical Quakers, the Brethren of the Free Spirit, and others who took the radical libertarian and social-justice message of Judeo-Christianity seriously. The opposition of "New England anarchism" to authority, land monopoly and usury has its roots in this tradition. Out of the common critique the streams individualist mutualism and anarchist communism emerge and go their separate, but at times parallel, ways. Benjamin R. Tucker, who published the first English edition of *The Anarchists,* honored this radical egalitarian sense of life when he referred to the author, in the pages of his journal *Liberty*, as "Comrade Mackay." Likewise, and in spite of being a scathing critic, Tucker referred to other fellow anarchists, whether he agreed or disagreed with them, and regardless of their brand of anarchy, by the same title: "Comrade."

Camaraderie is hard to come by in this world dominated by the need to compete and survive. But it is camaraderie that is needed above all, if survival is to have any meaning. It is also a way to engage in the struggle itself. For it is as comrades that we resist the dominant monopoly capitalist culture's attempt to reduce the gifts of life to commodities, to alienate us from ourselves, to divide-and-conquer. Mackay, while a bold critic of coercive communism, was an equally bold troubador-champion of voluntary cameraderies of all kinds—as shown by the friendships depicted in *The Anarchists* and his other writings, based on his own life.

Now, over a hundred years later but perhaps not too late, it is time to heed the song of the troubador, and to sing songs of our own: To let go of *all* the isms, individual*ism* as well as commun*ism*—and to live, instead of an ism, a *life*: a life of true individuality in the free spirit of camaraderie.

It is with great joy that I thank all those who collaborated in this centenary edition of John Henry Mackay's great work: the contributing writers Hubert Kennedy, Edward Mornin, Sharon Presley, and Peter Lamborn Wilson; the financial supporters and prepublication subscriber for their long suffering patience of Job—may this book be found well worth its "wait"—and the untiring friends at Autonomedia, especially Jim Fleming, Raffi Khatchadourian, Dave Mandl, and Ben Meyers—without whom it would not have happened—Comrades All!

Mark A. Sullivan
New York City
Autumn Equinox 1996

A Postscript and a Dedication

It is now more than two and a half years since completing the editor's introduction, and one hundred and eight years since Benj. R. Tucker published the first English edition of *The Anarchists*—making this centenary edition now six years past the mark! Truth to tell, the editor must bear the brunt of responsibility for the long time taken and offer this sincere apology to all, especially to the pre-publication subscribers. The project was conceived one year before the centenary, already too close for comfort. Invitations were sent to the contributing authors whose response was generous—and more than generous on the part of Hubert Kennedy. But *The Anarchists* competed with various other commitments on the part of the publishers and, especially, the editor, who was going through significant and demanding changes in his personal and spiritual life. Throughout these years, the inspiration and moral support of a friend—whose friendship now goes back some twenty years—was invaluable. That friend is Ian Young.

One could well dub Ian Young "Canada's Poet-Anarchist" as John Henry Mackay was Germany's. Born in London during the German blitzkrieg, Ian escaped the Nazis who, just a dozen years earlier, had condemned Mackay's works and perhaps even drove him to his death. Like his half-Scottish predecessor, Ian was raised outside the land of his birth and travelled much in his youth. Ian finally settled in Toronto, as Mackay did in Berlin. Similarly, each in his own way became a poet and storyteller, advocate of anarchy and homosexual liberation, social critic and psychohistorian. In this regard one remembers Ian's June 1989 Libertarian Book Club presentation in New York City on "AIDS and the Fate of Gay Liberation"—which then grew into a major work, *The Stonewall Experiment: A Gay Psychohistory*, published in 1996 by Cassell. In the spirit of Mackay's *The Anarchists*, one might well consider Ian's work "A Picture of Civilization at the Close of the Twentieth Century"—since "AIDS" has now replaced "Anarchy" as society's terrifying "A-word."

There are other similarities, and of course differences—at least one that is very ironic. Mackay parted company with his one-time close friend Rudolf Steiner (at whose wedding Mackay served as best man) as the latter developed his Anthroposophical movement. Ian, on the other hand, is keenly interested in Steiner's role as a central figure in the German esoteric metaphysical opposition to Nazi occultism.

For these reasons and more, it is fitting and indeed a pleasure to dedicate this centenary edition of John Henry Mackay's *The Anarchists,* with love, to a dear comrade and champion of liberty, Ian Young.

MAS - NYC
Summer Solstice 1999

Morgan Edwards: An Anarchist Comrade

(6 November 1949 — 29 March 1998)

THIS LIBERTARIAN FEMINIST, renaissance man, and "anarchist without adjectives," then known as Robert Cooke, was an active participant on the scene when John Henry Mackay and *The Anarchists* were rediscovered by a new generation of radicals in the late 1960s and early 1970s.

Morgan, your friendship over the decades has encouraged this present work, and your contribution to the free spirit of this new edition is gratefully acknowledged and recorded here:

> ANARCHISM, though a political philosophy, is not a doctrine. Some anarchists have been doctrinaire, even dogmatic, but none of their doctrines or schools have encompassed more than a part of anarchism. Each anarchist thinker and actor has contributed and passed on. As a result, anarchism is a melange of ideas and practices, some elaborate, some incomplete, some half-baked.
>
> Anarchist ideas surface periodically in many or even most societies (although they may not bear the label "anarchist"). Wherever people create an anarchistic culture — that is, whenever they live free of, or resist, all authority and express in words their ideals and way of life, the philosophy of anarchism appears.
>
> — Morgan Edwards
>
> "Maculate Origins: themes of failure and success in american Anarchism"
> *The Storm! A Journal for Free Spirits* #9/10, 1980

An Illustrated Guide to John Henry Mackay's *The Anarchists*

London, June 1887, Victoria's Jubilee Parade: One of "those ridiculous celebrations… of the fiftieth anniversary of a woman who allows herself to be called *Queen of Great Britain and Ireland, and Empress of India.*"

THE ANARCHISTS

A PICTURE OF CIVILIZATION AT THE CLOSE OF THE NINETEENTH CENTURY

BY

JOHN HENRY MACKAY

WITH A PORTRAIT OF THE AUTHOR, AND A STUDY OF HIS WORKS BY GABRIELE REUTER

TRANSLATED FROM THE GERMAN

By GEORGE SCHUMM

BOSTON, MASS.
BENJ. R. TUCKER, PUBLISHER
1891

John Henry Mackay

Portrait of the author and title page from the 1891 Tucker edition

Benj. R. Tucker, Mackay's mentor, comrade and publisher, from his *Instead of a Book,* 1893. He edited and published *Liberty*, out of Boston and later New York City, from 1881 to 1908. After his publishing works, his large stock of avante garde books and bookshop in Greenwich Village were destroyed by fire, Tucker retired to France and later Monaco, where he died in 1939, survived by his wife Pearl Johnson and daughter Oriole. Mackay's correspondence with Tucker is documented by Hubert Kennedy in *Dear Tucker*. In his introduction to *The Anarchists,* Mackay paid tribute to his closest friend in cause of anarchy.

Max Stirner, drawn from memory by Frederich Engels. The influence of this Young Hegelian rebel philosopher on Mackay and Tucker is acknowledged by both. In the publisher's preface to the first English edition of Stirner's *The Ego and His Own* (1907), Tucker writes: "…there has been a remarkable revival of interest in both the book and its author. It began in this country with a discussion in the pages of the Anarchist periodical, 'Liberty,' in which Stirner's thought was clearly expounded and vigorously championed by Dr. James L. Walker.… But the chief instrument of the revival of Stirnerism was and is the German poet, John Henry Mackay. Very early in his career he met Stirner's name in Lange's 'History of Materialism,' and was moved thereby to read his book. The work made such an impression on him that he resolved to devote a portion of his life to the rediscovery and rehabilitation of the lost and forgotten genius…and his biography of Stirner appeared in Berlin in 1898.… During his years of investigation Mackay's advertising for information had created new interest in Stirner, which was enhanced by the sudden fame of the writings of Friederich Nietzsche, an author whose intellectual kinship with Stirner has been a subject of much controversy."

Sturm.

Zweite, durchgesehene und vermehrte Auflage.

Zürich 1890.
Verlags-Magazin
(J. Schabelitz).

Left: The title page to the second (1890) edition of Mackay's revolutionary poetry "Sturm," which was dedicated to the memory of Max Stirner. The first edition, as noted in his introduction to *The Anarchists,* brought early fame to Mackay as the "first singer of Anarchy."

Below: Dr. James L. Walker, who introduced the readers of Tucker's *Liberty* to the ideas of Max Stirner. From his book *The Philosophy of Egoism,* published by Tucker in 1905. Walker may have been the model for Dr. Hurt in Chapter VII.

Yours sincerely
James L Walker

Peter Kropotkin, "a little man, a long coat, with a long, heavy beard" as described in Chapter I. A major theoretician of anarchy, along with Stirner, Proudhon and Bakunin.

"Two little portraits, however, hung above the fireplace. The one represented the great fanatic of the revolution whose wild force had spent itself against the walls of west European life; and the other, the great thinker on the century behind whose mighty brow a new world seemed to be in travail,—Michael Bakounine and Pierre Joseph Proudhon. The pictures were gifts to Auban from the only person who had loved him ever since he knew him."

—Chapter IV.

These two portraits had been published by Benjamin Tucker, and indeed may have been given by him to Mackay.

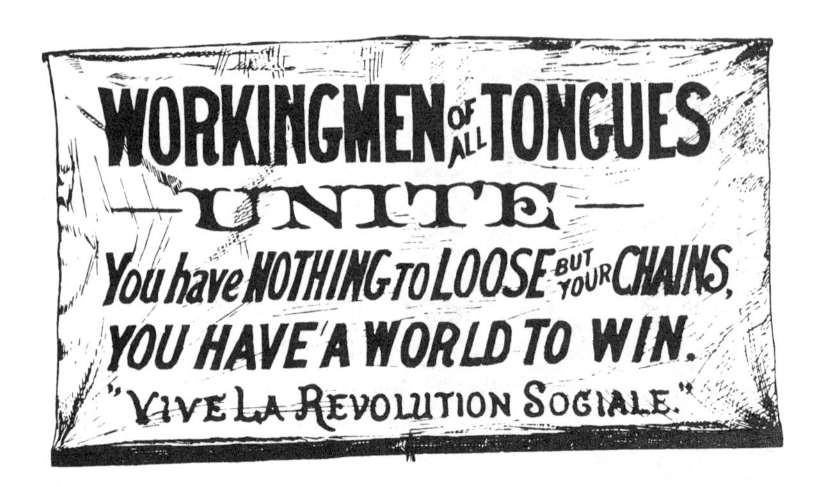

The call to social revolution and subsequent labor rally in the Chicago Haymarket at which the explosion of the proverbial anarchist bomb led to one of the most controversial trials in United States history. The incident, the trial, and the execution (right) form the centerpiece of *The Anarchists* as movingly described by Mackay in the Chapter VI, "The Tragedy of Chicago."

119
120

The Anarchists

(Clockwise from top left) Albert Parsons, August Spies, Samuel Fielden, George Engel

of Chicago

(Clockwise from top left) Louis Lingg, Adolph Fischer, Oscar Neebe, Michael Schwab

Liberty

NOT THE DAUGHTER BUT THE MOTHER OF ORDER — PROUDHON

Vol. V. – No. 8. BOSTON, MASS., SATURDAY, NOVEMBER 19, 1887. Whole No. 112

They never fail who die
In a great cause: the block may soak their gore;
Their heads may sodden in the sun; their limbs
Be strung to city gates and castle walls
But still their spirit walks abroad. Though years
Elapse, and others share as dark a doom,
They but augment the deep and sweeping thoughts
Which overpower all others, and conduct
The world at last to freedom.

Tucker's periodical *Liberty*, subtitled "Not the Daughter but the Mother of Order" (quoting Proudhon), published from 1881 to 1908. This is the November 19, 1887 edition published after the execution of the Haymarket Anarchists in Chicago.

The first issue of the German language edition entitled "Libertas" published on March 17 1888. Mackay's debt to Tucker and Liberty is expressed in his introduction to *The Anarchists*: "For more than seven years my friend Benj. R. Tucker of Boston has been battling for Anarchy in the new world with the invincible weapon of his 'Liberty.' On in the lonely hours of my struggles have I fixed my gaze upon the brilliant light that thence is beginning to illumine the night."

Libertas

FREIHEIT, NICHT DIE TOCHTER, SONDERN DIE MUTTER DER ORDNUNG — PROUDHON

1. Jahrgang. BOSTON, MASS., SAMSTAG, den 17. MAERZ 1888. Nummer 1.

"Denn stets in deinem Aug, o Freiheit,
Erstrahlt ein hehres Licht, der Welt zum Heil;
Ob du uns tödtest auch, vertraun wir dir."
John Hay.

FREIHEIT.

[Aus dem Englischen für Libertas übersetzt von H. F. Lüders.]

Wer dürfte wol zu sagen sich erkühnen:
"So, so allein soll mir das Meer erscheinen"?
Sei's, dass es liegt in stiller Friedenspracht,
Die Erde küssend und des Himmel's Blau
Rings wiederstrahlend von smaragdner Flut;
Sei's, dass vom Wind bewegt, auf seiner Brust
Es unsre weissbeschwingten Boten trägt
Zu Zielen blut'gen Ruhms und ernster Not;
Sei's, dass gepeitscht vom Sturme, es sich beugt
Der Macht der Elemente, brüllend schlägt
An seine Felsenkerkermauern; wild
Lebend'ger Wesen Blut voll Mordlust trinkt
Und seinen Strand mit Trümmern übersä't:
Stets ist's das Meer und Alle beugen sich
Vor seiner schrankenlosen Majestät.

So auch umsonst versucht der feige Mann,
Der Freiheit enge Grenzen aufzubauen.
Denn schrankenlos zu sein ist ein Gesetz,
So sich die Freiheit schuf und das im Sturm
Und Frieden gleich sie unentwegt befolgt.
Verachtet sie drum nicht, wenn sie im Schlaf
Gleich einem Leuen ruht, indess ein Schwarm
Von Uebeln sie umflattert harpyengleich;
Noch zweifelt, wenn sie in verworrner Zeit
Des Schreckens Fackel schwinget und ihr Ruf
[illegible]
In der Empörung Wut ihr Riesenleib
Erscheinet auf dem Richtplatz, wo das Beil
Als Grabgeläute der Tyrannen tönt:
Denn stets in deinem Aug, o Freiheit,
Erstrahlt ein hehres Licht, der Welt zum Heil;
Ob du uns tödtest auch, vertraun wir dir.
—John Hay.

Zur Klarstellung.

Nach der herrschenden Ansicht ist Anarchismus gleichbedeutend entweder mit Chaos, Mord und Raub oder aber mit eitler Schwärmerei. Dass der Pöbel an dieser Auslegung des anstössigen Wortes hartnäckig festhält, kann ich verstehen; dass aber auch ehrliche und im Allgemeinen intelligente Volkslehrer und Zeitungsschreiber dieselben Begriffe mit dem Worte verbinden wie der Pöbel, kann ich nicht verstehen. Und gleich von vornherein bestreite ich diesen Volkslehrern und Zeitungsschreibern die Zulässigkeit, den Begriff einer Sache sich beim Pöbel einzuholen. Will ich Etwas über das Gesetz der Schwere lernen, so wende ich mich an Newton und nicht an die Leute, die mit sicherm Instinkt in der Verbreitung der neuen Lehre eine Gefahr für den sie ernährenden Aberglauben erblicken. Will ich mich bezüglich der Descendenztheorie informiren, so gehe ich zu Darwin und Hæckel und nicht zu den Professoren im Solde Derjenigen, die nichts als ihre Ahnen besitzen, worauf sie stolz sein können. Und um den Anarchismus als das zu erfassen, was er in Wahrheit ist, frage ich, falls mir die eigene Beobachtung und das eigene Denken keine befriedigende Antwort zu geben vermag, bei Proudhon, Josiah Warren, Herbert Spencer, Lysander Spooner, Max Stirner u. A. an und verschliesse mich gegen die Verdrehungen und Verleumdungen desselben seitens Derjenigen, die ganz richtig in ihm den unerbittlichen Feind ihrer Privilegien wie den strengen Strafrichter ihres frevlen Tuns und Treibens sehen.

Das ist gerade das Traurige, dass sich die Bekämpfer des Anarchismus der Mühe nicht unterziehen, denselben auf seinen Kern zu prüfen, oder sich auch nur mit den Werken seiner grossen und genialen Fürsprecher vertraut zu machen, sondern sich willkürlich einen anarchistischen Strohmann zurechtstutzen und dann wacker auf denselben losschlagen. Damit beweisen sie nur, wie wenig sie von der Sache verstehen, die sie so von oben herab abzutun sich unterfangen. Hier denke ich an einen Mann, der den Anarchismus allwöchentlich vernichtet und doch noch nie ein anarchistisches Werk gelesen, geschweige denn gewissenhaft studirt hat. Und dieser Mann ist der Typus einer ganzen Klasse. Wäre es nicht löblicher, wenn er die Sache, die er nicht versteht, auf sich beruhen liesse bis er einmal wirklich "hinter sie gekommen" wäre?

Wäre dieser Mann, den ich im Geist vor mir sehe, in der Bildung seines Begriffs vom Anarchismus gewissenhaft zu Werke gegangen, so müsste er wissen, dass die Gewalt nicht nur nicht ein integrirendes Moment desselben bildet, wie er seinen Lesern nicht müde wird zu verkünden, sondern von ihr geradezu ausgeschlossen ist. Die Gewalt ist vielmehr das eigentliche Wesen des Staates, und die Anarchie ist die Verneinung der Gewalt, mithin des Staates.

Die Tatsache, dass manche Anarchisten der herrschenden Gewalt des Staats ihrerseits wieder Gewalt entgegenstellen, macht die Gewalt doch gewiss nicht zu einem wesentlichen Bestandteil des Anarchismus. Die Frage, wie man die Gewaltherrschaft des Staates am erfolgreichsten bekämpfen kann, hat mit der Frage nach dem Anarchismus selber gar nichts zu schaffen.

Und noch einmal, wäre der Mann, den ich im Geiste vor wir sehe, in der Bildung seines Begriffs vom Anarchismus gewissenhaft zu Werke gegangen, so müsste er ebenfalls wissen, dass derselbe, weit entfernt, den Boden des Tatsächlichen verlassen zu haben, wie er gleichfalls seinen Lesern beizubringen versucht, gerade auf demselben fusst und auf nichts weniger abzielt als ein unerreichbares Wolkenkukuksheim. Der Anarchismus gibt sich bezüglich der menschlichen Natur keinen Illusionen hin. Ihm sind die Gebrechen und Schwächen derselben so bekannt wie nur irgend einem Menschen mit offenen Sinnen. Er setzt keine vollkommenen Menschen voraus, wie ihm fälschlich untergeschoben wird, er postulirt die Selbstherrlichkeit des Individuums und die Freiheit als unumgängliche Bedingung der fortschrittlichen Entwicklung des Einzelnen wie der Gesellschaft. Diese Entwicklung vollzieht sich in Gemässheit mit natürlichen Gesetzen und weisst alle willkürliche Einmischung fremder Autorität, wie immer sich dieselbe auch motivire, entschieden zurück. Das Maas von Ordnung, das wir heute haben, ist nicht irgend welcher gesetzlichen Feststellung zu Gute zu schreiben, sie ist wesentlich das Resultat eines natürlichen, durch Jahrtausende sich erstreckenden Entwicklungsprozesses. Und wenn sich die heutige "Ordnung" in immer höherm Grade als unsicher und hinfällig zu erweisen droht, so ist das einzig dem Umstand zuzuschreiben, dass die Menschen aus guten wie schlechten Absichten dem natürlichen Verlauf der Dinge Etwas am Zeuge flicken wollten und demselben grosse Hindernisse in den Weg stellten. Daraus folgt von selbst die Forderung nach der Beseitigung dieser Hindernisse oder nach der Abschaffung des Staats, in welchem die freie Entwicklung hemmenden Mächte ihre Verkörperung finden. Worin die Forderung des Anarchismus gipfelt, wenn auch nicht, wie ich hier betone, in Rousseau'schem Sinn, ist in den Worten des Telldichters die Rückkehr des alten Urstands der Natur, wo Mensch dem Menschen gegenübersteht, — d. h. frei von allen kirchlichen und staatlichen Satzungen.

Die Richtung der gesellschaftlichen Entwicklung deutet auf die Auflösung des politischen Staats im ökonomischen Organismus. Der Anarchismus stellt Produktion und Konsumption, Handel und Wandel, Kunst und Wissenschaft, Litteratur und Erziehung der Privatinitiative anheim, und überlässt ruhig die Sorge für die immer höhere Entfaltung und Vervollkommnung dieser Dinge dem freien Uebereinkommen der dabei interessirten Individuen. Er hat die unerschütterliche Ueberzeugung, dass das gemeinsame Interesse, welches nicht weggeleugnet werden kann, sondern mit der wachsenden Intelligenz immer offenbarer werden wird, die Menschen fester aneinander anschliessen wird als aller gesetzliche und polizeiliche Zwang. *Laissez-faire* ist sein leitendes Prinzip, aber das bedeutet nicht, um mich der Worte eines neuern Schriftstellers zu bedienen, "wie die Gegner verächtlich hinzuwerfen pflegen, Anarchie im üblen Sinne des Wortes, oder freies Schalten aller bösen Triebe der menschlichen Gesellschaft, sondern die Freiheit ist auch hier geregelt, aber von einem andern Gesetzgeber als dem hinter dem grünen Tisch sitzenden, nämlich von den ewigen und unabänderlichen, im freientwickelten Verkehr sich deutlich offenbarenden Naturgesetzen, denen alle Interessenten bei Strafe der Vernichtung ihres Wohlergehens sich unterwerfen müssen."

Dieser Entwicklungsprozess in der Richtung des Anarchismus wird nun voraussichtlich nicht so friedlich verlaufen, wie es zu wünschen wäre. In dem Grade, in welchem er infolge des erwachenden Volksbewusstseins vorwärts schreitet, wird er unvermeidlich in immer heftigern Konflikt geraten mit der herrschenden Gewalt, die er notwendig bedroht und auf deren gänzliche Vernichtung er abzielt. Aber so lange uns das Recht der freien Presse und der freien Rede unbenommen bleibt, wird sich Libertas mit der energischen Betreibung der geistigen Agitation begnügen, die Anwendung aller Gewaltmittel zwecks Beseitigung der herrschenden Ordnung verwerfen, und sich auf die Macht des passiven Widerstands verlassen. Mit der Beseitigung der geistigen Misere und Versklavung, die wir mittels der Weckung der Intelligenz und eines erleuchteten Egoismus anstreben, zerstören wir zugleich auch die Pfeiler der herrschenden Gewalt und verursachen den Zerfall der ökonomischen Misere. Wenn das auch langsam geht, so gedulden wir uns bei dem Gedanken, dass wir in dem sich vor unsern Augen abspielenden Entwicklungsprozess einen mächtigen Bundesgenossen haben und der Erreichung des gesteckten Zieles versichert sein dürfen.

Und so begibt sich denn Libertas an ihre Aufgabe mit "dem Ernst, den keine Mühe bleichet."

G. S.

An die Leser.

Eine Menge kleinerer Notizen, unter dem gemeinsamen Titel "Auf der Wacht," mussten wegen Raummangels zurückgestellt werden. Ebenso auch eine Anzahl von längern Artikeln, die wir aber später zum Abdruck bringen werden.

Wir verschicken diese Nummer von Libertas an zahlreiche Adressen im ganzen Lande. Nicht Alle werden ihr eine freundliche Aufnahme gewähren. Umsomehr erwarten wir die prompte tatkräftige Unterstützung aller Derjenigen, die mit uns denken und fühlen. Man zögere nicht mit der Einsendung des jährlichen Abonnements.

A Nearly Complete File of Liberty To the Highest Bidder

I hereby offer for sale, to the highest bidder, for the benefit of the " Propaganda of Individualistic Anarchism " in the German language, a nearly complete file of Liberty, lacking only 23 numbers,—*viz.*, of Vol. I, Nos. 1, 3, 4, 5, 6, 7, 10, 16, 17, 18, 19, 26; of Vol. II, Nos. 3, 6, 7, 13, 21, 25, 26; of Vol. IV, Nos. 6 and 7; of Vol. VI, No. 4; and of Vol. X, No. 14.

The file will be awarded to the person making the highest of such offers as may be received by me not later than December 31, 1907, provided such highest offer is not less than Fifty Dollars. The money thus realized will be devoted to the " Propaganda " specified above.

John Henry Mackay
166 Berlinerstrasse
Berlin-Charlottenburg, Germany

Mackay's advertisement in 1907 in *Liberty* (October, November, and December, numbers 400, 401 and 402 — the penultimate issue) to raise funds for the "Propaganda of Individualistic Anarchism."

Propaganda des individualiſtiſchen Anarchismus in deutſcher Sprache.

Viertes Heft.

Sind Anarchiſten Mörder?

Von

Benj. R. Tucker,

Herausgeber der Zeitſchrift „Liberty" in New-York.

Mit einem Vorwort.

Aus dem Engliſchen von John Henry Mackay.

Drittes bis fünftes Tausend.

Preis: 10 Pfg.

Berlin-Baumſchulenweg 1907.
Verlag von B. Zack, Kiefholzſtraße 186.

The cover of one of Mackay's pamphlets translating Tucker into German: the 1907 edition of "Are Anarchists Thugs?" This response to the image of anarchists as violent bomb-throwing assassins first appeared in the New York Tribune on December 4, 1898, then reprinted in *Liberty* number 359, January 1899. Mackay's German publisher, Bernhard Zack, was enough of a comrade and friend to also publish Mackay's books and pamphlets in defense of sexual liberty, particularly male homosexuality or "the nameless love," written under the pseudonym "Sagitta" (Latin for "Arrow").

In 1893 John Henry Mackay made a pilgrimage to the United States to visit the graves of the Haymarket Anarchists in Chicago, and to meet anarchist friends for the first time, particularly Tucker in New York. On September 28th, he had lunch with Emma Goldman, as mentioned in her *Living my Life*. He admired and shared her sexual radicalism. Her journal *Mother Earth* (1906 – 1918) succeeded *Liberty* as the leading American anarchist journal. Although Goldman was considered a "communistic" anarchist, she published favorable treatments of individualism such as those of Stirner, Nietzsche, and the French egoist E. Armand. Goldman opened her 1917 collection, *Anarchism and Other Essays* (frontispiece above) with Mackay's poem "Anarchy" (below). The German original appeared in "Sturm," and had been first published in English by Tucker in *Liberty*, number 216, January 30, 1892, as translated from the German by Harry Lyman Koopman. The poem has since been reprinted many times, keeping alive the name of the "first singer of Anarchy."

ANARCHY.

Ever reviled, accursed, ne'er understood,
  Thou art the grisly terror of our age.
"Wreck of all order," cry the multitude,
  "Art thou, and war and murder's endless rage."
O, let them cry. To them that ne'er have striven
  The truth that lies behind a word to find,
To them the word's right meaning was not given.
  They shall continue blind among the blind.
But thou, O word, so clear, so strong, so pure,
  Thou sayest all which I for goal have taken.
I give thee to the future! Thine secure
  When each at least unto himself shall waken.
Comes it in sunshine? In the tempest's thrill?
  I cannot tell—but it the earth shall see!
I am an Anarchist! Wherefore I will
  Not rule, and also ruled I will not be!

JOHN HENRY MACKAY.

A large share of whatever of merit this translation may possess is due to Miss Sarah E. Holmes, who kindly gave me her assistance, which I wish to gratefully acknowledge here. My thanks are also due to Mr. Tucker for valuable suggestions.

G. S.

Introduction

The work of art must speak for the artist who created it; the labor of the thoughtful student who stands back of it permits him to say what impelled him to give his thought voice.

The subject of the work just finished requires me to accompany it with a few words.

First of all, this: Let him who does not know me and who would, perhaps, in the following pages, look for such sensational disclosures as we see in those mendacious speculations upon the gullibility of the public from which the latter derives its sole knowledge of the Anarchistic movement, not take the trouble to read beyond the first page.

In no other field of social life does there exist to-day a more lamentable confusion, a more naïve superficiality, a more portentous ignorance than in that of Anarchism. The very utterance of the word is like the flourish of a red rag; in blind wrath the majority dash against it without taking time for calm examination and consideration. They will tear into tatters this work, too, without having understood it. Me their blows will not strike.

London and the events of the fall of 1887 have served me as the background for my picture.

When in the beginning of the following year I once more returned to the scene for a few weeks, principally to complete my East End studies, I did not dream that the very section which I had selected for more detailed description would soon thereafter be in everybody's mouth in consequence of the murders of "Jack the Ripper."

I did not finish the chapter on Chicago without first examining the big picture-book for grown-up children by which the police captain, Michael Schaack, has since attempted to justify the infamous murder committed by his government: "Anarchy and Anarchists" (Chicago, 1889). It is nothing more than a—not unimportant—document of stupid brutality as well as inordinate vanity.

The names of living people have been omitted by me in every case with deliberate intent; nevertheless the initiated will almost always recognize without difficulty the features that have served me as models.

A SPACE OF THREE YEARS has elapsed between the writing of the first chapter and the last. Ever newly rising doubts compelled me again and again, often for a long period, to interrupt the work. Perhaps I began it too soon; I do not finish it too late.

Not every phase of the question could I treat exhaustively; for the most part I could not offer more than the conclusions of chains of reasoning, often very long. The complete incompatibility of the Anarchistic and the Communistic *Weltanschauung*,[1] the uselessness and harmfulness of a resort to violent tactics, as well as the impossibility of any "solution of the social question" whatsoever by the State, at least I hope to have demonstrated.

THE NINETEENTH CENTURY has given birth to the idea of Anarchy. In its fourth decade the boundary line between the old world of slavery and the new world of liberty was drawn. For it was in this decade that P.-J. Proudhon began the titanic labor of his life with *Qu'est-ce que la propriété?* (1840), and that Max Stirner wrote his immortal work: *Der Einzige und sein Eigenthum* (1845).

It was possible for this idea to be buried under the dust of a temporary relapse of civilization. But it is imperishable.

It is even now again awake.

For more than seven years my friend Benj. R. Tucker of Boston has been battling for Anarchy in the new world with the invincible weapon of his "*Liberty*." Oft in the lonely hours of my struggles have I fixed my gaze upon the brilliant light that thence is beginning to illumine the night.

WHEN THREE YEARS AGO I gave the poems of my "*Sturm*" to the public, I was hailed by friendly voices as the "first singer of Anarchy."

I am proud of this name.

But I have come to the conviction that what is needed to-day is not so much to arouse enthusiasm for liberty as rather to convince people of the absolute necessity of economic independence, without which it will eternally remain the unsubstantial dream of visionaries.

In these days of the growing reaction, which will culminate in the victory of State Socialism, the call has become imperative upon me to be here also the first champion of the Anarchistic idea. I hope I have not yet broken my last lance for liberty.

John Henry Mackay
Rome, in the spring, 1891

1. *Weltanschauung*: world view.

Chapter I.
In the Heart of the World-Metropolis

A wet, cold October evening was beginning to lower upon London. It was the October of the same year in which, not five months before, had been inaugurated those ridiculous celebrations which gave the year 1887 the name of the "Jubilee Year"—celebrations of the fiftieth anniversary of a woman who allows herself to be called "Queen of Great Britain and Ireland, and Empress of India." On this evening—the last of the week—a man coming from the direction of Waterloo Station was wending his way to the railroad bridge of Charing Cross through labyrinthine, narrow, and almost deserted streets. When, as if fatigued from an extended walk, he had slowly ascended the wooden steps that lead to the narrow walk for pedestrians running beside the tracks on the bridge, and had gone about as far as the middle of the river, he stepped into one of the round recesses fronting the water and remained standing there for a short time, while he allowed the crowd behind him to push on. Rather from habit than genuine fatigue, he stopped and looked down the Thames. As he had but seldom been on "the other side of the Thames," notwithstanding his already three years' sojourn in London, he never failed, on crossing one of the bridges, to enjoy afresh the magnificent view that London affords from them.

It was still just light enough for him to recognize, as far as Waterloo Bridge to his right, the dark masses of warehouses, and on the mirror of the Thames at his feet, the rows of broad-bellied freight boats and rafts coupled together, though already the lights of the evening were everywhere blazing into the dark, yawning chaos of this immense city. The two rows of lanterns on Waterloo Bridge stretched away like parallel lines, and each of the lanterns cast its sharp, glittering light, deep and long, into the dark, trembling tide, while to the left, in a terrace-shaped ascent, the countless little flames which illumine the Embankments, and the Strand with its surroundings, every evening, were beginning to flash. The quiet observer standing there saw yonder on the bridge the fleeting lights of the cabs; to his rear he heard the trains of the South East road rumbling and roaring while madly rushing in and out of the station of Charing Cross; saw beneath him the lazy waves of the Thames, with almost inaudible splashing, lapping against the dark, black, slimy masses stretching far into the deep; and as he turned to pass on, the gigantic station of Charing Cross, that centre of a never-ceasing life by night and by day, opened before him, flooded by the white glare of the electric light....

He thought of Paris, his native city, as he slowly passed on. What a difference between the broad, level, and clear embankments of the Seine and these stiff, projecting masses, on which not even the sun could produce a ray of joy!

He longed to be back in the city of his youth. But he had learned to love London with the passionate, jealous love of obstinacy.

For one either loves London or hates it....

Again the wanderer stopped. So brightly was the gigantic station illumined that he could plainly see the clock at its end. The hands stood between the seventh and the eighth hours. The bustle on the sidewalk seemed to have increased, as if a human wave was being washed from the one side to the other. It seemed as if the hesitating loiterer could not tear himself away. For a moment he watched the incessant play of the signals at the entrance of the station; then, across the tracks and through the confusion of iron posts and cars, he tried to reach Westminster Abbey with his eye; but he could not recognize anything except the shimmering dial on the steeple of Parliament House and the dark outlines of gigantic masses of stone that arose beyond. And scattered in every direction the thousands and thousands of lights....

Again he turned to the open place where he had before been standing. Beneath his feet the trains of the Metropolitan Railway were rolling along with a dull rumbling noise; the entire expanse of the Victoria Embankment lay beneath him, half illumined as far as Waterloo Bridge. Stiff and severe, Cleopatra's Needle rose in the air.

From below came to the man's ears the laughing and singing of the young fellows and the girls who nightly monopolize the benches of the Embankments. "Do not forget me—do not forget me," was the refrain. Their voices sounded hard and shrill. "Do not forget me"—one could hear it everywhere in London during the Jubilee Year. It was the song of the day.

If anybody had observed the features of the man who was just now bending over the edge of the bridge, he would not have failed to catch a strange expression of severity that suddenly possessed them. The pedestrian no longer heard anything of the now suppressed, now subdued noise and the trivial song. Again a thought had seized him at the sight of the mighty quays at his feet; how many human lives might lie crushed beneath these white granite quarries, piled one upon the other so solid and unconquerable? And he thought again of that silent, unrewarded, forgotten toil that had created all the magnificence round about him.

Sweat and blood are washed away, and the individual man, on the corpses of millions of unnamed, forgotten ones, rises living and admired....

As if goaded by this thought, Carrard Auban passed on. Leaving behind him the stony arches at the end of the bridge—the remains of the old Hungerford Suspension Bridge—he looked down and walked faster. Again as always he lived in the thoughts to which he also had dedicated the youth of his life, and again he was impressed by the boundless grandeur of this movement which the second half of the nineteenth century has named the "social": to carry the light where darkness still prevails—among the toiling, oppressed masses whose sufferings and slow death give life to "the others."...

But when Auban had descended the steps of the bridge and found himself in Villiers Street, that remarkable little street which leads from the Strand down past the city station of Charing Cross, he became again fascinated by the bustling life around him. Incessantly it was surging past him: this one wanted to catch the train which had just discharged those who were hurrying towards the Strand—belated theatre-goers who had perhaps again miscalculated the distances of London; here a prostitute was talking at a gentleman with a silk hat, whom she had enticed hither by a word and a look of her weary eyes, in order to come to an agreement with him concerning the "price"; and there a crowd of hungry street urchins were pushing their dirty faces against the window panes of an Italian waffle-baker greedily following every movement of the untiring worker. Auban saw everything: he had the same attention of a practised eye for the ten-year-old youngster who was seeking to beg a penny of the passers-by by turning wheels before them on the moist pavement, and for the debased features of the fellow who, when he came to a halt, instantly obtruded himself on him and tried to talk him into buying the latest number of the "Matrimonial News"—"indispensable for all who wished to marry"—but immediately turned to the next man when he found that he got no answer.

Auban passed slowly on. He knew this life too well to be confused and stupefied by it; and yet it seized and interested him ever anew with all its might. He had devoted hours and days to its study during these years, and always and everywhere he found it new and interesting. And the more he learned to know its currents, its depths, and its shallows, the more he admired this matchless city. For some time this affection, which was more than an attachment and less than love, had been growing into a passionately excited one. London had shown him too much—much more than to the inhabitant and the visitor; and now he wished to see all. And so the restlessness of this wish had driven him in the afternoon of this day to the other side of the Thames, for extended wanderings in Kennington and Lambeth—those quarters of a frightful misery—to allow him to return fatigued and at the same time discouraged and embittered, and to show him now in the Strand the reflection as well as the reverse of that life.

He was now standing at the entrance of the dark and desolate tunnel which passes underneath Charing Cross and leads to Northumberland Avenue. The shrill and vibrant sounds of a banjo struck his ear; a group of passers-by had collected: in their midst a boy in a ragged caricature costume and with blackened face was playing his instrument—who has not seen the bizarre forms of these "negro comedians" executing their noisy song-dances at the street corners of London?—while a girl was dancing to the sounds of the same with that mechanical indifference which seems to know no fatigue. Forcing his way along, Auban cast a glance also at the face of this child: indifference and at the same time a certain impatience lay upon it.

"They support their whole family, poor things!" he murmured. The next minute the crowd had dispersed, and the little couple forced their way to the next street corner, there to begin anew, play and dance, until the policeman, hated and feared, drove them away.

Auban passed through the tunnel whose stone floor was covered with filth and out of whose corners rose a corrupt atmosphere. It was almost deserted—only now and then some unrecognizable form crept along the walls and past him. But Auban knew that on wet, cold days and nights, here as well as in hundreds of other passageways, whole rows of unfortunates were lying about, closely pressed against each other and against the cold wills, and always expecting to be driven away the next moment by the "strong arm of the law": heaps of filth and rags, ruined in hunger and dirt, the "Pariahs of society," creatures in truth devoid of will.... And while he was climbing the steps at the end of the gloomy passages a scene which he had witnessed on this same spot about a year previous, suddenly rose before him with such terrific clearness that he involuntarily stopped and looked round as if it must repeat itself bodily before his eyes.

It was on a damp, cold evening, towards midnight, the city enveloped by fog and smoke as by an impenetrable veil. He had come hither to give some of the shelterless the few coppers which they need in order to pass the night in a lodging-house, instead of in the icy cold of the open air. When he had descended these steps—the tunnel was overcrowded by people who, after they had passed through all the stages of misery, had reached the last—he saw a face rise before him which he had never since forgotten: the features of a woman, frightfully disfigured by leprosy and bloody sores, who, with an infant at her breast, was dragging, rather than leading, a fourteen-year-old girl by the hand, while a third child, a boy, was clinging to her dress.

"Two shillings only, gentleman; two shillings only!"

He stopped to question her.

"Two shillings only; she is still so young, but she will do anything you want," and with that she drew the girl near, who turned away, trembling and crying.

A shudder ran through him. But the beseeching and piteous voice of the woman kept on.

"Pray, do take her along. If you won't do it, we shall have to sleep out doors—only two shillings, gentleman, only two shillings; just see how pretty she is!" And again she drew the child to her.

Auban felt a terror creeping over him. Stunned and unable to speak a word, he turned to pass on.

But he had not yet gone a step, when the woman suddenly threw herself shrieking before him on the ground, let go of the girl, and clung to him.

"Don't go away! Don't go away!" she screamed in frightful despair. "If you won't do it, we must starve—take her along!—no one else will come here to-night, and in the Strand we are not allowed—please do it—please do it!"

But when, without intending to, he looked round, the woman lying before him suddenly sprang up.

"Don't call a policeman! No, don't call a policeman!" she cried quickly, in fear. Then, when she arose, Auban regained his composure. Without a word he reached into his pocket and gave her a handful of money.

The woman uttered a shout of joy. Again she took the girl by the arm and placed her before him.

"She will go with you, gentleman—she will do anything you want," she added in a whisper. Auban turned away, and hurried as quickly as possible through the rows of the sleeping and the drunken people towards the exit: no one had paid any attention to the scene.

When he reached the Strand, he felt how violently his heart was beating, and how his hands were trembling.

A week later he came evening after evening to search in the tunnel of Charing Cross and its surroundings for the woman and her children, without being able to find them again. There had been something in the eyes of the girl that disquieted him. But the time had been too short for him to discern what this abyss of fear and misery concealed.

At last he became so absorbed in thinking of the immense wretchedness that daily presented itself to him that he forgot this one scene, and daily he saw again upon the streets the children of poverty—children of thirteen and fourteen years—offering themselves—and he was unable to help.

Who was more to be pitied, the mother or the children? How great must be the misery, how frightful the despair, how insane the hunger, that impelled both! But the woman of the *bourgeoisie* speaks with loathing of the "monster of a mother" and of the "degraded child"—the Pharisee who under the weight of the same misery would travel exactly the same paths.

Pity! Most miserable of all our lies! This age knows only injustice. It is today the greatest crime to be poor. Very well. The more quickly must the perception come that our only deliverance consists in omitting this crime.

"The insane ones!" murmured Auban, "the insane ones!—they do not see whither pity and love have brought us." His eyes were dimmed, as if by the memory of the struggles which this perception had caused him.

How plainly, in passing through the tunnel this evening, did he recall the piteous, despairing voice of the woman and her urgent: "Do it! do it!" And again out of the gloomy darkness emerged the shy, sickly eyes of the child.

He turned round, and again passed through the tunnel. But before starting for the Strand, he turned into one of the side streets that lead down towards the Thames. He knew them all: these streets, these corners, these entrances and alleys: here was the sober-gray rear of a theatre whose front flooded the Strand with light; and yonder narrow three-storied house with the sham windows was one of those notorious resorts whose inner walls nightly witness scenes of depravity such as even the most degraded fancy dare not fully picture to itself. Here misery still lived, and, in yonder quiet street hard by, comfort—and thus the two alternated as far as the little church of Savoy in the midst of its bare trees—and as far as the aristocratic, exclusive edifices of the Temple with its splendid gardens....

Auban knew all; even the forever-deserted broad, vaulted passage which leads underneath the streets to the Embankments, and from whose forsaken, mysterious stillness the life of the Strand sounds like the distant dying rush and roar of an ever last and ever first wave upon a desolate, sandy shore....

The cold became more piercing as the hour fled, and trickled down in the foggy dampness of London. Auban was getting tired, and decided to go home. He turned towards the Strand.

The "Strand!" Connecting the West End and the city, it lay before him, lit up by the countless lights of its shops, filled with the rush of a never-stagnant and never-ceasing human tide; two separate streams, the one surging up to St. Paul's, the other down to Charing Cross. Between both, the deafening confusion of an uninterrupted traffic of vehicles; one after another, 'busses, clumsy, covered with gaudy advertisements, filled with people; one after another, hansoms, light, running along easily on two wheels; thundering freight wagons; red, closed mail coaches of the Royal Mail; strong, broad four-wheelers; and winding their way through all these, hardly recognizable in the dark mass, swiftly gliding bicycles.

The East End is labor and poverty, chained together by the curse of our time—servitude; the City is the usurer who sells labor and pockets the profit; the West End is the aristocratic idler who consumes it. The Strand is one of the most swollen arteries through which courses the blood turned into money; it is the rival of Oxford Street, and struggles against being conquered by it. It is the heart of London. It bears a name which the world knows. It is one of the few streets where you see people from *all* sections of the city; the poor takes his rags there, and the rich his silk. If you lend your ear, you can hear the languages of the whole world; the restaurants have Italian proprietors, whose waiters talk French with you; more than half of the prostitutes are

Germans, who either perish here or save enough to return to their fatherland, and become "respectable" there.

Along the Strand are located the immense court buildings, and one is puzzled to know whether these are actors or lunatics whom one sees passing under the lofty archways—the judges in their long cloaks and their powdered wigs with the neatly ridiculous cues—respectable badges of a disreputable farce which every sensible man in his heart scorns and despises, and in which everybody plays a part if he is called; and in its cold Somerset House the Strand gathers a bewildering number of magistrates of whose existence you have never heard in your life until you hear them mentioned; and the Strand has its theatres, more theatres than any other street in the world.

Thus it is the first walk of the stranger who arrives at the station of Charing Cross, and whom its mostly narrow and crowding buildings disappoint; so will it be his last when he leaves London, the one to which he will give his last hour.

Auban disappeared in the sea of humanity. Now he was passing the Adelphi, and the electric light—far eclipsing the gas-jets—was filling the street with its clear white radiance, one could see that he limped slightly. It was hardly noticeable when he walked rapidly; but when he sauntered along slowly, he dragged the left foot slightly, and supported himself more on his cane.

At the station of Charing Cross the crowd had become blocked. For a few moments Auban stood near one of the gates. The gate nearest Villiers Street, which a few minutes ago he had crossed further down, was besieged by flower-girls, some of whom were cowering behind their half-empty baskets, cold and worn out, and some trying to persuade the passers-by to purchase their poor flowers, with their incessant "Penny a bunch!" A policeman pushed one of them brutally back; she had ventured to take a step upon the pavement, and they were not allowed to go an inch beyond the limits of the side street. The shrill cries of the newsboys who wished to get rid of their last special editions, in order to be able to see Charlie Coborn—the "inimitable"—in his "Too Lovely Black Eyes" in "Gatti's Hungerford Palace," would have been unbearable, had they not been drowned by the hoarse cries of the omnibus conductors and the rumble and clatter of wheels on the stones of the Charing Cross entrance, which the West Ender, accustomed to asphaltum and wooden pavements, has almost forgotten.

With a confidence which only a long familiarity with the street life of a great city can give, Auban improved the first second in which the rows of wagons offered a passage across the street; and while in the next the tides closed behind him, he passed the Church of St. Martin, cast a glance upon Trafalgar Square reposing in the stillness of the grave, cut through the narrow and dark Green Street without paying any attention to the "cabby," who from his box was calling at him in a suppressed voice that he had "something to say"—something about "a young lady"—and found himself three minutes later in the lighted lobbies of the "Alhambra," from which belated frequenters would not allow themselves to be turned away, as they still hoped to secure standing room in the overcrowded house. Auban passed indifferently on, without glancing at the shining photographs of the voluptuous ballet-dancers—

advertising specimens from the new monster ballet "Algeria," to which half of London was flocking.

The garden in the middle of Leicester Square lay shrouded in darkness. From the gratings the statue of Shakspere was no longer recognizable. "There is no darkness but ignorance," was graven there. Who read it?

The north end of the square was the scene of a boisterous life. Auban had to force his way through crowds of French prostitutes, whose loud laughter, screaming, and scolding, drowned everything. Their gaudy and vulgar dresses, their shameless offers, their endless entreaties: "Chéri, chéri," with which they approached and followed every passer-by, reminded him of the midnight hours on the outer boulevards of Paris.

Everywhere this age seemed to show him the most disfigured side of its face.

Before him two young English girls were walking along. They were scarcely more than sixteen years old. Their disheveled blond hair, wet from the moisture in the atmosphere, was hanging far over their shoulders. As they turned round, a look into their pale, weary features told him that they had long been wandering thus—forever the same short distance, evening after evening; at a street corner a German woman with the Cologne dialect and a far-sounding voice—all Germans shout in London—was telling another that she had not eaten anything warm for three days and nothing at all for one: business was growing worse and worse; at the next a crowd was gathering, into which Auban was pushed, so that he had to witness the scene that took place: an old woman who was selling matchboxes had got into a quarrel with one of the women. They screamed at each other. "There," shrieked the old one, and spat in the face of the other before her, but at the same instant the indignity was returned. For a moment both stood speechless with wrath. The old one, trembling, put the boxes in the bag. Then, amid the wild applause of the spectators, they thrust their finger-nails in each other's eyes and, blackguarding each other, rolled on the ground, until one of the spectators separated them; whereupon they picked up their things—the one her broken umbrella, the other her rag of a hat—and the crowd laughingly dispersed in all directions.

Auban passed on, towards the Piccadilly Circus. This scene, one among countless—what was it other than a new proof that the method of keeping the people in brutality, in order to talk about the "mob" and its degeneracy, was still very successful?

Music halls and boxing-matches:—these occupy the few free hours of the poorer classes of England; on Sundays prayers and sermons: excellent means against "the most dangerous evil of the time," the awakening of the people to intellectual independence.

Involuntarily Auban struck the ground with his cane, which he held in a firm grasp.

The square which he had just left, Piccadilly, and Regent Street—these are evening after evening and night after night the busiest and most frequented markets of living flesh for London. Hither the misery of the metropolis, assisted by the "civilized" states of the Continent, throws a supply which exceeds even an insatiable demand. From the beginning of dusk until the dawn of the new day prostitution sways the life of these centres of traffic, and seems to constitute the axis around which everything exclusively revolves.

How beautifully convenient the leaders of public life arrange things for themselves, mused Auban. If their reason brings up before a barn door, and they can go no farther, they instantly say: a necessary evil. Poverty—a necessary evil; prostitution—a necessary evil. And yet there is no less necessary and no greater evil than they themselves! It is they who would order all things, and who put all things into the greatest disorder; who would guide all things, and who divert all things from their natural paths; who would advance all things, and who hinder all progress.... They have big books written—it has ever been so, and must ever remain so; and, in order, nevertheless, to do something, at least seemingly, they devote themselves to "reform." And the more they reform, the worse things get. They see it, but they do not wish to see it; they know it, but they dare not know it. Why? They would then become useless, and nowadays everybody must make himself useful. A life of mere material ease will no longer suffice. "Deceived deceivers! from the first to the last!" said Auban, laughing; and his laughter was now almost without bitterness.

But this man who knew that there has never anywhere been justice on this earth, and who despised the belief in heavenly justice as the conscious lie of hired priests, or feared it as the unconscious and thoughtless devotion to this lie, felt, whenever he placed his hand in the festering sore of prostitution, with a shudder, that here was a way along which a tardy justice was slowly, inexpressibly slowly, creeping from the suffering to the living.

What to the wealthy are the people—the people who "must not be treated too well," lest they become overbearing? Human beings with the same claims on life and the same wishes as they themselves? Absurd dreams! A labor machine which must be attended to that it may do its work. And the verse of an English song ran through Auban's mind:

Our sons are the rich man's serfs by day,
And our daughters his slaves by night.

Their sons—good enough for labor. But at a distance—at a distance. A pressure of the hand that labors for them? Labor is their duty. And these hands are so soiled—by the labor of a neverending day.

Their daughters—good enough to serve as conduits for the troubled stream of their lusts which would else overflow on the immaculate and pure souls of their own mothers and daughters. Their daughters by night! What will money not buy of hunger and of despair?

But here—here alone!—the one thus sacrificed draws her murderers into the whirlpool of their ruin.

Our whole sexual life—here wildly riotous, there pressed into the unnatural relationship of marriage—is being overspread, as by a dark, threatening cloud, by a legion of terrible diseases, at whose mention everybody grows pale, because no one is secure against them. And as it has corrupted an incalculable portion of the youth of our time, so it is already standing as the fulfilment of an unuttered curse over a generation still lying in slumber.

Auban was forced to look up. A crowd of young men of the *jeunesse dorée* were staggering out of the London Pavilion, whose gas torches scattered their streams of light over Piccadilly Circus. Their sole employment was only too plainly written on their dull, brutally debauched faces: sport, women, and horses. They were of course in full dress; but the tall hats were crushed in, and shirts, crumpled and soiled by whiskey and cigar ashes, furnished a conspicuous contrast to their black frock coats. With coarse laughter and cynical remarks some of them surrounded a few of the *demi-monde,* while the others called for hansoms, which speedily came driving up; the noisily protesting women were forced in, and the singing of the drunken men died away in the clatter of the departing cabs.

Auban surveyed the place. There before him—down Piccadilly—lay a world of wealth and comfort: the world of the aristocratic palaces and the great clubs, of the luxurious stores and of fashionable art—the whole surfeited and extravagant life of the "great world,"...the sham life of pretence.

The lightning of the coming revolution must strike first here. It cannot be otherwise....

As Auban crossed the street, he was attracted by the ragged form of an aged man, who, whenever the traffic of the wagons permitted, cleared the street of the traces left by the wagons and horses, and, when his broom had done the work, modestly waited for the thoughtfulness of those whose feet he had protected against contact with the filth; and Auban became curious to see how many would even as much as notice the service. For about five minutes he leaned against the lantern post in front of the arched entrance of Spiers and Pond's restaurant at the Criterion, and watched the untiring labor of the old man. During these five minutes about three hundred persons crossed the street dry-shod. The old man no one saw.

"You are not doing a good business?" he asked, as he approached him.

The old man put his hand in the pocket of his ragged coat and drew forth four copper pieces.

"That is all in three hours."

"That is not enough for your night's lodging," said Auban, and gave him a sixpence.

And the old man looked after him, as he slowly crossed the place with difficult steps.

Behind Auban disappeared the lights of the place, the light-colored, similarly built houses of the square of Regent Street; and while the distances behind him grew narrower and the roar died away, he walked on confidently farther and farther into the dark, mysterious network of the streets of Soho....

At the same hour—it was not far from nine—there was coming from the east, from the direction of Drury Lane towards Wardour Street, with the unsteady haste which shows that one is in a strange and unknown quarter and yet would like to reach a definite place, a man of about forty years, in the not striking dress of a laborer, which differs from that of the citizen in London only by its simplicity. As he stopped—convinced that he would hardly gratify his impatience by proceeding in the direction he was going—and asked his way of one of the young fellows congregated in front of one of the innumerable public houses, it was to be seen by his vain efforts to make himself understood that the inquirer was a foreigner.

He seemed, nevertheless, to have understood the explanations, for he took an entirely different route from the one which he had been following. He turned towards the north. After he had passed through two or three more of the equally dark, filthy, and in all respects similar streets, he suddenly found himself in the midst of the tumult of one of those market-places where on Saturday evenings the population of the poorer quarters supply their needs for the following days with the wages of the past week. The sides of the street were occupied by two endless rows of closely crowding carts with tables and stands, heavily laden with each of the thousand needs of daily life, and between them, as well as on the narrow sidewalks beside the open and overstocked shops, a turbulent and haggling mass was pushing and jostling along, whose cries and noise were only surpassed by the shrill confusion of the voices of the vendors praising their wares. The street in its entire length was dipped in a dazzling brightness by the flickering blaze of countless petroleum flames, a brightness such as the light of day never brought here; the damp air filled with a thick, steaming smoke; the ground covered with sweepings of all kinds which made walking on the slippery, irregular stone pavement still more difficult.

The laborer who had made inquiry concerning his way became entangled in the throng, and was trying to extricate himself as quickly as he could. He hardly gave a look at the treasures stored round about—at the stands with the huge, raw, bloody pieces of meat; at the heavily laden carts with vegetables of all sorts; at the tables full of old iron and clothing; at the long rows of foot-wear bound together which hung stretched above him and across the street; at the whole impenetrable hodge-podge of retail trade that here surrounded him with its noise and violence. When, accompanied by the curses of the crowd, a cart pushed recklessly through the multitude, he availed himself of the opportunity to follow it, and thus reached sooner than he had hoped the corner of the next cross-street, where things again took their even course and offered the possibility of standing still for a moment.

Then, as he looked round, he suddenly saw Auban on the other side of the street. Surprised to see his friend so unexpectedly in this quarter, he did not at once hasten to him; and then—as he had already half crossed the street—he turned back into the crowd, impelled by the thought: "What is he doing here?" The next minute he gazed at him attentively.

Auban was standing in the middle of a row of half-drunken men who were laying siege to the entrance of a public house, in the hope of being invited by one of their acquaintances: "Have a drink." He was standing there, bent forward a little, his hands resting on the cane held between his knees, and staring fixedly into the passing throng, as if waiting to see a familiar face emerge from it. His features were severe; around the mouth lay a sharp line, and his deep-sunken eyes wore a fixed and gloomy look. His closely-shaved cheeks were lean, and the sharp nose gave the features of his narrow and fine face the expression of great will-power. A dark, loose cloak fell carelessly down the exceptionally tall and narrow-shouldered form; and as the other on the opposite street corner saw him so standing, it struck him for the first time that for years he had not seen him otherwise than in this same loose garment of the same comfortable cut and of the same simplest dark color. Just so plain and yet so striking had been his external appearance when—how long ago was it: six or seven years already?—he made his acquaintance in Paris, and just as then, with the same regular, sharp, and gloomy features which had at most grown a little more pale and gray, he was standing there today careless and unconcerned, in thoughtful contemplation in the midst of the feverish and joyless bustle of the Saturday evening of Soho.

Now he was coming towards him, fixedly gazing straight ahead. But he did not see him, and was about to pass by him.

"Auban!" exclaimed the other.

The person addressed was not startled, but he turned slowly to one side and gazed with a vacant and absent look into the face of the speaker, until the other grasped him by the arm.

"Auban!"

"Otto?" asked he then, but without surprise. And then almost in a whisper, and in the husky tones, still half embarrassed through fear, of one awaking and telling of his bad dream, softly, lest he call it to life: "I was thinking of something else; of—of the misery, how great it is, how enormous, and how slowly the light comes, how slowly."

The other looked at him surprised. But already Auban, suddenly awake, burst out in laughter, and in his usual confident voice asked:

"But how in the world do you come from your East End to Soho?"

"I have gone astray. Where is Oxford Street? There, is it not?"

But Auban took him smilingly by the shoulder and turned him round.

"No, there. Listen: before us lies the north of the city, the entire length of Oxford Street; behind us, the Strand, which you know; there, whence you came—you came from the east?—is Drury Lane and the former Seven Dials, of which you have surely already heard. Seven Dials, the former hell of poverty; now 'civilized.' Have you not yet seen the famous Birddealers' Street? Look," he continued, without awaiting an answer, and made a gesture with his hand toward the east, "in those streets as far as Lincoln's Inn Fields, a large portion of the misery of the West End is quartered. What do you think they would not give if they could sweep it off and push it to the east? Of what use is it that they build broad thoroughfares, just as Haussmann, the prefect of the Seine, did in Paris, in order thus more readily to meet the revolutions—of what use is it? It crowds only more closely on itself. There is not a Saturday evening that I do not go through this quarter between Regent Street and Lincoln's Inn, between the Strand and Oxford Street; it is an empire in itself, and I find just as much to see here as in the East End. It is the first time you are here?"

"Yes, if I am not mistaken. Did not the Club meet here formerly?"

"Yes. But nearer to Oxford Street. However, a lot of Germans are living here—in the better streets near Regent Street."

"Where is misery worst?"

"Worst?" Auban reflected a moment. "If you turn in from Drury Lane—the Courts of Wild Street; then the terrible jumble of almost tumbledown houses near the Old Curiosity Shop which Dickens has described, with the dirt-covered alleys; in general, along the side streets of Drury Lane, especially in the north along the Queen Streets; and further this way, above all, the former Dials, the hell of hells."

"Do you know all the streets here?"

"All."

"But you cannot see much on them. The tragedies of poverty are enacted behind the walls."

"But still the last act—how often!—on the street."

They had slowly walked on. Auban had placed his arm in that of the other, and was leaning wearily against him. Notwithstanding this, he limped more than before.

"And where are you going, Otto?" he asked.

"To the Club. Will you not come along?"

"I am a little tired. I spent the whole afternoon over yonder." Then, as it occurred to him that the other might see in these words only a pretence for declining, he added more quickly: "But I'll go with you; it is a good chance; else I should not get there so very soon again. How long it is since we saw each other!"

"Yes; it is almost three weeks!"

"I am beginning, more and more, to live for myself. You know it. What can I do in the clubs? These long speeches, always on the same subject: what are they for? All that is only tiresome."

He saw very well how disagreeable his words were to the other, and how he nevertheless tried to come to terms with the justice of his remark.

"I am still at home every Sunday afternoon after five o'clock, as I used to be. Why don't you come any more?"

"Because all sorts of people meet at your place; *bourgeois*, and Social Democrats, and literary people, and Individualists."

Auban burst out laughing. "*Tant mieux.* The discussions can only gain thereby. But the Individualists are the worst of all, aren't they, Otto?"

His face was completely changed. Just before gloomy and reserved, it now showed a kindly expression of friendship and friendliness.

But the other, who had been addressed as Otto, and whose name was Trupp, seemed to be affected only disagreeably by it, and he mentioned a name which, although it did not remove the calm from Auban's brow, made the smile die away from his lips.

"Fifteen years! And for nothing!" said the workingman, wrathful and indignant.

"But why did he go so carelessly into the trap of his enemies? He must have known them."

"He was betrayed!"

"Why did he confide in others?" asked Auban again. "Everyone is lost from the start who builds on others. He knew this too. It was a useless sacrifice!"

"I fear you have no idea of the greatness of this sacrifice and his devotion," said Trupp, angrily.

"Dear Otto, you know very well that I am altogether lacking in the feeling of appreciation of all so-called sacrifices. Of what use has been the defeat of the comrade, the best, the most honest, perhaps, of all? Tell me!"

"It has made the struggle more bitter. It has shaken some out of their lethargy; others—us—it has filled with new hate. It has"—and his eyes flashed, while Auban felt how the arm which he was holding was trembling in convulsive wrath—"it has renewed within us the oath to claim on the day of reckoning a hundredfold expiation for every victim!"

"And then?"

"Then when this accursed order has been razed to the ground, then upon its ruins will rise the free society."

Auban looked again at the violent talker, with the sad, serious look with which he had before greeted him. He knew that in the distracted breast of this man but one wish and one hope were still living—the hope of the outbreak of the "great," of the "last," revolution.

Thus, years ago, had they walked over the boulevards of Paris and intoxicated themselves by the sounding words of hope; and while Auban had long ago lost all faith, except the faith in the slowly, slowly acting power of reason, which will finally lead every man, instead of providing for others, to provide for himself, and had thus more and more come back to himself, so the other had more and more lost himself in the fanaticism of a despair, and conjured daily anew the shimmering ghost of the "golden future" before his eyes, and let slip from his hands, which longingly and confidingly entwined the neck of love, the last hold upon the reality of things.

"In fifteen years," thus again broke forth, blazing, the flame of hope from his words, "much can happen!"

Auban made no further answer. He was powerless against this faith. Slowly they walked on. The streets grew more and more deserted and quiet. The atmosphere, growing denser and denser, was still charged with the teeming dampness of three hours ago. The sky was one misty, gray mass of clouds. The lanterns gleamed with an unsteady flicker. Between the two men lay the silence of estrangement.

They were also externally very different.

Auban was taller and thinner; Trupp, more muscular and well-proportioned. The latter wore a short, brown, full beard, while the former was always carefully shaved. When they were alone they always, as on this evening, talked in French, which Trupp spoke without trouble, if not quite correctly, while Auban spoke it so rapidly that even Frenchmen often found difficulty in following him. His voice had a strange, hard sound, which occasionally yielded to the warmth of his vivacity, but still oftener to a fine irony.

Before them the tangle of small and narrow streets was beginning to disappear. They ascended a few steps. There lay Oxford Street!

"In fifteen years," Auban broke the silence, "the chains of servitude will have nearly cut through the wrists of the nations in the countries of the Continent, so that they will no longer be able to strike a blow. Here the same hands will be manacled on the day on which the right of speech is denied the mouth which now protests and talks itself hoarse."

"I know the workingmen better than you. They will have risen long before then."

"Only to be mown down by cannons, which automatically fire one shot every second, and sixty in a minute. Yes. I know the *bourgeoisie* better, and its helpers."

They were standing in Oxford Street: in the light and life of night.

"Look there—do you believe this life, so entangled, so perplexed, so enormously complicated, will fall at one blow, and at the bidding of a few individuals?"

"Yes," said Trupp, and pointed to the east. "There lies the future."

But Auban asked: "What is the future? The future is Socialism. The suppression of the individual into ever-narrower limits. The total lack of independence. The large family. All children, children.... But this, too, must be passed through." He laughed bitterly, and as he followed the gaze of his friend: "There lies—Russia." Then both were again silent.

Oxford Street stretched away—an immeasurable line of blending light and rushing darkness up and down.

"There are three Londons," said Auban, impressed by the life, "three: London on Saturday evening, when it gets drunk in order to forget the coming week, London on Sunday, when it sleeps in the lap of the infallible church to sober up; and London, when it works and lets work—on the long, long days of the week."

"I hate this city," said the other.

"I love it!" said Auban, passionately.

"How different was Paris!"

And the common memories rose before them.

But Auban hurried on.

"We shall never reach the Club."

They crossed Oxford Street straight ahead, and walked up the next cross-street towards the north. Auban again rested heavily on the arm of his friend. "But tell me: how are matters?"

"Very well, notwithstanding we are still without a 'council.' Do you still remember what a fuss was made at the time we organized the Club wholly according to the communistic principle: without council, without officers, without statutes, without programme, and without fixed compulsory dues? Complete failure through disorder was prophesied, and all other possible things besides. But we are still getting on very nicely, and in our meetings things proceed just as in others where the bell of the president rules—it is always one talking after the other, if he has anything to say."

Auban smiled.

"Yes," said he, "that the fanatics of order cannot understand, how sensible people can come together and remain together in order to deliberate on their common interests, unless the individual has been guaranteed his membership with rights and duties on a bit of paper. But the fact that this attempt has not failed is surely not a proof to you of the possibility of constituting human society at large on like foundations? That would be pure insanity."

"So? that would be pure insanity? We don't think so. We cherish this hope," protested Trupp, tenaciously.

Auban broke in: "How is your paper going?"

"Slowly. Do you read it?"

"Yes. But rarely. I have forgotten the little German that I learned in school."

"We edit it together, too. Without a committee, without an editor. On one evening in the week those who have time and who feel inclined come together, and the communications sent in are read, discussed, and put together."

"But that is why the matter differs so extraordinarily in point of excellence and is so heterogeneous. No, back of a paper must be a personality, a complete, interesting personality."

Trupp interrupted him violently.

"Yes, and then we should again have 'leadership.' A manager always turns into a governor"—he did not notice the assenting nod of Auban—"here in the small way, there in the large! Our whole movement has terribly suffered therefrom, from this centralism. Where in the beginning there was pure enthusiasm, it has changed into self-complacency; genuine pity and love into the desire of each to act the part of the saviour. Thus we already have everywhere high and low, the flock and the bell-weather, on the one side conceit, on the other thoughtless and fanatical echoing of the party principles."

"But you have indeed totally misunderstood me. As if I had ever believed anything else! On general principles I distrust everyone who would presume to represent others, to provide for others, and to take upon his own shoulders the responsibility for the affairs of others. Mind your own business and let me take care of mine—that is a good saying. And really Anarchism."

"I, too, am an Anarchist."

"No, my friend, you are not. You champion in every respect the opposite of truly Anarchistic ideas. You are a thorough-going Communist—not only in your opinions, but in your whole way of feeling and wishing."

"Who would dispute my right to call my opinions Anarchistic?"

"Nobody. But you do not consider what lamentable confusion arises from the mixing of totally different conceptions. But why quarrel now over the old question? Come on Sunday. We might again discuss. Why not?"

"Very well. But you are, and you will remain, the Individualist that you have become since you have studied the social question 'scientifically'! I wish you were still the same that you were when I met you in Paris, my friend!"

"No, not I, Otto!" said Auban, and laughed out loud.

Trupp was annoyed.

"You do not know what you are defending! Is not Individualism synonymous with giving free reign to all the low passions of man, above all, egoism, and has it not produced all this misery—liberty on the one—"

Auban stopped and looked at the speaker.

"Liberty of the individual? Today when we are living under a Communism more complicated and brutal than ever before? Today when the individual, from the cradle to the grave, is placed under contribution to the State, to the community? Go to the ends of the world, and tell me where I can escape these obligations and be myself. I will go to this liberty that I have sought in vain all my life."

"But your views only furnish new weapons to the *bourgeoisie*."

"If you will not use these weapons yourselves, the only ones in which I still believe. Only then. And surely, they—these slowly ripening thoughts of egoism (I use this word deliberately)—they are in the same way dangerous to the present conditions as they will be dangerous to the conditions prevailing when we shall have entered the haven of the popular state that will make all things happy, the haven of condensed Communism—more dangerous than all your bombs and all the bayonets and *mitrailleuses* of the present rulers."

"You have greatly changed," said Trupp, seriously.

"No, Otto. I have only found myself."

"We must come back to this. It must be decided—"

"Whether I still belong to you or not? But this is surely only talk. For the free man—and you want the whole, undivided autonomy of the individual—can only belong to himself."

They had now entered Charlotte Street, which lay before them in its length and gloomy darkness.

They turned into one of the side streets, into one of the almost deserted and half-lighted passages which stretch along towards the noise of Tottenham Court Road.

"Now we must talk German," said Auban in that language, which sounded odd and unfamiliar on his lips.

They stopped in front of a narrow, light-colored house.

Above the door, upon the pane illuminated by the flickering light behind it, stood the name of the Club.

Trupp quickly opened the door, and they entered.

Chapter II.
The Eleventh Hour

On Friday evening of the following week Carrard Auban was riding down the endlessly long City Road in an omnibus. He sat beside the driver—a gentleman in a silk hat and with a faultless exterior—and watched impatiently the gradual lessening of the distance which separated him from his destination. He was excited and out of sorts. As the omnibus stopped at Finsbury Square, he quickly alighted, hurried down the pavement as far as the next cross-street after he had satisfied himself about the direction, and found himself a few minutes later on the steps of South Place Institute.

Even from a distance an unusually large concourse of people was noticeable. At short intervals policemen were standing round. The doors of the dark, church-like building were wide open; as Auban slowly pushed his way in with the stream, he exchanged hasty words of greeting with some acquaintances who were stationed there to sell the papers of their society or their party. The responses frequently told of surprise or pleasure at seeing him.

He took what came in his way of the papers offered for sale: "Commonweal," the interesting organ of the Socialist League; "Justice," the party organ of the Social Democratic Federation; and a few copies of the new German paper, "Londoner Freie Presse," the enterprise of a number of German Socialists of the various schools, which was to form a common ground for their views, and to serve the propaganda among the German-speaking portion of the London population. Auban never returned from these meetings without having filled his breast-pocket with papers and pamphlets.

At the inner entrance the resolution of the evening was being distributed: large, clearly printed quarto sheets.

The hall was of about equal width and depth; a broad gallery, which was already nearly filled, extended along the walls. At an elevation of several feet, a platform rose in front, on which were placed a number of chairs for the speakers. It was still unoccupied. The hall gave the impression of being used for religious purposes. The shape of the seats also indicated this.

This evening, however, nothing was to be noticed of the indifferent, mechanically quiet routine of a religious meeting. The seats were occupied by an excited, strongly moved multitude loudly exchanging their opinions. Auban rapidly surveyed it. He saw many familiar faces. At the corner of the hall, near the platform, a number of the speakers of the evening had gathered. Auban cut through the rows of benches that were incessantly being filled, and approached the group. With some he exchanged a quiet pressure of the hand; to others he nodded.

"Well, you will of course speak, too, Mr. Auban?" he was asked.

He shook his head, deprecatingly.

"I do not like to speak English, do not like to speak at all. That's past. And what should I say? What one would like to say he is not allowed to say. It is a mixed meeting?" he then asked more softly of a man standing near him, the well-known agitator of a German revolutionary club.

"Yes, radicals, free-thinkers, liberals—all sorts of people. You will see, most of the speakers will disavow all sympathy with Anarchism."

"Have you not seen Trupp?"

"No; he surely will not come. I have never yet met him at one of these meetings."

Auban looked round. The hall was already crowded to suffocation; the aisles between the seats were filled; a number of working-men surrounded the large group photograph of the Chicago condemned, which, in a broad gilt frame, was suspended beneath the speaker's table. On the table adjoining, several newspaper reporters were putting their writing-pads in order.

At the entrances the crowd became more and more excited. The doors were wide open. From the pushing and jostling it could be seen that large masses were still demanding admission. Some succeeded in forcing their way to the front, where there still was room on the seats if people crowded closer together. When Auban saw this, he also quickly secured a seat for himself, for his lame leg did not permit him to remain standing for hours.

He planted his cane firmly and crossed his legs. So he remained sitting the entire evening. He could overlook the whole hall, as he sat on one of the side seats: the platform lay right before him.

He took the resolution from his pocket and read it through carefully and slowly, as well as the list of speakers: "several of the most prominent Radicals and Socialists." He knew all the names and the men to whom they belonged, although he had scarcely met any of them during the past year.

"The right of free speech," was on the programme. "Seven men sentenced to death for holding a public meeting." The resolution read: "—that the English workingmen in this meeting earnestly wish to call the attention of their fellow-workingmen in America to the great danger to public liberty which will arise if they permit the punishment of citizens for attempting to resist the suppression of the right of public assembly and free speech, since a right for the exercise of which people may be punished, thereby clearly becomes no right, but a wrong.

"That the fate of the seven men who are under sentence of death for holding a public meeting in Chicago, at which several policemen were killed in an attempt to forcibly disperse the people and suppress the speakers, is of the greatest importance to us as English workingmen, since their case is today the case of our comrades in Ireland, and perhaps tomorrow our own, if the workingmen on both sides of the Atlantic shall not unanimously declare that all who interfere with the right of public assembly and free speech do so illegally and at their own peril. We cannot admit that the political opinions of the seven condemned men have anything whatever to do with the principles cited, and we protest against their sentence, which, if it is executed, will make a capital crime of meetings held by workingmen in the United States of America, since it is always in the power of the authorities to incite a public gathering to resistance by threatening their lives. We expect of our American comrades, however greatly their political opinions may differ, that they will demand the unconditional release of the seven men in whose persons the liberties of all workingmen are now threatened...."

When Auban had finished, he saw beside him an old man with a long, white beard and friendly expression.

"Mr. Marell," he exclaimed, visibly pleased, "are you back again? What a surprise!"

They shook hands heartily.

"I did not mean to disturb you—you were reading.

They spoke English together.

"How long since you returned?"

"Since yesterday.

"And were you in Chicago?"

"Yes, fourteen days; then in New York."

"I had not expected you—"

"I could not bear it any longer, so I came back."

"You saw the condemned?"

"Certainly; often."

Auban bent over to him and asked in a low voice:—

"There is no hope?"

The old man shook his head.

"None. The last lies with the governor of Illinois, but I don't believe in him."

They continued in an undertone.

"How is public sentiment?"

"Public sentiment is depressed. The Knights of Labor and the Georgeites are holding back. Altogether, many things are different from what one imagines here. Here and there the excitement is great, but the time is not yet ripe."

"Everything will be done?"

"I don't know. In any case, everything will be useless."

Both were silent. Auban looked more serious than usual. But even now it was not to be discerned what kind of feeling it was which ruled him.

"How are the prisoners?"

"Very calm. Some don't want a pardon, and will say so. But I fear the others are still hoping."

It was past eight o'clock. The meeting began to grow impatient; the voices became louder.

Auban continued to inquire, and the old man replied in his calm, sad voice.

"You will speak, Mr. Marell?"

"No, my friend. There is another, a younger one here; he also comes from Chicago, and he will have something to say about them there."

"Will you be at home tomorrow?"

"Yes; come. I will give you the proceedings, and the latest papers. I have brought much with me. Everything I could get. Much. If you were to read everything, you would get a good picture of our American conditions."

"A new trial will not be granted?"

"I hope not. For it wouldn't be of any use; the torture, which already is unendurable, would be uselessly prolonged; new, immense sums would have to be raised by the people—again fifty thousand dollars, composed of labor pennies—and to what end?—no; the hyena wants blood."

"And the people?"

"The people doesn't know itself what it wants. It does not yet believe in the gravity of the situation, and when the Eleventh has come, it will be too late."

A young Englishman, who knew Mr. Marell from the Socialist League, joined in their conversation. Auban looked up. The former said seriously:—

"No; I still will not believe it. At the close of the nineteenth century, in full view of the nations, they will not murder seven men whose innocence is as clear as day;

thousands upon thousands are slain, but people no longer have the courage to simply boast of power and mock all laws in a country with the institutions of the States. No; they will not do it, for the reason that it would be madness from their standpoint thus to enlighten and arouse the people. No; they will not dare. Just look; all this number of people here, and so every day in all liberal countries, here and on the other side, these meetings, these papers, this flood of pamphlets! Where is the man with a mind and a heart who does not revolt?—are the hosts to be counted that are rising on the other side? And their will would not be powerful enough to fill those hired scoundrels with terror and make them desist from carrying out their wicked designs? No; they will not dare, comrade! It would be their own ruin!"

The two whom he addressed shrugged their shoulders. What could they answer him?

In the struggle of the two classes, both of them had seen those who hold the power in their hands commit so many outrages that they had to ask themselves what could happen that might still surprise them and excite their indignation.

Auban saw how the hands of the old man, holding a gray, shabby hat, trembled, and how he was trying to conceal this slight trembling, which told of his emotion, by carelessly playing with his hat.

"They believe they will strike Anarchism in the heart if they hang a number of its champions," he said. Auban noticed that he did not care to go on with the conversation at this time, and remained silent.

But he again pondered: "What is Anarchism?" The condemned of Chicago? Their views were partly social-democratic, partly Communistic, no two of them would have given the same answer to any question put to them involving first principles, and yet all called themselves and were called "Anarchists"; but when had Individualism ever spoken more defiantly than out of the mouth of that young Communist who had thundered at his "Judges": "I despise you, I despise your laws, your 'order,' your government," and: "I stand by it: if we are threatened by cannon, we will answer with dynamite bombs."

And further, the old man who was sitting beside him! He, too, called himself "Anarchist."...

And what was it that he was ever anew preaching in his countless pamphlets? Love. "What is Anarchy?" he asks. And he answers: "It is a system of society in which no one disturbs the action of his neighbor; where liberty is free from law; where there is no privilege; where force does not determine human actions. The ideal is one with that proclaimed two thousand years ago by the Nazarene: the brotherhood of all mankind." And pained, he again and again exclaims: "Revenge is the lesson preached by the pulpit, by the press, by all classes of society! No, preach love! love! love!"...

It occurred to Auban, in recalling these words, how dangerous it was to speak in such general, such hazy, such superficial terms to those who were as yet so little prepared to discover the meaning and the import of the words. Thus did the incongruous and foreign elements more and more form themselves into a coil whose unravelling frightened away many who would else gladly have followed the individual threads.

Auban had only recently made the acquaintance of the old man. It had been at a debate in which the differences between individualistic and communistic Anarchism were discussed. Mr. Marell had been the only one who—as he himself believed—championed the former. His reasoning had interested Auban. Notwithstanding its inconsistencies, he found much in it that was in close relation to his own conclusions. So they had become acquainted with each other and met a few times before the former returned to America, to do there, as he said, what was yet in his power to do. As he never talked about himself, Auban did not know of what nature these efforts were to be, and from what he had heard this evening he could see further that they had been unsuccessful. But so much was clear: that this man seemed to be at the head of a very extended ramification of connections of all kinds; for he knew all the eight persons implicated in the trial, and appeared likewise to be well informed in regard to the spread of the Anarchistic teachings in America.

All his pamphlets were signed: "The Unknown." In London, the old man was not a striking figure: he rarely spoke in public, and the tide of the revolutionary movement of London casts too many individuals on the surface today only to swallow them up again tomorrow, to permit of paying special attention to the transient visitor in this ceaseless coming and going.

He now made inquiry of the Englishman concerning some of those present. Auban leaned back.

"Who is that?"

He pointed to a woman in a simple, dark dress, who was sitting near them. Her well-defined features betrayed the liveliest interest in everything that was going on about her, and she spoke animatedly and laughingly with her neighbor.

"I don't know," replied the Englishman. But then he remembered once having seen her in a German club, and he added:—

"I only know that she is a German, a German Socialist. Ambitious, but with a good heart. In Berlin she agitated a long time for the abolition of the medical examination of prostitutes."

The old man, curious, continued to put questions to the one standing before him.

"And to whom is she talking now?"

The Englishman looked. It was a young man whom he also knew only slightly.

"I believe he is a poet," he said. Both smiled.

"He has written a poem on social life."

"Have you read it?"

"Oh, no; I don't read German."

"He looks neither like a poet nor like a Socialist. Does he believe he can improve the world with his poems? He will one day see how useless they are, and that people must have bread before they can think of other things. If one has nothing to eat, poetry is at an end."

The younger man smiled at the zeal of the older, who continued, undisturbed, while Auban studied the crowd.

"It is possible to write the tenderest love poems and like a butcher to witness the bloodiest atrocities. And one will write a public hymn in honor of the 'brave soldiers,' the murderers, who return from the battles dripping with blood. One can sing of the 'sufferings of the people,' and the next hour, in the ball-room, kiss the hand of 'her ladyship,' who has just before boxed the ears of her servant. But what are we talking about? Tell me rather who is the gentleman yonder?"

"One of our parliamentary candidates. A scamp without character. A declaimer. If he had the power, he would be a tyrant. But as it is, he does enough mischief."

NOW BOTH BEGAN TO give their attention to the meeting. Auban was still absorbed in his thoughts. The chairs on the platform had become occupied by the representatives and delegates of the societies which had called the mass-meeting. Among them were several women. The chairman's seat was occupied by a pale man in the dress of a High Church clergyman, about forty years old. He was greeted with applause when his election as chairman was announced. Auban knew him; he was a Christian Socialist, who had for many years been active among the poor of the East End. On account of his opinions he had been deprived of his living. The Church is the greatest enemy of character.

He now called the meeting to order. He said that it was composed of people of the most divergent views, of Radicals and Anti-Socialists as well as of Anarchists and Socialists, but who were united in the one wish to protest against the violation of the right of free speech. He was no Anarchist like the Chicago condemned; he had a strong aversion to their doctrines; but he demanded for their disciples and followers exactly the same or even greater liberty than he—the minister of a Christian church—claimed for himself in the expression of his opinions. All had an equal right to serve what they had learned, and what they held to be the truth, and therefore he demanded in the name of his God, and in the name of humanity, the release of these men.

When he had finished, a large number of telegrams, addresses of sympathy, and letters from all parts of England were read. Many of them were received with enthusiasm.

Auban knew that many of these societies had a membership of thousands; among the names he heard read were some of the greatest influence. The writers whose works everybody read—what were they all doing, all who were as surely convinced as he was of the atrocity of that sentence? They quieted their conscience with a protest. What could they have done? Their influence, their position, their power—these might perhaps have been strong and impressive enough to make impossible the execution of that deed in the face of an excited and general indignation that had arisen. But their name and their protest—these died away here before the few without effect. They, too, were the slaves of their time who might have been its true masters.

Auban was roused from his thoughts by a voice which he had often heard. Beside the table on the platform was standing a little woman dressed in black. Beneath the brow which was half hidden as by a wreath by her thick, short-cropped hair, shone a pair of black eyes beaming with enthusiasm. The white ruffle and the simple, almost monk-like, long, undulating garment seemed to belong to another century. A few only in the meeting seemed to know her; but whoever knew her, knew also that she was the most faithful, the most diligent, and the most impassioned champion of Communism in England. She, too, called herself an Anarchist.

She was not a captivating speaker, but her voice had that iron ring of unalterable conviction and honesty which often moves the listener more powerfully than the most brilliant eloquence.

She gave a picture of all the events that had preceded the arrest and conviction of the comrades in Chicago. Clearly—step by step—they passed before the eyes of the listeners....

She told of the rise and progress of the eight-hour movement in America; of the efforts of former years to enforce the eight-hour labor day among the government employees; of their successes.... She explained how it had happened that the revolutionaries of Chicago joined the movement without deceiving themselves as to its significance and real importance; of the untiring efforts of the International Workingmen's Association; and how those men who were now facing death had been forced to take the lead in the movement....

Then she attempted to describe the tremendous excitement which had preceded the May days of the previous year: the feverish tension in the circles of the workingmen, the rising fear in those of the exploiters.... The rapid growth of the strikers up to the day, the first of May, which, looked forward to by all, was to bring about the decision....

Then she conjured before the eyes of the meeting the days of May themselves; "more than twenty-five thousand workingmen lay down their work on one and the same day; within three days their number has doubled. It is a general strike. The rage of the capitalists is comparable only to their fear. Evening after evening meetings are held in many places of the city. The government sends its policemen and orders them to fire into one of these peaceable gatherings: five workingmen are left dead on the spot....

"Who has called the murderers of those men to account? Nobody."

She paused. One could hear her emotion in the tone of her voice when she continued:—

"The following evening the Anarchists call a meeting at the Haymarket. It is orderly; notwithstanding the occurrences of the previous days, the addresses of the speakers are so little incendiary that the mayor of Chicago—ready to disperse the meeting on the first unlawful word—notifies the police inspector that he may send his men home. But instead of doing so, he orders them again to march upon the meeting. At this moment a bomb flies from an unknown hand into the attacking ranks. The police open a murderous fire....

"Who threw the bomb? Perhaps the hand of one who in despair wished thus to defend himself against this new slaughter; perhaps—this was the prevailing opinion in the circles of the workingmen of Chicago—one of the commissioned agents of the police themselves; who does not know the means to which our enemies resort in order to destroy us? If this was the case, he did his business even better than had been expected.

"Who threw the bomb? We know it as little as those eight men know it, who, in the tremendous consternation which spread over Chicago from this hour, were seized at hazard, as they bore the best-known names of the movement, although several of them had not even been present at the meeting. But what of that? The court was as little deterred from arresting them as later on from finding them guilty of secret conspiracy, notwithstanding some of them had never before seen each other.

"Why were they convicted?" she closed. "Not because they have committed a crime—no; because they were the champions of the poor and the oppressed! Not because they are murderers—no; because they dared to open the eyes of the slaves to the causes of their slavery. These men whose spotless character could not be soiled even by the most venomous attacks of the 'organs of public opinion,' will be hanged because they followed their convictions unselfishly, nobly, and faithfully in an age when only he goes unharmed who as a liar keeps the company of liars!"

She stopped. All had listened attentively. Many applauded.

Auban followed her with his penetrating eyes as she descended the steps of the platform into the hall and, on finding all the seats occupied, carelessly seated herself on one of the steps. It seemed as if he wished to look through the hand which she was holding before her eyes as if in bodily pain, into her very soul, to find there also the confirmation of his deepest conviction, which is the last to be acquired—the selfishness of all being. And even here he did not for a moment hesitate to confess that this woman must be happier in this life of toil, sacrifice, and privation, than she would have been had she continued in that other in which she had grown up, in wealth and ease, and which she had left—as she and all others believed—to serve "the cause of humanity," while in reality, even if entirely unconsciously, she followed the call of her own happiness.

The noise and talking in the hall which had lasted several minutes subsided, and Auban again turned his thoughts and his attention upon the platform, where the chairman announced the name of the next speaker.

"Look," said Mr. Marell to Auban. "That young man comes from Chicago. He will tell you something about things there. He has just come from Liverpool."

Auban listened attentively: the American told of some of the details of the trial which gave a better ideas of the nature of the proceedings against the indicted men than anything else. He described the empanelling of the jury by quoting the words of the bailiff: "I have this case bound to be hanged. I summon such men as the defendants must challenge—until they come to those whom they must accept." He described the persons of the State's witnesses, the lying scoundrel who was bribed by the police to say anything that was required of him...the two other witnesses for the prosecution who had been given the alternative, either to hang with the rest or to go free and tell the "truth." "Will such people not say anything that may be required of them if they see before them death or liberty?" exclaimed the speaker, and loud applause from all parts of the hall greeted his words. Then when he quoted the words of that brutal and notorious police captain: "If I could only get a thousand of these Socialists and Anarchists together, without their damned women and children, I would make short work of them"; and when he spoke of that corrupt "paid and packed jury" whom the money lords of Chicago had offered a reward of a hundred thousand dollars for their "services" through the mouth of one of their organs, a mighty storm of indignation and contempt broke forth. Cries rose from the audience, threats were heard; and the excitement in the ranks of the audience was still great. When the young American had already stepped down and given place to a little man, in a long coat, with a long, heavy beard, hair growing already thin, and of unmistakable Slav type, the cries of indignation and wrath suddenly changed into jubilant exclamation of recognition and veneration, of enthusiasm and affection.

Evidently there were not many among these thousands that did not know this man, who was given a warmer reception that any one of the English leaders; that had not already heard of his remarkable life and fate, of his miraculous escape from the forts of Petersburg which was to land him in France, there again to be imprisoned, and to finally offer him a last retreat here in England—heard of him those contradictory and conflicting rumors which of themselves shed a shimmer of the strange and the exceptional over one of high rank; that did not know what this man had done and was still doing for "the cause." It was his writings, scattered throughout the revolutionary organs of "Anarchistic Communism" of all nationalities, which had for many years formed the inexhaustible and often sole source of the Communistic Anarchist. Everybody knew them; everybody read and re-read them. His personal power, which he had once devoted to the secret movement in Russia, now belonged to the International; and certainly the latter had gained as much in him as the former had lost. This power could never be replaced; and because everybody knew this, everybody was grateful to him who saw him.

He was a Communist. The paper which appeared in Paris, and which, after his stay there became impossible, he managed from London, called itself "Communistic-Anarchistic." In splendid essays, which appeared in one of the foremost English magazines, he had attempted to lay down the "scientific foundations" of his ideal, which he believed was rightly called Anarchy. But even these labors, which gave a general idea of the extent of the information of the author in all matters of Socialism and of his enormous reading, did not enable Auban to picture to himself the possibility of the realization of these theories. And he saw also the delusive faith in this new and yet so old religion yielding nothing except a new evil harvest of despotism, confusion and most intense misery....

In the meantime he who had roused these thoughts was waiting in nervous excitement—how many, many times had he thus been standing by the shore of the surging sea of humanity!—for the burst of applause that rose to him to subside. Then he began in that hard, clear English of the Russian who speaks the languages of the countries in which he lives. At first it seemed as if one could not understand him; three minutes later it was impossible to lose a single word of his animated and effective address. "What is the meaning of the events in Chicago?" he asked. And he answered: "Revenge upon prisoners who have been taken in the great conflict between the two great classes. We protest against it as against a cruelty and injustice. It is the fault of our enemies," he exclaimed, "if such crimes make the conflict ever more terrible, ever more bitter, ever more irreconcilable. This is not an affair that concerns only the American people; the wrong done against the workingmen of the country is equally a wrong against us. The labor movement is by its whole nature international; and it is the duty of the workingmen of every country to call upon their fellow-workingmen in other countries and to uphold them in their resistance to those crimes which are committed against all alike!"

He did not speak long; but his speech excited both himself and his listeners. The unmistakable earnestness of his words, his flashing eyes, his passionate vehemence, awakened in the indifferent listener a presentiment of the significance of a cause which he did not understand, and strengthened in its followers the belief in its justice and its grandeur. He left the platform almost before he finished speaking, as if he wished to avoid the applause which was newly bursting forth, and the next moment was again sitting among the audience, serious and pale, attentively following the words of his successor on the platform, who—as a delegate of one of the great London liberal clubs—remarked that the events which were today transpiring on the other side might tomorrow take place in their own country....

Auban no longer heard what any of the speakers were saying. He was absorbed in thought. He was still sitting, as an hour ago, motionless, his feet crossed over the projecting cane, his hands resting on the handle, and staring fixedly before him. The voices of the speakers as well as the applause of the crowd—all this seemed to him afar off. Often—while wandering through the roaring streets—had he been overcome by this feeling of absence; then he thought of those days when, with a sigh of relief, mankind had once again rid itself of one of its tyrants, and of the days when that worthless and curse-laden life had been avenged upon many dear and priceless ones. And he thought of the heroic forms of those martyrs, of their silent sacrifice, and of their single-hearted devotion to an idea. He thought of them whenever he saw one of those upon whose brow there still seemed to hover the shadow of those days. But no longer did it appear to him as surpassingly grand and enviable so to live and so to die. The glow of passion which had consumed his young had fled, and lay in ashes beneath the cool breath of the understanding which constantly and ceaselessly battles against all our confused feelings until with the belief in justice it has taken from us the last, and has itself become the only rightful guide and director of our life.

Too much blood had he seen shed, not to wish at last to behold the victories of peace. But how was that possible if the goal became ever less clear, the wished ever more impossible, the passions ever more unbridled?

Again those days of which he was thinking were to be repeated! Again was the blood of the innocents to flow in streams, to conceal the countless crimes committed by authority against the weak, the irresolute, the blind! What was it that all these people wanted who seemed to be so enthusiastic, who spoke in such eloquent accents of truth? Protest? When had privileged wrong, acquired by the power of authority, ever heeded a protest?

But why were they the downtrodden ones? Because they were the weaker. But what is to blame? It is not as great a blame to be weak as to be strong if there is any blame about it? Why were they not the stronger?

With the cruel severity of his penetrating logic he continued to examine and dissect. The pain which here spoke so eloquently through the looks and words of all, the pain of being obliged to witness the crime, was it not less than that which the attempt to actually prevent its commission would have caused? Why else did they content themselves with protesting, with merely protesting?

Surely, they might have been the stronger. But for what other reason were they not the stronger than that they were the weaker?

There was a great emptiness and coldness in him after the flaming passion. It seemed to him as if he were suspended in an icy eternity without space and limits, and in the anguish of death trying to catch hold of airy nothing.

The old man who was sitting beside him looked into Auban's face at this moment. It was of an ashen gray, and in his eyes gleamed an expiring fire.

Meanwhile the speakers were untiringly following each other on the platform. The excitement seemed still to be increasing, although no one in the spacious hall had remained unaffected by it, except, perhaps, the reporters, who, in a business-like manner, were making notes.

Auban no longer heard anything. Once he had half risen as if he had decided to speak. But he saw that the list of speakers was not yet exhausted and he abandoned the intention of uttering the word which was not to be uttered that evening.

Only once he looked up during the last hour. A name had been announced which England had long ago indelibly inscribed in the history of her poetry of the nineteenth century among the most brilliant; of a man who was mentioned as one of the regenerators and most active promoters of industrial art; and who finally was one of the most thorough students and most prominent champions of English Socialism. This remarkable and incomparable man—poet, painter, and Socialist in one person, and a master in all—notwithstanding his white hair, had the animation and freshness of youth. Auban had never forgotten one of his countless lectures, which he was now delivering before hundreds, in one of the many small club-rooms of the Socialist League branches in London, now before thousands in public meeting in Edinburgh or Glasgow—"The Coming Society." And never had the pictures of the free society risen enticingly and delusively before Auban's eyes than under the spell of these words which the poet had attempted to gift with magic and beauty, the artist with plasticity and volume, the thinker with argumentative power and conviction. "How beautiful it would be if it could be so—how everything would be dissolved in harmony and peace," had been his thoughts then.

An old bard and patriarch, and yet on the other hand the most natural, the most healthful old Englishman—the self-made man—in blue, collarless shirt and most comfortable dress, he was standing there and talking rather than speaking of the days of Chicago.

The applause with which his coming and going had been greeted gave proof of the popularity of this man whose interest and energy for the cause of the social movement seemed to know no fatigue.

It was long past ten o'clock when the chairman rose to read the resolution in his clear, loud voice. The hands flew in the air—there was not one in opposition; the resolution was unanimously carried. A cablegram was sent to New York, where on the same occasion a demonstrative meeting was to take place the next day: it bore the good wishes of the assembled across the ocean.

Then the hall began slowly to be vacated. The eagerly talking, excited crowd pushed gradually through the doors into the open air: the reporters gathered their sheets, comparing points here and there; the platform was being deserted. Only the woman who had spoken first was still standing beside the chairman, the Atheist and Communist beside the minister of the Church and Christian Socialist Democrat.

She had probably asked for some names and notes for her little four-paged monthly paper. As Auban observed the two, it occurred to him how in their innermost nature their views touched each other, and how it was after all only sham walls that they saw standing between them. And further, in what irreconcilable and sharp opposition he stood to what bound them together!

After he had warmly taken leave of the old gentleman, whom the young American was still holding back, he walked away slowly and alone.

THE COMRADES WITH their publications were still standing at the door, each calling out the name of his paper.

Auban recognized one of them who belonged to the "Autonomie," a young man with a blonde beard and friendly features. He inquired of him concerning Trupp, and received the assurance that he had not been present. As he was about to pass out he felt a slap on his shoulder. He turned round. Before him stood a strange old man whose face certainly no one ever forgot after having once seen it. It was an old, sunken, wrinkled, sharply cast face; the mouth lay back, so that the unshaved chin stood out prominently; the upper lip was covered by a closely cropped, bristly moustache; the eyes were hid behind a pair of large steel spectacles, but flashing in moments of excitement and still giving an expression of boldness to this old face which trouble and care had changed, only to bring out more sharply its characteristic features without being able to erase them. But otherwise the form of this old man seemed bent by the heavy burden of an immense, over-stocked leathern bag which hung down at his side. Around his neck he wore a bright-colored woollen cloth tied into many knots, which covered his shirt, and which even in the hottest days of summer he no more thought of putting aside than his threadbare brown cloak.

"Hello, old friend!" exclaimed Auban, and shook his hand; "are you here, too? Come, let's have a drink."

The old man nodded.

"But no ale, comrade, no brandy; only a glass of lemonade."

"Have you become a temperance man?" asked Auban, smiling. But the old man was already going ahead.

They stepped into the large public house on the next street-corner. The spacious private apartment at its further end was nearly empty, while the others were overcrowded. Auban recognized a group of English Socialists, who had also just attended the meeting. They shook hands. Then he took the bag from the old man, gave his order, and they sat down on one of the benches. No meeting of Socialists was held in London at which this old man was not to be seen. How many years was it already? No one knew. But everyone knew him. Hearing one of his original speeches or addresses, the question may have been raised by one or another, who was the old, gray-headed man with the sharp features, who was hurling his wild accusations against the existing order with such youthful passion and defending his ideal of fraternity and equality with such youthful warmth; then he might have received the answer that he was an old *colporteur* who made his living by peddling Socialistic pamphlets and papers.

But who he really was only few people knew.

He was fond of talking, and so he had once told Auban that he had taken part in the Chartist movement; and Auban knew also that his pamphlets and elaborations were to be found among the millions of books of the British Museum—the one really social institute of the world—bound, numbered, and catalogued just as carefully as the rarest manuscript of past centuries.

"Well, what new thing have you?" he asked when they had seated themselves.

The old man drew up his leathern bag and unpacked it. At ease with himself and indifferent to the people standing about, he spread out his pamphlets and papers on the table before him, while he selected for Auban what the latter did not yet possess, and in a loud voice made his original remarks concerning the worth and the worthlessness of the different things. "What is this?" asked Auban, taking up a small pamphlet that aroused his attention. "Impeachment of the Queen, Cabinet, Parliament, and People. Fifty years of brutal and bloody monarchy." Auban looked surprised at the get-up of this strange work; it was set throughout in uniformly large, coarse letters, only a few of which showed out clearly, while the rest were recognizable in consequence of their disproportionately large size; as the paper was nearly cut through by the irregular print, only one side was printed, and each two leaves pasted together; the whole pamphlet—eight such leaves—was laboriously and unevenly trimmed with the scissors, and Auban examined it with some surprise. He read a few lines which, by a strange display and use of punctuation marks, formed a violent impeachment of the Queen in the lapidary style. "Revolt, workers, revolt! Heads off!!" he read in letters a centimetre high on one of the following pages.

"What is this?" he asked.

A smile crept over the face of the old man. "That is my jubilee present to the Queen," he exclaimed.

"But why in this primitive form?"

The old man shook his gray head.

"Look," said he, taking off his spectacles. "My old eyes no longer see anything. So I must have recourse to an expedient and use large letters which I can *feel*, with my finger tips, one after the other. There is no printer's mistake, only the punctuation."

"And you printed this yourself?"

"Set it with my fingers, without eyes—and without manuscript, out of my head—printed without a press, always one side at a time, stitched and published."

"But that was a tremendous piece of work."

"No matter. But it is good. The workingmen must read that!"

Auban looked astonished at the unsightly print, and thought with a sort of admiration of the immense toil which the getting up of these few pages must have cost the old man. He wondered whether in the age of the Marinoni press there was another such print, so grotesque in its exterior, recalling the beginnings of the printer's art of Gutenberg. Auban read: "Fifty years of increasing luxurious debauchery and crime, committed by the royal aristocratic and damnable classes." Thus it began, with a confused enumeration of the costs of the wars, a haphazard list of names gathered from personal recollections, to close with a violent imprecation: "Oh, may the curses of a thousand murdered, starved people come over you, Victoria Guelph, upon your brutal and bloody monarchy"; and with growing astonishment Auban read also the last page, from which in formless and confused words shot forth a hot revolt.

The Englishmen, too, who knew the old man, approached him, filled with curiosity. Laughingly they bought what copies he had with him.

Then the old man put his things into the bag again, threw it over his shoulder with a powerful jerk, pulled his hats—he always wore two felt hats, one drawn over the other; this was one of his obstinate peculiarities—over his gray head, and left the place, accompanied by Auban, with a loud, harsh laugh. They went together to Moorgate Station. The old man talked continually, half to himself, and so indistinctly that Auban could understand the other half only with difficulty; but he knew him and quietly let him have his way, for it was in this manner that the old man always relieved himself of his anger.

After he had already taken leave of him, Auban still saw him walking on, gesticulating and muttering, before him. Then he disappeared in the flowing stream, and Auban stepped to the ticket-office of Moorgate Station.

On the middle platform of the immense underground space, he again met a number of acquaintances who were waiting there and talking together.

Among them were some of the speakers of the evening. Auban sat down wearily on one of the benches.

Trains came rushing in and out; up and down the wooden steps the crowds jostled and thronged. The station was filled by the white-gray smoke of the engine. It floated over the platforms and the people standing there, curled round the countless blackened pillars, rafters, and posts, laid itself caressingly like a veil against the ceiling far above, and finally sought its way through the ventilators into the open street; into the life, the bustle, and roar of London.

Auban followed it with his eyes. "Well, comrade," suddenly asked a man sitting beside him, an English writer of social essays and works, "what do you think of Chicago?"

He was not sympathetic to Auban, and it was not unknown to him that the latter never made a secret of his sympathies and antipathies. Nevertheless, he obtruded himself on him on all occasions. Auban knew very well that, like everything else, he would work up these terrible events about which he had inquired, with an indifferent heart. He looked at him coldly, and without answering him.

This steady and indifferent look became intolerable to the other.

"Well," he said again, "don't you think that in the defence of its contemptible privileges no infamy will be infamous enough to the *bourgeoisie*?"

"Certainly, sir," said Auban; "would you, if you were at the helm, pursue a different policy?" and he looked at his questioner, with that sarcastic and contemptuous smile for which he was so hated by all whom he did not love. And without a further word he rose, nodded, and boarded, heavily and slowly, the puffing train, which, after a minute of noise, confusion, and slamming of doors, carried him in mad haste in the direction of King's Cross.

Chapter III.
The Unemployed

The metropolis on the Thames, the "greatest wart of the earth," was again having its annual show: the gloomy spectacle of those crowds whom only excess of misery—the spectre of starvation—could drive forth from their dens, into the heart of the city, to that spot of world-wide fame which is dedicated to the memory of past days of "glory and greatness," there to consider the question: "what must we do to live tomorrow? How pass this long winter without work and without bread?"

For these unfortunate creatures who had long ago learned that there are no rights for them on earth, either to a foot of its soil, or to the least of its goods, had now lost even their last "right"; the right of slaving for others—and were standing face to face with that terrible spectre which is the most faithful companion of poverty throughout their whole life—hunger.

It was despair that drove these people, whose modesty and contentment were so great as to cease to be comprehensible, out into public view.

The damp, cheerless October was approaching its end. The days were growing shorter and the wild hours of night-life longer.

The broad, cold area of Trafalgar Square was beginning to fill with the forms of misery already in the early morning hours.

From all parts of the city they came: happy he whom misery had not yet forced to give up his own home, the filthy hole in the cellar or in the fifth story, or the corner of a room; happy he, too, who by the aid of a lucky chance had been able to scrape enough together on this day, to find shelter in one of the lodging-houses; but in most of these sickly, pale, and tired faces was but too plainly to be read that they had "rested" through the cold night on one of the benches along the Thames Embankment, or in a gateway, or passage-way of Covent Garden.

The "unemployed!" Yes; they were again causing a great deal of talk in this year of grace! For thirty-five years already had they thus, year after year, at the beginning of winter, stepped into the presence of wealth. And every year their numbers increased, every year their assurance became more confident, every year their demands more definite! The February riots of 1886, which had not passed without attacks upon property, were still in everybody's memory. They had nothing in common with any party; they had no avowed leaders in Parliament House who "championed" their rights: hunger was their leader and driver; no organization bound them, but misery welded them together. Whence in the days of political and social convulsions come suddenly the unknown helpers, like rats from their holes? Ah! they are the recruits of the great army of silence who were never counted and who yet so often turned the scales.... They are the members of that great mass which is called *the people*: the disfranchised, the outlawed, the nameless ones, those who never were and suddenly are; a secret disclosed and a shadow turning into substance, the apparently dead coming to life, an ever-disregarded child unexpectedly grown to manhood—that is the people!

It was never taken into calculation, as it had no rights; now it calculates on its own account, and its numbers are crushing....

You liars who became great in its name, who committed the crimes of your power behind its cloak, how you have suddenly been swept away! You deceived, betrayed, and sold it; it was a word, a phantom, a nothing, which you manipulated at your own will and pleasure; and now it suddenly rises before you! Bodily before you!...

As ever before, so in this year the *bourgeoisie* and its government met the unemployed with indifference, ignorance, and hard-heartedness. When the sight of them daily began to become uncomfortable, it called its police to drive them from the Square. They went to Hyde Park; they were permitted to return to the Square, to be again brutally dispersed.

They drove them mad that they might arrest them; and when they appeared before the judge, he declared their processions as "theatrical," and no hand was lifted to strike this villain in the face; they addressed themselves to the State with their humble petition for work, and the State answered that it could not help them—but their sight was not keen enough to enable them to see that it was the State itself that ruined them; only more tired, more hungry, more embittered, they returned from their fruitless petitioning of the magistrates—for work; and when the early morning dawned, crowds of them were standing hungry and terribly excited before the gratings of the docks, where daily a not inconsiderable number of strong arms were in demand for the loading and unloading of steamers. Whoever by long waiting and a more reckless use of his fists and elbows succeeded in forcing his way to the front and securing a job, was helped for one day. But comparatively—how few were these! Most of them, despair in their hearts and a curse upon their lips for this wretched life, returned to their comrades in misery, to hear what they would propose; they had "nothing to do."...

For weeks already they had been coming together, and for weeks the London daily papers, delighted at having new matter with which to fill their endless columns, were publishing long editorials on the question of the "unemployed": much wise precept—and not a trace of understanding of the real causes of this misery; many fine words—and not a single way out for the unfortunate ones. Each had another remedy for the evil, and proposed it with the ridiculous air of infallibility; but all agreed that it was a disgrace for our "orderly commonwealth" that this degraded rabble should undertake to parade its misery in public. What of it that they were starving by day and freezing by night, silently in their remote corners and holes, where no one either saw or heard; but so to hurt the aesthetic, tender feelings of good society by the daily exhibition of all this misery and filth, what insolence!

It was on a Sunday—the one before the last of this cheerless and gloomy month—that Trupp determined to devote his free afternoon to an attempt to get a more correct picture of the extent and the significance of these gatherings than he was able to form from the accounts of his comrades and fellow workmen in the shop. At about noon he had been at Clerkenwell Green, the old-time meeting-place of so many parties and years, and had there listened with indignation to the latter portion of the speeches, and was now going with an exceptionally large procession of unemployed, headed by a red flag, down the Strand towards Trafalgar Square. He had not yet met an acquaintance, but entered into conversation with a man marching beside him, who, on seeing that he was smoking, asked him for a little tobacco, "not to feel the hunger so"; and the conversation, notwithstanding the fact that Trupp could not readily express himself in English, and hardly understood one-half of what was said to him, while he had to guess at the other, soon took a lively turn after he had bought a few sandwiches in the nearest of Lockhart's cocoa-shops, with his last pennies, for the sickly and sleepy-looking man. He still had work—for how long, of course, he did not know. It was a long, daily repeated story of suffering which the other was telling him: miserably paid work the whole summer through; its sudden suspension; piece after piece of the scant furniture carried to the pawnbroker's; soon the want of even the most necessary means of support; his little child dead for the want of food; the wife in the workhouse—and he himself: "I will hang myself before I'll go there too," he concluded.

Trupp looked at him; he was an intelligent-looking, rather elderly man; then he asked him:—

"How many unemployed, do you think, are there in London?"

"Very many!" said the other. "Very many! Certainly more than a hundred thousand, and if count the women and children, still more! Half a million! The people who meet on Trafalgar Square form only a small part, and of those a fifth consists of professional beggars and tramps, of pickpockets and idlers, and has nothing to do with the unemployed, who only want honest work. But they don't give us any, and let us starve. Yesterday again we called on the Board of Works."

"What's that?" interrupted Trupp, who knew little of the ramified institutions of the city.

"They are the authorities who have in charge the erection of the great city buildings—their office is quite near the Square—and there was one of the speakers who explained that they might make a beginning with the works on the Thames, of which so much has already been said, and give employment to a good many people; and another one, he spoke of the building of sewers, and the founding of villages for the poor in the vicinity of London—but they don't want to, they don't want to."

Trupp listened attentively.

"And at the same time two and a half million pounds sterling are yearly raised in London for poor-rates; two million alone by voluntary contributions. Where the money goes, I should like to know!"

"Yes," said Trupp; "those are your servants, the servants of the people and the trustees of its affairs."

"And we also called at police headquarters, and got the answer that anyone who was found without work and shelterless, and who refused to go to the workhouse, would be punished with imprisonment at hard labor."

"What are you?"

"Oh, I have done many things when I was hungry and couldn't get my work. The last time, till two months ago, I worked in a canning factory, made tin boxes—every day twelve hours—never less but often fourteen."

"And how much?"

"Well, when things went well, eight shillings, mostly seven shillings, often only six shillings per week."

For some time Trupp had been living at the East End. He knew the wages of the English workingmen. He knew families of eight persons who together did not earn more than twelve shillings a week, of which they had to pay four for their hole of a room.... He knew that among the women and girls who make match-boxes and bags a perpetual famine was raging.

Famine in the richest city of the world! He clenched his fists.

He himself earned more. He was a very well-informed and competent mechanic, whose work required good judgment. From childhood he had grown to manhood in this immense misery, the sight of which had never forsaken him in any country, in any city. But what he saw in London of mad luxury on the one side, and hopeless misery on the other, surpassed everything.

He drew from his pocket a crumpled piece of paper, which he suddenly remembered, and hastily scanned it while walking on. It was the "Jubilee Manifesto" of the Social Democratic Federation.

He scanned the following figures:—

Four million people in Great Britain dependent on charity...the workingmen not in a position to get more than one-fourth of what they produce...thirty percent of the children of the Board Schools half starved...fifty-four persons died in one year of famine in London...eighty thousand women—ten in a hundred—prostitutes.

Pictures from the "Fifty Years of Progress!"

"You are yourselves to blame," he said to his companion, while they were passing through Fleet Street, the street of the great newspapers whose names were calling down from all the roofs and all the walls; "you are yourselves to blame," and the roar of the ever-swelling procession, which was seriously and threateningly moving towards the Strand, seemed to emphasize the force of his words—"you are yourselves to blame if the earth which belongs to you is not yours. Your own thoughtlessness and cowardice—these are your worst enemies. Not the handful of miserable money-bags and idlers," he said, contemptuously.

"Ah, are you a Socialist?" said the other, smiling.

Trupp shrugged his shoulders.

"Look," he exclaimed aloud, in his bad and faulty English, "those stores which you have filled with bread and which you pass by hungry; those magazines which you have filled to bursting with clothes, to whom do they belong if not to you and to your shivering children?"

There was none among those who, in the irresistible tide of the procession, had heard and understood these simple words who had not assented to them; but, silently, worn out, and infirm of will, they all bore their gnawing hunger past the exhibitions of superfluity. None of these hands which had always toiled for others only, which had always filled the pockets of others only, and which, themselves empty, were forever to remain empty, was now stretched out to take back a small, an insignificantly small, part of what was being withheld from them.

Silently and without confidence they were moving on, down the long thoroughfares of wealth—they who had been robbed of everything, and left with nothing; left with not a foot of soil, with not one of the boasted rights of man, with not even the most necessary means of support, as a terrible arraignment of all the institutions of an earthly justice, as an unavoidable, unanswerable denial of the existence of a divine justice—and they, they were described as a disgrace of their age, they who were only the victims of the disgrace of their age. Such was the terrible confusion of ideas at the close of the nineteenth century, and the guilty believed to escape their guilt by sophistically confounding cause and effect of the prevailing conditions.

These were Trupp's thoughts as he silently marched down the endless street in the silent procession. The throng seemed to grow greater and greater the nearer it came to Trafalgar Square. Trupp and the workingman with whom he had been talking were still marching side by side. But they no longer talked. Each was occupied with his own thoughts. The words of the former had been heard, and he noticed how they were being discussed.

"Those damned Germans," exclaimed a young man, "are to blame for everything. They force our wages down." And he looked round at Trupp threateningly.

The latter knew at once what the other meant.

He had already too often heard of the "bloody Germans," not to understand this old grievance which came in such fine stead for the exploiters to divert the attention of workingmen from the real causes of their misery.

His strong figure, his gloomy, bearded face, his whole attitude, seemed, however, too little encouraging for the young man to strike up a quarrel with him; and Trupp left him and the others in their belief in the baseness of the German workingmen who "come to England only to steal the bread from the English."

But it did not lessen his pain and his bitterness when he recalled who it really was that came from Germany to England. He knew those multitudes whom not only the hope of better wages, but also the hope of a freer and truer life, compelled to leave their country; for how was it possible for them to live under the constant pressure of a mad law—the disgraceful law, as popular opinion named it—which presumed to murder thought, to stifle speech, and to keep watch over every movement?

When the procession reached the Square, Trupp was surprised to see the great crowds already assembled there. The large, broad space of the interior was almost filled by a surging mass, and in all the surrounding streets the traffic of wagons and people seemed to be as great as on week days.

The approaching procession was received with stormy shouts. Trupp left it, and remained standing near Morley's Hotel. He saw the files of men entering the Square, saw the man who was carrying the red flag, with several others mounting the pedestal of the Nelson Column, and a hundred-headed crowd gathering round the next moment, attentively listening to the words of a speaker.

He had secured a standing-place a little above the crowd, on the street leading to St. Martin's Church. He could see the pedestal of the column, which was densely crowded. He saw the violent gesticulations of the speakers, the waving of the red flag, and the black helmets of the police, who in large numbers had taken their position directly below the speakers.

Sometimes he was shut off from the view by a passing cab or a closely packed omnibus.

Suddenly he saw a tremendous commotion arising in the crowd that occupied the Square; a cry of terror and of indignation from a thousand throats at once broke into the air, and like a mighty, dark billow, the crowd surged back, far overflowing the steps on the north side and the streets.... The police, with their whole force, had suddenly and without warning made an attack on the quietly listening meeting, and were now recklessly driving the screaming crowd before their closed ranks.

Trupp felt a frightful rage rising within him. This cold and deliberate brutality made his blood boil. He crossed the street and stood by the stone enclosure of the place; beneath him lay the Square already half emptied. With blows and kicks the police were driving the defenceless ones before them. Whoever made the least show of resistance was pulled down and led away.

A young man had escaped from their hands. In mad haste he sought to gain the exit of the place. But those stationed there pulled him instantly down, while the scattered crowd outside accompanied this act of repulsive brutality with exclamations of contempt and rage.

As Trupp saw this, he jumped with one leap over the wall which was still several yards high at this place—it slopes gradually from the north to the south. He hurried to the pedestal of the column, on which several of the speakers were still standing.

The flag-bearer had placed himself against the column and held the flag with both hands. He was evidently determined to yield only to the most extreme force.

Now the police again slowly drew back to the column and again took up their position there; and the crowd followed them from all sides and all the entrances of the Square. In a few minutes the entire area was again covered by a dark sea of humanity, whose indignation had increased, whose calls for the continuation of the speech had grown more impatient, whose excitement had become more intense.

Again the pedestal of the column was occupied: people mutually lifted and pulled each other up. Before the flag stood a young man of about thirty years. He was one of the best speakers and very well known among the unemployed. He was deathly pale with excitement, and looked with an expression of implacable hatred down upon the forms of the policemen at his feet.

One of the constables shouted up to the speakers that on the first incendiary word he should arrest each one of them on the spot.

With an indescribable expression of contempt the young man looked down upon him.

Trupp was standing just before the line of policemen, so near that he was almost forced by the thronging multitude to touch them. But notwithstanding this, he raised his arm in the air, and called loudly to the men on the pedestal: "Go on!" This at once became the sign for loud applause among those standing round and for countless similar exclamations.

It seemed at first as if the police intended to make a fresh attack in consequence of this outbreak of the feelings of the multitude. But they refrained, and the speaker began. He spoke on the right of free speech in England, and on its attempted suppression, which had so far remained unsuccessful. He saw before him a throng such as Trafalgar Square had not held that year. Here, before the eyes of the entire world, they had placed themselves with their demand: "Bread or Labor." And here, in the face of this prodigal riches and wealth which they themselves had created, they would continue to assemble until their demand should be fulfilled. They had not broken a window, and had not taken a piece of bread to appease their hunger; whoever said so was a liar. "It would have been very agreeable to them if we had done it; in that case the police would have a convenient excuse for having disturbed our peaceable meetings, and for having most brutally incited us to excess."

Beside Trupp was standing the reporter of a newspaper, who was laboriously jotting down cipher notes. He could have torn the paper out of the indifferent man's hands. Disgusted, he tried to force his way through the crowd surrounding him. He could proceed only step by step. The assembly no longer consisted exclusively of the unemployed: mixed up with them was the riffraff of London that gathers on all occasions in incredibly large numbers, many curious ones who wished to see what would happen, and a number of really interested persons. Women with their children on their arms, tired and hungry, stood close by the tawdry dress dolls of the West End, of whom a few had ventured on the Square after they had been assured that it was "not yet dangerous"; and in the throng Trupp saw one face that made him indignant: the brazen, scornfully smiling face of a gentleman in a tall hat who was standing near the column, and who now interrupted the words of the speaker with: "Nonsense!" Clearly a prominent official who—relying as much on the patience and forbearance of the people as on the clubs and revolvers of the police—permitted himself this bit of insolence. An indignant muttering rose, while he looked over the surrounding crowd with his impudent smile.

"Just wait, fellow," Trupp was thinking to himself; "some day you won't feel like smiling"; but almost at the same time he joined in the laughter that broke forth when a powerful blow from behind drove the stove-pipe hat of the tall gentleman down over his eyes and ears. The crowd scattered, and an empty space quickly rose round the chastised offender, who already felt no longer like smiling. The police came forward, although they had not seen anything of the incident. Trupp had been carried away with the crowd; he was now standing on the east side of the Square.

Meantime the other three sides of the column had also become covered with people, and the meeting was being addressed by some of their numbers. Some things that were said had no bearing on the purpose of the meeting, and the voice of many a speaker was more expressive of his self-complacency and of the childish pleasure he took in his own words than of the indignation over the conditions which he was to criticise, and of the endeavor to arouse this same indignation in the hearts of his hearers and to fan it into a flame.

With an angry smile Trupp was watching one of those violently gesticulating professional popular speakers, who, with tiresome verbosity, was telling the starving Londoners of their starving comrades in India, and recounting the atrocities committed by the English government in that unhappy land, instead of revealing to them the equally arbitrary acts of the same government by which they were condemned to suffer and slowly to die.

Loud laughter and jeers, however, suddenly caused him to transfer his attention from the speaker to one of those pitiable fanatics who believe they have a mission at all such gatherings to lead the misguided people back into the lap of the infallible Church; to sustain the poor in their trials and troubles, and the rich in their pleasures. Trupp looked at the black-coated man curiously. The closely shaved sallow face, the cowardly look of the eyes, and the honeyed tone of the drawling voice would have been repulsive to him, even if the man had not stood in the service of what he hated, because he saw in it the chief agency for keeping the people in ignorance and mental slavery.

But the words of the missionary were received only with scorn and laughter. From all sides his voice was drowned by loud cries. Threats were heard: "Go away!" Then orange peel and nut shells were flying at him. But he let everything pass over him and drawled out his carefully committed phrases, to which nobody paid heed, as calmly and monotonously as if the whole affair did not concern him at all. He was pushed from the spot where he was standing. Hardly had he gained a foothold again when he continued with his speech. The conduct of this new Christ was at once ridiculous and pitiable. Suddenly an admirably well-aimed egg was hurled at the speaker—a rotten, pasty mass closed his mouth with a clapping sound. That was too much for even this martyr. He no longer held his ground. Soiled from top to toe, spitting and rapidly ducking his head, he slipped through the crowd standing round, followed by the coarse laughter of the excited and screaming people.

Trupp shrugged his shoulders. He wished the mouth of every corrupter of the people and falsifier of truth might be closed in an equally drastic manner.

He turned away and allowed the swarm to carry him past the fountains, whose dirty water-basins were strewn with refuse of every kind, back again to the north side. There also, holding themselves by the lantern posts of the broad railing, a number of speakers were shouting their excited, jumbled, and exciting phrases down to the crowd far beneath them in the Square.

One of them seemed familiar to Trupp. He remembered having seen him in the meetings of the Social Democratic Federation. He was a party Socialist. Trupp listened. Again he did not understand everything, but from disjointed catchwords he could infer that he was speaking of the rapid development of capitalistic exploitation, of the ever more threatening bread riots incident to it, of the uselessness of the means employed for their suppression, and that he was attacking that old superstition which, first put forth by a prejudiced mind, has since taken such deep root—that it is the insufficiency of the means of subsistence which necessitates the misery of certain classes. Then he passed to the familiar theories—holding the balance between Social Democratic and Communistic ideas—of the distribution of goods of which there is a superabundance: all in sentences whose separate words, by the repetitions of many years, seemed as if cast in brass and to have turned into mere phrases.

The effect, however, was small. There were but few who followed every word or who were even able to follow. The majority allowed themselves to be driven from one place to another by the incessant commotion which swayed them to and fro as the wind sways the grass of the field. The voices of the speakers tried in vain, for the most part, to struggle against the roar.

Around the benches on the north side of the Square a boisterous lot of children had gathered: street Arabs who at every hour of the day flood the principal streets of

London by hundreds—cast out by their parents, if they still have any, and pushed on by the dreaded fist of the policeman. Children who never have a youth; who in their life have never seen anything of nature except the dust of Hyde Park, where on a summer's evening they bathed in the Serpentine with hundreds of their comrades; who have never in their life eaten their fill, and who never have anything but dirty rags on their bodies; who have never been spoiled, as they have never been unspoiled.

Laughing and screaming, they were standing and jumping about the dirty and battered benches. One little fellow held himself for a minute on the back of one of them: with comical gravity he imitated the movements of the speaker, and screamed senseless words to the throng. His dirty, prematurely old face was radiant with pleasure. Then he was pulled down by his exulting comrades.

Trupp smiled again, but bitterly. This little scene seemed like the most cutting satire on the most serious business. He looked at the dirty, vicious faces of those standing round him; wherever he looked: misery, hunger, and depravity. And they were his brothers. He felt as if he belonged to them all; inseparably bound together with them by a common fate.

Above Trafalgar Square lay a monotonous gray, heavy, sunless sky. This cold dome seemed farther away than usual.

Again a great commotion surged through the masses from the foot of the Nelson Column. Evidently it was being deserted. Over the dark sea of heads the red flag could be seen turning in the direction of Westminster. And without a word having been said, thousands followed it of their own accord. The separate individuals formed and condensed themselves into one immense serpent. So it moved down Whitehall, past the seats of so many magistrates, past the historical memorials whose bloody traces had been washed away by time from the stones of this famous street, past the two sentinels of the Horse Guards, who in their ostentatious uniforms and on their well-fed horses were keeping watch over the entrances of that low structure; and up through the crowds of spectators on both sides, who followed the strange procession as soon as it had gone by....

In the midst of the ranks walked Trupp. His pulses beat somewhat faster as he felt himself drawn away and down by the currents of this day.

The towers of Parliament House rose ever more distinctly and impressively out of the fine mist. Then suddenly Westminster Abbey lay before the countless multitude that was irresistibly pouring itself upon its doors. Trupp made an attempt to get a view of the head of the procession beyond the black hats that surrounded him. If it would only come to a crisis!—was his glowing wish.

But quietly he saw the red flag turn away from the main entrance and pass around the corner: the procession followed it in closed rank and file.

All kinds of exclamations were heard about him. He did not know what it all meant. And suddenly he found himself—the procession had to gain admission through the eastern entrance—in the great silence of those vast walls which were filled with the dust of ages and consecrated with the glory of centuries.

He stood in the Poets' Corner of Westminster Abbey, jammed in the throng that found no room in the narrow pews. He saw the busts and read the names which he did not know. What were they? And what were they to him? He knew only one English poet, and his name he did not find—Percy Byssche Shelley. He had loved liberty. Therefore he loved him and read him, even where he did not understand him. He did not know that English narrow-mindedness and illiberality had distinguished him, like Byron, by obstinately denying him the honor of a place in this half-lighted corner among so much genuine genius and so much false greatness.

Divine service was being held. From the middle of the space, as from a great distance, came the gloomy, monotonous, half-singing voice of a clergyman, who continued his sermon after an imperceptible interruption in consequence of the unexpected intrusion, thus again quieting the congregation, his frightened audience.... Trupp did not understand a word. The crowd around him exhaled a pungent odor of sweat and dust. They became more excited after the great feeling which had overpowered them on their entrance had again disappeared. Some had kept their hats on; a few others, who had removed theirs, now put them on again. Some climbed on the pews and looked over the rest. Only a few low words fell upon the grand sublimity of this silence. Trupp sat down. In spite of himself he was seized by a strange, inexplicable feeling, such as he had not experienced in a long—in an indefinitely long—time.... The more we are hedged in by space, the more we suffer when the wings of our thoughts beat against its walls until they bleed; the farther it circles around us, the more we forget it and all its limits. Trupp looked down, and for half an hour forgot entirely where he was.

His whole life rose before him again. But the embrace of this memory was not gentle and consoling as that of a mother to whom her son returns, but violent, relentless, crushing, as must be the fatal kiss of a vampire!

His whole life! He was now a man of thirty-five, in the zenith of his life, in the possession of his strength.

He sees his childhood again—the starved, joyless years of his childhood, as the son of a day-laborer in a dirty village on the flats of Saxony; the father a numbskull; the mother a quarrelsome woman, forever dissatisfied, from whom he inherited his iron energy and uncontrollable passion; with whom he was in continual conflict, until one day, after a frightful scene in which his ripening sense of justice had rebelled against her groundless accusations and complaints, he ran away from her—the father never being considered....

He sees himself again as a fifteen-year-old, neglected boy, without a penny, wandering from place to place for two days; he feels the ravenous hunger again which finally, after two days, gave him the courage to beg a piece of bread in a farmhouse; and again the dejected despair which finally drove him—it was on the morning of the third day, a wet, cold, autumn morning (*how well* he remembered that morning!), when he rose shivering with cold and wholly exhausted from the ground—to ask for work in the next village. It was in the vicinity of Chemnitz. He enters a blacksmith shop. The boss laughs and examines the muscles of his arm. He can stay, he may sit down to breakfast, a thick, tasteless soup, which the journeymen ate sullenly, but which he devours greedily. The others make fun of his hunger; but never had ridicule disturbed him less. Then, with mad zeal, with burning pleasure and love for all things, he works and studies.

Days, weeks, months, pass on.... Nobody concerns himself about him. The hours of the evening after his day's work seem longest to him. He does not know what to do. Once he gets hold of a book and then spells out sentence after sentence. It happens to be "The Workingmen's Programme," by Lassalle. He had found it in a corner of his garret. Somebody must have forgotten it there. He does not understand a word of it. But one day the boss sees him bent over the soiled leaves, and tears them out of his hands and boxes his ears. "Damned Social Democrats!" he cries; "do they want to ruin even the child!" The boy does not understand this, either. He cannot imagine what bad thing it is that he has done. But he has heard the word "Social Democracy" for the first time. That is twenty years ago....

So he forms his first friendship. For from this hour one of the workmen, an orthodox follower of the prosperous General German Workingmen's Society, which at that time was still in irreconcilable opposition to the Eisenachian movement of the Workingmen's Party, took an interest in him, and instead of the heavy, scientific treatise of that gifted champion of German Socialism he slipped into his hands a sheet printed on thin, oily paper, which illustrated the social evils of the time by the light of daily events more successfully to the awakening spirit than even the most simple treatise on political economy could have done. There he read the descriptions, collected from all sources, of hostile antagonisms: the hate-filled accounts of insolent revelry, of brutal heartlessness, of shameful arrogance on the one side, the passionate portrayals of despairing poverty, of deceived labor, and of downtrodden weakness on the other, the radically opposite side; and his young heart bubbled over with pain and indignation. Hate and love divided it forever: hate of the former, and love for those who were suffering like him. Mankind soon resolved itself into *bourgeoisie* and workingmen, and soon he saw in the former nothing but calculating rogues and lazy exploiters; in the latter, only victims, the nobler the more unfortunate they were....

Years pass by. When at the age of nineteen he leaves the gloomy, cheerless city, he has advanced far enough by dint of hard work in the evening hours to read fluently and to write correctly, if not easily. He is a journeyman. His certificate is excellent.

Every fibre of his being urges him to travel. The great war has spent its rage. While in Paris, the fires and flames of insurrection paint the heavens as with a lurid glare until they are extinguished in streams of blood, he, cutting his way through the Thuringian forest, wanders towards Nürnberg and Munich, where for a year he finds a favorable opportunity in a large factory for perfecting himself in his calling.

As yet an enthusiastic follower of the "most advanced" party, an instinctive feeling of revolt is nevertheless already beginning to rise within him against its authoritative principles, which do not permit of even the least deviation from the sanctioned form.

He is urged abroad, to foreign lands. He turns to Switzerland. After many delays he reaches Zurich, then Geneva. And there for the first time he hears the word

"Anarchism." He had never heard it in Germany.

Nowhere as yet is it spoken aloud. Only here and there it is heard in a whisper. No one yet probably knows what it means. No one yet dares attempt to explain it. No one yet dreams of its significance for the future....

At the age of twenty-two he is a revolutionist!

Hitherto he had been a reformer.

For the first time he came in contact with people of all nationalities, whom a strong fate had brought together there: emigrants, conspirators, sappers and miners—the men and the women of the European revolution, some still bleeding from fresh wounds, others already covered with scars: all filled by that feverish impatience, that trembling passion, that painful longing "to do something," but here growing more and more away from their former life.

They talk to him: the young of their hopes, the old of their disappointments and—their hopes. Occasionally one of them disappears: he has a "mission" to fulfil. Another one comes. Their names are scarcely mentioned, never remembered.

These are strange times for Trupp.

In 1864 Marx had founded the "International," in London. Its great successes went hand in hand with ever-increasing dissensions among the members who defended private property here and denied it there; who championed Collectivism here and were already beginning to lose themselves more and more in the misty regions of Communism there. Their differences came to light at their congresses.

Then an iron hand is thrust into the breach and makes it deeper and wider. Bakunin, the Russian officer, the disciple of Hegel, the leader of the Dresden insurrection, for three days "King of Saxony," the Siberian exile, the tireless conspirator, the eternal revolutionist, the prophet and the dreamer, enters the lists against the iron tyrant, the gifted *savant,* the celebrated author of the Bible of Communism. The struggle of two lions mutually devouring each other!

In 1868 rises the "Alliance of Socialistic Democracy"; and hardly a year before Trupp had come to Switzerland, the Jurassian Confederation, the "cradle of Anarchy." Almost three years he remains in Switzerland; he learns French.

As he comes to Berne once more before leaving the country for years, the curtain is there slowly falling over the last act of that prodigious life.... Death had already opened its gates for Mikhail Bakunin. Although he has already been deserted by almost all, the dying giant is still making convulsive efforts of despair to gather new hosts round him and send them forth in the hopeless conflict.... It is past. Only fools still swear by a flag which the storm of decades has torn into shreds.... Never did he who had held it aloft achieve what he wished: to overthrow the world. But he did succeed in hurling the torch of dissension into the stronghold of the "International."

Otto Trupp is one of his last disciples.

At the age of twenty-four he is a terrorist. He has learned them by heart, those mad eleven principles "concerning the duties of the revolutionist to himself and to his fellow-revolutionists," which begin with the frightful words of the greatest illiberality:

> The revolutionist is a self-immolated person. He has no common interests, feelings, or inclinations, no property, not even a name. Everything in him is devoured by a single, exclusive interest, a single thought, a single passion—the revolution.

Filled by this single interest, this single thought, this single passion, the twenty-three-year-old Trupp returned to his native country. Wandering through it from south to north, his bitterness increased with the greatness of the misery which he saw wherever he went.

It was the year in which the two schools of Socialism joined their forces on that soil which was destined to bear one of the best organized, most active, and most compact parties: the one that will perhaps claim the immediate future....

He journeys from city to city. Everywhere he tries to undermine the existing order of things. He invites the workingmen to leave the snail-paced course of reform; he points out to them the way of force as their saviour and liberator. And many a one who is incapable of curbing the impatient desires of his passionate heart with the reins of reason, follows him.

Now he calls himself an Anarchist!

Henceforth he battles under this sign. The word seems to him to indicate with sufficient clearness what he aspires after: he wants no authority, neither that of an individual, nor of a majority. While he ventures upon all possible sciences with an iron will, he erects for himself the shapeless structure of a general philosophy in whose dark chambers he would have gone astray had he not seen through the ill-formed roof, shimmering with promise, the blue sky of an ideal of brotherly love....

He trusts only in the revolution henceforth. With one blow it will create the paradise of peaceable social life. Therefore every impulse of his longing is directed to it. For it he gathers recruits: for the great revolution of his class which will be the last.

So he journeys from city to city under how many assumed names, with passports exchanged how often, he no longer knows.... He is forever a refugee: not a day passes on which he must not keep his eyes open, his lips closed, to escape pursuit. Often the prison claims him. But it always releases him again after short intervals: nothing can be proved against him.

Then in quick succession follow the shots at the Emperor in Berlin. He applauds the regicides, both of whom were fanatics; the one, moreover, an idiot, the other a lunatic. The reaction triumphs. Its terrible period of degradation begins: the lowest feelings venture abroad. The spirit of persecution, the lust of denunciation, hatred, fill all hearts.

When Trupp—one of the first—is arrested, he despairs of being ever again released from prison.

The threads are being drawn together above him. A miraculous accident saves him. While still in search of the arch-traitor and conspirator, they sentenced him for insulting his Majesty, to half a year, not dreaming who it was whom they held in their hands. Every day during this half-year he saw the sword drawn over him, ready to descend.... But it does not descend. He is again free. Amidst great privations he reaches the boundary, reaches Paris. The other period of his life begins: that of the refugee abroad. He knows he cannot venture a step into Germany that would not prove fatal....

The secret plotter and agitator who silently scatters his fermenting seed in every direction becomes the public propagandist, the debater in the clubs, the speaker on the street-corners, and in the meeting-halls.

The French Anarchists have founded the first Anarchistic Communistic organ, "*Le Révolte!*" The followers of the new creed, which is slowly but surely spreading, take the initiative in the Anarchistic organization of "free groups," for the first time building on the principle of decentralization. The workingmen's congress of Marseilles, 1879, is communistic; its significance is not yet to be estimated; the split between Communism and Collectivism—externally hardly noticeable—is internally already completed.

Trupp is everywhere. His thirsting heart never beat more restlessly than in these years of the great, awakening movement which carries everything before it. What he hears among the Frenchmen, he repeats to the small but already expanding circle of his German comrades.

Then he makes the acquaintance of Carrard Auban.

He sees that pure, almost childlike enthusiasm on the brow of the young man of twenty-five, that reckless courage which delights him, and that self-denying devotion which seems to grow from day to day. But hardly has he made his acquaintance and won his friendship, when he loses him again for a long time. Auban is convicted. The ringing words of his great speech before the judges accompany Trupp through the two years during which they are separated....

When in 1884 they meet again in London—both refugees—Auban has become another; Trupp remained the same. Only the memory of the great, glorious days of revolt still unites them.

Auban understands him now for the first time; but he can no longer understand Auban.

In Germany, the creed has become deed. Suddenly there appeared upon the frightened world the face of horror. Vienna, Strassburg, Stuttgart, the Niederwald, and the assassination of Rumpff—all these deeds have happened which have been infinitely harmful to the spread of the idea of liberty, which have placed many a new murderous weapon in the hands of the enemy, so that from now on—for an indefinite time—the word "Anarchist" has become synonymous with "murderer." Will it ever be cleared there? Is it not lost for Europe: abandoned to eternal misunderstanding, to insatiable persecution, to newly aroused hatred?

Trupp is in London—in the exhausting and petty quarrels of the day his energies have been wasted until now.

SUDDENLY TRUPP AWOKE. He again came to himself. He fixed his hat. He looked round and up to the dizzy vaulted ceiling.

The drawling words of the clergyman were still dying away in plaintive tones scarcely audible in that immense space. In fine and rich tones rose the boy voices in response. Then once more the walls—tremblingly blending the reverberating waves of sound into a deep beauty—threw down the tones on the silent people below....

Trupp found himself again wedged in the multitude whose clothes were ever more strongly emitting a vaporous odor which mingled with the mouldy dust to form an oppressive sultriness.

Now they had all become silent, the unemployed. Some were tired, others stupefied; almost all taken captive by the strangeness of the situation. Most of them had probably not been inside a church since their boyhood. Now in spite of themselves they were being held captive by memories which they had buried long ago.

Many were leaning against the backs of the pews, closely pressed together, in a restless half-slumber; others, in a suppressed voice, hardly breathing, were whispering questions to each other: they wanted to know who were those marble figures in the garb of past ages, the wonderful head-dress, with the serious expressions, in the challenging attitudes.... Were they those who had the power to make them happy, to destroy them?

The daring spirit of revolt with which not an hour ago they had started from Trafalgar Square had vanished. Wedged together, they were standing here—how much longer were they to remain standing so? Why did they not go away? What were they doing here? Here no help was to come to them. Here was no other consolation than words. But they wanted work, work and bread.

Bitterness spread among the lingering ones. In Trupp it blazed forth like fire. From the chancel came, monotonous and uniformly slow like trickling drops, the words of the clergyman. He did not understand them. Perhaps no one understood them. They told of things that are not of this world....

"Put all your trust in God!" said the plaintive voice.

"In God!" came back softly, in wonderful strains of hope and rejoicing, the youthful voices.

"He alone can save you!" the clergyman again.

Was there a suspicion in the minds of the starving ones of the unconscious mockery of this terrible faith which was a lie from beginning to end? A movement of unrest rose among them. All had become awake; all shook off the slumber of stupefaction.

Then a shrill laugh sounded from Trupp's lips, in which infidelity, hatred, and bitterness mingled. Cries answered him from different sides. Some also laughed. Then fitful laughter, here and there. Confused cries.

The reluctantly and mechanically uncovered heads were again covered. There was pushing and jostling.

The majority were crowding towards the door. Quickly the throng poured into the open air. The worshippers gave a sigh of relief. The Lord God, without whose will not a hair falls to the ground, had turned the danger away from his children. They were freed from the impious. They were again by themselves. The clergyman, who had stopped for a moment at the outbreak of the noise, went on, and those remaining again turned their eyes, full of confidence and serene calm, towards him, their shepherd.

Trupp was exasperated. He would have liked nothing better than a scandal in this place.

The dull light of the damp, cold October afternoon again enveloped the throng emerging from the twilight of Westminster Abbey, from its "sacred silence" into the noise of the day. The greater part of the unemployed had been obliged to wait outdoors. They had sullenly and doubtingly followed the pacifying words of a high dignitary of the Church, or listened with applause to the bitter truths of the disloyal Christian Socialist.

They again formed into a procession headed for the Square which they had left hardly an hour ago. They followed the waving of the red flag. They crowded together in closed ranks as if so to feel their hunger less, their power more.

Trupp was pushed on.

In regular steps their heavy feet struck the hard ground. They supported each other. An immense procession was filing through the narrow Parliament Street.

And out of this procession rose as by premeditation a song. Low, sombre, sad, and defiant, it burst from a thousand throats to the sky like the cloud of smoke which presages the outbreak of the conflagration.

They sang the old immortal song of "The Starving Poor of Old England":—

Let them bray, until in the face they are black,
That over oceans they hold their sway,
Of the flag of Old England, the Union Jack,
About which I have something to say:
'Tis said that it floats o'er the free, but it waves
Over thousands of hard-worked, ill-paid British slaves,
Who are driven to pauper and suicide graves—
The starving poor of Old England!

And in a mighty chorus the refrain in which every voice joined:—

'Tis the poor, the poor, the taxes have to pay,
The poor who are starving every day,
Who starve and die on the Queen's highway—
The starving poor of Old England!

Another stanza and still another:—

'Tis dear to the rich, but too dear for the poor,
When hunger stalks in at every door—

And closing with a terrible, daring menace, exulting in hope:—

But not much longer these evils we'll endure,
We, the workingmen of Old England!

Trupp tore himself away from the ranks and turned into a side street.

Behind him Westminster Abbey sank away in the ever-deepening shadows. The sombre, sorrowful tones in which the hungry and starving expressed their sufferings grew fainter and fainter in his ear....

> 'Tis the poor, the poor, the taxes have to pay,
> The poor who are starving every day,
> Who starve and die on the Queen's highway—
> The starving poor of Old England!

No judge, either in heaven or on earth, heard the terrible arraignment of these wretched ones who were still waiting for justice.

With bent head, his lips firmly pressed together, occasionally casting a sharp glance round to assure himself of his way, Trupp walked on, probably for an hour, towards the north of London.

Chapter IV.
Carrard Auban

During that same afternoon on which so much seething blood flowed back to the heart of the metropolis, Carrard Auban was sitting in his quiet, lofty room on one of the streets north of King's Cross, which are never very lively on week days, but seem as if haunted by death on holidays.

He had been living here since he was again alone. For more than a year already.

It was one of those bare, plainly furnished rooms, without modern improvements, for which one pays ten shillings a week, but in whose quiet seclusion one can live without being disturbed by the noise of the life outside. Room after room of the entire three-story house was thus rented; the occupants saw their landlady only when they paid the weekly rent, while they hardly ever met each other. Occasionally they would meet on the stairs, to pass rapidly on without greeting.

Auban's room was divided into two unequal parts by a screen, half as high as the ceiling; it hid the bed, and left free the greater half, which was chiefly occupied by an unusually large table. The size of the table corresponded with the enormous bookcase, which reached to the ceiling, and which held a library that was probably the only one of its kind.

It contained, first, the philosophical and politico-economical works of the great thinkers of France, from Helvetius and Say to Proudhon and Bastiat; less complete in number, but in the best editions, those of the English, from Smith to Spencer. Prominence was given to the champions of Free Trade. Further, a very incomplete, but very interesting collection of publications, pamphlets, papers, etc., concerning the history of the revolutions of the nineteenth century, especially those of the fourth decade. The present possessor, who had for a long time almost entirely neglected this legacy of his father, now valued it daily more and more according to its true worth.

Then the library contained an almost unclassifiable wealth of subordinate material dealing with the social question: surely a precious mine for the future student of the history of the labor movements. It had been collected by Auban himself: there lay piled up whatever the day had pressed into his hand. It was a living piece of the labor of his age, and surely not the worst....

To acquire insight was Auban's highest aim. It was more to him than all knowledge, which he regarded only as an aid and a stepping-stone to the former.

The works of poetic art filled only one shelf. Here was Victor Hugo beside Shakespeare, Goethe beside Balzac. But only in rare moments of recreation was one or the other of these volumes taken down.

This table, whose top was one huge piece of mahogany, and this library, each separate book of which was of special value to its possessor—for he had the habit of instantly burning every book which he had read and which did not appear important enough to be read by him again—constituted the sole wealth of Carrard Auban. It had accompanied him from Paris to London, and it made these cold walls in the foreign land seem like home to him.

No work of art of any kind adorned the room: every object bore the trace of daily use.

Two little portraits, however, hung above the fireplace. The one represented the great fanatic of the revolution whose wild force had spent itself against the walls of west European life; and the other, the great thinker of the century behind whose mighty brow a new world seemed to be in travail—Mikhail Bakunin and Pierre-Joseph Proudhon. The pictures were gifts to Auban from the only person who had loved him ever since he knew him.

Auban's eyes rested on Proudhon's large, thoughtful features, and he thought of the mighty life of that man.

He was sitting before the fireplace, on a low armchair, and stretching his feet towards the warm flames. So his long, thin figure had been reclining for two hours, his eyes now fixed upon the gently crackling fire, now wandering about the room as if following the thoughts that again and again took flight.

He was not dreaming. He was thinking, restlessly and incessantly.

He was very pale, and on his brow lay, like morning dew, fine pearls of cold perspiration. The usually unvarying, impassive expression of his face was disturbed by the labor of thought.

It was a cool, damp, foggy October afternoon, from which the sun had turned away discouraged.

Auban stared motionless into the glow of the fire which illumined the room in proportion as the growing dusk outside enveloped his windows in closer folds.

For some time he had been troubled by a restlessness which he could not explain. The harmony between his wishes and his power was disturbed.

Sometimes of late he thought he resembled the man who had squandered a princely fortune, and now, a beggar, did not know how to live.

But today he felt how a superabundance of power and ideas was urging him on to extraordinary deeds.

It was not yet clear to him: was his will not equal to his power, or was it only necessary to give the first impulse to the latter which was urging him on?

It would be decided.

Ever since Auban began to think, he had struggled—struggled against everything that surrounded him. As a boy and youth, like one in despair, against external fetters, and like a fool, against the inevitable; like a giant against shadows, and like a fanatic against the stronger. As a man he had struggled with himself: the persistent, exhausting, hard struggle with himself, with his own prejudices, his own imaginations, his exaggerated hopes, his childish ideals.

Once he had believed that mankind must radically change before he could be free. Then he saw that he himself must first become free in order to be free.

So he had begun to clear his mind of all the cobwebs which education, error, promiscuous reading, had deposited there.

He felt that there must again be light and clearness in his head, if he did not wish to sink away into night and gloom. The important thing was to find himself, to become mentally free from all fetters.

He again became himself. It again grew light and clear within him; from all sides the sun came flooding in upon him: and happy, like a convalescent, he basked in its rays.

Now he could think without bitterness of his youth; smile over its errors, and no longer mourn over years apparently lost in a struggle which in this age each must fight out who would rise above it....

WHO WAS CARRARD Auban? And what had been his life until now?

He was now nearly thirty years old. In these thirty years he had acquired externally an imperturbable calm and superiority, internally a cool tranquility, which, however, did not yet save him from violent emotions of pain and wrath.... He was, in one word, a relentless critic who recognized no other laws than those of nature.

He had never known his mother. The only thing almost and the last that he remembered of his earliest youth was the wild, confused, passionate stories and declamations of an old passionate man, pining away in ideals, who had occupied with him a small, narrow, always disorderly room in the vicinity of the Boulevard Clichy—in one of those streets in which so often a profligate life hides itself under the air of greatness. This man was his father.

How his father had come to marry the young German who had lost the years of her youth in the ever-joyless and ever-depressing position of a governess in Paris was known really but to one person. This person was his only friend, and his name was Adolphe Ponteur. After Carrard was left an orphan at the age of six, he became his sole protector, and what he told the boy in later years about his father was as follows:—

The cradle of Jean Jacques Auban—he had never been baptized with that Christian name, but he never called himself otherwise—had been rocked on the last waves of the great revolution: his father had been a grain merchant, who, by shrewd speculations under the first Napoleon, had retrieved his fallen fortunes tenfold. By the aid of the same, Jean Jacques grew to be almost fifty years old without learning that one needs money in order to live. When he was brought face to face with this truth, he was a man wholly unacquainted with life, thoroughly happy and thoroughly alone, although not isolated. A man who in these fifty years had done an enormous amount of reading and learning without ever thinking of utilizing what he had learned; a revolutionist of the ideas of mankind without embittering hopes and almost even without wishes; a child and an idealist of touching simplicity and surprising freshness of body and mind. He had always lived in his ideas, never in life, and had never touched a woman.

Half a century had passed by this man without having drawn him into its whirlpool and devouring him. The clash of arms of the Corsican conqueror, raised as he was by might and struck down by it—by might great and small—pursued him throughout his entire youth. But he paid no more attention to the events of the day than children do to the tales of antiquity told by their nurses and teachers.

The revolution of 1830—it was to him only a shadow that fell disturbingly on his work....

For he was occupied with examining anew the terrible mistakes of Malthus—that there was not enough space and food on the earth for all—without being able to detect them.

He had a suspicion of the approach of a new conflict, compared with which the political dissensions of the day were as boys' quarrels. Therefore he listened with the same attention to the prophetic words of the gifted St. Simon as to the wild imprecations of Baboeuf, the Communist; therefore he studied with the same zeal Fourier's Phalanstère, those impossible fancies of a lunatic, and the labors of the reformers during the *régime* of Louis Philippe; and alternating between the one and the other he beheld today in the Icaria of "Father Cabet" the promised land, and tomorrow in Louis Blanc, the hypocritical rhetorician, the redeeming saviour.

He saw nothing of the proletariat which in the gray dawn of those decades, as one awakening, heaved its first heavy sighs, and still unconscious of its power stretched its mighty limbs.

But from the moment in which the necessity of earning his own living overwhelmed him, all was changed: ten years sufficed to make of the retired, healthy, and studious man an embittered, rapidly aging individual, who was yet daily more awakening to life. It was no longer the great idols whom he loved; he began to make fun of them, and to participate in the ideas and petty struggles of the day which had disgusted him for fifty years. It was exceedingly difficult for him to put his knowledge and talents to practical use; he lived poorly, in subordinate positions of the most various kinds; too old to acquire the full meaning of life, and too young, in his young awakening, not to seize it with all the impetuosity of the inexperienced youth of twenty, he was driven from one disappointment to another, which did not make his judgment clearer or his step firmer.

So the February revolution saw the aging man on the barricades among the crowds of the insurgents who fought for the phantom of political liberty. His enthusiasm and his courage were no whit less than those of the workingmen in their blue blouses, beside whom he stood.

The fall of the July government filled him with boundless hopes. His books were covered with dust; the past of his quiet life of contemplation lay extinguished behind him.

He was now a workingman. The Luxembourg, where the delegates of his class were enthroned on deserted cushioned seats, was the heaven to which he also looked for counsel and assistance. Daily he went to the *mairie* of his *arrondissement* to claim the sum which the State was compelled to pay to all unemployed workingmen—what work could Jean Jacques have done in the national workshops?

He did not see the madness of this decree which was destined to lead to new and more bloody conflicts. For there were two things which he had not yet learned in the fifties: that the State can pay out only what it has taken in; and that therefore all attempts to solve the social question through the State from above are doomed from the start.

But when he might have learned it from his own experience, during the days of the June insurrection, in which labor took up its first real struggle with capital, and drew the lesson from the terrible defeat of that most remarkable of all battles, that the privileges of authority must be met by more deadly weapons than those of force, he was lying ill under the strain of the unusual excitement.

It was his good fortune. For he who had taken part in the political revolution of February—the day of reckoning of the *bourgeoisie* with royalty—the unimportance of which he was incapable of recognizing, how could he have held aloof from the days in which the proletariat would fain have had its reckoning with the *bourgeoisie*? Would he not have met with a sad end, thirsting and rotting in the frightful cellar holes in which the prisoners were penned, or perishing as a banished convict in one of the trans-oceanic penal colonies of his country?

He was spared that fate. When he arose, trembling Paris was in a state of terror before the red spectre of Socialism.

A man had appeared upon the scene who penetrated men and things more deeply than any before him. Proudhon had founded his first paper, the "*Représentant du Peuple*," and delivered his celebrated and notorious address on the gratuity and mutuality of credit in the National Assembly amidst scorn and ridicule.

But Auban saw in the greatest and most daring man of his time nothing but a traitor to the "cause of the people," because he had not taken part in the battles of July.

Blind as he was, he could just as little appreciate the project—perhaps the most important and far-reaching which ever sprang from a human brain—which Proudhon discussed for half a year as the *Banque d'échange*, and which from December, 1848, till April of the following year he sought to realize as the *Banque du Peuple*, in his second paper, "*Le Peuple*," until the brutal hand of power completely demolished the almost finished structure by imprisoning its author.

What in the confusion of the day the father could not comprehend, perhaps because it was too near him, the son was to grasp in its entire range and tremendous significance: that each one by means of the principle of mutualism, and independently of the State, could exchange his labor at its full value, and thus in one word—make himself free!

This last, greatest, most bloodless of all revolutions, the only one that carries with it the guarantee of a lasting victory—Jean Jacques passed through its first awakening almost with indifference.

The election of Louis Napoléon destroyed the last of his hopes. From that time he hated Cavaignac, the faithless one, no more than that usurper.

It took a long time before he could recover from his gloomy torpor. It took years. He lived through them in constant care for his daily bread. Perhaps it was this care that kept him alive. His late marriage was more the result of an accident than of deliberate intention. He met the woman whom he loved in the house in which she was a governess, and into which he came to complete the education of two stupid boys. The sad dependence of their position brought them closer together: she took an interest in him, and he loved this girl of twenty-seven years sincerely.

They lived together in a quiet and not great, but secure, happiness. Carrard was born, the son of a man who had long passed the meridian of his life, and of a woman who was still far from it.

The mother died at his birth. Jean Jacques broke down completely. He was now indeed an old and a weary man. He had lost his faith with his vigor. His passion had fled, and what he tried to give out as such was only vehement, excited declamation. In the midst of this and the clumsy tenderness of Adolphe Ponteur, the little Carrard grew up, and was six years old when his father died with a terrible curse upon the third Napoléon, and without a look for him. Such is the story, in rough outlines, which Adolphe Ponteur told the child about his parents in the years when he was a better father to him than the real one could ever have been. He shared his scanty bread, his narrow room, and his old heart with the boy; he wished to teach him to read and write himself, and took a great deal of pride in carrying it out; but it became evident that it was not Carrard, but he himself who lacked the talent therefor. So he sent him at his ninth year into the large city school of his *arrondissement.*

The war of 1870 came, and the boy had reached his thirteenth year. Adolphe dreamed of the *gloire* of his countrymen, and Carrard continued to live on unconcerned.

The days of the Commune had come, in which all Paris seemed again to be a chaos of blood, smoke, noise, rage, and madness; with terror Adolphe saw a flame leap from the dark eyes of the boy which, for the first time, reminded him of Jean Jacques, and he, the honest *bourgeois* who had always seen only the external horrors of a revolution without being able to recognize its internal blessings, was so frightened by it that he resolved to separate himself from him, and to send him away from that "poisoned" Paris—that Paris without which he himself could not live.

He took him to Alsatia, to Mulhausen, that dull, large factory city which, after the "great war" had spent its rage, found itself in the difficult position of steadying itself on the boundary line between the exhausted but not conciliated enemies. Ponteur had a relative there who stood alone, a genuine Frenchwoman, who had never learned a word of German, and Carrard had relatives on his mother's side—a German government official, who had secured the call to that higher position by extraordinary diplomatic gifts, *i.e.,* by the fine art of hiding his thoughts and feelings behind words.

Mademoiselle Ponteur treated Carrard with exceeding care and kindness, gave him a little room and board, and for the rest allowed him to do as he liked. In the four years in which he lived under her roof, which had nothing more to protect than the quiet memories of the past, he did not once approach her with a request, nor did she ever venture to offer him advice. She was entirely at sea concerning what to do with him, and felt very much relieved when she noticed—and she noticed it at once—that the boy had already very well learned to take care of himself.

The relatives on his mother's side fulfilled their duties towards him by inviting him once a week to their family table, where he sat in the midst of a spoiled and noisy lot of children whose language he understood at first not at all, and later only with difficulty, where he always felt very uncomfortable, and where he again succeeded in having no further notice taken of him and no criticism passed when his visits became fewer and fewer.

At Mademoiselle Ponteur's he learned to appreciate his solitude and independence; at his relatives he conceived an inextinguishable repugnance to German middle-class life.

He remained five years in that place—five years in which he did not once return to Paris. He spent his vacations making excursions through the southern Vosges mountains, which are so little known and so beautiful in their solitude and chaste severity. He looked towards Paris when he walked along the summit of the mountains.

At the age of fifteen he found a friend in the strange city. He was a French workingman who had known his father, and who had in some way heard of Carrard, and spoke to him one day as he was coming from school. From that day Carrard sat every evening, after work, in a small inn, in the midst of a circle of workingmen, among whom there was none who was not at least double his years, and of whom each thought it was his special duty to show some kindness to the "*pauvre enfant*" who was here "so alone." One made cigarettes for him, another taught him to play billiards, and a third told him of past glorious days when the nations had attempted to make themselves free: "Vive la Commune!"...

Carrard heard about the hopes and the wishes of the people out of the mouths of those who belonged to them. He began to suspect, to see, to think. But only as through a veil.

The school became a prison to him, because it compelled him to learn what he considered useless and did not teach him what he wanted to know. It gave him no answer to any of the questions which he never asked.

He had no friends among his schoolmates. He was not popular, but no one would have dared to put an obstacle in his way.

Only one sought his friendship: it was the oldest son of his relatives. His name was Frederick Waller—Waller had also been the maiden name of Carrard's mother—and he was the same age as Carrard, with whom for years he attended the same classes in the same school. He was intelligent without special gifts, indifferent without being able to wholly suppress some real interest in Carrard, and possessed of the desire to win his confidence, which the latter, even in matters of the most common concern, never gave him; and notwithstanding that this inaccessibility often embittered him, he never in these years lost a feeling of sympathy for Carrard which was composed of interest, admiration, and curiosity.

Carrard was, in his eighteenth year, tall and pale, outwardly perfectly calm, inwardly consumed by thoughts and passions, passing his days in gloomy resignation on the school benches and in free and easy intercourse with his friends, the workingmen, at Père François, and his nights in mad pondering over God and the immortality of the soul, and those thousand questions which every thinking man must once in his life have solved for and in himself.

When he had reached his fifteenth year, he received the report from Paris of the death of his old friend—it was the last time in his life that he was able to soothe his pain by tears; two years later the woman died in whose house he had lived for years, and with whom he had never exchanged an intimate, but also never an unfriendly word. She had really come to like him, but never possessed the courage to tell him so. He had never been able to offer her either more or less than an unvarying distant respect.

He passed one year more in another family. Then he returned to Paris with a passably fair certificate, with which he did not know what to do, and with an unshaken belief in the future. He greeted the city of his childhood like a mother already given up as lost: for days he did nothing but wander blissfully through the streets of the city with wide-open eyes and a beating heart, and let the odor of the metropolis act on his excited senses—that odor which is as intoxicating and stupefying as the kiss of a first love in the first night....

He was looking for work and felt glad not to find any during the first four weeks. What mattered it that in those four weeks he spent the small sum which he possessed as a legacy from the man who had tenderly loved him? He lived in Batignolles. Often he rose with the sun and wandered through the dewy paths of the Parc Monceaux, and past the antique, serious structure of the Madeleine, upon the broad, clear place which in the last two centuries has drank so much blood, and yet was lying there in its broad, gray, clear area, shone upon by the sun, flooded by the roaring life, like a serene calm in an eternal riot; wandered down to the beautiful river with its broad shores, and looked at the work which from there fructified Paris, until he sat down tired on one of the benches in the gardens of the Tuileries, surrounded by the laughter of the children, while he turned the leaves of a book which he did not read. Then, when noon had come, and he had taken his meal in one of the countless modest restaurants of the Palais Royal, he could again sit for hours before one of the cafés on the great boulevards and let this nervous, ever-excited life pass by his half-closed eyes in a sort of somniferous, sweet insensibility, until he roused himself, and sauntering down the Champs Élysées, sought the shady paths and sequestered stillness of the Bois for the late hours of the afternoon, to return in the evening—after hastily partaking of some refreshments in one of the small public houses of Auteuil—to the *cité* in one of the steamboats on the Seine, where in silent devotion he greeted the steeples of Notre Dame disappearing in the dusk. He was seldom attracted by the amusements offered for the evening; but he loved to saunter through the Quartier Latin, from one café to another, and to watch the noisy life of the students and their girls; or in the neighborhood of his dwelling, to end the evening in a small inn in conversation with a workingman or a retail dealer on the politics of the day, when the mighty bustle of the boulevards had stupefied, and their endless rows of lights blinded him....

It was the honeymoon of his love. A confused, intoxicated bliss had entirely captured him. After the past years of solitude and monotony he drank of this goblet of joy which was filled to the rim and seemed as if it could not be drained.

"O Paris!" Carrard Auban then said, "how I love you! How I love you! Do you not belong to me also? Am not I also your child?" And pride swelled his young bosom and shone from his eyes which had never been so young. He was still like the growing vine which climbed upwards on foreign grandeur and embraced it with the arms of longing and hope to grow strong on it alone....

But when his pleasure and his money were, nevertheless, on the wane, and he saw himself forced to think how he was henceforth to live, he was not frightened. It did not seem to his courage as a matter too difficult. And yet it was only a very rare and happy accident which led him into a conversation on that day in the Jardin des Tuileries with a gentleman who was looking for a secretary, and offered him that position.

Auban worked with him—a rather free and not overtaxed life—for two years, receiving a modest salary, which was, however, sufficient for his needs. He was not interested in the work. He was not a methodical and, therefore, not a good workman in the matter of copying letters and keeping the library of his employer in order. But he became indispensable to him by helping him—the English specialist, a strange mixture of thoroughness in the settling of some unimportant scientific question and of childish superficiality in drawing conclusions from his work—to improve his faulty French, in which language he was fond of recording his worthless discoveries.

When he returned to England, he gave Auban—although he had never even by a question evinced the slightest interest in his secretary, or showed that he saw in him anything but a tool for his work—a number of letters of recommendation, which were entirely useless, and a sum of money, large enough to be of great service to him in the immediate future.

Auban was again free for some time. Although he had already in these two years followed the social movement of his country with the liveliest interest and made the acquaintance of a number of its moving spirits, he now threw himself—with a great shout of joy—into its tide.

It took him up as it takes up and devours everything.

Broad, dark, mysterious, like the impenetrable thicket of the primeval forest, the domain of the social question—of the future of mankind—lay before his eyes. Fresh, young, ready, he was standing before it.

Behind him a confused childhood—roads across fields, already trodden, and paths across mown meadows, already again overgrown—and before him the great mystery, the ideal to which he would dedicate his life.

The rustling of the voices in the wilderness before him seemed to give answer to those confused lamentations that had sounded about his cradle in the garret.

And he began.

It was impossible to enter with purer intentions, with hotter wishes, and with a bolder will upon the conflict which is the conflict of the present and the coming time.

Auban, not yet twenty-three years old, saw in this conflict two armies: on the one side were those who wanted the bad; on the other those who aspired to the good. The former appeared to him wholly corrupt, already in a state of dissolution, already half conquered; the latter, the healthy soil, ready to receive the seed of the future.

He was overwhelmed by the imperiousness of the movement, and wholly unable to exercise his judgment. He was intoxicated by the idea of being one in these ranks who were challenging the world to conflict. He felt himself raised, filled by new, glorious hopes, strengthened, and as if transformed.

Is there anyone who on joining the movement has not sometime experienced similar, the same, emotions?

He attended the meetings and listened to the words of the various speakers. The farther they inclined towards the "left," the greater was his interest and his applause. He became a guest in the clubs in which the workingmen associated. He listened to the wishes as he heard them from their own mouths. He read the papers: radical, socialistic, the dailies and the weeklies. In every prater of liberty he saw a god; and in every political phrase-monger a hero....

Until now he had shown no marked energy. Especially the latter years had made him commonplace. Now his capacity for work grew. He did really work—the whole, laborious work which the entrance into a new world of ideas exacts of one.

From all sides the tide of new ideas was streaming in upon him. He mastered slowly the chaos of pamphlets in which a diluted set of scientific investigations is often offered to the undisciplined mind in such a strange way. Then he took up the study of some of the principal works of Socialism itself.

His habits of life changed. He did not wish to be a *bourgeois* or appear like one for any consideration. He exchanged his little room for one in the workingmen's quarter of the Buttes Chaumont. He simplified his dress until it was extremely modest, though never disorderly. He ate in the taverns with the workingmen. However, his expenses did not grow less in consequence. Only the feeling of shame at being "better" than his starving brothers he no longer experienced under these perpetual, self-imposed privations.

True to the teachings which he accepted, he began to work as a manual laborer. As he had not learned a trade, he was obliged to look about a long time before he could gain a firm footing. He first became a typesetter, then a proof-reader, in the office of a Socialistic daily paper.

It was at this time, too, that he wrote his first articles. Nothing brings people more quickly and more closely together than the struggle in the service of a common cause. Quickly the noose of a programme is thrown round one's neck. Instantly it is drawn together: henceforth your energies must be directed at the one fixed aim; your course has been determined for you; the use of your powers preordained.

Such is the party!

Auban had joined the ranks voluntarily. Now he was no longer anything more than the soldier who had sworn to follow the waving flag at the front: whither it points, there lies the goal. If your reason revolts, appeal is made to your sense of honor, to your loyalty. You are no longer free—you have sworn to free others!

But also for Auban the time soon came when he was able to exercise his own judgment. He saw the tremendous dissensions of this movement. He saw that ambition, envy, hate, and trivial vulgarity covered themselves here with the same pomp of idealism—the word-garments of fraternity, justice, and liberty—as in all other parties of public life.

He saw it with a pain such as he had never before experienced.

He was still very young. He still did not want to understand that the prominent leaders of the parties never dreamed of mutually taking these words seriously; that to the Conservatives the "welfare of the country," the "public peace and security"; to the Radicals the "free constitution" "loyal citizenship"; to the workingmen's parties the "right to labor," and the fine phrases about equality and justice, were simply but a bait with which to draw to their side, in the largest possible numbers, the mentally blind, and so by the right of the majority to become the stronger.

Had not he himself, during the year in which he almost daily wrote something for the paper of his party, fought with these words—the battle in the air!—without ever having carefully scrutinized them? And he had fought with enthusiasm and honesty, in the good faith that there was no other and better way to free the oppressed and persecuted.

He wanted only one thing, only one thing: liberty! liberty! The voice of his reason, the wild lamentations of his passionate heart, called out to him that the happiness and the progress of mankind lay only in liberty. This incessant thirst for liberty drove him through all the phases of the politico-social movement. No creed satisfied him. Nowhere did he find the premises invulnerable, the conditions fulfilled, the guarantees secured.

He was constantly haunted by the searching thought, by the unsatisfied feeling: it is not liberty, complete liberty! He felt how his aversion to all authority was growing. Therefore he resigned his position.

It was at this time that he made the closer acquaintance of Otto Trupp, whom he had already often seen, and formed friendship with him. Through him he learned about the movement of the workingmen in Germany and Switzerland, of which he had hitherto heard but little. Trupp's accounts made a deep impression on him.

It was in the year 1881. The idea of Anarchism was rapidly spreading in France. From the party ranks of Socialism, it tore crowds of the more independently thinking workingmen, of people dissatisfied with some of the actions of the prominent leaders, then all those whose feverish impatience could not abide the time of the revolution—of deliverance.

If the State, private property, and religion were no more, if all the institutions of authority were abolished, could authority still continue? The thing to be done was to oppose force to the ruling force!

The idea of the destruction of the old world took possession of him. Only on its ruins, if all was destroyed, could arise that society which recognized equality as its first principle. "To each according to his needs, from each according to his powers!" Now he had found the formula in which he could seek refuge. And his dreams reared the structure of the future of humanity: they built it high, broad, and beautiful.... Everybody would be contented: all hopes fulfilled, all desires satisfied. Labor and exchange would be voluntary; nothing henceforth to determine their limits, not even their value. The earth belongs to all equally. Each has a right to it as he has a right to be a human being. And he reared the proud structure of his thoughts—reared it into the heavens!...

This creed of Communism which is as old as the religions that have made of the earth not a heaven, but a hell, he called Anarchism, as his friends called it Anarchism.

Never had his words been more impressive, never had they aroused greater enthusiasm. He was now standing on the outermost boundary of the empire of parties! It was impossible to go further. He sacrificed himself. He was more active than ever before, organizing and agitating. Everywhere he found new comrades.

It was the wildest year of his life. Not a day for introspection and not a night for rest.

He was too much a man of energy who liked to see positive results, to be satisfied with this hasty, feverish activity of the propaganda. Meanwhile the circle of his practical experiences was enlarging without being noticed by him. He understood his comrades: their passionate denunciations, their crying sufferings, their embittered imprecations. Daily he saw here the needy and the starving about him, himself often hungry and in despair; daily there shameless debauchery, baseless insolence, scornful arrogance—maintained only by force. Then he clenched his fists, while his heart contracted in convulsions; then he preached without hesitation and from his deepest conviction the creed: to destroy force by force; then it appeared to him as of the first importance that the starving should have bread, the shivering fuel, and the naked clothing. What were all the achievements of science, of art, what was all the progress of mankind, beside these prime and absolute requirements? Everywhere he preached force, in all meetings, in all societies. He attracted attention. But—as usually happens—it was only an accident that turned the scales in this case.

One of the meetings which he also wished to address was suppressed. On dispersing the crowd, a policeman seized him by the arm and pushed him brutally against the wall. He struck the officer in the face with his fist.

True to the principles which make it obligatory upon the revolutionist "to serve the propaganda in every possible case, especially in court if the circumstances in any way permit," Auban delivered a speech before the judge which created a sensation. Again and again had prisoners, when arraigned, raised the question of the jurisdiction of the court, but never had anyone in like manner denied the authority of all law.

People were surprised—some indignant, some amused. They considered him irresponsible. So Auban was sentenced to only a year and half of imprisonment.

Today the courts of the civilized countries of Europe, when they hear such language, know that it is an "enemy of order" who is before them, and do not again let him go.

In 1883, hardly a year after Auban's conviction, the great Anarchist trial of the Sixty-Six at Lyons stirred up the entire community and directed general attention to the new creed. This blow, which the government went far out of its way to deal, would undoubtedly have struck Auban also, had he not already been inside the walls of a prison. In the view of "public opinion" the name "Anarchist" was almost synonymous with assassin from that time in France too....

When Auban felt the fists of the police hirelings on his body, the essence of force became clear to him in all its brutality. His pride rose in revolt. But he was—"powerless." The idea of suffering in the cause of humanity sustained him. He saw neither the cold smile of the judges, nor the dull, curious looks of the spectators who viewed him as a strange variety of their race. Not a muscle of his face twitched as he heard his sentence. A year and a half! That was nothing. What a paltry sacrifice compared with the thousand-fold sacrifices of the martyrs—to think only of the heroic death of the murderers of the Czar!—who had suffered before him! With proud contempt he entered the prison.

Never was the first period of a man's sentence more heavily borne, the last more lightly, than by him.

At first it seemed to him that he could not live a month without the air and the sun of liberty. He was mistaken. In the beginning a dull and heavy rest took possession of him: the rest of exhaustion after these last stormy years! It did him good. He drank it almost as some healing medicine. Gone were the hourly excitements! Gone the conflicting noise! For a long time the blood continued to flow from all the wounds which these years of struggle had inflicted on him. When it ceased, he felt more calm than ever before.

It was possible for him to secure some books. With the thoroughness which the quiet and solitude of his days and nights forced on him, he studied the investigations of the great political economists of his country.

The picture of the world took another shape before his eyes, the more reflective he grew. Removed as it were from his age, no longer in the midst of the tumult of its contentions, he gained a point from which he could survey its currents. It was at this time that he came back to himself.

In the fall of 1884 he left the prison. He was no longer his former self. It was difficult for him to find his way. His powers had lost their elasticity. He was joyfully welcomed back by his comrades. Trupp was in London. They assisted him according to their means. But it was no longer the same. His faith had been shaken. He thirsted to fathom the truths of political economy. He wished to know what promises it held out. *This* was the most important thing to him now. He knew that he could not learn it from the passionate discussions of the meetings, nor from the newspaper articles dealing in commonplaces, nor from the flood of pamphlets brought to the surface by the movement.

Paris became unendurable to him. Everywhere he looked into the mirror of the follies of his youth. He was repelled, disgusted by the frivolous, noisy, boasting life. He longed after some great, free silence.

The only thing that offered itself was a position in a large publishing house in London, where he could be employed in the publication of a comprehensive work of French compilations. He decided quickly.

But he did not go alone. He took with him a girl whom he had learned to know before his arrest, and who had remained true to him during all that long time.

The year which Auban passed with her was the happiest of his life. But the frail flame of this brief happiness was extinguished when the dying mother gave him a still-born child.

The whole character of this simple woman whose judgment was as natural as it was keen was brought out by her reply to a Communist, who in a tone of bitter reproach once asked her:—

"Did you ever contribute anything to the happiness of mankind?"

"Yes, I have myself been happy!" she replied.

When Auban had lost her, he grew still more serious and settled. More and more did he begin to hate and to fear the dreams of idealistic inexperience. He rejected them with a caustic analysis, often with a bitter scorn. Therefore he was now being attacked by parties who had formerly greeted him with joy. He saw in this nothing but a gain. He now became what he had never been: sceptical. If he had formerly exaggerated the party dissensions of the day, he was now—when he no longer could take seriously the political farce—inclined to underrate them.

Since he came to London, he had taken up in his free hours the study of the latest daughter of science—political economy, that sober, serious, severe study which exacts so much of the head, so little of the heart. It compelled him to dispel the legion of value wishes; it compelled him to think logically; and it compelled him to scrutinize words as to their value and meaning.

It was Proudhon who first attracted him powerfully, that gigantic man whose untiring investigations encompass all domains of human thought; Proudhon, whose impassioned, glowing dialectics seems so often to go astray in the obscure mazes of contradiction where only the spirit enthroned above all parties can follow the master exclusively bent on seeking the complete liberty of the individual; Proudhon, the "father of Anarchy," to whom ever and ever all must go back who would lay bare the roots of the new creed of no authority.

"Property is robbery!" That is all most socialists know about Proudhon. But the scales were falling from Auban's eyes.

He now saw what it was that Proudhon had meant by property: not the product of labor, which he had always defended against Communism, but the legal privileges of that product as they weigh upon labor in the forms of usury, principally, as interest and rent, and obstruct its free circulation; that with Proudhon equality was nothing but equality of rights, and fraternity not self-sacrifice, but prudent recognition of one's own interests in the light of mutualism; that he championed voluntary association for a definite purpose in opposition to the compulsory association of the State, "to maintain equality in the means of production and equivalence in exchange" as "the only possible, the only just, the only true form of society."

Auban now saw the distinction Proudhon made between possession and property.

"Possession is a right; property is against right." Your labor is your rightful possession, its product your capital; but the power of increase of this capital, the monopoly of its power of increase, is against right.

"*La propriété, c'est le vol!*"

Thus he recognized the true causes of the terrible differences in the distribution of weapons of which nature knows nothing when it places us on the battleground of life; how it happens that some are condemned to pass a life of trouble and toil and hopelessness within the limits unalterably fixed by the "iron law of wages," while the others, removed from competition, throw out playfully, as it were, the magnet of their capital, to attract whatever of foreign labor products fall within its field, and so steadily add to their wealth—all that he now saw clearly under the light of this examination.

He saw that the minority of the latter were in a position, by the aid of anciently received opinions, to coerce the majority into a recognition of their privileges. He saw that it was the nature of the State which enabled that minority to keep a portion of the people in ignorance concerning their interests, and to prevent by force the others who had recognized them from pursuing them.

He saw consequently—and this was the most important and incisive perception of his life, which revolutionized the entire world of his opinions—that the one thing needful was, not to champion the creed of self-sacrifice and duty, but rather egoism, the perception of one's own interests!

If there was a "solution of the social question," it lay here. All else was Utopia or slavery in some form.

So he grew slowly and quietly into liberty: during the day bound in the slavery of his toilsome labor and in the evening in the company of the woman to whom belonged his love. Then, when he had lost her, again alone; only more alone, but quieter and stronger than ever....

Trupp was and remained his best friend. He had more and more learned to appreciate the earnestness, the firmness, and the instinctive tenderness of that man. Nevertheless there was no longer any real understanding between them. Trupp always viewed men from the standpoint of what they ought to be and one day would be; but Auban had penetrated the nature of liberty far enough to know how little one can force people to be happy who do not wish to be happy.

He placed all his hope in the slow progress of reason; Trupp, all in the revolution which would flood the world with the light of liberty, illuminating all, because fulfilling all wishes. Auban had come to himself and wished that each might so come to himself; Trupp lost himself more and more in the generality of mankind. Trupp had placed himself in the service of his cause and felt as belonging to it in life and in death; Auban knew that liberty does not bind one to anything.

So the one was more and more fired to a life of action, like a horse by the spurs of his rider, like a soldier by the "Forward!" cry of his general, while the other became more and more convinced of the significance of the policy which awaits the approach of the enemy to repulse his attacks. So the one saw all lasting good proceeding only from a bloody, the other only from a bloodless, conflict....

Chapter V.
The Champions of Liberty

Auban jumped up.

There was a rap at the door. The bar-boy who came every Sunday thrust his head through the door: "Sir?" He might call again in half an hour.

Auban looked at his watch. He had again been musing away a whole hour.... It was almost five o'clock. It was already getting dark, and Auban lit a large lamp which illuminated the room from the mantlepiece. Then he stirred up the fire to a fresh glow; pushed the table with an effort towards the window, so that there was a large space before the fireplace; and finally placed a number of chairs round the latter in a semicircle. Now there was room for about eight or nine persons.

He surveyed the room which, now that the curtains were drawn, warmed by the blazing fire and illumined by the mild light, gave the appearance almost of comfort.

But how different it used to be: in the two small rooms in Holborn, when his wife was still living—his wife who knew so well how to make things comfortable for everybody in the Sunday afternoon hours: how to prevail upon the most timid to speak his thoughts, the babbler to check his tongue, the bashful to join in the conversation, the phrasemonger to think, without their noticing it.

It was not a rare thing at that time for women to attend these gatherings. But the tone had always remained perfectly natural and free from all conventional constraint.

Her brief illness had suddenly interrupted the gatherings; her death left the greatest gap in the circle. Auban could not give up the idea of these afternoons which had originated with her.

They again came to him. She was never mentioned, although everyone who had known her felt her loss.

How many had come and gone in these two years: surely a hundred persons! They were all more or less in the international movement of Socialism. Their ideals were as different as the paths along which they pursued them.

But all were suffering from the pressure of present conditions and longed for better ones.... That was the only bond which in a loose way united them in these hours.

Many thought ill of Auban for opening his doors to so many different characters. Some regarded it even as disloyalty. "To whom?" he asked them, smilingly. "I own no bodily or spiritual master to whom I have sworn loyalty. How can I have become disloyal?"

So the political talkers, the party men, and the orthodox fanatics remained away: all those who fancied they could enjoy the heaven of liberty only *after* their ideal of liberty had become the ideal of all.

Again and again the few came—Auban's personal friends—whom the experiences of their lives had taught that liberty is nothing but independence of one another: the possibility for each of being free in his own fashion.

The conversation was usually carried on in French. But not infrequently also in English, when the presence of English friends made it necessary.

Of late, strangers were again coming and going more frequently. Auban asked no one to come again; but everybody felt by the pressure of his hand with which he took leave that he would be just as welcome next week.

All had the right of introducing their friends, which they sometimes exercised to such a degree that there were more persons than chairs. But often, too, Auban was alone with one or two of his friends.

It was mostly some issue of the day which formed the centre of the common conversation. Or a discussion arose, separating the gathering into talkers and listeners. But it also happened that small groups were formed, when two or three different languages filled the room.

Once a man came, no one knew whence, who sometime later proved to be a decoy. The lust of ferreting out some conspiracy had led him to this place, too. But when he saw that there was no talk here about dynamite, about bombs, about the "black hand," executive committees, and secret societies, but that scientific and philosophical questions which he did not understand were being discussed, he disappeared as he had come, after he had been unspeakably bored for several hours.

A similar disappointment awaited several youthful Hotspurs who imagined that the throwing of a bomb was a greater deed and would more speedily abolish all social misery than the laborious examination into the causes of this misery. The contempt with which they henceforth spoke of this "philosophical Anarchism," which was entirely fruitless and had nothing in the least to do with the liberation of starving humanity, was as sovereign as it was easily to be explained.

Auban usually held aloof from the discussions. But he did not like to see them depart from the firm ground of reality and degenerate into a useless war of words, alike without end and aim.

But today—urged by his friends and not held back by his own feelings—he wished to set forth in all their sharp contrast the outlines of two philosophies, whose illogical intermingling had produced a night of contradiction and confusion....

Today he wished to destroy the last misunderstanding about himself and his position, and thereby enter upon a conflict to which he was firmly resolved for a long time to devote his best powers....

HE WAS JUST LOOKING, somewhat impatiently, at his watch, when he heard a rap at the door. But the visitor was an entire stranger to him. He was a man of forty, who walked up to him, introduced himself, and handed him a letter.

Auban ran through it after he had both taken seats. It was a recommendation of the bearer, in an easy, bright style, and it came from a man with whom, in years past in Paris, Auban had often stood on the same platform in defence of the rights of labor, but who was now on the editorial staff of a great opposition paper of the day, and much feared on account of his predatory pen.

Half excuse, half jest, the letter toyed back and forth between unforgotten memories and the delight in present achievement.... It recommended to the good will of Auban a friend who felt himself attracted by the study of the social movement as "the butterfly by the flame," and who was especially desirous of gaining some information about the obscure region of Anarchism during his short stay in London, regarding which Auban would surely prove a better guide to him than the writer, "who lived too much in the charmed circle of the day, to be still allured by a forlorn future...." Then he felicitated Auban upon his publisher's success, jested once more over their common follies, which "experience had deprived of their last bloom," and made a ceremonious bow.

Auban asked a few questions, to enable him to complete the picture of this changed man. Then in a friendly manner he said that he was ready to give any information which might be desired of him. He was delighted by the tones of his mother-tongue; he was secretly delighted by this visit which brought an odor of Paris into his room....

This stranger was sympathetic to him: his plain dress, his calm, confident manner, his serious face.

He began with a question.

"You wish me to explain to you the teachings of Anarchism. Would you first tell me what you have hitherto taken Anarchy to mean?"

"Certainly. But I confess that I have no clear picture of it before me. The opposite rather: a bloody and smoking chaos, a heap of ruins of all existing things, a complete loosening and severance of all ties that have hitherto bound men together: marriage, the family, the Church, the State, unbridled men and women no longer held in order by any authority, and mutually devouring each other."

Auban smiled at this description, which he had heard a thousand times.

"That is indeed the picture most people nowadays still form of Anarchy," he said.

"It is represented so on every occasion by the press, the political parties, in our encyclopedias, by the professional teachers of political economy, by all. However, I have always taken it for the conscious misrepresentation of enemies and for the unconscious, parrot-like talk of the masses."

"You were right," said Auban.

"But I further confess that the opposite ideal—the simple, peaceable, undisturbed community life of mankind, where each constantly sacrifices voluntarily his interests in favor of his neighbor and the general welfare—I confess that such an ideal of a 'free society' appears to me wholly incompatible with the real nature of man."

Auban smiled again: "I confess the same."

The other was surprised. "What?" he said. "And yet this is the ideal of Anarchy?"

"No," answered Auban; "on the contrary, it is the ideal of Communism."

"But—both have one aim."

"They are opposed to each other as day and night, as truth and illusion, as egoism and altruism, as liberty and slavery."

"But all Anarchists of whom I have heard are Communists?"

"No; the Communists whom you know call themselves Anarchists."

"Then there are no Anarchists among us in France, none in Europe?"

"As far as I know, none; at any rate, only in small numbers here and there. However, every consistent Individualist is an Anarchist."

"And the whole, daily changing movement of Anarchism which causes so much talk?"

"Is Anti-Individualistic, and therefore Anti-Anarchistic; is, as I have already said, purely Communistic."

Auban noticed what a surprise his words caused. The former had wished to be informed by him concerning the nature, distance, and aim of a road, and now he had shown him that the guide-board on the road bore a false inscription....

He saw the serious, thoughtful expression in the features of his visitor, and was now convinced that it was indeed his interest in the solution of a doubtful question which had brought him here.

There was a short pause, during which he quietly waited until the other had completed his train of thought and resumed the conversation.

"MAY I NOW ASK YOU TO tell me what you understand by Anarchy?"

"Gladly. You know that the word, An-archy, is derived from the Greek language, and means, in literal rendering, 'no authority.'

"Now the condition of no authority is identical with the condition of liberty: if I have no master, I am free.

"Anarchy is consequently liberty.

"It is now necessary to define the conception 'liberty,' and I must say that it is impossible for me to find a better definition than this one: liberty is the absence of aggressive force or coercion."

He stopped a moment as if to enable his listener to carefully note each one of his slowly and clearly spoken words. Then he continued:—

"Now, the State is organized force. As force constitutes its essential nature, robbery is its privilege; so the robbery of some for the benefit of others is the means of its support.

"The Anarchist sees therefore in the State his greatest, yes, his only, enemy.

"It is the fundamental condition of liberty that no one shall be deprived of the opportunity of securing the full product of his labor. Economic independence is consequently the first demand of Anarchism: the abolition of the exploitation of man by man. That exploitation is made impossible: by the freedom of banking, *i.e.*, liberty in the matter of furnishing a medium of exchange free from the legal burden of interest; by the freedom of credit, *i.e.*, the organization of credit on the basis of the principle of mutualism, of economic solidarity; by the freedom of home and foreign trade, *i.e.*, liberty of unhindered exchange of values from hand to hand as from land to land; the freedom of land, *i.e.*, liberty in the occupation of land for the purpose of personal use, if it is not already occupied by others for the same purpose; or, to epitomize all these demands: the exploitation of man by man is made impossible by the freedom of labor."

Here Auban stopped, and there was again a pause. "It seems to me you are approaching the *laissez-faire, laissez-aller* of the champions of free competition."

"The reverse is true: the Manchester men are approaching us. But they are far behind us. However, a consistent advance along the lines they have chosen must unfailingly lead them to where we are standing. They claim to champion free competition. But in reality they champion competition only among the despoiled, while with the assistance of the State they remove capital from competition, monopolize it. We, on the other hand, wish to popularize it, to make it possible for everyone to become a capitalist, by making it accessible to all by means of the freedom of credit and by forcing it to enter competition, like all other products."

"These ideas are very new."

"They are not quite so new, but they have become so again today, today when people look for their deliverance to the ruling powers, and when they refuse to understand that the social question cannot be solved in any other way than by the initiative of the individual who finally resolves to assume the administration of his affairs himself instead of placing it in the hands of others."

"I have not been able to discern the full meaning of each of your words; but if I understand you rightly, you said that you do not recognize any duty of submission to the will of another or any right whatever compelling the observance of a foreign will?"

"I claim the right of free control over my person," replied Auban, emphatically. "I neither demand nor expect of the community a bestowal of rights, and I consider myself under no obligations to it. Put in place of the word 'community' whatever you wish: 'State,' 'society,' 'fatherland,' 'commonwealth,' 'mankind,'—it is all the same."

"You are daring!" exclaimed the Frenchman; "you deny all history."

"I deny the past," said Auban. "I have profited by it. Only a few can say as much. I deny all human institutions which are founded on the right of force. I am of greater importance to myself than they are to me!"

"But they are stronger than you."

"Now. Some day they will no longer be so. For in what does their power consist? In the folly of the blind."

Auban had risen. His large features shone with the expression of a free, calm pride.

"So you believe in the progress of mankind towards liberty?"

"I do not believe in it. Woe unto him who believes! I see it. I see it as I daily see the sun."...

The visitor had also risen. But Auban held him back.

"If you like and have time, stay here. I expect some friends today, as usual on Sundays. Especially today the conversation will turn on many points that may interest you.

The invitation was accepted with evident pleasure.

"It would indeed not be agreeable to me to be obliged to rise from a repast of which I have hardly finished the first course."

Auban again inquired about Paris, about some of the celebrities of the day, about many things that the newspapers did not tell him.

Then came the guests. First, Dr. Hurt, an Englishman, a physician, who had treated his wife, and who had since become a regular attendant at Auban's gatherings. He was curt, taciturn, without phrases, without sentimentality, a character whose prominent features a keen observer could easily recognize: an inflexible will, a strong tendency to ridicule, and an analytical incredulity.

Auban valued him exceedingly. There was none among his friends with whom he liked to talk so well as with this sceptical Englishman, whose courage was equal to his logic.

For awhile the conversation was now carried on in English, which the Frenchman understood. The doctor occupied the second place by the fire, his favorite place, and warmed his broad back, while he cursed that London where the fog and smoke covered everything with a sticky crust of disease germs....

He was interrupted by Mr. Marell, the American, who was accompanied by a young man of twenty, who—evidently struggling between embarrassment and curious interest—shook Auban's hand only with diffident reserve.

"How do you do, Mr. Marell?"

"Well, I bring you a young student of social science, a German poet; I think you have already seen him at the meeting of protest in Finsbury Hall; he would like to make your acquaintance."

Auban smiled. Again a new acquaintance. Where and how the old man made them was a puzzle to him. But a natural goodness of heart did not only not permit him to ever deny a request; it enabled him in kindly sympathy to instantly anticipate it. That may have been the case here too.

Almost always travelling between England and the States, he was on both sides personally acquainted with nearly everybody connected with the social movement, and nearly everybody, no matter what his opinions, knew and loved him. He brought most of the guests to Auban, who extended a cordial welcome to all alike.

"That's right," he said, as usual; "the poets have ever been the friends of liberty, and the German poets above all. When I had not yet quite forgotten my German, I used to read Freiligrath's splendid poems—ah, how magnificent they are! 'The Revolution' and the poem of the 'Dead to the Living'— is it not so?"

"Yes," said the German, with eyes beaming with joy, "and the 'Battle at the Birch Tree.'"

"They are a strange people, those Germans," said Dr. Hurt, "the land of Individualism, and yet that servile cringing. I cannot understand how an upright man can live there among those obsequiously bent necks."

"Well, there are not a few who emigrate. How many come even to America," the Yankee interrupted him.

Again the door opened.

It was Trupp, who, serious as ever, greeted those present with a nod; a Russian Nihilist, whose name no one knew, but of whose work in the propaganda his comrades talked a great deal; and finally, a follower of the New York "*Freiheit*," school, whose visits always gave Auban special pleasure, notwithstanding that on many questions he was still farther from an agreement with him than with Trupp.

Following upon their heels came the last visitor for the afternoon—a giant in stature, whose blonde hair and blue eyes at once betrayed the Norseman. He was a Swede, who belonged to the young Social Democratic party of his country, but who inclined strongly towards Anarchism, and always claimed that there was but one difference between the latter and his party, a difference of policy: what the Social Democrats sought to achieve by the way of political reforms, the Anarchists sought to accomplish by force; and as the former course seemed too long, he was inclined to choose the latter. He was entirely what is usually described as a "sentimental Socialist."

They formed a semicircle round the fire. The bar-boy came, and went from one to the other, taking orders. By thus relieving himself of the trouble and care of furnishing and offering refreshments, Auban secured to each the liberty of individual choice. The comfortableness of his guests justified him.

The conversation soon grew lively.

Auban avoided the ceremonious introduction of his guests. But he had a fine way of indirectly—in the course of the conversation—making one acquainted with another. And so on this afternoon it was not long before each of his eight guests knew who the other was, if he had not already met him on former occasions. They did not all talk with each other. Dr. Hurt kept perfectly silent, but listened attentively. Everybody knew these characteristics. The Russian did not join in. Thoughtfully looking before him, he allowed none of the words spoken in the room to escape him, seeking and finding behind each a deeper and more special meaning than was intended. It was the fourth time that he had been present; and he had come the first time four weeks ago.

But the kindliness of the old American, whose serious simplicity never changed, and Auban's calm unconcern, never allowed a feeling of uneasiness to rise or the conversation to flag.

Most of them smoked. In half an hour the room was filled with smoke: its white streaks curled like wreaths round those heads so variously shaped by nature, round those manly, serious brows, and then floated away towards the ceiling, where they disappeared.

After a pause, and after the glasses had been filled again, Auban, who was sitting between his French visitor and the young German of whom the American had said that he was a poet, bent forward and said in French:—

"Trupp and myself would like to ask you, gentlemen, the favor of an hour for a discussion of the question: What is Anarchism? this afternoon. And not, as usual, for a discussion of some special and sharply defined question, but for a discussion of the fundamental principles of Anarchism itself. For both of us feel that such an interchange of opinions has become necessary."

He waited to see if the meeting would assent to his proposition. The conversation had ceased. They nodded to him, and he continued:—

"'What?'—some of you will ask, 'what?—a discussion on the fundamental principles of Anarchy? Why, have not these principles been established long ago and so placed beyond all doubt?'

"Whereupon I answer, No! Notwithstanding fifty years have almost passed since the word 'Anarchism'—in opposition to the view prevalent; that Anarchy is nothing but the disorder of chaos—for the first time employed to designate a state of society; notwithstanding that in these fifty years Anarchism has in all civilized countries of the earth become a part of contemporary history; notwithstanding it has already laid the indestructible foundation of its own history; notwithstanding there are thousands of persons today who call themselves 'Anarchists' (here in Europe from ten to twenty thousand, and in America probably as many more); notwithstanding all that,

I say that there is but a very small number of individuals who have thoroughly mastered the idea of Anarchism.

"I will say right here who these few in my opinion are. They are the thinkers of Individualism who were consistent enough to apply its philosophy to society. They are—in the most intellectual and cultured city of the American continent, in Boston—a few courageous, strong, and thoughtful men wholly independent of all the current movements of the age—in the same city where Anarchism found its first and till now only organ. They are, finally, scattered in all directions, the disciples of Proudhon, to whom this giant is not dead, even if Socialism in ridiculous conceit fancies it has buried him...."

"I believe you may add," said Dr. Hurt, "that there are a few among the great monopolists of capital who have come to understand what it is that maintains their enormous fortunes and enables them to steadily increase, and who have therefore not remained wholly ignorant of their greatest enemy."

"So we, the workingmen, we who have always honored the name despite all persecutions, we are no Anarchists? What?" began Trupp, excitedly.

"In the first place, the question of Anarchism is not the concern of a single class, consequently also not of the laboring class, but it is the concern of every individual who values his personal liberty. But then,"—Auban rose, advanced a little towards the centre, and stretched his thin figure, while he continued in a louder voice—"but then I say that you—those whom you just had in mind, Otto, when you spoke of the workingmen—are indeed no Anarchists. And in order to prove that, I have asked you today to listen to me for a half-hour."

"SPEAK FIRST," SAID TRUPP, apparently calm. "I will answer you after you are through."

Auban continued.

"I can say that I have always wanted only one thing: liberty. Thus I came to the threshold of so many opinions; thus I also came into the movement of Socialism. Then I withdrew from everything, devoted myself to entirely new investigations, and I feel that I have now arrived at the last result of all study: myself!

"I no longer like to talk to many people. The times are past when the words came readily to me while thoughts were wanting, and I no longer lay claim to this privilege of youth, women, and Communists. But the time has come for firmly and strongly opposing those foolish attempts at uniting principles in theory which are practically as different as day and night.

"We must choose sides: here or there. For the one, and thereby against the other. For or against liberty!

"Better honest enemies than dishonest friends!"

The decided tone of these words made an impression on all present. By the earnestness with which Auban had spoken them everyone felt that a crisis was at hand.

Everyone, therefore, manifested the deepest interest in Auban's further remarks, and gave his undivided attention to the discussion which followed between him and

Trupp, only occasionally offering a suggestion or asking a question.

Word after word fell from Auban's lips without any sign of emotion. He spoke with unvarying precision that allowed of no misapprehension, but emphasized more strongly one or the other of his arguments, the fundamental axioms of a relentless philosophy.

Trupp spoke with the whole warmth of a heart thirsting for justice. Where his reason came to an obstacle, he raised himself above it on the wings of his imperturbable hope.

French was spoken today. There was none among them who did not understand that language.

Auban began again, and he enunciated each of his well-considered words so slowly that it seemed almost as if he read them or had learned them by heart.

"I maintain," he began, "that a great split has arisen in the social movement of the present day, and that it is perceptibly growing larger from day to day.

"The new idea of Anarchism has separated itself from the old one of Socialism. The professors of the one and the followers of the other are concentrating themselves in two great camps.

"As I have said, we are face to face with the alternative of making a choice one way or the other.

"Let us do this today. Let us see what Socialism wants, and let us see what Anarchism wants."

"WHAT DOES SOCIALISM want?

"I have found that it is very difficult to offer a satisfactory answer to this question. For ten years I have been watching the movement in each of its phases, and I have learned to know it in two countries by personal experience. I have followed its rise and growth in the history of the present century, but to this hour I have not succeeded in forming a clear picture of its aims. Otherwise I should perhaps still be a follower of it.

"Wherever I inquired after its ultimate aims, I received two answers.

"The one was: 'It would be ridiculous to already outline the picture of a future which we are only preparing. We leave its formation to our descendants.'

"The other was less reserved. It changed men into angels, pictured with enviable rapidity an Eden of happiness, peace, and liberty, and called that heaven on earth the 'future society.'

"The first answer was made by the Collectivists, the Social Democrats, the State Communists; the second, by the 'free Communists,' who call themselves Anarchists, and those genuinely Christian dreamers who belong to none of the social parties of the present, but whose number is much larger than is commonly believed. Most religious fanatics and philanthropists, for instance, belong to them.

"In this brief presentation, which will strictly keep inside the limits of reality and deal with men only as they are, have always been, and will always be, I must entirely ignore the last-mentioned classes. For the former of these, the free or revolutionary

Communists, would never have received any attention in the social movement—notwithstanding almost every decade of the present century witnessed their rise, growth, and disappearance: from Baboeuf and Cabet, via the tailor Weitling and the German-Swiss Communistic movement of the forties, to Bakunin—had they not championed a policy whose occasional application during the past twelve years has made of the name 'Anarchist,' falsely assumed by them, in the minds of the mentally blind (and these still constitute about nine-tenths of all mankind) a synonym for robbers and murderers; and the latter, the philanthropical Utopians—well, there have always been such, and we shall presumably have them with us as long as governments shall create misery and poverty by force.

"Ignoring, therefore, all purely ideal Socialists and their Utopian wishes, and concentrating my attention on the aspirations of the first-mentioned classes, which are the only tangible ones, I answer the question: What does Socialism want?—in their spirit and by their own words thus:—

"Socialism wants the socialization of all the means of production, and the societarian, systematic regulation of production in the interests of the community.

"This socialization and regulation must proceed in accordance with the will of the absolute majority and through the persons of the representatives elected and designated by it.

"So reads the first and most important demand of the Socialists of all countries, so far as they keep within the limits of reality and deal with the given conditions.

"It is of course impossible to treat here in detail:

"First, of the possibility of the realization of these principles, which is indeed conceivable only by the aid of an unexampled terrorism and the most brutal compulsion of the individual, but in which I do not believe; and second, of the consequences, in no manner to be estimated, which an unlimited—even if only temporary—dictatorship of the majority would entail upon the progress of civilization....

"And why should I? I need only point to the present conditions from which we are all suffering: to the privileges, forcibly created and maintained by the State, with which it invests capital in the form of interest, and land in the form of rent, on the one side, and to the useless internecine struggle of the labor dependent on that capital, the struggle in which labor irretrievably devours itself, on the other; I need only point to these abominable conditions, to give all thinking people an idea of how completely null and void must become economic, and consequently all personal, liberty, after these separate monopolies shall have become consolidated in the one, comprehensive, absolute monopoly of the community which is today called the State and tomorrow the collectivity.

"I say only so much:—

"The forcible exploitation of the majority by the minority today would become a forcible exploitation, no more justifiable, of the minority by the majority tomorrow.

"Today: Oppression of the weak by the strong. Tomorrow: Oppression of the strong by the weak.

"In both cases: Privileged power which does as it pleases.

"The best that Socialism might achieve would consequently constitute only a change of rulers."

"Here I put my second question:—

"What does Anarchism want?

"And starting from what has been said, I answer:—

"Anarchism wants the absence of all government which—even if it abolishes 'class rule'—inevitably separates mankind into the two great classes of exploiters and exploited.

"All government is based on force. But wherever there is force there is injustice.

"Liberty alone is just: the absence of all force and all coercion. Equality of opportunities for all constitutes its basis.

"On this basis of equal opportunities, the free, independent, sovereign individual whose only claim on society is that it shall respect his liberty, and whose only self-given law consists in respecting the liberty of others—that is the ideal of Anarchy.

"When this individual awakes to life, the knell of the State has sounded: society takes the place of government; voluntary associations for definite purposes, the place of the State; free contract, the place of statute law.

"Free competition, the war of 'all against all' begins. The artificially created conceptions of strength and weakness must disappear as soon as the way has been cleared and the perception of the first egoism has struggled into light that the happiness of the one is that of the other, and *vice versa.*

"When with the State the privileges maintained by it have become powerless, the individual will be enabled to secure the full product of his labor, and the first demand of Anarchism, the one it has in common with Socialism, will be fulfilled.

"When shall I be enabled to secure the full product of my labor?" Auban interrupted himself, as he caught the questioning glance of the Frenchman, and continued:—

"When I can exchange the product of my labor at its full value and with the proceeds buy back one of equal value, instead of being forced, as at present, to sell my labor below its value, *i.e.,* when I must submit to being robbed of a portion of it by force."

After this explanatory clause, Auban again took up the thread of his address.

"For after the disappearance of force, capital, unable any longer to levy the customary tribute, will find itself compelled to participate in the struggle, *i.e.,* to lend itself out for a consideration which the competition among the banks themselves in the business of furnishing mediums of exchange will force down to the lowest point, just as it will make impossible the accumulation of new capital in the hands of the few.

"The power of increase of capital is the death of labor: the vampire that sucks its blood. When it is abolished, labor is free.

"When the resources of nature shall no longer be obstructed by the violent arrangements of an unnatural government which is a mockery on all common sense, and which under the pretence of the care of the general welfare, purchases the mad luxury of an insignificant minority at the cost of the misery of an entire population, then only shall we see how bountiful she is, our mother. Then will the welfare of the individual in truth have become identical with the welfare of the community, but instead of sacrificing himself to it, he will have subjected it to himself.

"For it is this and nothing else that Anarchism wants: the removal of all artificial obstructions which past centuries have piled up between man and his liberty, between man and his intercourse with his fellow-men, always and everywhere in the forms of Communism, and always and everywhere on the basis of that colossal lie, designed by some in shrewd and yet so stupid self-infatuation, and accepted by others in equally stupid self-abasement: that the individual does not live for himself, but for mankind!

"Trusting in the power of reason, which has begun to clear away the confusion of ideas, I calmly look into the future. Though liberty be ever so distant, it will come. It is the necessity towards which, through the individual, mankind is ever moving.

"For liberty is not a condition of rest; it is a condition of vigilance, just as life is not sleep, but wakefulness from which death only can absolve us.

"But liberty raises its last claim in the name of Anarchism by demanding the sovereignty of the individual. Under this name it will fight its last battle in every individual who revolts against the compulsion of his person by the Socialistic world that is forming today. No one can hold aloof from this struggle; each must take a position for or against.

"For the question of liberty is an economic question!"

Auban's words had long ago lost their deliberate judicial tone. He had spoken his last sentences rapidly, with a voice full of emotion. But with his hearers the effect of his words varied with the individual.

No one rose to reply at once.

Then Auban added:—

"I have taken my position in the last two years, and I have told you where I stand. Whether I have made myself clear and whether you have understood me—I do not know. But I do know that my place is outside all current movements. Whom I am seeking and whom I shall find is, the individual; you—and you—and you—you who in lonely struggles have come to the same perception. We shall find each other, and when we shall have become strong enough, the hour of action will have come for us also. But enough."

He ceased, and stepping back, took his old seat.

Several minutes passed, during which various opinions were exchanged in low voices before Trupp began his reply. During Auban's address he had been sitting bent forward, his chin resting on his hand, and his arm on his knee, and had not allowed a word to escape him.

He spoke tersely and as one convinced of what he says, after he had once more surveyed the audience with his keen eye.

"We have just been told of two different Anarchisms, of which the one, we are assured, is none at all. I know but one; that is Communistic Anarchism, which has grown among workingmen into a party, and which alone is known in 'larger circles' as we say. It is as old, yes, older than the present century: Baboeuf already preached it. Whether a few middle-class liberals have invented a new Anarchism is entirely immaterial to me and does not interest me any more than any other workingman. As regards Proudhon, to whom comrade Auban again and again refers, he has long ago been disposed of and forgotten even in France, and his place has everywhere been taken by the revolutionary, Communistic Anarchism of the real proletariat.

"If the comrades wish to know what this Anarchism wants, which has risen in opposition to the State Communists, I will gladly tell them in a few words.

"Above all, we do not see in the individual a being separate from society, but we regard him as the product of this very society from which he derives all he is and has. Consequently, he can only return, even if in a different form, what in the first place he received from it.

"For this reason, too, he cannot say: this and that belong to me alone. There can be no private property, but everything that has been and is being produced is social property, to which one has just as much right as another, since each one's share in the production of wealth can in no manner be determined. For this reason we proclaim the liberty to consume, *i.e.,* the right of each to satisfy his wants free and unhindered.

"Consequently we are Communists.

"But, on the other hand, we are also Anarchists. For we want a system of society where each member can fully realize his own 'self,' *i.e.,* his individual talents and abilities, wishes, and needs. Therefore we say: Down with all government! Down with it even in the form of administration. For administration always becomes government. We likewise oppose the whole swindle of the suffrage and declare the leaders who have presumed to place themselves at the head of the workingmen as humbugs.

"As Communists we say:—

"To each according to his needs!

"And as Anarchists

"From each according to his powers.

"If Auban says such an ideal is possible, I answer him that he does not yet know the workingmen, although he might know them, for he has associated with them long enough. The workingmen are not such sordid egoists as the *bourgeois*—after they have had their day of reckoning with them, after the last revolution has been fought, they will very well know how to arrange things.

"I believe that after the expropriation of the exploiters and the confiscation of the bank, they will place everything at the disposal of all. The deserted places will quickly enough find occupants, and the well-stocked warehouses soon enough customers. We need not cudgel our brains about that!

"Then when each one shall be sufficiently supplied with food, clothing, and shelter, when the hungry shall be fed and the naked clothed—for there is enough for all for the present—they will form groups; will, impelled by the instinct of activity, produce in common and consume according to needs.

"The individual will at best receive more, never less, from society than he has given it. For what should the stronger who produces more than he can consume do with the excess of his labor except give it to the weaker?

"And that is not liberty? They will not ask how much or how little each produces and each consumes; no, each will carry his finished work to the warehouses and take therefor in return what he needs for his support. According to the principle of fraternity—"

HERE TRUPP WAS interrupted by a shout of laughter from Dr. Hurt. A general commotion arose. Most of them did not know what to think. Auban was angry.

"To me it is not a matter for mirth, but a matter for tears, doctor, when men rush into their destruction with open eyes," he said.

Trupp rose. Every fibre of his whole solid figure was in a state of tension. He was not offended, for he did not feel himself attacked, but his idea.

"With people like you we shall indeed make short work!" he exclaimed.

But Dr. Hurt, who had suddenly also become serious, entirely ignored these words.

"Where do you live?" he asked brusquely. "On the earth or on the moon? What kind of people do you see? Are you never going to be sensible?"

And turning away, he again broke out in laughter.

"One must hear such things in order to believe them! Two thousand years after Christ, after two thousand years of the saddest experience in the following out of a creed which has caused all the misery, still the same nonsense, in the same unchanged form!" he exclaimed.

At one blow the spirit of the gathering had changed. In the place of calm listeners who were recovering themselves from their astonishment at this interruption, excited participants took sides for or against.

Trupp shrugged his shoulders.

The success of his words with the majority had been unmistakable. Auban saw it with an uneasy surprise: what he himself had said had been strange and cold reasoning to them. They longed for the perfection of happiness—Trupp offered it to them.

Is it possible? This question came to none.

There is something evil about hope, thought Auban and Hurt, and their thoughts greeted each other silently in a glance—it despises reason, which laboriously indeed and only gradually, but with unfailing certainty, removes stone after stone and story after story from the giant structure of illusion.

With glistening eyes the young German had hung on the lips of Trupp. Still an entire stranger to the moment, the description of the ideal just heard filled *him* with enthusiasm. O surely, here was all that was good, noble, true!... He now stretched out his hand to Trupp and said: "Let me be your comrade!"

The Russian was sitting motionless. Not a line of his gloomy, youthful, and yet so manly face changed. The workingman who had come with him was waiting for an opportunity to speak.

The old American addressed himself to Dr. Hurt. He was trembling with deep emotion.

"Believe me, dear sir, Socialism is an affair of the heart. The ethical foundations of morality—"

But the incorrigible doctor interrupted him also, without respect for his white hair.

"I know nothing about the foundations of ethics, sir. I am a materialist. But a hard and bitter life has taught me that the question of my liberty is nothing but a question of my reckless power, and that sentimentality is the greatest of all vices!"

The excitement was perceptibly increasing. Talking back and forth, each wished to give expression to the surging thoughts within him. A circle had formed round Trupp, composed of the young German who wrote social poems, Mr. Marell, the American, the Swede who had trouble with the foreign language, and Trupp's German comrade. They listened to him as he continued to picture the future in ever more seductive colors.

Dr. Hurt and the Frenchman were again speaking together.

The Russian looked at Auban as if he wished to fathom him. But the latter thought to himself as he studied those eight heads in their restless moving: What a picture for a painter!

The gentle profile of the old white-bearded American and the soft, smooth features of the young German...the pale, gloomy face of the Russian, his brow overshadowed by his shaggy hair, and the bright face of the Frenchman with the modern half-beard...Dr. Hurt's narrow head, his brow protruding as by ceaseless mental labor, the head of a logician, of a Roman imperator, and the hair-crowned head of the Norseman, with the childlike blue eyes and their confiding expression, which did not change during the heated discussion....

What a difference there is between us men! he thought further; and we should be able to submit to a common law of compulsion? No; liberty now and forever, in the least as in the greatest....

Prevailing on the group round Trupp to resume their former places, he said in a loud voice:—

"I am sorry that you were interrupted, Otto."

But Trupp said quickly:—

"I had said what I had to say."

"Well, so much the better. But shall we not attempt to bring out our opinions somewhat more in detail? Let us look more closely at special points."

The calm attention of awhile ago soon returned. But it was now forced, not natural as before. Several persons took part in the discussion.

Auban began anew, turned towards Trupp:—

"I will attempt to prove that the philosophies of Communism and of Anarchism are also irreconcilably opposed to each other in their conclusions."

"YOU WANT THE autonomy of the individual, his sovereignty, and the right of self-determination. You want the free development of his natural stature. You want his liberty. We agree in this demand.

"But you have formed an ideal of a future of happiness which corresponds most nearly to your own inclinations, wishes, habits. By naming it 'the ideal of humanity' you are convinced that every 'real and true man' must be just as happy under it as you. You would fain make your ideal the ideal of all.

"I, on the contrary, want the liberty which will enable each to live according to his ideal. I want to be let alone, I want to be spared from any demands that may be made in the name of 'the ideal of humanity.'

"I think that is a great difference.

"I deny only. You build anew.

"I am purely defensive. But you are aggressive.

"I battle exclusively for my liberty. You battle for what you call the liberty of others.

"Every other word you speak is abolition. That means forcible destruction. It is also my word. Only I mean by it: dissolution.

"You talk about the abolition of religion. You want to banish its priests, extirpate its teachings, persecute its followers.

"I trust to the steadily increasing perception which puts knowledge in the place of faith. It is economic dependence that forces most people nowadays into recognizing one of the many still existing churches, and prevents them from leaving them.

"After the chains of labor have fallen, the churches will of themselves become deserted, the teachers of a delusive faith and folly will no longer find listeners and their priests will be forsaken.

"But I should be the last to approve of the crime against the liberty of individuals which would by force seek to prevent a man from adoring God as the creator, Christ as the saviour, the pope as infallible, and Vitzliputzli as the devil, so long as he did not trouble me with his nonsense and demand tribute from me in the name of his infallible faith."

They laughed: perplexed, amused, irritated, pitying such weakness in dealing with the enemy.

But Auban continued unconcerned, for he was firmly resolved, now he had begun, to say the best that he had to say.

"You want free love, like myself.

"But what do you understand by free love?

"What else can you understand by it, if you are consistent enough to apply the principle of brotherhood—as you represent it in the devotion to and renunciation of labor—also to that field, than: that it is the duty of every woman to yield to the desire of every man, and that no man has the right to withdraw himself from the desire of any woman; that the children resulting from those unions belong to human society, and that this society has the duty of educating them; that the separate family, like the individual, must disappear in the great family of humanity: is it not so?

"I shudder when I think of the possibility that this idea might ever prevail.

"No one hates marriage more than I. But it is only the compulsion of marriage which induces men and women to sell themselves to each other, which affects and obstructs free choice, which makes difficult, and for the most part impossible, a separation, which creates a state of misery from which there is no deliverance except death—it is only this compulsion of marriage that I loathe. Never should I dare raise an objection to the free union of two people who are brought together by their free choice and whom free choice keeps together for life.

"But just as well as the free union of two persons do I understand the inclination of many people to change in the object of their love; and unions for a night, for a spring time—they must be as free as the marriages for life, which alone are sanctioned by public opinion today.

"The commands of morality appear ridiculous to me, and to have arisen from the morbid desires of narrow men for regulating natural relations.

"And finally, you throw overboard private property with the same royal ease and such a superficiality of thought as we find only in Communism.

"You say the State must fall in order that property shall fall, for the State protects it.

"I say the State must fall in order that property may exist, for the State suppresses it.

"It is true you do not respect property: *your own* property you do not respect; otherwise you would not allow it to be taken from you day after day. Expel illegitimate property, *i.e.,* that which is not really property, but alienism. But expel it by becoming proprietors yourselves. That is the only way in which to really 'abolish' it, the only reasonable and just way, and at the same time the way of liberty.

"Down with the State in order that labor may be free, which alone creates property! So I exclaim also.

"When money shall be freed from all forcibly protected privileges—"

But now Trupp's patience was at an end.

"What?" he cried, indignant, "even money is to remain, wretched money which has corrupted, debased, and enslaved us all?"

Auban shrugged his shoulders. He was about to become vexed, but then he laughed.

"Allow me a counter-question. Would it make you indignant to be an employer and employee at the same time? A receiver and a payer of wages, and, as a co-operator, master of the capital instead of as at present only its slave? I think not. What arouses our indignation is only the fact that in consequence of forcible robbery it is possible at present to get something without work."

"But what, according to your opinion, is to determine the value of labor?"

"Its utility in free competition, which will determine its value of itself. All fixing of value by authority is unjust and nonsensical. But I know very well that Communism solves this question, too, without much trouble: it simply lumps everything."

"But free competition prevails today!" cried Trupp.

"No; we have the competition of labor, but not in the same way the competition of capital. I repeat: You see the pernicious effects of that one-sided competition and of property forcibly invested with privileges, and you exclaim: 'Down with private property!' You do not see that it is this very property which makes us independent, and you do not see that it is therefore only necessary to remove the obstacles in the way of acquiring it in order to abolish the false relation of masters and servants. Believe me, the organization of free credit, *i.e.,* the possibility of each coming into possession of the means of production—this bloodless, thorough-going and greatest of all revolutions—will be followed by a change of all the conditions of life which no one can adequately picture to himself today."

He stopped and saw how coolly his words were received. Only Dr. Hurt sat collected, logically examining word after word, calculating. To the majority a revolution was only a chaos of corpses and ruins, and they shook their heads at Auban's words. Therefore he tried to make his meaning clearer.

"Do you know what effect the abolition of interest, and thereby of usury, would have? A steady demand for human labor; the equilibration of supply and demand; the reduction of prices to the lowest point, and consequently an enormous increase of consumption; the exact exchange of equivalents, and consequently the most equitable distribution of wealth possible. But as a result of this great economic revolution, the country as well as the individual growing more prosperous daily."...

Trupp laughed, indignant and irritated.

"A fine revolution! And you want to make us workingmen believe in these crack-brained fancies? Did I not see you before me, I should think I was listening to a *bourgeois* economist. No, dear friend, the revolution that we shall some day make will reach the goal more quickly than all your economic evolutions! We will make shorter work: come. and take back what has been stolen from us by open force and scientific cunning!"

"If only the *bourgeoisie* do not make still shorter work of you!" remarked Dr. Hurt. "*Exempla docent*! That is: Learn from history!"

That was his answer to Trupp's previous threat, which he had apparently neglected.

The excitement produced by these words subsided only gradually. They saw in them a defence of the *bourgeoisie,* and showered replies to them.

THE GERMAN, WHO OCCUPIED the ground of the New York "*Freiheit*" and the "Pittsburg Proclamation," and who was a member of the "Communistic Workingmen's Educational Society" now took the floor.

"Nothing has so far been said of the real Anarchism which was in existence before anything was known of the Boston middle-class liberalism advocated by Manchester men fifty years behind their times, or of the eccentric cavilling of the 'Autonomists'"— he aimed at Auban and Trupp—"and which still has the most numerous following. It wants the Communism of free society based on the co-operative organization of production. It does not deny the duty of labor, for it declares: No rights without duties. It demands, moreover, the exchange of equivalent products by the productive associations themselves, without middle-men and profit-takers, and that the communes shall regulate all public affairs by means of free contract. But in a free society, so organized, in which the majority will feel very comfortable, the State will be useless."

"Then you grant the majority the right of establishing its will by force?"

"Yes. The individual must give way before the general welfare, for that is higher."

"That is a position, one of the two which I have described. You are on the road to Socialism."

"A fine position for an Anarchist!" said Trupp. "And what becomes of the liberty of the individual? It is nothing but the centralistic Communism which we have left far behind." The flame of dissension which some time ago had broken up the clubs and led to the founding of a new paper, threatened to blaze forth again. "It is my belief, and I stand by it, that in the coming society each will perform his share of labor voluntarily."

The Frenchman now asked him courteously:—

"But assuming the case that men will not labor voluntarily as you expect, what then becomes of the right to satisfy their wants?"

"They will. Rely on it," was Trupp's answer.

"I think it is better not to rely on it."

"You don't know the workingmen."

"But the workingmen become *bourgeois* as soon as they acquire property, and then they will be the first to oppose the expropriation of their property. You ignore human nature, sir; egoism is the spring of all action. Remove that spring, and the machine of progress will cease to operate. The world would fall into ruins. Civilization would have reached its end. The earth would become a stagnant pool; but that is impossible as long as human beings inhabit it."

"Why do you not take the initiative, and demonstrate the possibility of realizing your theories in practice?" Trupp was further asked.

He evaded this question by asking it himself. It was Auban who at once replied:—

"Because the State has monopolized the circulating medium, and would prevent us by force from furnishing one ourselves. Therefore, our attacks are primarily directed against the State, and only against the State."

The discussion between Auban and Trupp seemed to have come to an end, and threatened to entirely break up. Then Auban made a last attempt to force back upon the ground of reality what vague wishes had raised into the empty spaces of phantasy.

"One last question, Otto," sounded loud and hard voice—"only this one:—

"Would you, in the system of society which you call 'free Communism,' prevent individuals from exchanging their labor among themselves by means of their own medium of exchange? And further: Would you prevent them from occupying land for the purpose of personal use?"

Trupp faltered.

Like Auban, everybody was anxious to hear his answer.

Auban's question was not to be escaped. If he answered "Yes!" he admitted that society had the right of control over the individual and threw overboard the autonomy of the individual which he had always zealously defended; if, on the other hand, he answered "No!" he admitted the right of private property which he had just denied so emphatically.

He said, therefore:—

"You view everything with the eyes of the man of today. In the future society, where everything will be at the free disposal of all, where there can be no trade consequently in the present sense, every member, I am deeply convinced, will voluntarily abandon all claim to sole and exclusive occupation of land."

Auban had again risen. He had become somewhat paler, as he said:—

"We have never been dishonest towards each other, Otto. Let us not become so today. You know as well as I do that this answer is an evasion. But I will not let go of you now: answer my question, and answer it with yes or no, if you wish me ever again to discuss a question with you."

Trupp was evidently struggling with himself. Then he answered—and it was a look at his comrade who had just attacked him, and against whom he would never have violated the principle of personal liberty, that impelled him to say:—

"In Anarchy any number of men must have the right of forming a voluntary association, and so realizing their ideas in practice. Nor can I understand how anyone could justly be driven from the land and house which he uses and occupies."

"Thus I hold you and will not let go of you!" exclaimed Auban. "By what you have just said you have placed yourself in sharp opposition to the fundamental principles of Communism, which you have hitherto championed.

"You have admitted private property, in raw materials and in land. You have squarely advocated the right to the product of labor. That is Anarchy.

"The phrase—everything belongs to all—has disappeared, destroyed by your own hands.

"A single example only, to avoid all further misunderstanding: I own a piece of land. I capitalize its product.

"The Communist says: That is robbery committed against the common property.

"But the Anarchist Trupp—for the first time now I call him so—says: No. No earthly power has any other right, except that of force, to drive me from my possessions, to lessen the product of my labor by even a penny.

"I close. My purpose is accomplished.

"I have demonstrated what I wished to demonstrate: that there can be no reconciliation between the two great antagonisms in which human society moves, between Individualism and Altruism, between Anarchism and Socialism, between liberty and authority.

"I had claimed that all attempts at uniting the irreconcilable must leave behind the solid ground of reality, and disappear in the clouds of Utopianism, and that every serious man must declare himself: for Socialism, and thereby for force and against liberty, or for Anarchism, and thereby for liberty and against force.

"After Trupp has long sought to examine this alternative, I have compelled him by my last question to explain himself. I might repeat the experiment with each one of you. It is infallible.

"Trupp has decided himself for liberty. He is, indeed—what I should never have believed—an Anarchist."

Auban ceased. Trupp added:—

"But we will practically carry out the principles of Communism in Anarchy, and our example will so thoroughly convince you of the possibility of realizing our principles that you will accept them as we do, and voluntarily abandon your private property."

Auban did not say anything in response.

He knew very well that this external conciliation was only a fresh and last attempt on the part of his friend to bridge over the deep chasm that had long ago separated them inwardly, as it separated the new from the old, and assigned them outwardly their respective positions.

"Neither I nor anybody else can save anyone from his own doom," he thought to himself. From this time forth he joined in the conversation only when he was directly asked. It grew exceedingly lively.

Never had they remained so long as today. It was long past eight o'clock, and still no one thought of leaving except Dr. Hurt and the Frenchman.

When the doctor took leave of Auban, he said in a low voice: "I am not going to come again to your Sundays, dear friend. Anything that is right. But the performances that I am asked to attend must not be too crazy. Your 'comrade' jumped with both feet straight into heaven. That's too high for me."

Saying which he went, and Auban looked after him, smiling. The Frenchman also rose, once more expressing his thanks. But Auban said deprecatingly:—

"We have only driven in the posts and erected the bare scaffolding. But it was impossible to do more today."

"You will have a hard battle to fight, which you might make easier for yourself if you would drop that word which frightens away innumerable persons who are otherwise near you, yes, who entirely agree with you."

"The word Anarchy describes precisely what we want. It would be cowardly and imprudent to drop it on account of the weaklings. Whoever is not strong enough to study its true meaning and to understand it, he is not strong enough either to think or to act independently."

"I shall return to Paris in a few days. May I convey your good wishes to our friend, Monsieur Auban?"

"Yes. Tell him he is a poor egoist, because he has become a traitor to himself. He has assumed a great responsibility. But the true egoist dreads every responsibility except that for his own person."...

The stranger took his leave with a courteous bow.

"Who was that?" asked Trupp.

Auban mentioned his name.

"He arrived shortly before you and today for the first and the last time."

"Then you do not know him?" Trupp shook his head disapprovingly.

"No, nothing more about him."

"You should have told me that at once!"

But Auban replied sharply:—

"We have no secrets here. We are not Freemasons. What we have said anybody may hear who wishes!"

He took Dr. Hurt's vacant seat by the fire, and held his head in his hands. All spoke now, even the Russian. The variously pitched voices struck his ear as from a distance....

From what was being said he heard of Trupp's victory and of his own defeat.

Then rose the enthusiastic voice of the Swede:—

"It may be that there will be fewer geniuses. That is no misfortune. There will be more talents. Each will be a hand and brain worker at the same time. Capacities will be distributed instead of concentrating themselves. On the average, they will be greater."

"And a thousand donkeys will be wiser than ten wise men. Why? Because they are a thousand!" Auban added to himself.

They had forgotten him. While he had been speaking, the cool breath of reason had descended on them. Now it was warm again: the warmth of a future, winterless, paradisean life. And they rivalled each other in the description of that life; their words intoxicated them; they forgot where they were....

Auban continued to hear.

They ridiculed the eternal question of their opponents: who would do the dirty and disagreeable work in the future? There would be enough volunteers for everything, remarked one; and another: There would no longer be any such work to do; machines would be invented for everything.

Never had Auban been more strongly convinced than at the present moment that most people are themselves their greatest enemies, and never had he more strongly felt that the authority of love would prove to be vastly more terrible than was the authority of hate.

He was striving to destroy privilege. But these Communists denied with the excellences also all values, even the value of labor. His warfare was directed against men and what they had established in folly and ignorance—victory was inevitable; but their warfare was directed against nature itself—victory was forever impossible!

The chasm went deeper, far deeper than it lay uncovered before him today. It was a battle between an old and a new philosophy. And the old was Christianity in all its forms!

The greatest criminal against mankind had been he who had pretended to love it most. His creed of self-sacrifice—it had produced those who renounce: the misery that was now clamoring for deliverance.

God must fall in every shape!

They remained together for more than an hour longer. The conversation gradually drifted to the events of the day: Chicago and serious riots in London were at hand. It was agreed to suspend the meetings at Auban's for several weeks.

When the American rose, and thereby gave the signal for a general breaking up, most of them were surprised to see how late it was.

Auban shook hands with each one; that of Trupp he held a moment longer than usual, with a firm pressure, as if he wished to say once more: Choose! choose! For he had indeed a high opinion of him.

The young German was evidently not satisfied with Auban, and did not attempt to conceal the fact, either. Auban only smiled thereat. Mr. Marell was the more friendly.

"Well, Auban," he said, and took both his hands, "you are a strange man. There is a good deal of sense in everything you say; but what you teach is icy and cold, icy and cold; the heart gets nothing."

"Oh, no, Mr. Marell, liberty is warm like the sun. Cold alone are the walls of the prison. The heart will have richer treasures to bestow when it no longer beats and keeps silent in conformity with commands. But it should never take from reason the guidance of our lives—only today did we see again how incapable it is of following reason in the domain of economics."

Auban was alone. He opened both windows. While the smoke fled in dense clouds from the room and the waiter behind him removed the glasses, he leaned against the window-sill and looked down upon the street. Now while the evening air was cooling his brow, he felt how warm he had become, and how deeply the talk had affected him.

And *for that* your youth!—he thought to himself. The sacrifice seemed again, as so often, too great for the perception it had given him. Yes, it was cool and bitter, this perception, as the American had said. But had it not been like a refreshing iron bath after the enervating half life of faith in hope without deeds?

And he remembered how young he still was, and how much there was yet before him to do, and even if his work should prove apparently as useless as the attempt which he had made today in a small circle—nevertheless, he was filled by a great power and a great joy, and, re-entering his room, he said aloud:—

"Yes, for this perception of liberty your youth!"

And the walls, terrified by the sudden silence after the noise of the discussion, gave back his words:—

"Yes, *for that* your youth!"

Chapter VI.
The Empire of Hunger

The East End of London is the hell of poverty. Like an enormous, black, motionless, giant kraken, the poverty of London lies there in lurking silence and encircles with its mighty tentacles the life and the wealth of the city and of the East End: those on the left side extending over the Thames and embracing the entire Embankment on the other side—Rotherhithe, Deptford, Peckham, Camberwell, Lambeth, the other London, the South separated by the Thames; those on the right side stealing round the northern limits of the city in thinner threads. They join each other where Battersea rams into Chelsea and Brompton across the Thames....

The East End is a world in itself, separated from the west as the servant is separated from his master. Now and then one hears about it, but only as of something far off, somewhat as one hears about a foreign land inhabited by other people with other manners and customs....

It was the first Saturday in November on which Auban had promised to visit his friend Trupp. He intended to go with the latter through the East End and then to the club of Russian revolutionists. They had chosen Saturday, because there is no work in London during the afternoon of that day; because Auban's business and Trupp's factory were closed for thirty-six hours.

Auban left his business about one o'clock in one of the side-streets of Fleet Street. The hurry and scurry of business life seemed to have increased tenfold. He could hardly make his way to Fleet Street through the throng of carts, heavily laden with fresh printed paper rolls which emitted a strange odor of dampness; of truck-wagons whose cursing drivers could not get from the spot; of hurrying, excited, jostling crowds of clerks, workingmen, messengerboys, and merchants. To save time he decided not to go home. He ate in one of the nearest overcrowded restaurants, and ran through the latest papers. Everywhere the unemployed.... Trafalgar Square: police attacks; the assembled dispersed by force; new arrests on account of incendiary language.... Shelterless women in Hyde Park: sixteen nights in the open air; starved and frozen; some sent to the hospital, some to the workhouse, others die.... Preparations for the murder of the Chicago Anarchists: as there are not enough gallows, it has been decided to hang them in two divisions, first four, then three; extraordinary measures to preserve order; petitions for pardon by the condemned, signed by four of them; the governor relentless.... Auban let the papers drop.

Here it was, daily and hourly: the enormous debasement of life which makes of one a butcher, of another a victim! The one like the other overcome by illusion.... And nowhere an escape for either! Both obeying the idol of duty created by men. And both dominated by it, in life and in death!

Auban took the next omnibus going to Liverpool Street Station. He sat on the top. As he passed the statue of the Queen and the Prince of Wales, which has been erected in the place of the obstructive gate of Temple Bar, where in former, darker ages, the bloody heads of executed criminals were exhibited before the people, he thought of the slow ascent of struggling and climbing humanity from slavery. How grandly it would some day develop in liberty!—How long might it be yet, before those sculptured idols would be overthrown, the crowns and purple robes destroyed, the sceptres broken, the last remains of mediævalism effaced!...

Then must be fought that other tyrant, more blind: "the sovereign people." It would be the age of dullness, the age of mediocrity, of dead-levelism in the strait-jacket of equality, the age of mutual control, of petty quarrels in the place of the great struggles, of perpetual annoyances...then the fourth estate would have become the third, the class of the workingmen "promoted" to the class of the *bourgeois*, and the former would then exhibit the characteristics of the latter; commonplace, of thought, pharisaical complacency of infallibility, well-fed virtue! And then would again appear the genuine insurgents, great and strong, hosts of them, the champions of the ego threatened in every moment....

THE OMNIBUS MOVED slowly but surely down Fleet Street. At Ludgate Hill there was an enormous throng of people. In the direction of Holborn Viaduct, that wonder of modern street-engineering, fogs were rising; the iron bridge of Farringdon Street was already enveloped by them. In the opposite direction, where the Thames rushes along beneath Blackfriars Bridge, it was clear. As the horses, stamping on the wet wooden pavement, were drawing the packed omnibus under the railroad bridge of the London, Chatham and Dover Road, towards St. Paul's, the throng seemed impenetrable.

But St. Paul's rose in the air with its dark masses, from whose black background the white marble figure of Queen Anne stood out in relief.... The heart of the city, here it was beating....

Farther. Past the gigantic masses which in their fixed calm seemed to belong to a forgotten past.

A black stream of humanity was flowing down Cheapside. Finally the great strong-box, the windowless, low, lazy building of the Bank came in view. It was already closed. Now it lay there as if dead.

Auban was again seized by the monstrous life that surrounded him.

The countless banks, grouped around the Bank of England like children about their foster-mother, were closed. Everybody was hastening to get dinner, reach home, enjoy rest.... Thousands and thousands of people, exhausted by the week's toil, were rushing along in wild confusion, each impelled by the wish to forget for a few hours the columns of figures which constituted his life, which filled his brain to the last nook and corner.

Young clerks, small messenger-boys in the most various uniforms, careworn book-keepers, serious trades-people, "solid" business men, speculators, usurers, great money-kings at whose feet the world worships—who would dare oppose them?—all mingling here in wild chase, in mad confusion, apparently a chaos of disorder, but really issuing in the most admirable order.

The omnibus stopped here for some time. People got off and on. Crowds thronged after, but had to remain behind. But all found the place they were looking for in the almost endless line of omnibuses, one close upon the other....

From his seat Auban surveyed the sea of humanity. He followed an individual here and there with his eyes; here, a young merchant, evidently a stranger, who seemed like one lost in the swarm, not knowing which way to turn; there, an elderly gentleman in a tall hat, a faultless, simple black coat, with a white beard, and an expression made up of haughtiness and prudence which seemed to say: "I am the world. I bought it. It is mine. What do you want? I keep you all in pay: the King and his court, the general and his army, the *savant* and his ideas, and all my people who work in order that I may be. For men are stupid. But I am wise, and I understand them...."

AUBAN TURNED TO LOOK at the Bank again. There was the hiding-place of that great mystery which held all happiness and all unhappiness. Inscrutable to the majority, it was to them the higher power which determines their fate. With awe, with admiration, with speechless astonishment, they heard about the immense wealth in which they had no share. Whence came it? They did not know. Where did it go? Into the pockets of the rich; that they saw. What gave it the mighty power to shape the world as its possessors saw fit? No, they would never solve it, that frightful riddle of their own wretchedness and the happiness of others. There lay the vampire that sucked their last drop of blood, the monster that drove their wives to dishonor, and slowly choked their children. And they passed more rapidly by the dark walls behind which lay the gold that had been their own blood.

When they were told that the country in which they lived was burdened with a national debt of so and so many millions, and that each of them was in part responsible for this debt, the nonsense of it left them completely indifferent; what a million was they did not know, but the last unpaid room-rent and the five shillings' debt in the meatshop weighed heavily upon them, and filled them with fear and trembling for the following day.

Socialism began to talk to many of them. When it told them that nothing in the world had any value except labor, and when they saw that those who did not work were in the possession of all values, it was no longer difficult for them to draw the simple conclusion that it must have been *their* labor which created the possessions of the former; in other words, that the former lived by their labor, robbed them of their labor; what it was that enabled them to do this was again an impenetrable mystery to most of them; for they were in the majority, and the others only a few against their masses! The more intelligent ones suspected that probably nothing would promise help except to place in opposition to the protective and defensive union of the robbers a similar union of the robbed. So they became Socialists.

For Auban the mystery had long lost its terrors, the sphinx face of power its awfulness. His studies had torn veil after veil from the hidden picture, and he now stood eye to eye with the doll of the State deprived of the tinsel trappings of idealism. The god before whom all worshipped, what was he but a wooden doll, empty and hollow, an enormous humbug, a bugbear? Wound up by a few skilled hands, automatic movements were to make a show of real life!

The ignorance of the deluded masses put into the stiff figures of that skeleton the terrible weapons of privilege. This bank, the greatest in England, was invested by the State with the monopoly of issuing paper money. Thus enormous fortunes arose which gave a false picture of the true condition of the country. Beyond the reach of competition as it was, this one principle alone enforced by power, suppressed free intercourse, undermined confidence in one's own and others' powers, rose destructively between supply and demand, and created those frightful differences in possession which elevated some into masters and degraded others into slaves.

The monopoly of money, the authority of the privilege to create the only legal medium of exchange;—if it fell, the State fell, and the track was cleared for the free intercourse of men.

BUT AUBAN'S THOUGHTS were interrupted.

The omnibus finally started again, leaving the immense buildings of financial traffic behind it, the Bank and the stock exchange, on which as in bloody scorn shone the words of the Bible: "The earth is the Lord's and the fulness thereof."

As he wound his way through the narrow streets to Liverpool Station, turning aside from the roar and bustle of Broad Street to reach his destination by a longer but quieter route, Auban, walled in by those high, silent, forbidding houses which seemed never to have been cheered by a ray of the sun, felt as if he were riding through the cool, dark passes of a narrow valley.

The omnibus stopped at the giant buildings of the stations of Liverpool Street. Auban entered the large bar-room on the corner of the street. Its apartments were over-crowded. People jostled each other, standing, holding in their hands glasses and pewter mugs, speaking in a lively manner, discussing, drowning each other's voices. In perpetual motion the doors opened and shut; the money jingled on the counter.

Auban sat in the corner for a while, drinking his half-and-half in small draughts. Then he pushed through the swarms of people to the station. Leaning against the grating of the entrance, in the midst of a crowd of screaming newsboys, bootblacks, flower girls, venders of all sorts, old and young, stood a small deformed boy, noticed by no one, staring before him with gloomy sullenness, his hands buried in his dirty trousers, ragged, debased, the face of an old man on the thin body of a child. Auban saw him, and his practised eye at once recognized hunger in those looks. He bought a few oranges at the nearest cart. With speechless greed the little fellow ate the fruit, without looking up, like a starving dog that pounces upon a bone. How long was it since he had eaten anything? How long already had he been standing here, his little heart filled with scorn, bitterness, and despair, apathetically staring before him at his bare feet growing stiff on the cold stones?

A cold shudder ran through Auban. It was the beginning of the horror which had always turned him into ice when he returned from the home of the "disinherited," the silent desolation of the East End of London....

AS THE TRAIN BORE HIM the short distance to Shoreditch, there rose before him in gigantic outlines from a hundred separate recollections the shadowy picture of that monstrous life: gloomy, threatening, silent, shapeless, intangible.

He thought of many another walk during which he had for long hours journeyed through the empire of hunger: of that interesting afternoon in the present summer when he had crossed the Isle of Dogs from end to end on foot, stupefied by the magnificence of its improvements made within less than twenty years, horrified by the wretchedness of those abandoned streets in whose rickety houses and miserable huts a tired race seemed to have hid its burdens of care. Then of that evening in Poplar which brought the afternoon to a close, when he had watched the enjoyments of the poor in a song and dance hall of the lowest order, among half-grown boys in shirtsleeves, and girls in fine hats with feathers, a pewter mug of ale before him, his pipe in his mouth, in the three-penny seat, the best and also the last, listening to the screaming voices of some hoarse female singers and negro imitators, and in the midst of the noisy accompaniment of a hundred voices. Then of that other afternoon in Wapping, through which he had loafed with the old sailor who showed him the enormous London docks, who took him in the evening to St. George Street, that notorious sailors' resort; to the dance hall where tall Malayans, silent Norsemen, negroes, and Chinamen, the entire strange and heterogeneous society thrown together here by the ships from all lands, mingled in dance and dissipation; and to the opium den at the Mint, that dark hole where the haunting silence of death seemed to rest over deathlike forms lost in their vice. And Auban thought of his solitary evening walks in the terrible misery of the districts of Whitechapel and Bow, where there was hardly a street through which he had not walked in amazement at the frightful things he saw, and in horror of the still more frightful things he suspected behind the dirty walls and the broken window-panes.

Auban had neither costly habits, nor any special claims on daily life that took much of his time. His days were mostly given to his calling, which, however, did not slavishly bind him to the hour; his evening hours mostly to his studies in political economy and watching the course of the movement. Then the Sunday afternoons to his friends. What leisure was left he devoted to walks through the immense city. These walks constituted his only genuine pleasure, his greatest enjoyment. He was happy if he could get away an afternoon for such a walk; then he would bend over the large map of the city, let his finger move from one point to another, until he had fixed the starting-point and the destination of that day's walk. When he plunged into the mysterious life of a strange neighborhood, he was seized, carried away, inspired by the greatness of the age which in ceaseless activity had created all those mighty things; when he returned to his quiet room, he was as if crushed beneath the pressure of this overpowering life that lifted some to the summit of happiness, to hurl the rest into the abyss of misery....

He had often thought of transferring his room, for a time at least, into the wretchedness of this life, in order to learn to know it better than he should ever be able to by mere outside observation, but he could never find the time. So he had to rely on what he saw and heard when occasion took him there. And even that was indeed enough.

Now Trupp had carried out this plan. He had written a card to his friend: he had given up his work in consequence of some trouble with his boss, and was now living in the neighborhood of Whitechapel. He suggested a *rendezvous* near Shoreditch.

At four o'clock. It had just struck half-past three. Auban awaited him without impatience.

Trupp arrived at the appointed time. His solid, broad-shouldered form was safely making its way through the throng. Again as on that evening in Soho he saw Auban; his hands resting on his cane, gently leaning against the entrance pillar of Shoreditch Station, not lost in revery this time, but closely observing men and surroundings.

They exchanged greetings. The last Sunday afternoon was not mentioned.

Trupp was more gloomy than usual. Full of bitterness, he told of the insolent brutality of his boss, the contemptible servility of his fellow-workingmen, the dull inactivity of his comrades. An example must again be set, else everything would fall asleep. He looked pale, as if he had had little rest of late. There was an unsteady flicker in his eye.

They turned into Hackney Road, that sad, long street of trouble and care where the small shopkeepers live. Then Trupp turned southward, toward the district of Bethnal Green.

The bustle round them suddenly ceased. The streets grew narrower, darker, duller; the filth greater and greater. Only here and there an insignificant store with knicknacks and old rubbish. Else nothing but locked doors and windows, whose panes had long ago been blinded by the filth.

They passed through several streets; then at a sudden turn they entered a narrow passage that led through under a house. It seemed to grow lighter, for the many-storied houses were at an end.

They stood on a small square. Three streets started thence which were formed by narrow houses, all two stories high, whose backyard adjoined each other.

It had taken them hardly five minutes to reach this place.

TRUPP STOPPED, WAITING. He did not say a word but Auban suspected that it was just this spot he wanted him to see.

He took his stand on a pile of heaped-up earth and surveyed the picture that presented itself.

Never in his life, it seemed to him, had he seen anything more sad, more depressing, more disconsolate than the stiff uniformity of those filthy holes of which one adjoined the other in horrid symmetry until the twentieth disappeared in the gray gloom of this chilly November afternoon. The yards that were separated from each other by crumbling walls reaching to a man's breast, and whose narrowness hardly permitted one to stretch out his arms, were filled with muddy pools of slimy filth; heaps of rubbish were piling up in the corners; wherever one looked, he saw broken things and furniture lying about; here and there a rag of gray linen was hanging motionless in the chilly air. The stone steps leading to the doors were worn out; the blinds of the windows, mostly broken, were swinging loosely on their hinges; the window-panes were cracked, hardly one was whole; the holes pasted over with paper; where the windows were open, bare walls were seen.

Not a human soul far or near. It seemed as if death had just passed in giant strides through these streets and touched all breathing things with his redeeming hand....

Then Auban saw something move in the distance. Was it an animal, a human being? He fancied he recognized the bent form of a woman. But at this distance he could not distinguish anything clearly. A thin smoke rose from a few of the many chimneys and mingled with the leaden gray air.

No artist has ever attempted to paint this picture, Auban thought, and yet he would need to put only *one* color on his palette: a dirty gray.

He listened. From a great distance an uninterrupted dull roll came rumbling into this forsaken stillness: the thousand-fold noises of bustling London consolidated into one portentous muttering. But here it found no echo in answer.

Meanwhile Trupp had been walking up and down: he had stood before the rotting carcass of a dog, looked at the hidden, rusty lantern at the street corner which had lost its panes to the last splinter, and was now seeking in vain for a trace of something green in this dusty sand—not a single blade of grass found sustenance in this cursed soil....

Everywhere neglect; wherever the eye turned, the neglect of hunger which daily fights a frightful battle with death.

SLOWLY THE FRIENDS TORE themselves away from the wretched sight, and silently walked down the middle street. Sometimes a window was half opened, a bushy head thrust out, and shy, curious eyes followed half in fear, half in hate, the wholly unusual sight of the strangers. A man was hammering at a broken cart which obstructed the whole width of the street. He did not respond to the greeting of the passers-by; stupefied, he stared at them as at an apparition from another world; a woman who had been cowering in a door corner, motionless, rose terrified, pressed her child with both hands against her breast hardly covered with rags, and propped herself, as if to offer resistance, against the wall, not once taking her eye off the two men; only a crowd of children playing in the mud of the street did not look up—they might have been taken for idiots, so noiselessly did they pursue their joyless games.

Trupp and Auban walked faster. They felt like intruders upon the secrets of a strange life, and they hastened to get away from all those looks of fear, hate, envy, astonishment, and hunger.

At the end of the street another group of children was gathered: they were amusing themselves by the sight of the dying fits of a cat whose eyes they had gouged out, and whom they had hanged by the tail. When the bleeding, tortured animal jerked with its feet to get away, they struck at it with the cruel, awful pleasure children take in visible pain. Trupp quickly stepped among them: "Cut it down!" he commanded. But he might just as well have spoken in German, so little were the words understood, which in his mouth sounded hard and unnatural. In speechless astonishment the children looked up at him, without knowing what he wanted of them. He had to take the dying animal away himself. Returning to Auban, he loudly expressed his indignation at such shameful cruelty to animals. The other sadly shrugged his shoulders: "Better conditions, better manners," he said; "what else can avail here?"

Trupp seemed to know every nook and corner of these streets. He led the way back and forth, often standing still when they came to a house whose cracked walls seemed as if they would tumble down if one leaned against them; then again finding narrow passages of an arm's width, from whose walls a filthy moisture trickled down, gathering on the ground below in pestilent, nauseous pools; so, surely and without a word, he led Auban through the dark labyrinth of this immense misery, whose gloomy monotony seemed to be without end, no matter what direction they chose.

They came into a court-like space which was enclosed by tall, gray houses; Gibraltar Gardens was to be read on a sign on the street corner. "Gibraltar Gardens!" said Trupp; "they mock the misery which they have created!" On the cracked asphaltum of the court a number of the children were amusing themselves with roller-skating—in the "Gardens of Gibraltar," where not a blade of grass grew!

The friends walked on through narrow streets of very old, bent, low, small houses, whose doors one could enter only with bowed head: pedlers lived there, and they had filled the street to suffocation with their second-hand rubbish; and then suddenly the wanderers came upon the roaring life of Church Lane. At a blow the physiognomy of the surrounding was changed: from deathlike desertion into the rushing life of trade on a Saturday afternoon!

Auban was tired. He limped more heavily. At his suggestion they spent a half-hour in the nearest public house, where he sat down in a corner. They still did not talk much together; at most, indicating some observation to each other. It was a gin palace of the lowest order which they had entered. It was called "The Chimney Sweep," as Auban laughingly noticed. The sawdust-covered floor reeked with filth and saliva; the bar was swimming with all sorts of drinks running together, which dried up into a sticky crust; behind it, where the large barrels were piled against the wall from the floor to the ceiling, the waiters had all they could do to fill the hands stretched out towards them; the stupefying odor of tobacco smoke and brandy, the moist warm vapors of unwashed clothing and bodies crowding each other, filled the space to the last corner.

Here misery was in search of its frightful happiness by drowning its hunger in drink. It was a genuine East End crowd; men and women, the latter almost as numerous as the former; some with infants on their withered breasts, but most of them old or at any rate appearing old. Through the grown people ragged children were forcing their way. Almost all were drunk, in the first stages of the Saturday drunk from which they sober up in sleep on Sunday. Auban called Trupp's attention to an inscription on the wall: "Swearing and bad language strictly prohibited!"... It was simply ridiculous, that injunction whose threat no one minded.

The confusion of noises was overwhelming. It did not cease for a moment, and rolled in swelling waves back and forth from one apartment to another. The stammering words of a drunken man were drowned by the coarse abuse of an excited old fellow, who declared somebody had drunk out of his glass; and the neighing laughter with which the two men were incited against each other, by the mad screams of a woman who was standing with clenched fists before her husband who did not want to go with her. Young men, almost boys, were singing in a corner with their dressed-up sweethearts or showing them "nigger dances" by stamping the resounding floor with their heavy shoes in measured time and throwing their upper body back and forth. But suddenly the attention of all women was aroused: a baby had begun to cry; perhaps he found no more nourishment at the breast of his drunken mother.

From all sides they bent over the little wrinkled, gray face, and each woman rivalled the others with suggestions about quieting him. Natural good-heartedness broke forth; they wished to help. Despite this, the infant cried louder and louder, until his lamentations died away in a low whimpering.

The grotesque spectacle of this life was nothing new to Auban. He had often been in these last haunts of misery, where the appearance even of a man not dressed in rags is an event.

Today, however, most of the people were already too much occupied with themselves in their drunkenness, or engaged in quarrels and disputes with one another, to concern themselves greatly about the strangers. An old woman only obtruded herself on Trupp with tenacious persistence, staring at him in a repulsively tender way with her bloodshot, bleared eyes and stammering her wishes in the idiom of the East End, a slang of which he did not understand a word. He took no notice of her. When she fell against him, he pushed her calmly aside. In doing so his face showed neither disgust nor contempt. This woman too was a member of the great family of humanity and his sister.

On the bench, opposite to Auban, sat a young, completely neglected girl. Out of her large dark eyes shot forth bolts of wrath at Trupp. Why? From hatred against the foreigner whom she had recognized in him? From anger at the obtrusiveness of the old woman, or at his cool defence? From jealousy? It was not to be learned from the abuse which she showered upon him from time to time.

Auban studied her. Her debased features, in which contempt mingled with meanness and hatred, were still beautiful, notwithstanding her right cheek was scratched bloody and her hair fell over her forehead in wild disorder. Her teeth were faultless. Her disorderly dress, the dirty linen sacque, was torn open, as if with brazen intention, and revealed to view the still childlike white breasts. "Why should I be disturbed about you?" all her movements seemed to say.

How long before the last traces of youth and grace would be wiped away? What difference was there still between her and that old woman, always drunk, into whose ear Trupp shouted, as she again fell against him with the whole weight of her body, that he did not understand English; he was a German.

"Are you, darling?" she stammered, and put her face close to his own. But at this moment she was completely overcome by her drunkenness. Uttering a gurgling sound, she fell down, head foremost, and lay motionless, on the slippery floor. The gray braids of her hair half-covered her distorted face.

The men laughed loudly; the woman shrieked and covered Trupp with a flood of abuse.

Auban had risen. He wanted to lift up the old woman. But Trupp prevented him. "Let her lie. She lies well there. If you should want to lift all the drunken women on their feet whom we shall see today, you would have much to do."

He was right. The woman was already sleeping.

"Let us go," said Auban.

The young girl had come up to Trupp and placed herself breast to breast against him. She looked at him with her large eyes sparkling with morbid desire. But she did not say a word. Trupp turned aside from her toward the door.

"You are a fool!" she then said with an indescribable expression. Auban saw her return to her place and cover her face with her hands.

WHEN THEY STOOD ON THE street, the roar and the bustle seemed like stillness after the bluster that had surrounded them.

It had grown darker and cooler. The air was impregnated with moisture. The nearer the evening approached, the noisier and livelier grew the street. The vendors on the wagons who monopolized the edge of the street, one after the other, cried louder. The mountains of vegetables and oranges were crumbling together; the old clothes and footwear were thrown pell-mell together, touched by so many scrutinizing hands; the leaves of the second-hand books were turned over, held close to the faces in the increasing darkness.

The dealers in clams and snails, the abominable food of the poorest classes, monopolized the street-corners. The sight of their loathsome wares filled one with nausea....

"Brick Lane!" said Trupp suddenly.

They stood at the entrance of that street so much talked about.

Whitechapel! The East End in the East End! The hell of hells!

Where do you end, where do you begin?—Your original boundaries of a district have been effaced by your name—today its mention recalls the darkest portion of the great night of the East End, the most dismal of its dens and haunts, the deepest of its abysses of misery....

Here human bodies lie piled up highest and most inextricably. Here the crowds whom no name mentions and no voice calls mingle and creep over each other most restlessly. Here want huddles the human animals most closely together into an unrecognizable mass of filth and rubbish, and their poisoned breath lowers like a pest-laden cloud over this section of the immense city, whose narrower boundaries are only drawn in the south by the black streak of the Thames....

FROM NORTH TO SOUTH IN A slight curve extends Brick Lane. It begins where Church Street runs into Bethnal Green Road, ending at the Museum of the same name, which was founded to meet the desire of the "poorer classes" for education, just as Victoria Park near by was founded that they might not be compelled to entirely forego their scanty breath of fresh air. It ends where at Aldgate the interminable Whitechapel Road and Mile End Road branch off to the north, and the stately, broad Commercial Road East, running as far as the India docks to the south.

Whoever has once slowly sauntered through Brick Lane can say that he has been grazed by the pestilential breath of want; whoever has gone astray in its sidestreets, has walked along the edge of the abyss of human suffering. Whoever would like to see how much human nature can endure; whoever still believes in the childish dream that the world may be saved by love, poverty relieved by charity, misery abolished by the State; whoever would trace the last effects of the terrible deeds of the murderer State—let him visit the battle-field of Brick Lane, where men do not fall with skulls cracked and hearts shot through, but where hunger cuts them down easily, after want has deprived them of their last force of resistance....

It is a long walk down Brick Lane. The friends walked silently. Enormous warehouses, looming up in the distance, vaulted railroad tunnels of the Great Eastern Railway, broke the monotony of the crowded rows of houses. Frequently they had difficulty in elbowing their way through the surging crowds. Odors alternated: decaying fish, onions and fat, pungent vapors of roasted coffee, the foul air of filth, of decaying matter.... Shops with bloody meat, stuck on prongs—"cat's meat"; at every street-corner a "wine and spirits" house; torn posters on the walls, still in loud colors; a crowd of young men passes by—they shout and sing; down the side-street a drunken form is feeling its way along the wall, muttering to itself and gesticulating, perhaps overcome by a single glass of whiskey because the stomach had been without food for days....

The region grew more and more dismal. The Jews' quarter, the poorest of the poor. The victims of the exploiters, the "sweaters," tailors, and small tradesmen. Infinitely contented, beasts of burden bearing the impossible, satisfied with six, yes, four pence for eighteen hours' daily labor, completely lost in dull resignation, they are the most willing subjects of the exploiters and force wages down to far below the starvation point. So they are the terror and the abomination of the inhabitants of the East End, whom they kill by their tenacious perseverance and their calamitous capacity of living on nothing in this frightful struggle of a more than merciless, of a vicious competition.

They alone have been able to gain a firm footing in Whitechapel: so they are encamped in the midst of the East End like a decaying fungus at the base of some giant tree....

Again those frightful rows of two-storied houses, whose gray monotony offers no resting place to the eye, stretching toward the east in stiff uniformity.

Such is Brick Lane, whose end Auban and Trupp have now reached, indescribable in its apparent indifference and awful gloom: pass through it not once, as today, but a hundred times, and nothing else will it betray to you of its hidden secrets, of its silent sufferings, of its dead lamentations, except this one thing: that it never yet saw an heir to happiness.

Whitechapel! When the two friends were passing through dirty, narrow Osborne Street, the entrance to Brick Lane, it was nearly six o'clock. They found themselves in the midst of a mighty stream of humanity that was flowing up Whitechapel and Mile End Road;—thousands upon thousands of workingmen bent towards the outer, the outermost limits of the giant body of the city. Through the fog glowed the red eyes of the lanterns, in long rows, converging in the farthest distance. The north side of the street was densely occupied by two rows of traders of all kinds, their wagons and stands, from which smoking naphtha lamps threw flames of light upon the masses who were forcing their way through the narrow middle road, jostling, pushing each other, excited, half stupefied.... It is the great day, Saturday evening. Whoever still has a penny spends it.

For Whitechapel Road is the greatest public pleasure-ground of the East End, accessible to all. Large music halls with broad lobbies and high stories and galleries are located there, and small hidden penny gaffs, in which there is little to see on account of the tobacco smoke, and little to hear on account of the noise. There is the medicine man with his wizard's oil which cures all ills—no matter how taken, internally or externally—as well as the shooting-stand, whose waving kerosene oil flames make the gaslights unnecessary. There we meet the powerful man and the mermaid, the cabinet of war figures and the famous dog with the lion's claws—his forefeet have been split; all that is to be seen for a penny....

AUBAN AND TRUPP SAW nothing of all these splendors. They had to pass through this tide for a distance. Only step by step could they proceed. Turning again towards the north, whence they had come, Trupp led his friend through two or three dark streets, and again through one of those low passages where dust, lime, and mortar fall down on them from the walls which they graze.... Suddenly they stood in one of those quiet, secluded court-yards which no stranger ever enters. Nothing was recognizable here except the towering masses of stone, which during the day could hardly offer a passage to the light from above, so closely did they adjoin each other. But now they completely disappeared in the fog and the approaching night. Auban felt as if he were at the bottom of a deep well, walled in on all sides, buried alive, with no way out and no light.

But he felt Trupp's hand again on his. It drew him away. Here he had rented a room. His room was on the first floor, close by the door. When it was lighted, Auban saw that its entire furniture consisted of a bed of straw, a table, and a chair. The table was covered with papers, pamphlets, and letters.

While he contemplated this cheerless simplicity, Trupp was walking to and fro, his head bent, his hands in his pockets, as he always did when he was inwardly excited. Forcing Auban to take the chair, while he seated himself on his trunk, he broke the silence of the past hours by telling in a suppressed, almost choked voice what he had seen during the past days.

"You consider this a poor room? You are greatly mistaken. I live like a prince—I am the only person in this whole house who has his own room to himself. Yes, several hundred people, several dozens of families, are living in this 'family hotel.' Here and on the first floor things are still passable: one family only occupying a room, parents, children, large and small, all mixed together. Further up—I have not yet been there, for on the third floor the filth and the odor are such that one must turn back—things are not so well. Two families in one room not larger than this. Whether they avail themselves of the famous chalk mark, I cannot say. Suffice it that they get on: sleeping-room, drawing-room, dining-room, kitchen, sick and death chamber—all in one. Or a hole ten by six feet is inhabited by six, twelve workingmen—tailors. They work twelve, fourteen, sixteen hours, often still longer. They all sleep in that one room, on the floor, on a bundle of rags, if they do not work through the nights by the poisonous gaslight. Days may pass, weeks, before they get out of their clothes. What they earn? That varies. Twopence the hour? Very rarely. Most of the time not so much in three, but frequently only in six hours. They are glad if they get one or one and a half shillings when they must stop from exhaustion. For making a coat which sells at two guineas in the store, they get from four to five, sometimes—when a strike is favorable to the sweaters and enables them to make any offer—only two to three, yes, one shilling. Do you want to hear of anything more? It is the same in the shoemakers' branch, among the girls who make match-boxes, the seamstresses, the spinners. The making of a gross of match-boxes fetches about twopence—the work requires from three to four hours; the sewing of a dozen shirts four or even three, and two and a half pence; the polishing of a gross of lead-pencils—an hour and a half's work—twopence; there are hands for everything, which will not rest until they have torn their nails from their fingers."

Auban interrupted him. He knew his friend. If he allowed him to go on, he would, promiscuously thrusting his hand into the heap of collected experience, continue hour after hour to draw forth one fact after another, one argument after another, and, in bleeding pain and frightful joy at once, conjure up a picture against which all objections would prove futile. Again and again when he stopped exhausted and tremendously excited, his *ceterum censeo* was the revolution, the destruction of the old society; the overthrow of the existing order of things.

He was not to be checked in his mad career. Ever-new rocks did he find, out of which he smote the waters of his theories. Interrupted, he digressed, came to another subject, and without hesitation tore off the veil, putting to flight any ray of a possible hope of slow improvement, strangling every idea of peaceable reform, burying it under the burden of his impeachment.... Then, when he had enveloped his hearers in the shadows of his despair, he whispered, stepping before them, the one word: "Revolution!" and left them alone in the night with this single star.... So he had become the agitator whose words had always been most effective when born of the moment. Better than anyone else Trupp knew how to break the lethargy of indifference, to kindle discontent, to awaken hatred and revolt. Therefore his work among the indifferent was always successful. He was not an organizer. So he avoided the clubs more and more. He liked to get out of the way of discussions. He did not know how to convince. When the rapture and the enthusiasm of the hour had fled—in the dull monotony of the following day which made the struggle appear useless, the victory hopeless—many of those whom he had carried away were seized anew and more powerfully by the gloomy feeling of the vanity of all effort, which snapped asunder the drawn chord of hope. He could point the way; he could not take the lead.

When Auban interrupted him, his feverish spirit seized upon another side of the conversation. He told of the children of this misery who are born in this and die in yonder corner, more than thirty in a hundred, before passing their first year, missed by no one, hardly known by their own mothers, never dressed, never enough to eat; of the fortunate ones who are spared a life of uncertainty, the slow death of starvation; of the high prices the poor must pay for everything they need—four, five shillings weekly rent to the landlord for the hole of a room alone, while the earnings of the whole family do not amount to ten, twelve; of the comparatively high school money which they are compelled to pay for their children, whom they need so much to help add a few pence weekly to their earnings; of their complete helplessness in all things, at the death of their relatives, for instance. Of late, dark rumors of frightful occurrences had reached the public, so impossible that everybody regarded them as the abortion of a distempered brain, of a sensational imagination. They were based on facts. Trupp confirmed them.

It was not a very uncommon thing for corpses to remain unburied for days in the same room where the rest of the family lived day and night.

"When I came here," said Trupp, "a young man of about twenty had died. Of a fever; I think scarlet fever. At any rate, his disease was contagious. The husband was out of work; the wife consumptive. She coughed the whole day. They had four children; but the second, a girl, came home only when she found no other shelter. She and her brother were the only ones who occasionally brought something into the house. Besides, there is the old insane mother of the wife, who never leaves her corner in the room. Well, the son died. He had been ill eight days. Of course, no care, no physician, no food. The corpse remained on the same spot on which the sick boy had died. No one touched it. Instead of looking after work, the man ran a whole day from one magistrate to another. He was referred from one district to another; one had no cemetery, to the other he did not belong. He was a foreigner, could not easily make himself understood—in short, the body remained where it was, without a coffin, unburied. After three days, people in the house began to talk about the matter; after five, the stench came through the cracks of the door; after seven, it had grown so intolerable that the neighbors in the adjoining rooms revolted; only after eight days a policeman heard about the matter, and on the ninth finally, the corpse, in the last stage of putrefaction, was taken away! The papers published no reports about it. And why should they? It is all useless, anyway. Nine days! That is easily told, but *no* imagination can in reality paint the picture of that room!"

He ceased for a moment. Auban was cold. He drew his cloak more closely round him, and looked at the light which was going out.

But Trupp had not yet finished. "Sometimes they throw a corpse into a corner of the yard, let what will become of it. Not far from here is a street, which is inhabited by thieves, pimps, murderers, rabble of the first order. There are crowds of children there. When one of them died recently, it was left where it lay. No one claimed it. Who the parents were no one knew. The woman who lived yonder told me of another case. Up there—above us—lives a drunkard. He has a wife and seven children. The woman works for the whole family. Recently one of the children died—of that dreadful disease for which science has no name, 'slow exhaustion, in consequence of insufficient nourishment'—do not the newspaper reports usually call it so? The woman takes her very last thing to the pawnshop, only to be able to buy a coffin and a few green branches. But before she can get enough together a few days pass. One evening the husband comes home; of course, completely drunk. The coffin is in his way. He takes it and throws it, with the corpse, through the window of the third story. The following day the women almost killed the man; but over their gin the men laughed about the 'smart fellow.' Such is East End life."

Auban rose.

"Enough, Otto," he said. "Can you see the street of which you just spoke?"

"Now? I guess not! We should not get away again with a whole skin."

"Then let us go." As they stood by the door, he looked Trupp in the eye. "You will surely not continue to live here?"

"Why not?—Am I perhaps better? Have I earned more than those poor? One more or less matters nothing."

"Yes, it does. One less in filth is always better than one more."

As they stood in the narrow entry, the door opposite was opened. A thin streak of light faintly illumined the passage, and showed the person emerging to be a young woman. She muttered something as she saw Trupp. It sounded like an entreaty, and she pointed to the room. A suffocating, musty, corrupted vapor met the men as they approached—the vapor of clothing that had never been aired, of decaying straw, spoiling food, mixed and impregnated with the miasms of loathsome diseases produced by that uncleanliness which covered everything—the walls, the floor, the windows. In the cloud of vapor which, despite the cold, warmed the room that could not be heated, a bed was distinguishable which took up the whole length of a wall. On this bed rose a figure that would surely not have been regarded as a human being if it had not hurled towards the door a flood of incoherent abuse: his face entirely disfigured by vice, disease, drunkenness, his head bound up by a dirty, blood-soaked rag, emaciated, his exhausted limbs hardly covered by rags, the man resembled more a dead than a living person. He fell back with a rattling sound, exhausted by the exertion of his aimless wrath. Trupp spoke to the woman. Auban only heard that it was a case of taking the sick man to the hospital—the paradise of poverty. He felt tired and stupefied, and walked ahead. Trupp soon followed. He had to lead his friend by the arm, so full of holes was the creaking floor of the passage, so worn out the stone flagging of the stairs. "That is also one of those whom the police can take to the poorhouse every day—they have 'no visible means of existence'! They are terribly afraid of it," said Trupp.

The lighted yard was deserted as before. One might have believed that all those houses enclosing it were uninhabited, it was so still; there was no sign of life.

"It is always so," said Trupp. "During the day the children are never noisy in their play."

There was a group of people at the corner of the next street. They were talking together in a lively manner. Some of them were evidently very much excited. As

Auban and Trupp drew nearer, a woman came toward them. She was screaming for a physician. The crowd readily made way for them. They passed through a gateway. A yard, half dark, narrow, dirty, lay before them. Here also was a group of men and women, with children clinging to them. In regular paces, two policemen were walking up and down, as far as the space permitted.

Auban was about to turn back again, when his eyes fell on a lantern which stood on the ground and cast a dull light on a heap of straw, on which lay a human form. No one hindered him as he stepped closer. The people standing round crowded forward; the policemen paced up and down. Auban was taken for a physician. The corpse lying before them was that of a man of about fifty. It lay on the back, the arms half stretched out and hanging down on both sides, the open eyes turned upwards. The body of the dead man was covered only by a long, black coat. It was open and lay against the naked flesh, with the collar drawn up and enclosing the neck. From his tattered, dirty, and threadbare black trousers, his naked feet protruded, covered by blue frost-marks and filth. His worn silk hat with a ragged rim had rolled away. His unkempt gray hair had fallen over his forehead; the left hand of the dead man was clenched.

Auban bent over him. The body was frightfully emaciated: the ribs of his chest protruded sharply; the joints of his hands and feet were so narrow that a boy's hand might have encircled them. His cheeks were fallen in, and his cheek-bones stood out prominently; his nose was sharp and thin; his lips entirely bloodless, and a little opened as if in pain; the projecting teeth apparently in good condition. The temples and the region of the throat were deeply sunken—the corpse appeared as if it had been lying for months in a dry place, so thin and tight the yellowish skin covered the bones.

Auban looked up to the policeman who was standing beside him.

"Starved?" he asked in a low voice.

The policeman nodded, stolid and indifferent. Starved! A thrill of excitement ran through the crowd standing round, who had noiselessly followed every movement of Auban. The word passed from lip to lip, and each spoke it in a different tone of fear and horror, as if each had heard his own death sentence. The children clung more closely to the women, these more closely to the men. A young fellow uttered a scornful, loud cry; he was pushed away. The whole group was thus set into commotion. They jostled each other: each wished to cast a glance at the dead man.

The policemen resumed their walk, occasionally casting a scrutinizing look at some individual in the crowd.

Auban had risen from his kneeling position. The hand of the dead man had fallen back flaccidly after he had raised it. There was no longer a trace of life in the lifeless body.

As he was about to turn, he suddenly felt Trupp's iron grasp on his arm. He looked up and saw a thoroughly troubled face. Trupp's eyes were fixed upon the dead man in rigid fright and speechless amazement, as if he recalled to him some dreadful memory.

"Do you know him?" asked Auban.

Trupp made no answer. He steadily gazed at the corpse.

The dead man lay before them, and it suddenly seemed not only to Trupp, but also to Auban, as if a last ray of life were returning into his broken eyes, and as if they were now telling in silent speech for the last time the history of their life: the history of a descent from high to low....

Trupp pulled his friend away, startled from his thoughts. The crowd looked after them in dull expectation, as they still believed Auban to be a physician. Only the two policemen continued pacing up and down, unconcerned: presently an officer would come with a wagon, and tomorrow the dead would lie on the marble slab of a dissecting-table....

On the street Trupp said rapidly, with a voice still choked with fear:—

"I saw him—once—it was four weeks ago—in Fleet Street.... He was coming down that street—towards me—just as he lay there: without shoes, without a shirt, but with a tall hat and black gloves. The sight of him was not ridiculous; on the contrary, it was frightful. He looked like death personified—emaciated like a skeleton—like a shadow!— so he slunk along the wall, looking straight ahead, observing no one and unobserved by any. My feeling told me I should not do it; but I recognized hunger, and so I went up to him and asked him something. He did not understand me. I doubt if he heard me at all. But when I gave him a shilling, he cast a glance on the money, then one on me as if he wanted to strangle me on the spot, and flung what I had given him—my last shilling—to the next street urchin. I was of course so astonished that I let him go....

Auban shook his head.

"Is it really the same man?"

"Could we forget that face after we have once seen it?"

Auban remained silent. It was a strange coincidence, but it was not impossible. Trupp might be mistaken. But Auban did not himself believe that he was under a delusion.

He too was greatly agitated. That face—no, one could not forget it after having once seen it. But sadder than the bloodless cheeks and the reproachful eyes had been to him the emaciation of those enfeebled, completely exhausted, famished limbs. Hunger must have labored long and patiently before death could extinguish the blazing flames of that life!

Weeks ago passing all ordeals through the strength of pride, it succumbed only today; he had retreated into a corner, the dirtiest, most hidden of all—there, unseen by any of those millions, he had broken down; there, unheard by any, he had breathed his last sigh—tired, perplexed, stupefied, sick, despairing, he had—starved!

"Starved!... Starved!... Starved!..."

Again and again Trupp muttered that word to himself.

Then aloud to Auban:—

"To see that we had indeed not expected! Look, how everything justifies me! But the vengeance we shall take will efface everything!"

"Except folly," thought Auban. But of course he did not say it now.

"There can be no blame: what has the blind done that he is blind? Only folly, folly everywhere—yes, and it will take a terrible revenge!..."

SUDDENLY THEY STOOD AT the entrance to the large, broad living stream of Whitechapel Road.

They had been walking till now without knowing where. Absorbed in what they had seen, they forgot all else. Now they were startled by the light that suddenly flooded them. They looked about. Everything was as it had been two hours ago. Again the lights! Again life, flowing, rushing life, ever and ever again conquering life after the terrors of death!

"To the club!" said Auban. It was the first word that he spoke. He was tired, hungry, but outwardly and inwardly calm, congealed as it were. Trupp was neither thirsty nor exhausted. While he changed his course with the confidence of habit and crossed Commercial Road, he looked before him gloomily, apparently cold, but stirred by indignation, tortured by a dull pain.

They had only a few minutes more to walk. A street lay before them, enveloped in the darkness of the evening, illumined by not a single light. It was Berner Street, E.C. The houses ran into one another; doors and windows were hardly to be distinguished in the shadows of the night. Only one well acquainted here could have found a given house. Auban felt his way with his cane rather than walked.

Here was located the club of the Jewish revolutionists of the East End. Trupp stood before the door and pulled the iron knocker. It was opened at once. Heads emerged from a room on the right, friendly hands were extended to Trupp when he was recognized. Auban saw with what pleasure he grasped the hands and shook them again and again. He himself had not been here for a year. He doubted whether he would see any familiar faces. But he had hardly mingled with the lively groups which filled the small low rooms of the basement, some standing, some sitting round the table, and on the benches, when he felt a hand upon his shoulder and looked into the face of an old comrade whom he had not seen for years, not since his years of storm and stress in Paris.

"Auban!"

"Baptiste!"

Memories flew up like a flock of birds whose cage is suddenly opened by the hand of accident.

Except the "*Morgenröthe*," the third section of the old Communistic Workingmen's Educational Society, the "International Workingmen's Club" was the only club of revolutionary Socialists in the East End. The members, about two hundred of them, consisted mostly of Russian and Polish immigrants. The whole of Whitechapel, which for the most part was inhabited by their countrymen, constituted their wide field of propagandism.

Auban asked his friend to translate for him portions of the paper which the club published weekly at a great sacrifice, assisted by no one, bitterly hated and persecuted by the wealthy Jews of the West End (who once even succeeded by bribery in temporarily suppressing the paper). It was called "The Worker's Friend," and was printed with Hebrew letters in that queer mixture of the Polish, German, and English idiom, which is chiefly spoken by the Polish emigrants and understood only with difficulty by others.

Trupp was in the midst of a group of lively talking people. They asked him to speak. He evidently had no desire to. But he consented, and followed them to the upper hall, after he had hastily drunk a glass of beer.

Auban remained sitting, and ordered something to eat. The acquaintance who had recognized him overwhelmed him with questions. They learned many things from each other: one of their friends had been cast ashore here, another there, by the great, mighty wave of the movement. In the course of those few years everything had been moved out of its position, had changed, had taken on a new aspect.

Auban grew more serious than he had been. He felt again the whirr of the wheel rolling on and on, the tramp of the crushing footstep that had also passed over him.... No sword was any longer suspended above him. He no longer feared anything, since he battled only for himself. But still the drops of pain were flowing from the scars of his iron heart.

They talked of their former friends. One of them had been shown up as a decoy? Was it possible? None of them would have thought that. "He was a scoundrel."

"Perhaps he was only unfortunate," suggested Auban. But the other would not hear of that.

Thus they talked together for an hour.

Then they ascended the narrow stairs to the hall, which was completely packed with people. It was of medium size and held hardly more than a hundred and fifty persons. Plain benches without backs stretched through it crosswise and along the walls. Everywhere extreme poverty, but everywhere also the endeavor to overcome poverty. On the walls hung a number of portraits: Marx, Proudhon, Lassalle overthrowing the golden calf of capitalism; a cartoon in a black frame: "Mrs. Grundy"—the stingy, greedy, envious *bourgeoisie,* which, laden with treasures of all sorts, refuses the starving the pittance of a penny....

At the front the room was enclosed by a small stage. There Trupp was standing beside the table of the chairman. He spoke in German. Auban pushed a little forward to see him. He could understand only a few words; he could hardly guess what he was saying. Was he telling of his experiences that evening? Auban felt the tremendous passion flooding the meeting in hot waves from that point. Breathless, anxious not to lose a single word, they hung on the lips of the speaker. An electric thrill passed through those young people, hardly out of their teens; those women tired and crushed by the burden of their ceaseless toil; those men who, torn away from their native soil, had found each other here doubly and trebly disappointed. Rarely had Auban seen such devotion, such burning interest, such glowing enthusiasm as shone from those faces. He knew them. Questions that among the children of the West would have at most formed matter for calm, indifferent interchange of opinion, were discussed here as if life and death depended on them; in contrast with their own sorrowful, depressed, narrow life only the ideal of paradise! Nothing else! Highest perfection in Communism: above all, peace, fraternity, equality! Christians, idealists, dreamers, fools—such were those Jewish revolutionists of the East End—step-children of reason, banner-bearers of enthusiasm.

Trupp closed. They were preparing for the discussion.

"Be egoists!" Auban would like to have shouted at them. "Be egoists! Egoism is the only weapon against the egoism of you co-religionist exploiters; there is no other. Use it: cool, determined, superior, calm, and you are the victors!"

But he did not express his thoughts. The time when he himself, inspired and inspiring, had stood by the surging waves of excited masses had been followed by years of study. His course included but one study: men. Since he understood them, he knew that the effect of the spoken word is the greater, the more general, the more ideal it is, the farther it goes to meet the vague desires of the heart. It is the phrase that is everywhere received with wild joy by the crowds; the clear, sober word of reason, stripped of tinsel, addressing itself to individual interests, denying all moral commands of duty, dies away without being understood, and without effect.

Had not that been brought home again to him only last Sunday?

Therefore, if he should speak today, he would again reap only misunderstanding, instead of joyful applause.

The discussion was in full swing. Most everyone who approached the speaker's table spoke with the most glowing zeal to convince, to persuade: not a word was lost.

Trupp retreated to the background of the hall. There he was again surrounded on all sides. They wished to be enlightened on this or that point of his speech. He replied to each. Auban had sat down. His acquaintance had left him. He did not understand a word. He saw the excited faces that hovered about him through a thin veil of tobacco smoke.

"Today flaming enthusiasm, tomorrow sobering up and discouragement.... Today Haymarket, tomorrow the gallows.... Today revolution, tomorrow a new illusion and its old authority!" he thought.

Trupp asked him if he would go with him to the "*Morgenröthe*." There was a meeting at that place, and he wished to speak there also. Auban let him go alone.

The workingmen's Marseillaise was sung. The gathering began to break up. The crowd mingled together.

A tall, broad-shouldered German comrade. with a blonde beard and hair, his glass in his hand, with his head raised, sang in a clear, firm voice, giving the keynote, as it were, the first stanza of the song over the heads of the others:—

> Wohlan, wer Recht und Freiheit achtet,
> Zu unserer Fahne steht zu Hauf!
> Ob uns die Lüge noch umnachtet,
> Bald steigt der Morgen hell herauf!
> Ein schwerer kampf ist's, den wir wagen,
> Zahllos ist unserer Feinde Schaar—

Doch ob wie Flammen die Gefahr
Mög, Uber uns zusammenschlagen,
Tod jeder Tyrannei!
Die Arbeit werde frei!
Marsch, marsch,
Marsch, marsch!
Und wär's zum Tod!
Denn unsere Fahn' ist roth!

All joined in the refrain.

Auban hummed the French words of the Marseillaise.... How many times already had he heard it, how many times already joined in singing it? In hope, in revolt, in despair, in the confidence of victory? Who had not already sung it?

Auban chanced to see how the eyes of a young man—he was evidently a Pole or a Russian—were suspiciously resting on his strange form. He could not help smiling.

Should he tell him who he was? They did not know him any more. But still the mere mention of his name would have sufficed to at once put to flight all doubt and suspicion.

But he refrained from doing it. He looked at his watch: he must not stay much longer, if he still wished to catch the last train of the underground road for King's Cross at Aldgate.

He went. They had reached the closing stanza of the song. They sang:—

Tod jeder Tyrannei!
Die Arbeit werde frei!
Marsch, marsch,
Marsch, marsch!
Und wär's zum Tod!
Denn unsere Fahn' ist roth!
Denn unsere—Fahn' ist—roth!
Denn unsere—Fahn'—ist—roth!

Auban stood on the street. It was pitch dark. With difficulty he felt his way to where the great streets converged. But before he had yet reached the first gaslights, an enormous building suddenly rose before him in the darkness: in four rows, one above the other, twelve, fourteen, twenty brightly illuminated windows.... It was one of the large factories of which there are from forty to fifty in every parish of the East End of London. Was it a silk factory? Auban did not know.

That building, ugly, coarse, ridiculous in shape, a four-cornered monstrosity with a hundred red, glowing eyes, with the flitting shadows of human forms and the gigantic limbs of the machinery behind them, was it not the glaring symbol of the age, the characteristic embodiment of its essential spirit: industry?

The culmination of the evening was reached when Auban stood again on the spot where the two giant streets converge. Already here and there excessive fatigue was beginning to merge in the stillness of Sunday. Soon the public houses were to close. More and more the people constituting the great stream of humanity were disappearing in the side-streets.

But still the throng was almost impenetrable. In feverish haste most of them drained the last flat drops of the flat drink of their Saturday spree.

Aldgate could be reached in less than five minutes. There was still half an hour for Auban before the last train of the underground road for King's Cross would leave Aldgate Station, and overcome by an inward force against which he was helpless, he turned once more into one of the northern side-streets, into a night full of peculiar mystery....

Only a few lanterns were still burning here, only few people passed by him. Then he came upon streets running crosswise. He turned toward the west.

He passed a group of young people. They were carrying on a dispute in a low voice, in order not to attract the attention of a policeman, and took no notice of Auban. He kept close to the wall.

A light shone from a grated window. He stopped and looked through the dirt-covered panes. It was the kitchen, the common kitchen of a lodging-house which he saw, the common waiting-room for all frequenters before they retire to the sleeping-place rented for one night.

The room was overcrowded. More than seventy persons must have been there; they lay, sat, and stood around in smaller and larger groups: some cowered in the corners. A large number thronged round the fireplace. There they prepared their food—tea, a bit of fish, the remains of meat. Each was awaiting his turn. As soon as one made room by the fire, another took his place. The spare fire did not give out much heat, for many were cold in their rags and crowded closely together.

There was only one table in the middle of the room. Bent over it, head beside head, most of them were already asleep in confused disorder—men, women, and children together. Only a few ate there, and on the narrow benches along the walls. But the table was strewn with dirty tin dishes—cups, bowls, plates—which the exhausted ones had pushed away before sleep overcame them. The floor was covered with refuse of every kind; children who had slipped away from the laps of their sleeping mothers crept round like little blind dogs.

The faint glimmer of the embers hardly illumined the room. Two smoking lamps on the walls were going out.

Nothing that he had seen today, nothing that he had ever seen in the East End, had made a deeper impression on Auban than the silent, gloomy, dismal picture of that room.

Was it the late hour that was having its effect on him? Was it his overheated brain, exhausted by long hours of exertion, which produced that abortion? Or did that which he had so often seen come close to him now that he was alone: this night scene of the abandoned life of the outcasts?

He held his breath while he penetrated every corner of the picture with his eyes.

No imagination could have fancied a more disconsolate room, and in it a more grotesque grouping, than was presented here: the white-haired old man, whose cane had dropped from his hand while he fell asleep with his head bent forward; the young girl who was staring before her while her pimp covered her with abuse; that entire family forming a group: the father evidently out of work, and the mother in despair over their situation, quieting the children who were quarrelling about a broken dish; those sleeping rows—they seemed as if dead....

And above them all the gloomy cloud of eternal filth and eternal hunger. No longer any joy, any charm, any hope...thus day after day...thus night after night....

Auban forcibly tore himself away from the picture without color, without outline, without tone.

He knew those lodging-houses where one found shelter for single nights. But white letters on the red walls gave the additional information: threepence, fourpence, and sixpence a night. For sixpence—those were the "chambers" where one got his own bed, whose linen was changed once at least every few weeks, after it had served twenty different bodies. For fourpence they slept in rows, closely crowding upon each other, utilizing the space to the fullest extent. For threepence, finally—that was the large room with the empty benches on which one slept, or the kitchen where one remained on the spot where one fell asleep: protected against nothing but the icy cold of the night and the fatal dampness of the street pavement....

A man staggered out of the door. He had been turned away because he could not pay. Auban wished to speak to him, to help him, but he was completely drunk. He staggered on backwards and forwards, knocked about with his hands, and felt his way along the walls of the houses, muttering and reeling—into the night which devoured him.

Auban also walked on. He had forgotten where he was and at what hour.

Suddenly he reflected. He must retrace his steps to assure himself that he was on the right way. There was the street into which he had turned—therefore straight ahead, again towards the west....

From that point only an unsteady light every hundred paces. The streets grew narrower and narrower. The pavement worse and worse, larger and larger mud pools and rubbish heaps....

But Auban did not wish to go back again.

The door of a house stood open. Another lodging-house, but an unlicensed one. One of the notorious rookeries, as the people call them. It was overcrowded. The entire narrow, steep stairway, as far as Auban could see, covered with crouching dark human bodies. Over and beside each other, like corpses thrown on a heap, so they lay there. As far as the street, on the threshold even, they were cowering. Nothing was any longer plainly recognizable; the skin, peeping from under the rags and tatters, was as dirty as they were, soaked with dampness, filth, and disease....

Auban shuddered. He hurried on. A cross street; then a high wall; a monstrous seven-story tenement house, suddenly rising out of the darkness like a giant. He passed it. Straight ahead—towards the west.

In the next street again a number of stragglers, but scarcely recognizable: shadows painted on the walls, or sitting in the house doors petrified. No noise, no talk, no laughter, no singing...the stillness of the grave.

Auban began to doubt whether he was on the right way. Again the streets grew completely deserted.

But he knew this region. Had he not been here in the daytime? Everything seemed changed. That wall on the left—he had never seen it. Had he gone wrong?—Impossible! He taxed his excited brain, almost to bursting, while he stood still. He reflected—it *must* be so and *could* not be otherwise; if he turned toward the left, toward the south, he must reach Whitechapel High Street in three minutes; if he walked straight on towards the west, he must in the same length of time reach Commercial Street....

Forward, then, straight ahead!

He felt only now how tired he was. His lame leg pained him. He would rather lie down on the ground and sleep.

But he called his will to his aid and walked on.

A thought came to him: suppose he should now be attacked—who would hear his calls for help? Nobody. He had no other weapon with him than his cane, which was beginning to weigh heavily in his hand. If anybody should meet him and recognize a stranger in him, it was hardly conceivable that he should let the chance of robbing him pass by....

An entirely new feeling possessed him. It was not fear. It was rather the abhorrence of the thought of being attacked by a wild animal in human form in this night, in this filth, in this solitude, and compelled to engage in a struggle for life and death.

He saw how careless it had been of him to challenge this almost unavoidable danger. He remembered now, too, that he was on the very street at the entrance of which a policeman had told him a while ago, as he probably told every well-dressed man, to keep away from it.

Auban hurried on as fast as he could. But the wall seemed to be endless. The darkness was impenetrable. He could not have told the difference between a man and a wall at ten paces.

He held his cane with an iron grasp, without supporting himself on it. He fancied every moment that he saw a robber emerging from the darkness, feeling him at his throat or by his side.... But he was determined to sell his life dearly at least.

He ran and swung his cane before him. Perspiration dropped from his forehead. His horror increased....

Where was he? It was no longer Whitechapel. It was a night without beginning and end; the fathomless depth of an abyss....

Suddenly his cane struck against a wall. And now Auban could again distinguish homes and windows on his right. A short street opened, faintly illumined by a single lantern, and so narrow that no wagon could have passed through it. It led into a longer one....

Suddenly the whole width of Commercial Street lay before Auban. In five minutes he stood panting under the round glass globe of the light which illumined the entrance to the ticket-offices and the stairs leading below.

He had reached the last point of this day's walk, Aldgate Station.

He still had just ten minutes before the departure of his train.

The whole way from the Club had not taken more than half an hour. Auban felt as if hours had passed since the song of the Marseillaise had vibrated in his ear....

While he was resting to quiet his wild pulses, while the street vendors before him were removing their boards and boxes with the remains of their wares, and round him men were jostling and pushing each other in unconscious intoxication and feverish haste, he once more turned his eyes towards the east.... And in a flash the picture he had been longing to shape rose before him: the enormous mouth of the gigantic body of East End—such was Whitechapel, which lay yawning before him. Whatever came near its poisoned breath staggered, lost its hold, was crushed by relentless yawning, and devoured, while all the sounds of misery, from the rattle of fear to the sighs of hunger, died away in the pestilent darkness of its abyss. And all the countries of the entire world threw their refuse into that greedy mouth, so that at last that terrible, forceless, insatiable body might satisfy itself, whose hunger was immeasurable and seemed constantly to be increasing....

And while Auban retreated before the vapor, he suddenly saw in the last minute still remaining to him the grand vision of coming events: that gigantic mouth opened wide its foaming jaws and vomited forth in choking rage an enormous slimy wave of rubbish, filth, and corruption over London.... And—like a tottering mountain—that nauseating wave buried everything: all grandeur, all beauty, all wealth.... London was now only an infinite lake of rottenness and corruption, whose horrible vapors infected the heavens and slowly destroyed all life....

Chapter VII.
The Tragedy of Chicago

The days beginning the second week of November seemed shrouded in smoke and in blood.

While in London the cry for "labor or bread" grew more and more ominous in the ears of the privileged robbers and their protectors, the eyes of the world were fixed on Chicago, on the uplifted hand of power. Would it fall? or, "pardoning," relax?

The events of the day followed thick and fast, one precipitating another.

Auban had passed the first days of the week in his office, working hard, for he wished to have the last two as much as possible to himself.

When on Wednesday after luncheon he went to his coffee-house, he saw Fleet Street and the Strand covered with gay-colored flags and streamers, which stood out in strange relief against the melancholy gray of the sky, the slimy black of the street mud, the impenetrable masses of people who monopolized the sidewalks on both sides. Lord Mayor's show! According to ancient custom the procession of the newly elected mayor of the city was moving through the streets with great pomp and ceremony, and for a few hours the people forgot their hunger in the contemplation of the gay, childish farce.

What an age! thought Auban. The city pays this worthless talker ten thousand pounds annually for his useless labors, and while he dines at Guildhall in wasteful revelry, hunger for a piece of bread is gnawing at the vitals of countless thousands!

He did not wish to see the procession. He sought his way through half-deserted side streets. A fine rain was ceaselessly dripping down. Dampness, cold, and discomfort penetrated the clothing.

He bought a morning paper and rapidly ran through it. Trafalgar Square in every column! Meetings of the unemployed day after day—now permitted, now forbidden—Arrests of the speakers—Alarming rumors from Germany: the disease of the crown prince said to be incurable…faint, timid surmises as to its nature…cancer…the fate of a country for weal or for woe dependent on the life and death of a man!—France—nothing—Chicago!…Brief remarks on the petitions for pardon of four of the condemned to the governor of Illinois, in whose hands rests the final decision after the refusal of a new trial.... On the discovery of bombs in one of the cells.... Indeed, certainly! Public sentiment is too favorable to the condemned. So bombs were suddenly "discovered"— discovered in a prisoner's cell guarded by day and by night!—and it again takes an unfavorable turn! That discovery came too opportunely at a moment when the petitions for pardon—these petitions which, as the newspapers graphically described, would form a line eleven miles in length if attached one to another—were being filled with hundreds of thousands of signatures, to leave any doubt in regard to the conscious, deliberate intention of the report.

Auban crumpled the paper in his hands and threw it away. Now his last hope had fled. In terrible clearness the coming days rose before him, and the frosty air shook him like a fever.

THE ELEVENTH OF November fell on a Friday. Auban was sitting in his room at the table covered with papers, pamphlets, and books. It was about five o'clock in the afternoon, and the light of the day was fading away between the gloomy rows of houses.

Auban, aided by the abundant material which his American friend had placed at his disposal, had devoted the entire day to a review of the tragedy, on whose last act the curtain had just fallen, in each of its separate phases, from beginning to end.

What he had seen rise and grow in each of its parts now stood before him as a perfect whole.

But he was still looking through the piles of papers and turning the leaves of pamphlets in nervous haste, as if he wished to gain additional light on some of the points that seemed not yet to have been set forth in sufficient clearness.

The impossibility of his today's task of picturing to himself in perfect clearness the whole, as well as its separate parts, almost drove him to despair. The contradictions were too numerous. Tragedy on which the last veil had fallen today would never be thoroughly understood.

Nevertheless, the facts rose in tangible form before Auban.

Before his mind's eye stands Chicago, one of the largest cities of the United States: fifty years ago still a little frontier town; twenty years ago a pile of ruins, made so in a night by a great conflagration, but rebuilt in a day; today the magnificent city by the great lake, the granary of the world, the centre of a boundless traffic, exuberant with an energy of which the aging life of the East no longer knows anything.... In that city of rapid growth, with a population of almost a million, of which one-third are Germans, in all their terrible clearness the consequences of legally privileged exploitation of human labor: the accumulation of wealth in a few hands to a dizzy height, and in faithful correspondence with it ever larger masses driven to the edge of the impossibility of supporting their lives.... And hurled into that fermenting city, like a new and more terrible conflagration, the torch of the social creed: fanned by a thousand hands, the flames spread so rapidly as to make it appear that the days of the revolution are at hand....

The authorities send their police; and the people sends its leaders whom it follows. The former club and shoot down striking workingmen, and the latter call in a loud voice: "To arms! To arms!"—and point to the device: "Proletarians, arm yourselves!" as the only remedy.

Force against force! Folly against folly!

The movement in favor of the eight-hour workday in the United States, the "eight-hour movement," which dated back almost two decades, and the end of which a million workingmen, four hundred thousand "Knights of Labor," and an equal number belonging to the "Federated Trade Unions," expect to see in the first of May, 1886, a point around which both parties are engaged in equally hot contention.... What the agitation of former years had already here and there secured as a written "right" remained an unacquired right.

The "International Workingmen's Association," founded in 1883 by German revolutionists in Chicago who called themselves Anarchists, but who preached the Communistic creed of common property, although it regards universal suffrage simply as a means with which to cheat the workingmen out of economic independence by the pretence of political liberty, nevertheless takes a position on that question which is rapidly becoming the sole issue of the day, in order not to let slip an important field of propagandism....

The first of May is preceded by unexpected events in Chicago, the centre of the eight-hour movement; the closing of a large factory—in consequence of which twelve hundred workingmen are without bread—is followed by meetings that culminate in serious collisions with the official and unofficial police, the private detectives of the Pinkerton Protective Agency in the service of the capitalists, the notorious "Pinkertonians."...

Thus, after more than forty thousand workingmen had laid down their work in

Chicago alone, on the impatiently expected first of May, and three hundred and sixty thousand in the States, the police on the third of May made an attack on the workingmen, in which a large number of them were wounded. The object of the meeting, called for the fourth of May at the Haymarket by the "Executive Committee" of the I. W. A., was to protest against those outrages of the constituted authorities.

On the same day one of the leaders, the editor of the great German "*Arbeiter-Zeitung*," wrote a circular which was destined to achieve a terrible celebrity under the name of the "Revenge Circular."

It is written in two languages: the one in English addresses itself to the American workingmen, whom it exhorts to prove themselves worthy of their grand-sires and to rise in their might like Hercules; the one in German reads:—

> "REVENGE! REVENGE! WORKINGMEN, TO ARMS!
>
> "Working people, this afternoon the bloodhounds, your exploiters, murdered six of your brothers at McCormick's. Why did they murder them? Because they dared to be dissatisfied with the lot which your exploiters made for them. They asked for bread, and were answered with lead, mindful of the fact that the people can thus be most effectively brought to silence. For many, many years you have submitted to all humiliations without a murmur, have slaved from early morning till late in the evening, have suffered privations of every kind, have sacrificed even your children—all in order to fill the coffers of your masters, all for them! And now, when you go before them and ask them to lessen your burden, they send their bloodhounds, the police, against you, in gratitude for your sacrifices, to cure you of your discontent by means of leaden balls. Slaves, we ask and entreat you, in the name of all that is dear and sacred to you, to avenge this horrible murder that was perpetrated against your brothers, and that may be perpetrated against you tomorrow. Working people, Hercules, you are at the parting of the ways! Which is your choice? Slavery and hunger, or liberty and bread? If you choose the latter, then do not delay a moment; then, people, to arms! Destruction upon the human beasts who call themselves your masters! Reckless destruction—that must be your watchword! Think of the heroes whose blood has enriched the path of progress, of liberty, and of humanity—and strive to prove yourselves worthy of them.
>
> "YOUR BROTHERS."

The meeting at the Haymarket on the fourth of May is so orderly that the mayor of the city, who had come with the intention of closing it at the first sign of disorder, tells the police captain he may send his men home.

The wagon from which the speakers are talking is on one of the large streets that lead to the Haymarket. It is surrounded by several thousand people, who are calmly following the words, first of the writer of the manifesto, then of the elaborate address of an American leader on the eight-hour movement; there are many details touching the relation of capital to labor.

A third speaker also makes an address in English.

Clouds, threatening rain, rise on the sky, and the larger portion of the audience disperses. Then, as the last speaker is closing, the police, numbering about a hundred men, make a set attack on those remaining. At this moment a bomb falls into the ranks of the attacking party, hurled by an invisible hand; it kills one of them on the spot, inflicts fatal wounds on six others, injures a large number, about fifty. Under the murderous fire of the police, those remaining seek refuge in the side streets....

The frenzy of fear reigns in Chicago. No one of the enemy sees in the throwing of the bomb an act of self-defence on the part of one driven to despair.... And, while in labor circles, the false assumption is gaining ground that it is the deliberate deed of a police agent which was to enable threatened and terrified capital to deal a fatal blow against the eight-hour movement, the press, in the pay of capital, is inflaming public opinion by monstrous reports of bloody conspiracies against "law and order," by reprinting incendiary passages from labor editorials and speeches, while it had itself prescribed lead for the hungry tramp, and a mixture of arsenic and bread for the unemployed, in order to get rid of them....

The three speakers of the evening are arrested. Likewise, four other well-known individuals in the movement; the eighth, the American publisher of an American labor paper, the "Alarm," later surrenders himself voluntarily.... Of the many who are arrested and examined, these eight are held and summoned to appear before the court.

Thus stood the facts of the early history before Auban's eyes: a battle had been fought in the great conflict between capital and labor, and the victors sat in judgment on their prisoners.

But the conflict had been brought to a sudden halt for a long time to come.

The second act of the tragedy begins: the trial.

Slowly before Auban's eyes the curtain is lifted from the trial as he had followed it in all its stages by the aid of the countless reports of the newspapers, as he knew it from the speeches of the condemned, and as he had studied it again today in the brief submitted to the Supreme Court of Illinois.

It had indeed been a laborious task to which he had devoted the day. Doubly laborious for him in the foreign—to his mother tongue so entirely foreign—language. But he wished once more, and for the last time, to see if the enemy had not at least the *appearance* of right on his side.

From that standpoint, too, the conviction of the condemned is nothing but murder. If a conspiracy had really been on foot to meet the next attacks of the police with the throwing of a bomb, the individual act of the fourth of May was certainly in no relation to it. No one was more surprised by its folly than the men who were to suffer so terribly from its consequences.

In the first place, the selection of the jury is arbitrary. Although about a thousand citizens are summoned, they are men whose admitted prejudice against the movement of Socialism compels the attorneys of the defendants to reject them, until finally they must accept men who, by their own confession, have already formed an opinion before the trial has yet begun. Of nearly one thousand citizens summoned, only ten belonged to the working class, which alone represents a hundred and fifty thousand in a population of three-quarters of a million, and those ten live in the immediate neighborhood of the police station. The State challenges most of them; those whom it accepts it is sure of in advance. Such is the jury in whose hands is placed the power over life and death! Ignorance, joined by arrogance, is ever ready to play the part of the ridiculous and contemptible; it becomes terrible, when, as here, it is re-enforced by the brutality of authority. Then woe to all who fall into its clutches!

The remaining preliminaries consist of the arrest and torment of innumerable persons belonging to the working class; the chief of police, a vain demagogue of the commonest type, regards no brutality too brutal, no artifice too contemptible, to get from them what he wants to know—that there has been a conspiracy. He arrests whom he pleases; he lengthens or shortens the period of arrest as he sees fit; he treats his victims as he likes. No one prevents him. No emperor ever ruled with more sovereign sway than the bloated insignificance of this brutal demagogue.

By the middle of July these preliminaries, too, are completed. The State's attorney calls upon the defendants to answer to the charge of conspiracy and murder. The great trial which had begun in the middle of June, by the selection of the jury, enters its second stage. A day later the hearing of the witnesses begins in the presence of an unexampled throng of the public, which continues undiminished as long as the trial lasts.

The State has very different kinds of witnesses. Some are confronted with the alternative of being themselves indicted with the prisoners or of testifying against them. They and their families have received support from the police, and held long interviews with them. Even so, they cannot say more than that bombs have been manufactured and distributed, but they must add that the distribution was not for the purpose of use at the Haymarket meeting.

Another State's witness is a notorious liar of most ill repute among all who know him. His testimony proves the most decisive. He also received money from the police. He saw everything: who threw the bomb and who lit it; he knows who was absent and who was present; only of the speeches that were delivered he heard nothing. And he knows the whole conspiracy in all its details.

All these State's witnesses contradicted each other's testimony—but the bloody clothes of the killed policeman are spread before the jury; some of the defendants never saw a dynamite bomb—but the State's attorney reads some stupid passages from the conscienceless book of a professional revolutionist on "Revolutionary Warfare"; a number of the defendants have never stood in any relations with each other, hardly knew each other—but the jury is flooded with extracts from speeches and articles born of the excitement and passion of the moment, and which in many cases date far back....

For "Anarchy is on trial." By the sacrifice of these eight men a ruinous blow is meant to be dealt against the entire movement, which is to paralyze it for a long time, the *bourgeoisie* against the proletariat, class against class!

The attorneys of the defendants do their best to rescue the victims from the clutches of authority. But as they are compelled to meet the enemy on his own ground in order to fight him, the ground described as in mockery "the common law," they are necessarily doomed to defeat. And they are defeated.

By the end of August the jury brings in its verdict, which dooms seven men to an untimely death.

Thus finally the fool spectacle of that trial which lasted a quarter of a year is brought to a close. A new trial, urgently demanded, is refused.

The defendants deliver their speeches before the judge, those now celebrated speeches through which the sufferings, the complaints, the wishes, all the despair and all the hope, all the expectations and all the defiance of the people, speak in all the tones of an outraged heart so impressively and so boldly, so simply and so passionately, so vehemently and so—vaguely....

A whole year passes before the butcher State can roll up his sleeves to strangle these victims with his insatiable hands. And it almost seemed as if things were to take a different turn. For while the workingmen are cheerfully making all necessary sacrifices to accomplish the utmost that is still possible, a revulsion of popular feeling is gaining ground, and the conviction of the innocence of the condemned is taking the place of intimidated fear and of artificially produced hatred.

The weathercock of "public opinion" is beginning to turn.

Nevertheless the Supreme Court of Illinois, to whom the case was appealed in March of the following year, affirmed the judgment of the lower court in September.

And likewise the Supreme Court of the United States at Washington.

The day of the murder is at hand.

The power of staying the threatening hand of death rests not with a single man, the governor of Illinois. His is the power to pardon.

Three of the condemned submit a written statement in which they describe the indictment as alike false and absurd, but regret having championed violence; the remaining four, in letters full of pride, courage, and contempt, decline a pardon for a crime of which they are innocent. They demand "liberty or death." In those letters one of them writes:—

"—Society may hang a number of disciples of progress who have disinterestedly served the cause of the sons of toil, which is the cause of humanity, but their blood will work miracles in bringing about the downfall of modern society, and in halting the birth of a new era of civilization."

Another:—

"The experience which I have had in this country, during the fifteen years I have lived here, concerning the ballot and the administration of our public functionaries who have become totally corrupt, has eradicated my belief in the existence of equal rights of poor and rich, and the action of the public officers, police, and militia, has produced the firm belief in me that these conditions cannot last long."

And a third one, after leaving the governor the choice of being "a servant of the people" or "a mere tool of the monopolists": "Your decision in that event will not judge me, but yourself and those whom you represent...."

Thus they themselves press the martyr's crown more deeply into their defiant brows.

The governor is besieged on all sides. At hundreds upon hundreds of meetings, hundreds upon hundreds of resolutions are passed protesting against the sentence.

Expressions of sympathy, of indignation, are heard in all parts of the world; everywhere people call for a postponement, for pardon...only in Chicago itself the hand of authority closes the mouth of the people with brutal might.

Only in the case of three death is commuted into a living grave; five of them must die.

Then, at the last moment, when the waves of popular sympathy threaten to make the murder which is planned impossible, bombs are suddenly found in the cell of one of the condemned. The venal press does its share. It does not inquire in what other way than with the knowledge of the police the bombs could have been placed where they are discovered so opportunely; it sounds anew its cries of fear about "public order being endangered," and fabulous rumors about bloody plans contemplating the destruction of the jail, of the whole city, are having their effect of intimidation. The wave of sympathy recedes....

Another scene: Weeping women are lying before the man who embodies authority and power. They clasp his knees; a poor mother pleads for the life of her son; a woman, who could join hands in union with the man she loved only through prison bars, demands justice; a helpless wife points to her trembling children as her words fail her; but nothing can touch the soulless picture of stone, in whose heart only the desolation of barrenness, in whose brain only the prejudices of mediocrity hold sway.

Shuddering, liberty turns away.

The second act of the tragedy is closed. On the death agonies of eighteen months drops finally the black curtain of the past.

Auban rose and walked to and fro, his hands crossed behind his back. It had grown dark. The fire went out.

He was absorbed in his thoughts. The rustle of a paper startled him; the evening paper was pushed through the door. He bent down and took it up eagerly.

Death or life?

A cry of despair escaped from his lips. By the light of the dying fire he ran through a short cable despatch: "Special edition—6.15 P.M.—Chicago, November 10—Terrible suicide—One of the condemned—just now—in his cell—shattered his head—with a bomb—lower jaw entirely torn away—"

The atmosphere of his room lay oppressively on Auban. He felt as if he were choking. Away!—away!—Hastily he took his hat and cane and hurried away.

When he returned an hour later, he found Dr. Hurt at the fireplace, his pipe in his mouth, in one hand a newspaper, in the other a poker with which he was stirring the fire into a fresh glow. He was surprised. It was the first time since the death of his wife that the doctor had visited him, except on the Sunday afternoons.

"Do I disturb you, Auban? Had a call near by, thought it would be good to warm my feet and have a sensible talk in these days, when men are all again acting as if the world were coming to an end—"

Auban pressed his hand firmly.

"You could not have done anything better, doctor," he said. He spoke each word clearly and distinctly, but his voice was entirely toneless. Dr. Hurt looked at him as he lit the lamp, prepared boiling water, and brought out whiskey-glasses and tobacco.

Then they sat opposite each other, their feet stretched towards the fire.

Evidently neither of them wished to begin the conversation.

Finally Auban pointed to the newspaper which Dr. Hurt was holding in his hand, and asked: "Have you read?"

Hurt nodded gravely.

But when, looking at Auban, he saw how pale and troubled his face was from the suppressed pain within, he said solicitously:—

"How you look!"

Auban waved his hand deprecatingly. But then he bent forwards and buried his face in both his hands.

"I have passed through a night of illusion," he said slowly, and in a low tone, reciting the verse of a modern poet....

Dr. Hurt sprang up, and for the first time putting aside the mask of his icy reserve, placed his hand on Auban's shoulder. and said:—

"Auban, my friend, do not take it so hard! Things had to come to this pass sooner or later—"

"What would you expect?" he continued more impatiently. "What would you expect of the governments? That they should fold their hands and look calmly on while the tide of the movement devours them? No; you who like myself know that right is nothing but might, and the struggle for life nothing but the desire for might, no, you cannot see in the events of Chicago anything but the sad episode of a common struggle which to your reason must appear as a necessity."

Auban looked at the speaker. His eyes flashed and his lips trembled.

"But I abominate all cowardice. And I cannot conceive of any greater and more contemptible cowardice than this cold-blooded murder. Courage, indeed! To murder—with the fools behind you, with prejudice by your side, and with the 'divine consent' above you. What cowardice, to let a battle be fought for you! Not to stand man against man, but to hide yourself behind the robe of the law, the bayonets of soldiers, the fists of savage hirelings—stupid beasts who know of no other will than that of their masters! What cowardice, I say, to have the majority of ignorance on your side and then to declare you are in the right! Is there a greater?"

As his visitor made no reply, he continued:—

"For me there is but one truly noble and dignified frame of mind: the passive; and but one form of activity whose results I call great: that of one's own powers. I hold all those who have developed *out of themselves,* who stand and fall by themselves, in boundless esteem; but equally boundless is my aversion towards those whom folly elevates today, to let them fall back into their nothingness tomorrow."

"Yes, everything is thrown in a heap, true and false merit," said Dr. Hurt.

"Why are there still rulers on thrones? Because there are still subjects. Whence this social misery? Not because some raise themselves above others, but because the others renounce themselves. On our lives rests the curse of an entirely unnatural idea: the Christian idea. We have cast off some of the externalities of the religions. But little is yet noticeable of the blessings that would result if we threw overboard the idea of religion, of the stiff breeze that would then swell our sails. Believe me, doctor, there is an intrinsic relationship between a *bourgeois* and a Social Democrat. But there is no bridge leading from either of them to me. There is a chasm between us—between the professors of the State and those of liberty!"

"You think like nature," said the other, meditatively, "and therefore health and truth are on your side."

And taking up the thread of their former conversation, he asked:—

"And was not your abhorrence aroused when you heard of the throwing of the bomb?"

"No. I saw in it only an act of justifiable self-defence. On their own responsibility the police made an attack upon a peaceable assembly. For once their brutality was punished, while it usually goes unpunished. I deplore the act, not only as entirely useless, but also as harmful. But still more do I deplore those who will not understand that such acts are always only the outbreak of a despair which has no longer anything to lose because everything has been taken from it."

"And those who always incite only others to violence without ever taking part themselves—what is your opinion of them?"

"That they are pitiable cowards, and that the paper was not at all wrong in suggesting some time ago that the man in New York, who was incessantly clamoring for the head of some European prince, ought to be sent to Europe at the general expense, to afford him an opportunity to get it there himself..."

Dr. Hurt had again sat down, and a grave silence reigned. They talked about other things. Then Hurt said again:—

"I begin to hate the people. It is like a Moloch that has opened his arms and now devours victim after victim. This grown-up child, which has so long been chastised with the rod, is suddenly indulged to a ridiculous degree. It reaches manhood, and is surprised at the strength of its own limbs. When it shall have become fully conscious of it, it will trample on everything that comes under its feet. It has already learned all the attitudes of power: ridiculous infallibility, haughty conceit, narrow self-complacency. I tell you, Auban, the time is not distant when it will be impossible for any proud, free, and independent spirit to still call himself a Socialist, since he would be classed with those wretched toadies and worshippers of success, who even now lie on their knees before every workingman and lick his dirty hands simply because he is a workingman!"

Now Dr. Hurt was excited, while Auban seemed lost in a brooding sadness which was only intensified by what he heard, because he had to agree with it.

"Every age has its lie," continued Dr. Hurt. "The great lie of our age is 'politics,' as that of the coming age will be 'the people.' All that is small, weak, and not self-reliant, is caught in its rushing current. All men of 'today'! There in the current they fight their little, worthless, everyday battles. But the men of tomorrow, and to them we belong, remain on the shore or come back to it again, after the current has threatened to devour them for a time. And there, on the shore of truth, we stand, and so we want to let the daily events of our age, whose witnesses we are, pass before us. Is it not so?"

Auban was moved. For the first time in all these long years he had known him, this strange and singular man laid open his heart to him, and showed him its scarred wounds. What must he also have suffered before he became so firm, so hard, and so alone?

"You are indeed right," he said. "I too swam in the current, and I too stand on the shore. And at my feet and before my eyes are drifting the bloody corpses of Chicago."

"They are not the first, and they will not be the last."

"You are indeed right," said Auban again. "I was among those who struggled in the current. When I was twenty; when I knew nothing of the world; when, in my eyes, some men were conscious sinners, others innocent angels; when I mistook effects for causes, and causes for effects—then they listened to me as I talked to them. Where I got the courage to parade my phrases before those large audiences, I no longer know. I was proof against all harm; I stood in the service of the cause. How could I fail under such circumstances? I derived all my strength from that thought; not from myself. From it often I drew my indefatigability, my unshaken belief, my indifference towards myself. And the farther I got from the reality of things, the nearer I came to my hearers. Often I went farther than I intended."

"That was also the way of the leaders of Chicago; they were driven on, and could not go back. They had to outdo themselves in order to maintain themselves. That is so often the tragic fate of all those who look to others for the measure of their 'worth.'"

"My fate would have been theirs," said Auban further. "However, I was not happy. I do not believe that self-sacrifice can make us truly happy. And I should not have liked to die so—I felt it again today. No; I want to battle and conquer without receiving a wound."

"Many will say that is very convenient—"

"Let them say so. I say, it is more difficult than to sacrifice one's self to the delight of our enemies and to no good of our friends. Do you want to know what brought me to this perception? A smile, a scornful, frigid smile. It was on the occasion of my speech before the judges. I hurled truths at them that fairly startled some, while they enraged others. I spoke of the rights of man that were mine, and of the rights of might which were theirs; in short, it was a pompous, passionate, and entirely uncommon speech wholly without policy and of course also without any purpose, the childish speech of an idealistic man. It is always ridiculous to approach men with ethical commands, especially such half-wild, unreasonable, ignorant men who derive all their wisdom from paragraphs and formulas. But I had not learned that then. While I was speaking so—I really spoke more to those who did *not* hear me—I noticed on the shrewd face of an officer a smile, a scoffing, pitiful, cutting smile, which said: You fool, what do we care about your words, so long as they do not become deeds!

"But no; I must correct myself. I did not see the smile, for I kept on talking unconcerned. Only later, in prison, I remembered that I had felt it, and then it pursued me a long time; I can see it today if I close my eyes!

"It grinned at me through the cracks of the prison wall. It was an enemy that I had to overcome. But I saw it was not one that allowed itself to be put to flight by words. There was but one means to lay it: to acquire a like smile. Only against it would the other be powerless. I acquired it. I had time, and everything I had experienced and seen seemed changed in the light of this new way of looking at things. I see men as they are; the world as it is. No longer people smile at me."

"It was certainly the greatest deed of your life, Auban, that you had the strength to tear yourself away and get on your own feet; but the Communists—is it conceivable that most of them speak with indignation about the petitions for pardon of some of the condemned? To see treason, a debasement in the signing of a bit of paper with which I can save my life out of the hands of my murderer! I should sign a thousand such scraps of paper and laugh at the blockhead who expected 'honesty' of me, while he got me into his power by cunning and force. Auban, these Communists are fanatics; they are sick, confused, afflicted with moral spooks—"

"I said what I had to say last Sunday," Auban remarked calmly.

"And all to no purpose. No, those people must grow wise through experience. Let them alone."

"The experience will be a terrible one. It is sad for me to see how the very people who have already suffered so much, cause new sufferings to themselves."

Again there was a digression in the conversation, which during the following hour turned on things far from Chicago.

The doctor had filled the room with smoke which he sent in short, rapid puffs from his pipe, never letting it go out. The plain severity of the room was tempered by the rays of the lamp and the flames of the fire. A breath of comfort almost filled it as the hours wore on.

"Do you know the legend of the emperor's new clothes?" asked Auban. "It is so with the State too. Most people, I doubt not, are inwardly convinced that they could get along much better without it. They pay unwillingly the taxes which they instinctively feel as a robbery of their labor. But the notion that 'it must be so because it has always been so' prevents them from speaking the word that would save them; they look at one another, doubtful and hesitating. But it requires all the ingenuousness of an unspoiled character to overthrow this artificial barrier, the source of all our external misery, with the words: 'Why, he has nothing. The whole thing is a piece of clear humbug of the most stupid kind—and the saving word has been found; it is Anarchy!"

Auban continued, as his listener remained in silent meditation:—

"Or let us take the following example: It is on the morning of a battle. Two armies are facing each other, brought together for mutual destruction. In an hour the slaughter is to begin. How many on either side, do you think, if the individual could have his free choice, would remain to become murderers; and how many would throw aside the weapons forced on them and return home to the peaceful employments of their life? All would return, would they not? And only the small number of those would perhaps remain who make of war and the exercise of power a calling. And, nevertheless, all the others act against their own will, their reason, their better knowledge, because things have not become clear to them. They must; for the curse of illusion—a something, something intangible, something incomprehensible, something terrible—urges them on.... Tell me, doctor, what it is, that dreadful something?"

"Habit, ignorance, and cowardice," said Hurt.

"Oh, I do not object to war! Do not think that!" exclaimed Auban, and heaped up the papers on his writing-desk that the other might not see how excited he was growing. "Not in the least. There have always been rowdies and brutes. But let them fight out their battles and quarrels among themselves, and not compel other entirely innocent people who prefer to live in peace to take part in their brutal brawls under the lying pretence that it is for their own interest to mutually murder each other in the name of the 'holy war for the fatherland' and similar nonsense! I do not object to war," he exclaimed once more, "but let it be fought by those who want it. So much the better—pounce upon each other, you brutal butchers, tear yourselves into pieces, exterminate each other; the earth will breathe a sigh of relief when it is rid of you!"

"But for the present we are still sitting in the cages of our States, cowering in the corners, mutually watching and observing each other, always on the alert, pressing against the bars of the grating, growling at each other, until we grasp each other by the throat because there is not room enough for us, and the food falls too unequally to our lots," said the doctor, sarcastically.

Auban replied in the same tone.

"That is the struggle for existence, my friend; the strong crush the weak—thus nature has willed it!"

"Yes, that phrase, the catchword of a science not understood, came very opportunely for them!"

"It serves them as an apology for their despotic tyranny and the compression of nature within the unnatural limits of the compulsory organization of the State and the stupid laws which they consider infallible, although they themselves made them. It is always the same: labor may compete until it perishes in the midst of the superabundance it has created; capital is exempt from competition."

At Auban's words Hurt had again suddenly become very excited.

"I can tolerate anything, only not that science, clear, confident, relentless, incorruptible science, is placed in the service of those swindlers of power and the 'existing order,' and thus falsified!" he exclaimed.

Auban continued, sarcastically:

"And what splendid specimens of the genus man survive as the fittest in 'that struggle for existence'! For example: Here is one of the Upper Ten, a member of the *jeunesse dorée,* a tall hat, a monocle, buckled shoes. He does not do a stroke of work. But his capital works for him. It yields annually one thousand pounds. He is lazy, without interests, a wreck at thirty.

"On the other hand, there are a hundred workingmen, young fellows, energetic, fresh, full of courage and the will to put their powers to use; they are prevented from doing as they would like. Everything is closed against them. They flag, grow tired, get dull, succumb. When they die, their life has been nothing but work and sleep. They finished the former only to lie down to the latter; and they rose from sleep only to go to work.

"Some have the means not to work; others have not the means to work. Thus the vampire sucks up one after another: he is the product of the squandered labor of a hundred persons. A sickly, unproductive life has simply destroyed a hundred healthy, productive lives. The former has been enervated by idleness, the latter exhausted by overwork.

"What do they call it, eh? Struggle for existence? Divine wisdom? The order of nature?"

He paused a moment, and looked at the doctor, who was blowing great clouds of smoke from his pipe. Then he continued:

"Or, again, another picture, equally edifying. 'Her Ladyship!' During the day she reads novels, or meddles with the work of her "domestics" of which she knows nothing. In the evening she drives to the ball. What she wears on her body, the diamond ornaments, are in themselves without any value whatever—"

"In itself nothing has value," Hurt interrupted him.

"But it represents a fortune in value," Auban continued, unconcerned.

But he was again interrupted.

"Ah, let us have done with that, Auban!" muttered Hurt. "As long as the workingmen will not become more sensible, such lives, and even worse ones, will be the inevitable, entirely natural result."

It had grown late. The atmosphere of the room was oppressive and hot. The fire was weary. Hurt looked at his watch. But before he rose, the secret, bashful, hot, almost reluctant love of this peculiar man for all the oppressed and suffering burst forth suddenly and vehemently like a flame in angry words which passionately dropped from his lips:

"The fools! Will they never grow sensible? To throw bombs, what nonsense! To make it as easy as possible for the governments to destroy them! But it seems to me that these people make a point of excelling each other in sacrifices and of seeking their pride not in victory, but in defeat! Sacrifice upon sacrifice! No, I do not want to have anything more to do with them; if they do not want to become sensible, they need not!"

He had risen. Turning towards Auban, whose sad eyes seemed riveted on the table on which the crumpled newspapers lay like an unsolved problem, he added, in an apparently lighter vein:

"You must not expect too much of me, Auban. I am a daily witness of death-bed scenes—what is the life of a few individuals who are forcibly torn away against the crowds whom no one counts and no one mentions, but who are also only victims of the others, although they never tried to defend themselves!"

He extended his hand to him.

"Read history. Open it where you like. Everywhere the conquerors and everywhere the vanquished. The thing has always been the same, only the numbers were different. Whether they fall, shot on the battlefield, starved at the street corner, choked on the gallows—is it not one and the same thing? *Not* to fall, to conquer—it is for that we are here!"

Auban could not answer. He was seized by a restless fear of the night that was coming, in which he was to remain alone with himself.

Hurt was getting ready to go. But when he had already taken hold of the door-knob, he turned once more towards Auban, stepped up to him, and said:

"However, I wish to thank you. I wanted to do it long ago. You know I am an old sceptic. I believe in nothing, and all utopias are an abomination to me. Consequently, I do not believe in liberty as an ideal either. But you, you have had such a way of explaining to me liberty as a business, that I want to tell you, in case you care to hear it: in your sense I am an Anarchist!"

With that he firmly pressed his hand, and the eyes of the two men met for a moment; now they knew each other. It was not a union sealed by blood into which they entered. They gave no promise that was binding on them. They assumed no obligations towards each other.

But they said to each other by their looks: We know what we want. Perhaps the time is not too distant when we shall feel strong enough to hold our ground against authority. Then we may stand together. Until then, vigilance and patience!

AUBAN WAS ALONE. AND he arose with a violent movement and paced up and down his room for certainly an hour, while the fire entirely went out.

When fatigue overcame him, it was still ringing in his ears again: Read history!

Without choice he drew forth the next volume, and read through the night until dawn.

Up to his knees he waded through the blood of the past. He saw the rise and fall of nations. He saw the responsibility for their life rolled on the shoulders of a few, and he saw those few break down beneath its weight, or play with it like the child with his ball…

He saw how those who "wished the good" produced the bad: error.

He saw how those who "strove after the bad" brought about the good: destroyed error.

He saw how everything that had been could not have been different, precisely because it had been so and not different. It was not for us to mourn and to curse, therefore, but to understand.

To avoid recognized errors—such the watchword, such the use, such the blessing of history, such its lesson....

Auban read. And over the downfall and ruins of nations he forgot about Chicago....

Then sleep closed his eyes. Gently it drew the book from between his fingers. It slipped on the floor.

The light, however, continued to burn.

Heavy dreams sank upon the sleeper. Restlessly his breast rose and fell, and the pain at other times concealed by the sharp, hard lines about the mouth had crept from its hiding-place, and now lay on his thin cheeks. His pale lips were slightly open.

Thus the night came to an end, the dreaded night.

When Auban awoke morning had come. He changed his dress.

Then he took up the newspapers. He knew what he should read. When he saw how the hand trembled with which he turned the paper, he paced up and down a few times before he began. He wanted to be strong.

Then he read, without haste, pale, with a gloomy calm. But his heart stood still.

It was the last act of the tragedy of Chicago: the morning of the eleventh of November.

The city is in a state of siege, every public building is under guard; everything is feared; above all, incendiarism; the military is concentrated, the fire department called out; at the hotels every arrival is watched; the jurymen, the judges, the State's attorney, the chiefs of the police, are placed under protection.... The larger factories are closed.... The jail is surrounded by an impenetrable line of armed policemen.... A tumult arises: a despairing woman wanders along the living wall with her weeping children, and attempts in frenzied fear to reach her husband before it is too late. She is seized by brutal hands, and must pass the most terrible hours of her life inside the stone walls of a prison cell....

Silence, the silence of fear, reigns again. In the neighboring streets men are jostling each other. Where they form groups, they again separate. They are paralyzed under the burden of those hours....

In the interior of the jail:—

The condemned have awakened. They write their last letters; they are even now molested by the contemptible obtrusiveness of a clergyman whom they decline to see; they take their last meal; across the distance of their cells they exchange their last words of friendship and hope in behalf of the cause for which they die, and their emotions find expression in strophes which their memory awakens in them, and whose unfamiliar sound echoes powerfully along the rigid walls:—

Ein Fluch dem Götzen, zu dem wir gebeten—
Der uns geäfft, gefoppt und genarrt—
Ein Fluch dem König, dem König der Reichen—
Der uns wie Hunde erschiessen lässt—
Ein Fluch dem falschen Vaterlande—
Wo nur gedeihen Schmach und Schande....

And:—

Poor creatures! Afraid of the darkness
Who groan at the anguish to come?
How silent I go to my home!
Cease your sorrowful bell—
I am well!

And that immortal song in which all four join, the Marseillaise of Labor, of labor struggling for emancipation—

Von uns wird einst die Nachwelt zeugen!
Schon blickt auf uns die Gegenwart....

Yes; the present which was willing to pave the way for a better future, not the present which in impotent blindness was about to revive a buried past, had fixed its gaze upon them in this hour, in pain and in sorrow....

The sheriff appears. The condemned embrace each other, press each other's hands, which are shackled; the death warrants, dead words with which authority seeks to justify its murder, are read.

The death march begins.

They pass through the door which leads into the yard of the jail; the gallows rises before their eyes. One after another they ascend its steps, pale, but undaunted. White caps are drawn over their heads. In this last moment their voices are heard from behind the coverings:—

"There will be a time when our silence will be more powerful than the voices you strangle today!" exclaims the first.

"Hurrah for Anarchy!" accompanied by a laugh, the second. And:—

"Hurrah for Anarchy! This is the happiest moment of my life!" falls in the third.

Finally the fourth and last:—

"Will I be allowed to speak, O women and men of my dear America?"—

The sheriff gave the signal. Then once more:—

"Let me speak, sheriff. Let the voice of the people be heard! O—"

The trap falls.... And cowards see how heroes die.

So far Auban was able to read; the following sentence his eyes just grazed, for suddenly the jail yard of Chicago rose before him in tangible clearness: he sees the crowd of two hundred persons that fills it, the twelve of the jury, the higher court officers, the guard, the newspaper reporters—a herd of cowardly hirelings; he sees the gallows, the four men whose features he had so often seen in the picture, erect, defiant, great; and he sees their dying, the convulsive movements of their death struggle which lasts fourteen minutes.... Fourteen minutes! The butcher kills his cattle at one blow, the robber his victim at one stroke; only these murderers take a horrible delight in the "victory of justice," which they themselves personify, and fortify their own cowardice behind the word with which authority has hitherto always justified all crimes: "His will be done...."

So clearly, like a vision, the end of the tragedy stood before Auban's eyes that he could no longer endure it, and let his brow sink forward on his arms stretched across the table. So he lay a long time. For he had to fight down everything again that had newly risen in him, of pain, anger, wrath, of sorrow and of hatred.

When he arose he was again himself. But he again paced up and down the length and breadth of his room with his restless steps.

The tragedy of Chicago!

What an audience! All mankind who call themselves civilized! Not one who does not take a part; all compelled to make a choice....

On the one side: the thirst for blood satisfied, beastly joy; the jubilant victory of authority; a sigh of relief after anger passed; sordid philistinism boasting over the triumph of order; morality priding itself upon its own narrowness; awakening compunctions of conscience; new fear of coming events; and the first gleams of understanding.

On the other: cries of horror, strangled by fear and by awe; impotent rage and growling wrath; shame of one's own cowardice, anger and pain at that of the others; bitterness, sinking to the very bottom of all hearts; dull surrender to the inevitable; a thousand hopes of earthly justice buried, a thousand new ones risen in the final victory of the cause that has just been baptized in blood; the thirst for revenge on the day of reckoning intensified to an intolerable degree; sentimental sorrow; and the first gleams of understanding.

All the slumbering feelings of which the heart is capable aroused! All the passions called from their hiding-places, struggling in the frantic rage of death! All deliberation, all calm reason, obscured by the clouds of smoke and blood—these were the fruits of this murder....

The tragedy of Chicago!

What scenes! What changes in them!

In the first act:—

The trembling of the earth which presages the outbreak of the volcano.

The hosts gather on both sides for the conflict.

Deliberating, rousing themselves, resolving, suspecting the danger, calling all forces to aid, arming themselves.

The noise of the battle-cry: Eight hours!

The first collisions: the whiz of the bullets, the gnashing of teeth, the howl of rage, the cries of indignation, the groans of the dying, the weeping of women.

Over countless glowing heads and feverish hearts the uproar of feverish words full of fire and flame.

A thundering crash: smoke and shrieks. Death and destruction.

The mad dance of the passions rushes past.

***

In the second act:—

After the noisy, open battle on the public plain, the quiet, hidden, but far more terrible struggle in the "domain of the law."

Spacious court-rooms and narrow prison-cells. Iron gratings which separate friend from friend, and high prison walls, so high that the sun cannot scale them.... O golden sun of liberty—not to see you for eighteen months, and then without having caught one of your rays to sink into eternal night.

***

And finally in the last and third act:—

The curtain had dropped. But the tragedy was not at an end.

No; those who had put it on the stage had forgotten the epilogue!

An epilogue, an unexpected epilogue, had to follow with inevitable necessity. It was the propaganda which this damnable deed produced: the echo which the history of these lives and deaths would call forth as an answer in countless still slumbering hearts. Thousands would ask: "Why were these men forced to die?" Thousands would answer: "For the cause of the oppressed." And again: "We are the oppressed, every hour tells us that. But is it not our destiny to suffer?" And again the answer: "No; it is your destiny to be happy. The days of your emancipation have come. Those men died for your happiness. Read their speeches—here they are. Learn from them who they were, what they wanted, that they were no murderers, but heroes." And the oppressed are awakening. They lift their tired brows, and the chains on their hands rattle. And now they hear their rattle. Then rage seizes them, they revolt, and the chains break. And swinging the iron weapons high in the air, they pounce upon their oppressors, seize and strangle all crying for mercy. Their hands are about to relax, but a voice calls: "Chicago!" Only this one word: "Chicago!" And all thoughts of mercy vanish. The greatest conflict the trembling earth has ever seen is fought to an end without mercy....

To the graves of their dead go the victors. They uncover their heads and say: "You are avenged. Sleep in peace."

And returning home they teach their boys who those were whom they so honored, how they lived and how they died.

That would be the epilogue of the tragedy of Chicago....

Bent over the crumpled newspapers lay Auban, covering them with his arms and his brow, as if he could thus choke what rose from them, stupefying, like the vapor of fresh blood.... His beating heart cried for a word of deliverance from this hour.

"Folly!" his reason whispered to him.

But he felt that it was too cheap a word. And so it died on his lips.

Chapter VIII.
The Propaganda of Communism

Trupp was on the way to his Club.

It was the evening of the day on which the London newspapers had published the detailed accounts of the murder in Chicago, and since Trupp had read them, he had wandered—as if impelled by feelings for which he had no name, and as if hounded and pursued by invisible enemies whom he did not know—through the infinite sea of houses, without aim, without purpose, in all directions, without knowing what he did.

He saw neither the streets through which he passed, nor the streams of humanity through which he forced his way.... Where he had been, he knew not. Once the Thames had lain before him, and, leaning against the railing of a bridge, he had stood a whole hour, gazing fixedly and abstractedly down upon the black tide of the river; several times he had crossed the main arteries of traffic, and then each time instinctively sought quieter and more secluded streets, where nothing would interfere with the whirling thoughts of his over-excited brain....

He had not eaten anything the whole day except a piece of bread which he had bought almost unconsciously while passing a bakery, and not drunk anything.

He could not even have told what he had been thinking. In rapid succession thought had followed thought in his brain, forming an immense chain whose countless links all bore one and the same mark: Chicago!

As often as he had looked up, and his eyes met the indifferent faces of men, an unconquerable rage had risen within him to jump at their throats in order to shake them out of their calm with brutal force. But when with bent head he had sauntered along, nothing had told of the storm that stirred up his whole being to its innermost depths and drove waves of impotent rage to the surface....

Only when the shadows of night fell did he awake: as out of a dull stupor, as out of an opium sleep, only that his dreams had not been sweet and enticing, but torturing and bitter, like the iron grasp of a fist.

Then only had he looked about, for he had no idea where he was. He was in Edgware Road, in the north of Hyde Park—still far enough from the Club, half an hour and longer, but he might have found himself in the farthermost suburbs of Highgate or Brixton, hours away from Tottenham, and unable to reach the Club that evening.

Still half stupefied by the blow of this terrible day, but not yet feeling anything of the death-like fatigue which must have taken hold of his body after the day's mad walk, he started on his way with aching feet, his entire body covered with perspiration and trembling with cold in the chilly evening air.

He knew now exactly what route to take, and he was careful to choose the nearest.

Two feelings had in these last two days incessantly battled within him.

One was that of deepest dejection.... The murder of Chicago had been carried out without any attempt on the part of the comrades to prevent it. Or if not to prevent it, at least to interrupt it. He had indeed never looked forward to such an event with absolute confidence, for he knew but too well how rarely the performance agrees with the promise; but nevertheless, this unclouded victory of authority was a terrible blow to him.

The other was a feeling of satisfaction when he thought of the inexhaustible fountain of the propaganda that would flow from these martyr deaths. Chicago had become the Golgotha of workingmen. Eternally, as here the cross, would there the gallows rise.

But with the instinct which a twenty years' participation in the Socialistic movement had given him, he suspected also that the question of Anarchism had now been placed in a different light, where it would henceforth stand out clearly for all thoughtful men: in the light of day. Much that had hitherto remained doubtful—covered by a veil of a mysterious and for most people inaccessible reserve—had now to be settled. A temporary lull in the propaganda was quite inevitable. The lost time would again be made up—doubtless. But above the doorway of the coming years was graven for him and his comrades: discouragement, lethargy, disaffection!

All that, but also many other things, filled him with a leaden despondency. Foremost, the position of Auban. He no longer understood his friend. His motives, his aims, had become incomprehensible to him.

That he still agreed with him in regard to the means, as he believed, held them together.

But how was there to be any agreement between them henceforth, after Auban had taken up the defence of what he, the Communist, regarded as the ultimate cause of all misery and imperfection: private property?

No doubt could rise in regard to Auban's perfect honesty. It would have been ridiculous. Auban wanted liberty. He wanted also the liberty of labor. He loved the workingmen. He had given a thousand proofs of it. Their interests were his.

Such love never dies. Trupp knew that.

But for all that, he did not understand him. He would never understand him. Never would he be able to see in private property anything but the stronghold of the enemy. And on its battlements stood Auban, his friend, the comrade of so many years; he could not grasp the thought!

Then there were the personal wranglings and misunderstandings in his own camp, in the group to which he belonged. There was no end to them. They had always existed as long as he could remember, and they had never lost any of the repugnance for him with which they had paralyzed his best powers since he came to London. His comrades were too indolent, too inactive, too undecided for him. In these latter years he had immeasurably increased the demands he made on himself and on others. Now everything disappointed him; none of his expectations were henceforth satisfied.

Nothing came up to them. He had no longer had any other thought than that of his cause. That idea claimed all his thought and action. It pursued him during the toilsome labor of his days with the persistent tenacity with which usually nothing but love dominates the nature of man; it kept him awake till late in the night, and frightened away all fatigue over the manifold labors of the propaganda that had been placed on his shoulders; it pressed the pen into his hand so little used to writing when the columns of the paper were to be filled, and withheld from his thirsting mouth the glass in order to place the money for it upon the great altar which was laden with the sacrifices of labor....

It was this devotion to the cause which had made of him a character remarkable of its kind; it had increased his capacities tenfold, cast his energies in the mould of constancy and firmness, and given aim and direction to his life. It dominated him, and he was its slave, although a slave who never feels his fetters because he believes he is free. He had put the bridle of that devotion on his body and brought himself to obedience as a horse obeys its rider; it must know neither fatigue nor hunger if he did not wish it.

Not because he himself wished to remain free, but because he wished not to be disturbed in the service of his cause, had he remained unmarried, or, rather, never united himself for any extended period with a woman. He was an excellent man in almost every respect. He had none of the faults of narrowness; the grandeur of the cause stifled them. Of an uncommon, although a one-sided and little disciplined intelligence, of firm health, without nerves and with muscles of steel, with an iron will and a dash of simple greatness—thus he stood: at the head of the people, as it were, their best and most worthy representative, erect with the pride of the proletarian who, in the consciousness of his power, in the consciousness of being "all in all," claims the world from a class already declining, claims it with the vehemence of a child, the wrath of a revolutionist, the confidence of a general who knows his troops and feels sure that they are invincible, and who claims it without suspecting what he demands.

History requires such men in order to—use them. It is they with whom it fights its external battles, by placing them at the head of the masses whose strength is decisive.

Liberty sees in them only obstacles. For its battles are fought only by the individuals who represent nothing but themselves.

Trupp was an excellent man. But he was often blind with both eyes. He was a fanatic. He was, moreover, the fanatic of a fantasy. For a fantasy is Communism which must invoke force in order to become dismal reality....

Trupp walked on, and his wakeful thoughts cut still deeper, and he felt them more painfully than the narcotic stupor in which he had passed the day. He was nearing the Club.

The revolutionaries of Socialism are scattered over the entire world. They have already set foot on the most distant continents, and are knocking with their fists against the farthermost doors.

They think they are the early morning walkers of the new day which is dawning for mankind.

Everywhere they join hands: here they call themselves a party, and aim to get into political power by means of universal suffrage and strictly disciplined organization under the direction of elected leaders in order at some future time to solve the social question from above by force; and there they call themselves a group, and preach the forcible overthrow of all external relations as the only deliverance out of that intolerable misery which always appears to have reached its highest point, and yet always grows greater, like the cloud which comes nearer and nearer, which yesterday we hardly noticed, which today already lowers above us with its threatening shadows, and which will discharge itself tomorrow—surely tomorrow: only we do not yet know the hour, the spot, and the measure of its force.

Everywhere they scatter their publications, their pamphlets. Everywhere they start their newspapers.... Most of these enterprises indeed pass away again as quickly as they arose; they die of exhaustion, they are suppressed, but still their number is so large that it can no longer be ascertained. They are seed grains, fallen on sterile soil and among weeds: only a few strike root, grow, bear fruit for a few summers.... But the hand that sowed them does not grow empty; courage, perseverance, and hope fill it again and again....

The revolutionaries of Socialism are scattered over all the great cities of the world.

But in none is their swarm so mixed as in London. Nowhere does it draw so closely together; nowhere does it go so far apart. Nowhere are its own dissensions more bitter, and nowhere does it fight the common enemy with greater bitterness. Nowhere does it speak in so many languages, and nowhere does it give expression to a greater variety of opinions in a greater variety of accents.

It embodies all types; and it shows them all in their most perfect and interesting as well as in their most demoralized and commonplace forms.

For the novice it is a chaos. But it soon becomes a splendid field of learning, where he quickly feels himself at home.

The life of the refugees in London has a great history.

When English Socialism, whose growth has not yet reached maturity, still lay in its swaddling clothes, the refugees of the fourth decade came to London, and at the instigation of men like Marx and others founded the first society of refugees of German workingmen in London, the "Communistic Workingmen's Society," which became the parent society of such variously constituted children that they no longer recognize each other as brothers and sisters.

The Russians came, with Herzen at their head, who rung his "Kolokol" there; and Bakunin came from his Siberian exile. Freiligrath came with magnificent songs on his trembling lips; and Kinkel came for a short time from the prison of Spandau; and Ruge with the scattered remains of his "*Jahrbücher.*" Mazzini lived there, the great patriot, the republican conspirator. There finally the Frenchmen: Louis Blanc, Ledru-Rollin, and the comrades of their fate....

All found rest and peace there, the peaceless rest of exile and the scanty bread of the banished....

Then the great names cease. There is a pause.

When with the advent of the eighth decade the creed of free Communism, which assumes the name of Anarchism, comes to London in the person of one of its first and most active champions who founds "*Freiheit*" there as its first organ, the "Communistic Workingmen's Educational Society" has already separated into three sections, which soon meet only in bitter hostility: here the Social Democrats, the "blue," there the Anarchists, the "red." A few years later the publication of the new paper is transferred to New York; but London, where, since the passage of the law against Socialists in Germany in 1878, the movement has drifted into an entirely new channel, has again become the headquarters of all German refugees, although in a different way from that of thirty years ago....

Their physiognomies, their aspirations, their purposes, their aims, have totally changed. Everything is in a state of fermentation; all stand against each other; all who come—tired by hardships endured, embittered by terrible persecutions, driven into all forms of activity—are drawn into it: for in that bay of exile the waves ran more wildly than on the high seas.

It seems at times as if the refugees had forgotten their distant enemy, so bitterly they fight among themselves. Individual groups secede from the sections of the parent society, and refuse to retain even the old name. A few individuals, filled with restlessness and ambition, try to avail themselves of the dissension for the purpose of gathering up the severed threads and keeping them—in their own hands. The controversies for and against them are carried on for weeks and for months to the degree of exhaustion, when they cease and leave no other traces than estrangement, a pile of papers full of insinuations and suspicions, and a useless pamphlet.

In 1887, the year of the Chicago murder, the four German workingmen's clubs of London were bound together only by the thin and already damaged bond of affiliation. Only a few of the members still associated with one another. As societies they came together only when the object was to join the English Socialists in some grand demonstration, to make a brilliant affair of some meeting, or to celebrate the days of March.

TRUPP FOUND HIS CLUB that evening well attended. Usually its rooms were filled only on the Sunday afternoons and evenings when not alone the members, but also their wives and children and the invited guests, came to attend the regular musical and theatrical entertainments. Those entertainments, open to everybody at an admission fee of sixpence, had the double purpose of furnishing new sources of revenue for the propaganda, pamphlets, and the countless occasions necessitating pecuniary assistance, and of offering a diversion from the cares of the past and the thoughts of the coming week in dance and light conversation, which often gave no hint of the excited struggles at the discussions and closed meetings.

Trupp hardly could force his way through the narrow passage from the door to the steps leading to the basement hall below. The bar-room on the left of the steps was crowded. Most of the people were standing before the counter, alone or in groups, glasses in hand, while only a small number had secured places beside the few tables. But there was still a corner for Trupp on one of the benches. They crowded more closely together, and he quickly took the first glass held out to him, emptying it at one draught.

The spirit of the gathering varied with the people. While a number of groups were moved by the noisy discussion of some question, others were almost dumb. An oppressive silence reigned at the table where Trupp had found a place. A young man was sitting at its other end. He was reading from a newspaper, but his voice was not clear, and he shed tears when he came to the details of the execution. He was surrounded on all sides. A look of threatening determination lay on all faces. But only suppressed words escaped the lips pressed together, and only their looks gave evidence of what most of them were thinking.

Suddenly Trupp saw Auban in a group of comrades standing at the counter where the host and his wife were untiringly seeking to gratify the wishes of the guests. They had not seen each other for eight days, since their excursion through the East End.

Why had Auban come that evening? It had been more an accident than deliberate intention which led him in the neighborhood of Tottenham Court Road and gave him the thought of visiting the Club for half an hour. The day had passed more quickly in work than he had dared to hope. The storms of the morning were followed by the calm of victory. Whoever saw him now found him cool and composed as ever.

Immediately upon his entrance he had been greeted by acquaintances. They had shown him the new rooms of the house; the upper rooms, where there was a billiard table and where the small conferences in closed circle were held, and the large meeting hall in the basement, which was very roomy and made an agreeable impression with its bright, clean walls.

In former years the Club had had at its disposal only the gloomy and dirty back room of a public house, of which they grew tired, especially in consequence of the quarrels that filled it for weeks and for months. And in the spirit of sacrifice they had now rented this house, where they felt comfortable.

In the bar-room, which was too small for the crowds always gathering there first, Auban had entered into a conversation. They had heard about the last discussion held at his place, and had many objections to offer to his theories.

What? He wanted to leave private property intact and to abolish the State? But the very function of the State is the protection of private property. And one man asked in English:—

"As long as there is private property it will need protection. Consequently, the State can fall only when the former falls. What have you to reply to that?"

"It is possible that private property will require protection. I shall buy that protection, and I shall combine with others for the protection of our property, whenever it will be necessary. But I claim that ninety-nine percent of all so-called 'crimes of property' are committed by those who, driven to despair by the prevailing conditions, either cannot sell their labor or sell it only far below the limit of its price—assuming that cost forms the true limit of price. I assert, therefore, that they must become a rarity from the hour when each shall be able to secure the full product of his labor, *i.e.,* from the hour when State meddling shall cease.

"I assert, further, that self-protection will be more effective than the protection which the State forces on us without asking us if we want it. For example:—

"I could not kill a man, whether in war, in a duel, or in any other 'legal' manner. But I should not hesitate a moment to send a bullet through the head of the burglar who should enter my house with the intention of robbing and murdering me. And I believe that he would think twice before entering on the burglary if he were certain of such a reception, instead of knowing, as at present, that stupid laws make it difficult for me to protect my life and my property, and that at the worst he will receive but such and such punishment.

"I have chosen this example also for the benefit of those who still are unable to see the difference between a defensive and an aggressive action, and consequently between a voluntary association for mutual solidarity in definite cases which can be dissolved at any time, for instance, life insurance, etc., and a State which grants the individual neither the choice of entering nor of leaving it, except on the condition that he emigrates from the land of his birth."

Auban ceased. But those who had listened to him made each of his sentences a text for lively discussions.

They tried to draw him into them. But Auban was not disposed today to talk much, and he declined. He descended the steps leading into the meeting hall. It was now filled, and there were many impatient calls for the exercises to begin.

Auban remained standing near the steps, at the entrance to the hall, whose benches stretching along the walls were now filled to the last seat. As the centre remained free, the assembly formed an oval circle in which each individual was recognizable by all. So most of them remained sitting in their places when they spoke.

On that evening few women were present. The men were mostly young, in the twenties and thirties.

The meeting did not differ in any respect from similar gatherings of workingmen, except, perhaps, in the proportionally large number of bold and energetic heads which bore the stamp of exceptional intelligence and great force of will. However, as is always the case, so here it was only the few who stood out so prominently as to be at once recognizable as the hewers of new paths, the axe-bearing pioneers and heralds of a new and better age.

They talked about Chicago. Many spoke. As soon as one had finished another began, and many a hand still rose in the air in sign that the list of speakers was not yet closed.

Most of them spoke briefly but violently. Plans were already being suggested as to the manner in which the propaganda of the death of the martyrs was to be inaugurated.

All agreed that something extraordinary must be done....

Then the debate turned on the question of founding a school for the children of the members who did not want them to be poisoned by the belief in the Church and the State prevailing in the public schools.

THOSE LOUD VOICES suddenly disturbed Auban. They did not harmonize with his mood. About Chicago *this* evening—in a meeting of such size: he felt it was not right; and the school question—he could not be of any help in it any way; his task was a different one.

He withdrew, therefore, into the quieter background of the hall, where a few comrades were sitting beside their glasses and their newspapers. One was reading, while another was carrying on a conversation in a low tone with a third, and a fourth had fallen asleep, overcome by the exertion of the day's labor. A young, blonde man with a friendly expression was holding a child on his knees. The mother had died not long after his birth, and the father, who could not leave him at home alone, was obliged to take him with him to the Club, where he grew up: nursed and petted by rough hands, but watched over by good and faithful eyes, fostered by that tender spirit of love that dwells only in hearts which can not alone love, but also hate.... The young man had bestowed special care on the child, and he hung often for hours on his neck with his thin, small arms while the father took part in a discussion; and nothing was more beautiful than the care and goodness with which he and the others tried to replace the mother for him.

Auban smiled when he saw that picture again. He came nearer and played with the child, who did not show a trace of fatigue. But then he was again overcome by his own heavy and serious thoughts. For he had seen a face at the same table which he knew but too well. It was a comrade who had become insane under the pressure of constant persecutions. At first over-sensitive, then seized by melancholy, his insanity had broken out here, in London, where he had sought his last refuge; here, where he was in perfect security. He passed most of his time at the Club, where he usually sat in a corner, not disturbing anybody, and where he was treated with gentle sympathy by all who saw him. No one could help him any more; but they wished to save him, at least, from the insane asylum.

Intentionally Auban did not speak to him. It would only have troubled him. For the unfortunate man was most contented if left sitting alone in his corner, where, with murmuring lips, he could for hours stare before him, and with his nimble fingers draw incomprehensible figures on the table. He always recalled to Auban another comrade who had been overtaken by insanity in another way. It had been one of his young Parisian friends. Fiery, enthusiastic, devoted, he lived only for the cause. He could have given his life for it. He was thirsting to demonstrate his love, and he found no other way than that of a "deed." He had been influenced by passionate speeches and inspiring promises. But his nature which shrank from violence and bloodshed, revolted. And in the long struggle between what seemed to him as his holiest duty and that nature which made its fulfilment an impossibility, his mind gave way....

While Auban was under the spell of that memory, he heard Trupp's loud, clear voice, as it penetrated the hall from end to end.

"We must declare ourselves in solidarity, not only with the opinions of the murdered men of Chicago, but also with the deed of the bomb thrower of the fourth of May, that glorious deed of a hero!"—and noticed the enthusiasm which those words elicited on all sides.

His flesh began to creep. He felt like rising and holding up his hands entreatingly against the fools who were ready to jump into the abyss that had opened before them. But his reason also showed him at once the perfect uselessness of his intention: instead of tempering the passions, his words would have fanned them to a higher flame on that evening.

He supported his head with his hands.

If possible, he wished to have a decisive word with Trupp that very evening.

He felt that there was nothing further for him to do here. He believed only in self-help. They would have to proceed along their lines and make their experiences, from which neither he nor anyone else could save them.

And he again asked himself the question which had often come to him of late years: Have you any right whatever to help? to influence? to counsel? Was there any other way than that of experience? And did not all experience require time to be made? Was it right to forestall it?"

Auban had, therefore, but rarely taken part in any discussions since he came to London. But he always remembered with pleasure an evening when he had discussed the question of the gratuity of mutual credit with four or five others in the narrow bar-room above him. Each had taken part, not with long explanations, but with brief, concise questions; each had had an opportunity to formulate and express his ideas as he wished, so that, when they separated, all demanded the continuation of such meetings, so animated were they and enthusiastic over the profitable manner of exchanging opinions. Then they met again, this time not in the exceptionally small circle, but in the usual large number, everything had been led back into the old rut: one speaker rose, spoke for two hours—in accordance with the principle of personal liberty each had the right to speak as long as he wished, and none the right to interrupt him—digressed, took up entirely foreign subjects, tired some and bored others, so that Auban had given up the matter and gone away discouraged. It was the last attempt of the kind he had made.

He had not only sympathy, but also admiration for those men who occupied themselves after their day's hard labor with the most serious problems in the most devoted manner, while they saw others diverting themselves in a stupid game at cards or in shallow talk. He respected them from the bottom of his heart. But only the more deeply did he deplore the intangible vagueness of their aspirations, which would not achieve a single aim, would grow more and more desperate, and after a thousand sacrifices end like all similar ones before them—in blood and defeat.

For in reality they were not struggling for the improvement of their own lot. They struggled for ideals which were unattainable because utterly visionary. Moreover, they had only contempt and scorn for all "practical" aspirations of their class to help itself, which, in comparison with their "great aims" of the emancipation of mankind, etc., seemed paltry and prosaic.

Their mental confusion seemed almost incurable to Auban since he had recognized it. He had often made experiments to see how far it extended, and met with results that first amazed and finally discouraged him.

Thus he had once put the first and simplest of all questions to each of a number of his acquaintances:—

"To whom does the product of your labor belong?" he asked in turn, first a number of inveterate Social Democrats of strictest faith; several Communists, both those who championed compulsory Communism and those who saw in the autonomy of the individual the final aim, and regarded themselves as Anarchists; finally, a number of English Socialists. If they had all been logical thinkers, they would have been obliged to reply on the basis of their philosophy of Socialism: "My labor belongs to the others: the State, society, mankind.... I have no right to it." But a Social Democrat replied without hesitation: his labor belonged to him; and an Autonomist: his labor belonged to society; and Auban was surprised to learn that those who were most bitterly fighting among themselves agreed on this one question, of which all others are corollaries; and that those who occupied one and the same ground gave directly opposite answers....

Indeed, nothing had yet been cleared up. Most of them were bound together not by clear thoughts, but by dull feelings which had not yet shaken off the torpor of sleep. Revolutions are fought with those feelings, but no truths are fathomed by them. The cool, refreshing bath of experience must first have washed the sleep from the eyes of the awaking masses, before they would be able to proceed to the labor of the new day....

It was necessary to be patient and not to lose courage! Auban thought again of Trupp, and wanted to see him. He could not find him in the hall, and so went up stairs again.

When he entered the bar-room again, he found Trupp engaged in conversation with a man whose bearing and dress at once showed that he was no workingman, but wished to appear one. He stopped, therefore, and at the same time caught a look of his friend, which he instantly understood. The stranger, who had been drinking from the glass before him, could not have noticed anything of the rapid, silent exchange of ideas.

Most of the people had gone down into the hall. Only at the table a few comrades were still sitting, reading and playing cards. Auban joined them and sat down with his back towards Trupp. Then he took up one of the papers lying about, and appeared to be reading it attentively.

Of the conversation carried on behind him he could understand only a few words, especially as it was in German. Both speakers intentionally lowered their voices. But he had not been sitting there five minutes, when he felt Trupp's hand on his shoulder.

"Will you go with us? Let us have another glass of beer." He turned instantly, and noticed in rising how little the stranger could suppress his embarrassment at this invitation.

All three left the Club together. The stranger concealed his embarrassment in passing through the door by politely allowing Auban to take the lead.

When they were on the street, Trupp said in a loud voice to Auban: "A banished comrade from Berlin! A fine place, isn't it?"

Auban bit his lips. On such occasions his friend was an expert.

"What are you?" he asked the Berlinian, in German.

"I am a shoemaker, but I cannot find any work here."

"Oh, you are a shoemaker! But how do you wash your hands to get them so white?" Auban continued.

Now the stranger grew seriously alarmed. His timid look passed alternately from one to the other. He was walking between the two. He wanted to stop, but Trupp and Auban walked on unconcerned, so that he could only ask: "You do not believe me?"

Trupp burst into a loud laugh, which sounded as natural as that of a child.

"Nonsense, the comrade is joking. Who would not believe you?"

And he suddenly grew very talkative, so that the others could not get in a word. But all that he said turned on the unmasking of decoys, police agents, and similar shady characters. He made fun of the ignorance both of the authorities and their tools. He spoke also of the voluntary spies who had sneaked into the clubs and meetings, and thrust their noses into everything until they were thrown out, when they finally filled the newspapers with lying reports of things they had hardly seen and did not understand.

Trupp's intention was no longer to be mistaken, especially since he did not concern himself about Auban, who, apparently absorbed in his own thoughts, sauntered along, but step for step kept closely by the side of the stranger, who could not escape from him, and whom each of his words put in perceptibly greater alarm and fear.

The had reached a narrow and dark street, which was illumined only by a single lantern and entirely deserted. Here several houses stood considerably back, leaving a large open space before the street again grew narrow.

Trupp had reached his destination, and suddenly interrupted himself.

The decoy saw that all was lost.

"Where are we racing?" he uttered, with an effort, and stopped. "I do not want to go farther—"

Already Trupp's strong hands had seized him and pushed him powerfully against the wall.

"You scoundrel!" he broke forth. "Now I have you!"

And twice his free hand struck the face of the wretch—once from the right and once from the left, and both times Auban heard the clashing blow of that iron hand.

The stranger was stunned. He raised his arms only in defence, to protect his face.

But Trupp commanded: "Arms down!" and involuntarily, like a child that is punished by his teacher, he dropped his arms.

Again—and again—Trupp's hand struck out, and with every blow his wrath also found relief in words: "You knave—you contemptible knave—you wanted to betray us, you spy? Just wait, you will not come again!"

And again his hand descended.

"Help me; he is strangling me!" came gaspingly from the lips of the man, who was seized by the terror of death.

But Auban, unsympathetic, half turned away, his arms crossed on his breast, did not stir.

And Trupp shook his victim like a doll of straw. "Yes, one ought to strangle dogs like you," he again broke forth. "It would be the best thing one could do! All of you, decoys that you are, scoundrels!"—and while he lifted the fellow from his cowering position, he dragged him with the hand which he seemed to have inextricably buried in his breast, closer into the unsteady, flickering light of the lantern and showed

Auban the pale, cowardly face, distorted by the fear of death, and disfigured under the blows of that murderous iron fist: "See, Auban; so they look, those wretches, who pursue the lowest of all callings!" He opened his fist, which lay like a vice on the breast of his victim, who—exhausted and dizzy—staggered, fell down, picked himself up again, muttered some incomprehensible words, and disappeared in the darkness.

The two friends gave the fellow no further attention. While they were rapidly walking towards Oxford Street, Trupp related the details of this new case. The friends now spoke French.

One day the fellow had come to one of the members with a letter of recommendation from a comrade in Berlin. The member took the bearer into the Club, and inquiry in Berlin confirmed the recommendation. But then it became known that the real receiver of it was not identical with the bearer; that the latter had been given it by the former, and had introduced himself under an assumed name. Thereupon, one of the comrades, without arousing his suspicions, went to room with him, and managed to get hold of his entire correspondence, which showed him to be a decoy in the direct pay of the German police, who for a monthly salary had undertaken to give his employers all desired information regarding the proceedings in the London Anarchistic clubs. They wanted to avoid a scandal in the Club, in order not to give the English police the coveted opportunity for entering it. He had undertaken the chastisement of which Auban had just been a witness.

Exposures of this kind were neither new nor especially rare. Generally, the fellows devoting themselves to that most sordid and contemptible of all callings escaped with a sound thrashing; often they scented what was coming, and anticipated a discovery by timely flight. In consequence of ceaseless denunciation, vilification, and persecution the suspicion among the revolutionists had grown very great. Important plans were no longer discussed in larger circles, and mostly remained the secret of a few intimates, or were locked up in the breast of a single individual. But greater still than against unknown workingmen was the suspicion against intellectual workers, in consequence of the sad experiences that had been made with newspaper writers and *littérateurs*. Nothing was more justifiable than caution in regard to these people; out of every ten there were surely nine who, under the pretence of wishing to "study" the teachings of Anarchism, only tried to penetrate the secrets of the propaganda in order to spread before their ignorant and injudicious readers the most harrowing tales concerning those "bands of murderers and criminals." That many an intellectual *proletaire*, who was suffering just as much, if not more, than the handworker from the pressure of the prevailing conditions, and who was consequently filled by the same great hatred against them, was frightened away by that suspicion—when he came to place his talents in the service of the "most progressive of all parties"—was a fact which, as Trupp said, was "not to be changed." The greater were the hopes which Auban began to place in them: bound by no considerations, and in the possession of an education weighing heavily upon them, they would surely be the first and for the present perhaps also the only ones who are not alone willing, but also capable of drawing the conclusions of Individualism.

TRUPP HAD REACHED A point in the conversation which always excited him very much.

"The Social Democrats assert," he said, with his bitter laugh, "all Anarchists are decoys; or, if it happens to suit them better, that there are no Anarchists at all. Ah," he continued, indignant, "there is nothing too mean that was not done against us by that party, above all, by its worthy leaders, who lead the workingmen by the nose in a perfectly outrageous manner. First they mocked and ridiculed us; then they vilified and denounced us; they harmed us wherever they could. From the beginning till now they saw in us their bitterest enemies, all because we attempted to open the eyes of the workingman to the uselessness of his sacrifices, of the suffrage humbug, of political wire-pulling. You have no idea, Auban, how corrupt the party is in Germany: the loyal Prussian subjects are not less self-reliant and more servile in relation to their lord and master than the German workingmen, who belong to the party, in relation to their 'leaders'! How will it end?"

"Well," Auban observed, calmly, "there is an immense difference between the workingmen as a class and the Social Democrats as a party. It is hardly conceivable that the former will ever be completely absorbed by the latter. Therefore, we need not stand in too great fear of the future. I even believe that the most important steps in the emancipation of labor will not be initiated by the Socialistic parties, but by the workingmen themselves, who will here and there gradually come to understand their true interests. They will simply push the party aside.

"But still less will they have anything to do with you. You must make that clear to yourselves. For in the first place, they can understand you at best with the heart, but not with the intellect, and for the real improvement of their condition they need nothing more than their intellect, which alone can show them the right road: I mean Egoism. And in the second place, by your perfectly absurd blending of all sorts of views, but still more by the policy you pursue, you have challenged the prejudices of ignorance, and apparently justified them, to such a degree that it requires an exceptionally independent will and a very rare love of knowledge to study your ways. Or a warm heart—which you all have!"

"As if you did not have it?" Trupp laughed, bitterly.

"Yes; warm enough, I hope, to love the cause of liberty forever. But no longer warm enough to harm it by folly."

"What do you call folly? Our policy?"

"Yes."

"You say that?" said Trupp, almost threateningly.

"Yes; I."

"Well, then it is about time that we came to a thorough understanding of the matter."

"Certainly. But first let us be alone. Not here on the street."

They walked on rapidly. Trupp was silent. When the light of a lantern fell on them, Auban saw how his whole frame trembled as if shaken by chill, while he was sucking the blood flowing from a wound in his hand, which must have grazed the wall while he was punishing the decoy.

"You are shivering?" he asked, thinking the excitement was the cause of it.

But Trupp exclaimed sullenly that it was nothing: he had only been running about the whole day, and forgotten to eat in consequence. Auban shook his head.

"You are incorrigible, Otto! To eat nothing the whole day, what folly!"

He took him by the arm and drew him away. They entered a small, modest restaurant on Oxford Street. There they knew a little-frequented back quiet corner, and Trupp ate hastily and silently, while Auban watched him chewing his meat with his strong teeth, he reminded him that in that very room they had sat opposite each other after years of separation, and he said, smiling:—

"Is not everything as it was then?"

But Trupp cast a bitter look of reproach on him, and pushed aside his plate and glass. His temporary weakness had disappeared, and he was again entirely the iron man, whose physical strength was inexhaustible.

"Now let us talk. Or are you tired?"

"I am not tired," said Auban.

Trupp reflected a moment. He feared the coming conversation, for he suspected that it would be decisive. He wished with all his heart by means of it to win back his friend to the cause of the revolution, to the conflict of the hour, in which he and his comrades were engaged, for he knew how invaluable his services were. He did not wish intentionally to bring about a rupture by a rude attack, but neither could he suppress the reproaches that had been gathering within him.

"Since you have been in London," he began, "and out of prison, you are another man. I hardly know you any more. You have no longer taken part in anything: in any meeting, or scheme, or enterprise. You have no longer written anything: not a line. You have lost almost all touch with us. What excuse have you?"

"What excuse have I?" asked Auban, a little sharply. "What for? And to whom do I owe it?"

"To the cause!" replied Trupp, vehemently.

"My cause is my liberty"

"Once *liberty* was your cause."

"That was my mistake. Once I believed that I must begin with the others; I have now learned that it is necessary to begin with one's self and always to start from one's self."

Trupp was silent. Then Auban began:—

"Two weeks ago we talked about our opinions at my house, and I trust I showed you where I stand, although I may not hope to have made it clear to you where you stand. I desired to place the one side of the question in a glaring light. The other side is still in the dark between us: that of policy. In shedding a light on it, too, this evening, I assume you are convinced that it is not moral or kindred scruples that move me to say to you: I consider the policy which you pursue, the so-called 'propaganda of deed,' not alone as useless, but also as harmful. You will never win a lasting victory by it."

Trupp's eyes were firmly fixed on the speaker. They flashed with excitement, and his bleeding hand, wrapped in a cloth, fell clinched on the table.

"It is well that we talk!" he exclaimed. "You demand, then, that we should idly fold our hands and calmly allow ourselves to be killed?"

He sprang up.

"You defend our enemies!" he ejaculated.

"On the contrary, I have discovered a weapon against which they are powerless," said Auban, calmly, and placed his hand on the arm of his excited friend, forcing him back to his place.

"I hate force in every form!" he continued; and now he seemed to be the one who wished to convince and win the other over to his idea. "The important thing is to make force impossible. That is not done by opposing force by force: the devil will not be driven out by Beelzebub.... Already you have changed your opinions on some points. Once you championed the secret societies and the large associations which were to unite the *proletaires* of all lands and all tongues; then you became aware how easy it was for the government to smuggle one of its dirty tools into the former, who at once seized all your clews, and how in every instance the latter have broken up, yielded to time and to their own fate; and since then you have more and more fallen back on the individual and preach as the only expedient method the forming of small groups, which know next to nothing about each other, and the individual deed as the only correct thing; since then you even condemn confidence among the most intimate friends in certain cases. Once your paper was published in 'Nowhere' by the 'Free Common Press'; now it is published like every other paper with the name and address of the printer on the last page. And thus everything, the entire movement has been more and more placed in the light of publicity."

He paused a moment.

Then he said impressively:—

"Your entire policy is a false one. Let us never forget that we are engaged in war.

"But what is the alpha and omega of all warfare? Every lieutenant can tell you.

"To deal the heaviest possible blows against the enemy at the least possible cost to yourself.

"Modern warfare recognizes more and more the value of the defensive; it condemns more and more the useless attack.

"Let us learn from it, as we ought to learn from everything that can in any way profit us.

"But my objections are of a far more serious kind. I accuse you even of ignoring the very first condition of all warfare: of neglecting to inform yourselves concerning your own and the enemy's forces.

"It must be said: you overrate yourselves and underrate the enemy!"

"And what," asked Trupp, scornfully, "are we to do, if I may ask?"

"What you are to do, I do not know. You must know yourselves. But I assert: passive resistance against aggressive force is the only means to break it."

Trupp laughed, and a lively conversation arose between the two men. Each defended his policy, illustrating its effectiveness by examples.

It was late when they closed: Auban persuaded of the impossibility of convincing his friend, and the latter embittered and irritated by his "apostasy."

They left the public house, and quickly reached the place where Tottenham Court Road meets with Oxford Street and the streets from the south. Entering one of the narrower and less crowded thoroughfares they walked up and down, and said their final and decisive words.

"You work into the hands of the government by our propaganda. You fulfil their dearest wishes. Nothing comes more opportunely to them than your policy, which enables them to employ means of oppression for which they would else lack all excuse. Proof: the *agents provocateurs* who instigate such deeds in their service. There is a ghastly humor in the thought that you are—the voluntary accomplices of authority, you who want liberty!"

He ceased, while from afar the tumult of Oxford Street came into that dark and quiet side street which was frequented only by a few timid forms which had separated themselves from the stream of humanity of the main thoroughfare, like sparkling embers from an ash-heap.

Trupp stood still. By the suppressed tone of his voice, Auban knew how hard it was for him to say what he had to say.

"You are no longer a revolutionist! You have renounced the grand cause of humanity. Formerly you understood us, and we understood you. Now we no longer understand you, because you no longer understand us. You have become a *bourgeois.* Or rather: you have always been a *bourgeois.* Return whence you came. We shall reach our aim without you."

Auban laughed. He laughed so loudly that the passers-by stopped and looked around. And that loud, full, clear laugh, which showed how little those words hurt him, formed an outlet for what had oppressed his breast these last days.

"*I* not understand *you*, Otto!" he said, while his laughter yielded to the earnestness of his words. "You do not believe yourself what you say. I not understand you, I who for years felt with your feelings and thought with your thoughts! If you were to set fire to the cities in a hundred points at once, if you were to desolate the countries as far as your power extended, if you were to blow up the earth or to drown it in blood—I should understand you! If you were to take revenge on your enemies by exterminating them one and all—I could understand it! And if it were necessary in order to at last achieve liberty—I should join your ranks and fight unto my latest breath! I understand you, but no longer believe in the violent progress of things. And because I no longer believe in it, I condemn force as the weapon of the foolish and the blind."

And as he recalled what Trupp had just said, he again had to laugh, and he closed:—

"Indeed, after all you have told me today it is only necessary to add that I condemn the policy of force in order—to spare the enemy!"

But again his laughter was silenced as his look met that of Trupp, who said, in a hard and almost hostile voice:—

"He that is not with us is against us!"

The two men stood opposite each other, so closely that their breasts seemed to touch. Their eyes met in iron determination.

"Very well," said Auban; and his voice was as calm as ever, "continue to throw bombs, and continue to suffer hanging for it, if you will never grow wise. I am the last to deny the suicide the right of destroying himself. But you *preach* your policy as a duty towards mankind, while you do not exemplify it in your lives. It is that against which I protest. You assume a tremendous responsibility: the responsibility for the life of others.

"For the happiness of mankind sacrifices must be made," said Trupp, frowning.

"Then make a sacrifice of yourselves!" cried Auban. "Then be men, not talkers! If you really believe in the emancipation of mankind by means of force, and if no experiences can cure you of that mad faith, then act instead of sitting in your clubs and intoxicating yourselves with your phrases! Then shake the world with your bombs, turn upon it the face of horror, so that it shall fear you instead of only hating you as now!"

Trupp grew pale. Never had the sorest of all spots between them been touched so mercilessly.

"What I shall do, and I can speak only for myself, you do not know. But you will some day see," he muttered. Auban's words had not applied to him. His was a nature which knew neither cowardice nor indecision, and which was strong enough to accomplish what it promised. But he felt with bitterness how true the accusation was in general which he had just heard.

And he deliberately brought the conversation to a close by saying:—

"What are we to each other any longer? My life is my cause. You became my friend because you were my comrade. My comrades are my friends. I know of no other friendship. You have renounced the cause—we have nothing in common any longer. You will not betray it, but you will no longer be of any service to it, such as you now are. It is better we part."

Auban's excitement had again subsided.

"You must act as you consider best, Otto. If you want me, you will find me by following the course of liberty. But where are you going?"

"I go with my brothers, who suffer as I do!"

They took each other's hand with the same firm grasp as ever.

Then they separated: each going his own long, solitary way, absorbed in thoughts which were as different as the course they took. They knew that a long time would pass before they would meet again; and they suspected that on the present evening they had spoken together alone for the last time.

Till now they had been friends; henceforth they would be opponents, although opponents in the struggle for an ideal which both called by the same name: liberty.

Chapter IX.
Trafalgar Square

London was in a fever.

It reached its highest point on the second Sunday of November, the Sunday following the events of Chicago.

Among the many memorable days of that memorable year this thirteenth of November was destined to take a most prominent place.

For a month, according to the whim of the police authorities, the "unemployed" had been alternately driven from and admitted to Trafalgar Square, the most accessible public meeting ground of the city.

This condition was intolerable for any length of time. The complaints of the starving masses grew more and more desperate, while the hotel-keepers and pawnbrokers considered the meetings as harmful to their business and invoked the protection of their servants, the "organs of public power."

At the beginning of the month a decree of the police commissioner interdicted the further holding of meetings on Trafalgar Square.

For thirty years this place, "the finest site of Europe," had been used by all parties at innumerable gatherings on the most varied occasions. A stroke of the hand was to drive them all away.

The first question raised was that of the "legality" of this despotic measure. The columns of the newspapers were filled with paragraphs from antiquated statute-books, which were paralleled by some taken from still older volumes: those insignia of a usurped power which fill all who have been reared in the faith of human authority with the mysterious awe of the inscrutable.

It is said that every citizen of the State helps make the laws of his country. But is there a single man among the thousands who knows what 57 George III. cap. 19, sec. 23, or 2 and 5 Vic. c. 47, sec. 52 means? Hieroglyphics.

To the chief of police it was of course a matter of perfect indifference whether his decree was "legal "or "illegal." If he had the power to enforce it today, it was "legal," and Trafalgar Square the property of the queen and the crown; if the "people" was strong enough to drive him and his men tomorrow from Trafalgar Square, the place remained what it had been, the "property of the people," and everybody could talk on it as much and as long as he found hearers who listened to him, or longer.

The question of the unemployed was pushed into the background at a blow. The Tory administration was suddenly opposed by the radical and liberal parties in battle array, who re-enforced the Socialists, and raised against the "terrorism" of the former their cry of the inalienable "right of free speech."

They decided to hold a public meeting on Trafalgar Square on Sunday, the thirteenth, with the programme: "Protest against the recent imprisonment of an Irish leader."

The preparations for the battle were conducted on both sides with feverish zeal: the Tories were firmly resolved not to stop short of the shedding of blood in beating down any attempt at occupying the Square, while the opposition parties were equally determined on capturing it at any cost.

The excitement in the city had been growing daily. On Saturday the authorities published a second ukase interdicting the approach of the Square on Sunday in the form of a procession.

There were not a few who believed they were on the eve of a revolution....

Auban had risen later than usual. His head felt dull. Nevertheless, he had taken up his work. But he was interrupted by a caller.

He shrugged his shoulders as he read the name "Frederick Waller" on the card that was handed him. What did that man still want of him? As a boy he had offered him his friendship, which Auban had not desired. Later—he had built up a large business in Lothringia and travelled a great deal—he had twice called on him in Paris, and Auban had explained those visits by the fact of his temporary popularity, received him coolly, dismissed him coolly. Now, after years, this man again approached him, with whom he had not a thought, not a sentiment, in common, and who belonged to a circle of people who had always been hateful to him in his inmost soul. But now he wanted to learn what brought him to him.

He wanted to directly ask him what his intentions were. But the other anticipated him by remarking that it was his duty not to entirely lose sight of his relatives. It was the same curious interest in the strange life which had once drawn him to the boy. He knew little about Auban. But as he suspected his radical views, he said confidentially that he, too, was anything but conservative, but that Auban would certainly understand how much his position compelled him to exercise the greatest caution. But Auban had neither patience nor understanding for men of that stamp. He wrapped himself in his frigid superiority, entirely ignored the question of his relative after his own life, made no inquiries, and expressed his opinions with their original harshness. When the visitor went away, he felt as if he had been overtaken listening at a strange door, and he made up his mind never again to repeat the attempt to get at Auban, who had this time plainly shown him how little he thought of him and his entire kith and kin.

In Auban this call awakened memories of long past years, which he followed up for a long time.

What a difference between then and now!

And yet it seemed to him sometimes as if his present self were more like the boy who, alone and reserved, labored to open the iron gates of truth in the quiet nights when no one saw him, with his soft and unskilled fingers, than like the youth who once presumed to storm them with fire and sword.

His was not a nature capable of permanently occupying a position exposing him on all sides to the gaze of a thousand eyes. He did not possess enough of levity, of ambition, of conceit, of self-complacency for that.

It was well that his fate had taken such a turn....

It was about three o'clock in the afternoon.

Auban was slowly coming from the north of the city. All the streets he passed were almost deserted. Only Oxford Street showed stray signs of life. It was not far from four o'clock when he approached Trafalgar Square. At St. Martin's Lane he had to stop: crowds of men obstructed the neighboring entrances of the side streets. He had arrived at the very moment when one of the four processions which at that hour tried to get access to the Square from four different sides, the one coming from Clerkenwell Green, came into collision with the police awaiting it here. He forced his way to the front as far as he could, but it was impossible for him to break through the last line of the crowd. He had to look between the heads and over them to see what was going on beyond.

The procession was headed by a woman. She carried a red flag. Auban took her and the men surrounding her, who grasped their canes more firmly, for members of that League. Directly behind the flag-bearer came the music. They played the Marseillaise. The procession was pretty long. Auban could not see it all. Only waving flags rose above the black throng.

In closed ranks the police awaited the procession. Holding in readiness their oaken clubs, they watched for the sign of attack from the superintendent.

When the procession had come up to them within a horse's length, calls passed back and forth, while at the same time the police made such a savage attack that the closed ranks of the procession seemed as if torn asunder. A fierce hand-to-hand fight followed. One tall policeman had sprung upon the woman and torn the flag out of her hands, which she held high in the air with all her strength. She staggered and fell down in a swoon, while a violent blow of a cane struck the neck of her assailant. The musicians fought for their instruments, which were taken from them, trampled on, and demolished. Some tried to save them by flight. With iron might the police handled their clubs, unconcerned where they struck. The attacked made a desperate defence. Most of them carried heavy canes and struck about them in mad rage. The confusion was indescribable. The air was filled with curses, cries of pain, words of abuse, the shrill howl of the multitude which, wherever it could, threw itself into the fight, dull blows, the tramp of heavy shoes on the hard pavement, the breaking of lanterns struck by stones.... People beat, kicked, scratched each other, sought to trip one another up, got entangled in a tight grip, pulling one another down.

Farther and farther the police pushed forward, driving the crowd before them, surrounded by it, but, mutually rushing to each other's aid, scattering it by the blows of their clubs. Farther and farther the attacked receded. There was no longer a trace of discipline among them. Some escaped in disorderly flight, others fought on the spot where they stood until they were overpowered, seized, and led away. After ten minutes the victory of the uniforms was decided: the flags were captured, the musical instruments demolished, the entire procession routed.... Some of the last of its ranks were pursued through the whole length of St. Martin's Lane, some driven into the side streets, where they mixed with the howling crowd and were carried away by it in hopeless confusion.

Auban also. He saw how a small division of the police, with their clubs in the air, came rushing towards the entrance of the street where he stood, felt how the crowd enclosing him got into motion, and, irresistibly carried away by it, he found himself the next minute at the other end of the street, where angry speech, laughter, and howling gave relief to the terror of the outraged crowd.

Then everything again streamed in the direction of Trafalgar Square. Auban also. He wished to reach it without again getting into too great a throng. But he could go by no other route than that leading by the church of St. Martin.

After what he had just seen, he was convinced that none of the processions would ever be able to gain access to the Square....

TRAFALGAR SQUARE LAY before him: bounded on the north by the severe structure of the National Gallery, by great club-houses and hotels on the east and west, it slopes gradually towards the south, where it broadens once more before it ends in a number of wide streets.

Its interior lower surface, formed by the terraces of the streets and bearing as an imposing feature the Nelson Column at the south, that large, cold, empty surface, adorned only by two immense fountains, was today completely in possession of the authorities, as Auban saw at a glance.

He became alarmed as he thought that the attempt might be made to drive from the place a force which, if not in numbers, was infinitely superior in discipline and military skill. It was indeed an army that was stationed there: a superficial estimate fixed its strength at from three to four thousand men. Who could drive it away? Not fifty, not a hundred thousand.

He left his place, and slowly drifted past the National Gallery. Here the surging crowds were kept in constant motion by the police. Where the constables saw a crowd, there they directed their attacks, by driving the wedge of their men into it. Every man who remained standing was incessantly commanded to "Move on! Move on!"

Walking down the west side, Auban now became convinced, at every step he took, of the well-considered plan of all these preparations. The steps leading to the north were strongly garrisoned. Here, and along the two other enclosed sides, a double line of policemen made it utterly impossible to climb over the enclosure and jump into the Square.

A reporter who knew Auban gave him a few figures which he had just learned and was now putting in his note-book, while Auban furnished him with some details concerning the Clerkenwell procession. The police had occupied the Square already since nine o'clock in the morning; since twelve in full force. About one thousand five hundred constables and three thousand policemen had been summoned from all parts of London, besides several hundred mounted police. The Life and the Grenadier Guards were being held in reserve.

The southern open side of the Square, in the centre of which the Nelson Column rises on an immense base guarded by four gigantic lions, was most strongly garrisoned, since no wall obstructed the entrance there. The "protectors of order" guarded the place here in lines four and five men deep; and a long line of mounted police was stationed here, who from time to time flanked the streets.

Here, in the wide space in front of the column which is formed by the meeting of four large streets, here, around the monument of Charles I, the crowds seemed densest. The masses appeared to grow larger from minute to minute. From all sides portions of the scattered processions congregated here in smaller or larger bands, no longer with flags and music and courageous spirits, but clasped together arm in arm, incensed by their defeat to the last degree, no longer hopeful of still capturing the place, but determined to have their revenge in minor collisions.

Auban studied the physiognomy of the crowd. Out of every five certainly two were curiosity-seekers, who had come to enjoy a rare spectacle. They willingly went wherever the police drove them. But surely many a one among them lost his equanimity in witnessing the brutalities that were committed about him, and by taking side with the attacked, became a participant in the event of the day against his will. Another fifth certainly consisted of the "mob": fishers in troubled waters, professional pickpockets, ruffians, idlers who make a better living than the honest workingman, pimps—in short, of all those who are always on hand, as nothing binds them. They were mostly very young. As the most personal enemies of the police, with whom they are engaged in daily struggle, they allowed no opportunity to pass in taking their revenge on them. Armed with stones, sticks, and pocket-knives, they inflicted painful injuries upon the police; whereupon they escaped as quick as lightning, disappearing in the crowds without leaving a trace and emerging at another place the next minute with loud howls and shrieks, to vent their spite afresh. They were present, moreover, at all collisions, aggravating the tumult, intensifying the confusion, exasperating the rage to the highest pitch by their wild shrieks. There remained only two-fifths, who consisted of those who were directly interested in the present afternoon: those who saw in the struggle an important political action, the members of the radical parties, the Socialists, the unemployed.... And those truly interested persons who had not been attracted by curiosity, the observing and thoughtful spectators to whom he himself belonged.

He had arrived at the south end of the place, half jostled, half pushed. Here the crowding was intense and the masses were steadily growing more excited.

It had just struck four o'clock: Auban saw the hands on Dent's clock. At the foot a violent collision took place. Two men, a Socialist leader and a radical member of parliament, undertook to gain admission by force. After a short hand-to-hand fight, they were overpowered and arrested.

Auban could not see anything but clubs and sticks swinging in the air, and uplifted arms....

He tried to go on, but met with difficulties. The mounted police continually flanked the way between the column and the monument of Charles I, in order to keep it clear. The masses, wedged in as they were, began to scatter in all directions: gathered into small groups, filled with fear, around the lantern posts; fled down Whitehall; or were pushed close against the lines of the police, by whom they were brutally driven away.

Auban waited until the riders had galloped by, and then reached one of the crossings where he felt secure beside the lantern post. But a constable drove away the crowd gathering here. "Move on, sir!" he commanded Auban too. But Auban looked calmly into the flushed face of the angry man, and pointed to the horses that again came storming towards him. "Where to?" he asked. "Must I let those horses ride over me or rush into the clubs of your men?" His calmness made an impression. When the street was again clear for half a minute, he safely reached the sidewalk in front of Morley's Hotel on the east side of the Square.

There he was suddenly seized by the arm. Before him stood an English acquaintance. His collar was torn, his hat soiled. He was in a state of the greatest excitement. After a few hasty questions back and forth, he said that the long procession from the south had also been dispersed.

While they—kept on the move by the police—held closely together in order not to be separated, and drifted to and fro with the crowd into which they were wedged, the Englishman said, with breathless haste:—

"We gathered at Rotherhithe: the radical and other societies and clubs of Rotherhithe, Bermondsey, etc., met on our way the Peckham Radical Club, the associations of Camberwell and Walworth, and in Westminster Bridge Road also those of St. Georges—it was an enormous procession, with numerous banners, music bands, adorned with green, accompanied by an endless mass of people on both sides, which in the best of order crossed the entirely vacant bridge of Westminster.

"As was agreed, we were to meet with the procession from Lambeth and Battersea in Bridge Street at Parliament House. Then we were to march in a straight line from south to north, up Whitehall, to this place. Just imagine: a single great procession of imposing length, representing the entire south of London, the entire section of the city on the other side of the Thames—from Woolwich and Greenwich to Battersea and Wandsworth!

"But our two processions had not joined each other, we had not reached Parliament Street, when the battle began. I was pretty far in the front ranks. Ah, the brutes, galloping on their horses into our ranks, breaking and tearing our flags, knocking down whatever comes in their way!"

"It was fortunate you did not get farther," Auban interrupted him, "for I have heard that the Life Guards were held in reserve in Whitehall. I am surprised that they are not yet here, for the situation is getting more serious."

"But we defended ourselves," exclaimed the other, "with my loaded cane I gave one—"

He did not finish his sentence. For a division of the police began to clear the sidewalk, dispersed the throng congregated there, and the next minute Auban was again alone. He was again near Morley's Hotel; the steps had just been cleared to the last man, but were again occupied with the rapidity of lightning. Auban secured an elected position....

From here the place and its surroundings could be easily overlooked, and presented a grand view. For four hours the multitude that surged round it had been steadily growing and seemed now to have reached the limit of its size as well as the culmination of its excitement. The windows and balconies of the neighboring houses were occupied to the last corner by the spectators of this wholly unusual and singular sight who followed every collision between police and the people with passionate interest and applauded the brutalities of the former. On the balconies of the club-houses lying opposite, the gilded youth of London indulged in the innocent pleasure, as Auban had observed before, of spitting on the "mob," against whose wrath they felt as secure in their high position as in a church....

In the south of the place, there where the masses surged through the wide bed of the streets like a wildly swollen stream, the situation seemed to grow more and more serious. Nevertheless, the traffic of omnibuses, often interrupted, went on. Crowded to overflowing, the heavy vehicles moved on step by step. Like ships they floated through the black human flood. On their tops stood excited men who gesticulated with their hands in the air, and improved the opportunity of saying at least a few sympathetic words to the multitude below. The horses and wheels made passages for swarms of people, who followed each vehicle like so many tails.

There Auban suddenly saw an extraordinary excitement, like an electric current, passing through the masses and coming nearer and nearer. Faster than before, they scattered in all directions, and louder and more frightened grew the cries and calls. What was it?

Horsemen appeared.

And:—

"The Life Guards!" exclaimed a hundred voices. The police seemed forgotten. All eyes hung on the shining cuirasses and the tufted helmets of the riders, who, about two hundred in number, slowly approached the Nelson Column, then turned to the right, and in quiet march proceeded on the way to the National Gallery, past the steps where Auban stood.

A man in civilian's dress rode at the head, between the commanding officers, a roll of paper in his hand.

And:—

"The Riots Act!" exclaimed again the voices. The representative of the magistrate of the city was received with loud cries.

"We are all good Englishmen and law-abiding citizens—we need no—" cried one.

"You damned fool, put away your paper—" another.

Just as the troops were passing the steps where Auban stood, he heard how the heavy tramp of the hoofs on the hard pavement was drowned by the cries of applause, the clapping of hands, the jubilant shouts of the surrounding crowds, and he distrusted his ears. Were these really signs of applause? It was not possible. It could only be mockery and scorn. But the exultation of the crowd at the unexpected spectacle of that glittering tin, that pompous procession, was so spontaneous, and so well calculated was the effect of the latter, that he could no longer doubt: the same people who but a minute before had covered the police, who clubbed them and rode rough-shod into them, with the hissing of their hate and the howl of their rage, now hailed with senseless pleasure those who had been sent to *shoot* them down!

At first Auban had incredulously shaken his head. Now he laughed, and a thought struck him. He gave a shrill whistle. And behold: round about him the whistle was taken up and carried along farther and farther, so that for a minute the clapping of applause was drowned by that sign of contempt. And Auban saw that now the same people whistled who before had shouted their applause.

Then he laughed. But his laughter soon gave way to the disgust that overcame in the contemplation of that irresponsible stupidity.

What foolish children! he thought. Just now cruelly chastised by brutal hands, they go into raptures—like the child over his doll—over the gay rags of that ridiculous outward show, without even suspecting the terrible meaning of the childish play!

As he resolved to escape that disgusting farce by leaving the steps and the place, the reinforcement of the Grenadier Guards came moving along on foot with crossed bayonets, everywhere scattering fear and wild dismay by their glittering steel; the steps were filled by a double number of terrified people, who at last—as it seemed—began to understand what the issue was, and that perhaps an accident might change this play by a turn of the hand into the most deadly earnest. But everything seemed to pass off with a threat. Calmly the troops passed several times round the outside of the Square. Only once, when Auban had already reached the north end at St. Martin's, he heard a terrible outcry of fear, drowning the dull roar and tumult, rise from the midst of the crowd, who were being driven before the steadily advancing column of bayonets occupying the entire width of the street.

What had happened? Had anybody been stabbed? Had a woman been crushed in the infinite throng? The excitement was tremendous. Now, at the approach of dusk, everybody seemed to be seized by the dizziness of fear, although only a few could make up their minds to leave the place.

Auban walked towards the Strand. For a long time the noise behind pursued him. He walked until he came to the end of the crowds who surged through the streets surrounding the Square in a wide circle, and where the usual bustle began. He longed after rest and seclusion. Therefore he went to the dining-room of one of the large English restaurants and sat there a long time.

Here on the snowy linen of the tables glittered the silver, and flowers exhaled their perfume, while the whole was reflected from the high mirrors on the walls. The guests, most of them in full evening dress, entered silently and took their places with dignity, conscious of the importance of the moment which they devoted to the study of the menus. With inaudible steps the waiters passed over the heavily carpeted floor. Nothing was to be heard in this lofty, aristocratic room with its subdued colors, but the low clatter of plates and knives, the rustle of silken trains, and occasionally a soft, melodious laugh which interrupted the conversation carried on in low tones....

Auban dined as simply as ever, only better and at a tenfold price which he paid for his presence in these rooms. And while he observed the diners, he involuntarily compared their confident, easy, elegant, but monotonous and uncharacteristic appearance with the forms out of whose midst he had come: the heavy, rude forms of the people whom hunger and privation had crushed and often disfigured until they could no longer be recognized....

When after an hour's rest he again took the direction of Trafalgar Square, he happened to pass the doors of Charing Cross Hospital. The entrance, as well as the whole street, on which the hospital lay, was densely crowded: here the broken limbs were again set and the gashed heads mended, which had resulted from the conflict on the neighboring battlefield.

The spectacle was at once serious and comical: here, supported by two others, a man came tottering along, whose face was covered with blood streaming from an open wound on his forehead; there a man came out of the door, his wounds just dressed, his one arm in a sling, but still holding in the other his broken wind-instrument. Here a policeman limped along who had fallen down with his horse; and there a man who had fainted was carried on a stretcher.

Auban came closer and looked round in the hall of the hospital. Along the walls the enemies were peaceably sitting together, some with their wounds already dressed, others waiting until one of the assistants, driven with work, should take pity on them.

"So far, we have not met with any very serious injuries," said one of the bystanders.

What a comedy! thought Auban. First they crack each other's skulls, then they let the same hand mend them—an innocent pastime. *Pack schlägt sich, Pack verträgt sich.*

And he walked on, forcing his way with great difficulty through the curious throng at the entrance, attracted, as it were, by the fresh blood, and who made way only for the wounded.

When he had again reached the Strand, a screaming and unusually large crowd came rushing towards him and forced him to stop. The police were now driving the multitude far into the side streets....

Nevertheless, he did not wish to turn back now, when the wings of the evening were already spread over the earth, without having cast another glance at the spectacle, which must have assumed an entirely different character in the twilight.

So he wanted to try to reach the Square from the south; and in front of Charing Cross Station he turned on the left into Villiers Street, leading to the Thames. Then he passed through the tunnel under the railroad station. Just five weeks ago—on a Saturday evening in October, wet and cold as the present one—coming from the other side of the Thames he had passed through it, and, agitated by the sad memories of former experiences, fled from it the last time. Today he had no time for memories.

He hurried on. When he stood in Northumberland Avenue, that street of palaces, he saw that ever fresh enforcements were sent to the Square from Scotland Yard, the headquarters of the police. He took the same road.

Evening in the Square presented a changed aspect: the Nelson Column rose like the giant forefinger of a giant hand threateningly into the darkness; on the right lay the enormous rotunda of the Grand Hotel with its illuminated windows, behind which the curiosity-seekers had not yet disappeared; silent was the inner surface of the place, still occupied by the police; and in the streets round about still raged the struggle, which with the falling darkness seemed to grow more intense the nearer it approached its end....

The countless lights of the lanterns flashed and illumined with their trembling rays the dark masses who surged wildly past them in feverish haste.

The Life Guards were still riding up and down the streets in troops. Flooded by the light, their uniforms, their armor, their white pantaloons and red coats, glittered in the darkness.

The attacks of the police, especially the mounted police, had become more and more insolent, brutal, and unjustifiable. Riding into the densest crowds at full speed, they trampled upon all who could not escape quickly enough, using their clubs against the falling and those lying on the ground, indifferent where they struck, on the arms, the shoulders, or the heads of the defenceless. In an instant, the places where just now not a stone could have fallen on the ground, were strewn with rags and tatters, crushed hats, broken canes.

Notwithstanding the exhaustion of both parties was unmistakable, all seemed doubly embittered. Now that nothing could be clearly distinguished, the cries sounded more beastly than before.

Whichever way he turned, Auban saw scenes that made his blood boil.

He stood, unable to move, in a crowd petrified by fear, at the very front; an old man sought refuge with him. His white hair was stained with blood. One of the riders pursued him, again and again beating him with his club. Auban rushed forward, but he could not help, for he was carried along by those following him with such violence that he himself felt as if he were falling; the police had come riding up on the other side and put everything into commotion.

At the entrance of Charing Cross he could at last get a firm footing once more. The riders turned round and madly galloped back. Auban mounted some steps.

"London has not witnessed such scenes since the days of the Chartists!" exclaimed an elderly gentleman beside him.

"The Prince of Wales made the bloodhounds drunk with brandy, so that they would kill us!" screamed a woman.

And it really seemed to be so. But not only the police were drunk, but also the people, drunk with rage and hate.

AT THE ENTRANCE OF the same street where Auban stood, not far from the Grand Hotel, a new crowd was gathering, clearly determined to offer resistance and keeping close together in obedience to the instinct of a common interest. A new division of the police, on foot, came moving on apace. A mad hand-to-hand fight followed. Stones flew through the air, window-panes crashed, the wrestling of the combatants was heard and the dull thud of the canes, screams, and low mutterings.

The police were on the point of retreating. But already the mounted ranks arrived at full speed, and the struggle was decided. The fleeing crowd was driven far into Charing Cross. Again Auban was irresistibly carried away.

The sparks which the galloping horses struck on the pavement glittered in the darkness.

Thus the noise and the conflicts would continue to rage for another hour, at most two, and then subside; and then the battle, fought out along the whole line in favor of authority, would be brought to an end, and the right of free speech on Trafalgar Square lost to the people forever, for a long time....

Before Auban left the Square, he once more, with a long look, fixed in his mind the picture of this spectacle, which he would never forget. Once more his ears and his eyes, both tired, drank in the dark expanse of the place, the black sea of humanity, the rush and roar of its tides, the dazzling lights, the thousand tones of passion consolidated into one; and no longer ridiculous, but almost terrible was the howl which seemed to come from a single throat.

Auban fled. He longed for rest. He longed for a struggle, different from this one in which he had participated in its early days as passionately as anyone, for a struggle about whose success there was no doubt, because it would have to be relentless, in which other forces were to be tested than those which had today wrestled together in play, as if to make each other's acquaintance.

As he entered the carriage which was to take him to his quiet room, he heard the shrill voices of the newsboys offering for sale the evening papers, which contained descriptions of what he had seen in the afternoon.

CHAPTER X.
ANARCHY

WEEKS PASSED.

The "bloody Sunday" on Trafalgar Square no longer excited people to passionate discussions. On the following Sunday, indeed, a company of patriotic volunteers had come to offer their support to the police, but after they had been exposed a few hours in the Square to the scorn and ridicule of the curious crowd, who made no attempt at reconquering a lost right, they had to return home, drenched by the rain, and without having swung their newly turned clubs.

After the grand spectacle, the comedy of voluntary self-abasement; after the "bloody Sunday" the "laughing-stocks"!

The Square was and remained empty.

THE QUESTION OF THE "unemployed" was of course not solved, but it had been pushed into the background, and no longer cried for an answer in the shrill tones of hunger.

IN CHICAGO THE CORPSES of the murdered men had been followed to their graves by an unparalleled outpouring of the population. It looked like a wish to atone for a wrong.

THE TIME OF GREAT events had passed. Everything had taken again its usual course.

The days had grown more chilly and damp as the month approached its end.

Auban had not again seen Trupp, nor any of his other friends. Only Dr. Hurt had occasionally called on him, to "warm his feet" and smoke his pipe. They approached each other spiritually more and more closely, and understood each other better and better.

The Sunday afternoon gatherings seemed not only interrupted, but to have been suspended altogether. Nor did Auban think of reviving them. He was now convinced of their uselessness.

The clubs, too, he had not again attended since the evening of his talk with Trupp. And the greatest change in his life—he had also given up his walks through the districts of hunger.

He had much to do. He began now with the work of his life, compared with which all that he had previously done was only preparation.

For himself he had at this time won a little victory.

The management of the French compilation, to assist in which he had been called to London three years ago, had gradually passed into his hands. Thanks to his conscientiousness, circumspection, and independence, the enterprise, which was now approaching its completion, had been attended by brilliant success. Although he had become indispensable to the publishing firm, one of the greatest in England, they had failed to adequately reward his services and but slightly raised his salary.

He had waited long for the voluntary fulfilment of that duty. He waited until he held all the trumps in his hands. Then he turned them up one day, and handed in his resignation, to take effect by the end of the year.

A long interview followed with the two members of the firm. At the outbreak of their moral indignation at the breach of the contract which had not been entered into by Auban, either in writing or by any word of his, but by them, as they claimed, only in "good faith," Auban had begged of them to put all sentimentality aside in a business transaction. Then he demonstrated to them by the use of figures that the only service they had rendered in the publication of the work consisted in furnishing the capital, but that that service had been so profitable as to give them four-fifths of the product of his labor.

Then, when he was asked to remain a quarter of a year longer, till the preliminary completion of the work, he made his demands: first, his monthly salary to be increased threefold.

"Never had they paid any of their employees such a salary—"

"Never, surely, had any of their employees rendered them such services—"

Further—and that was Auban's principal move by which he hoped in a degree at least to secure his future—a share of the profit of each edition of the work.

"Was ever such a demand made?"

"That was immaterial to him. It was in their power to accept or reject it."

They did the former.

Finally, Auban's third demand: a compensation, in proportion to the success of his labor, for services hitherto performed, payable at once.

"That looks damnably like blackmail."

"They might call it what they pleased. He had learned of them. Were they surprised? Did they not also force down the wages of their workingmen as far as possible? He would resist, and in his turn force them—"

When he had gone, the partners gnashed their teeth. But as shrewd businessmen they tacitly admitted that they had never respected Auban more than at that moment....

Auban submitted the contract, which both parties had drawn up, to one of the best lawyers, for examination and approval, before he signed it and bound himself for three months.

Then he was free for some time; and never had he felt so clearly how necessary pecuniary independence was for what he now wished to do....

A quarter of a year, and he was in a position to return to Paris. To Paris! His heart beat faster at the thought.

He loved London and admired it, that wonderful, immense London, and he loved Paris. But he loved it differently....

London began to weigh heavy on him with its eternally gray sky, its pale fog, its gloomy darkness.

A sun rose. And that sun was Paris. Soon he would again bask in its rays, which were so warm, so animating, so beautiful!

The piles of papers and pamphlets on Chicago had disappeared from Auban's writing-desk, and it was covered by new works, which filled his few free hours.

He was clear concerning what he wanted.

He stood alone: none of his numerous friends had gone with him in the latter years; none had been able to draw the last conclusions.

So he had to leave them behind—he who had restlessly advanced towards liberty.

But he had formed new connections, and ever and anon he cast his glances towards America, where a small but steadily and surely increasing company of excellent men had already been engaged for years in the task which in the Old World had not yet been begun.

It was becoming urgent to begin it here too.

Two circumstances aggravated the difficulties in the way of the spread of the idea of Anarchy in Europe:—

Either people regarded every Anarchist as a dynamiter; or, if they had cast a glance at the philosophy of the new party, as a Communist.

While in America already some rays of light had begun to enter the dull eyes of prejudice and bias, all were still veiled in Europe.

It was necessary, above all, to newly examine, understand, and explain the misapprehended meaning of the word.

Those who accepted everything as it was offered them, and who saw in Anarchy only chaos, and in the Anarchist only the violent revolutionist, had to be taught that Anarchy was, on the contrary, the goal of human development, and designated that condition of society in which the liberty of the individual and his labor constitutes the guarantee alike of his welfare and that of mankind.

And those who rightly did not believe in the ideal of liberty in fraternal Communism, had to be shown that Anarchy, far from seeing liberty in Communism and sacrifice, sought, on the contrary, to realize it by the removal of definite forcible obstructions and artificial barriers. Then after this first crude and ungrateful preliminary work had been accomplished and after the perception had gained ground, even if at first only among the few, that Anarchy is not a heaven on earth and that men need only to understand their true nature and its needs, and not to "fundamentally change it," in order to make liberty possible, the next task would consist in designating the institution of the State as the greatest and only obstacle in the path of human civilization.

It was necessary to show: that the State is privileged force, and that it is force which supports it; that it is the State which changes the harmony of nature into the confusion of force; that it is its crimes which create the crimes; that it grants unnatural privileges here, while it denies natural rights there; that it paralyzes the competitive evolution of forces in all domains, stifles trade, and thus undermines the welfare of the whole people; that it represents mediocrity in all things, and that everything which it undertakes to do could be done far better, more satisfactorily, and more profitably without it if left to the free competition of private men; that a nation is the richer and happier the less it is governed; that far from constituting the expression of the will of the whole people, the State is rather only the will of those who stand at its head, and that those who stand at the head do indeed always look out for themselves and "their own," but never for those who are foolish enough to entrust them with their cares; that the State can only give what it has first taken, because it is unproductive, and that it always gives back less than it received—in short, it was necessary to show that, taken all in all, it is nothing but one immense, continued, shameless trick, by means of which the few live at the expense of the many, be its name what it will....

Then, after the faith in the infallible idol of the State had thus been shaken with regard to some points, and the spirit of self-reliance correspondingly strengthened, the laws dominating social economy had to be studied. The truth had to be established that the interests of men are not hostile to each other, but harmonious, if only granted free rein for their development.

The liberty of labor—realized by the fall of the State, which can no longer monopolize money, limit credit, withhold capital, obstruct the circulation of values, in a word, no longer control the affairs of the individual—when this had become a fact, the sun of Anarchy had risen.

Its blessings—they would be felt like warmth after the long night of cold and want....

But nothing ought to be promised. Only those who did not know what they wanted made promises. It was necessary to convince, not to persuade.

That required different talents from those of the flowing tongue which persuades the masses to act against their will instead of leaving the choice of his decisions to the individual and trusting to his reason.

All knowledge would have to be drawn upon in order to demonstrate the theory of the newly awakening creed: history, in order to avoid the mistakes of the past in the future; psychology, in order to understand how the soul is subject to the conditions prescribed by the body; philosophy, in order to show how all thought proceeds only from the individual, to whom it must return....

After everything had thus been done, in order to demonstrate the liberty of the individual as the culmination of human development, one task remained.

Not only had the ends and aims to be shown: the best and surest ways had also to be pointed out along which they were to be achieved. Regarding authority as the greatest enemy, it was necessary to destroy authority. In what way?

This also was found. Superior as the State was in all the appliances of power and armed to the teeth, there could be no idea of challenging it to a combat. It would have been decided before it had yet been begun. No; that monster which feeds and lives on our blood had to be starved by denying it the tribute which it claimed as a matter of course. It had to die of exhaustion, starve—slowly, indeed, to be sure, but surely. It still had the power and the prestige to claim its booty, or to destroy those who should resist. But some day it would encounter a number of men, cool-headed, calm, intrepid men, who with folded arms would beat back its attack with the question: What do you want of us? We want nothing of you. We deny you all obedience. Let those support you who need you. But leave us in peace!

On that day liberty would win its first victory, a bloodless victory, whose glory would travel round the earth with the velocity of the storm and everywhere call out the voice of reason in response.

What else were the strikes before which the exploiters trembled than passive resistance? Was it not possible for the workingmen to gain victories by means of them? Victories for which they would have to wait in vain if they continued to trust in the perfidious game of political jugglers!

Hitherto, in the history of the century resorted to only in individual cases here and there, and only temporarily for the purpose of certain political demands, passive resistance, locally applied as against the government—principally in the form of resistance to taxation—would some day constitute the presented bayonet against which the State would bleed to death.

But until then?

Until then it was necessary to watch and to wait.

There was no other way in which finally to reach the goal, but that of calm, unwearied, sure enlightenment, and that of individual example, which would some day work wonders.

THUS IN ITS ENTIRE outline lay before Auban the work to which he decided to dedicate his life. He did not overestimate his strength. But he trusted in it. For it had led him through the errors of his youth. Consequently it could be no common strength.

He was still alone. Soon he would have friends and comrades. Already an individualistic Anarchistic movement was noticeable among the Communists of Paris, championing private property.

The first numbers of a new periodical—founded evidently with slender means—had just come to him, which gave brilliant proof of the intelligence prevailing in certain labor circles of his native country. The "*Autonomie individuelle*" had extricated itself from Communism, and was now attacked as much by it as formerly by the Social Democrats. Auban became absorbed in the reading of the few papers which were imbued with a spirit of liberty that enchanted him....

A knock at the door interrupted him.

A letter was handed to him. It asked of him the favor of a *rendez-vous* that very evening, and bore no signature. At first Auban wanted to throw it aside But after reading it a second time his face assumed a more thoughtful expression. There must have been something in the style of the letter that changed his decision, for he looked at his watch and studied the large map of London that hung on the wall.

BY THE UNDERGROUND railroad he rode over Blackfriars from King's Cross to London Bridge. He had to change cars, and was delayed in consequence. Nevertheless, he arrived at the street and the appointed house before the time set. When he knocked at the closed door, it was at once opened.

Auban did not need to mention the name which had been told him. It died on his lips in an involuntary exclamation of recognition and fright when he saw the man who opened the door for him. Before him stood a man who had been one of the most feted and celebrated personalities in the revolutionary movement of Europe, but whose name was now mentioned by most people only with hate and contempt. Auban would have sooner expected to see anybody else than this man who received him silently and now led him silently up stairs into a small, low room.

There, by the only window, they stood opposite each other, and Auban's recognition yielded to a feeling of deepest agitation when he saw what the few years during which he had not seen him had made of his former acquaintance. Then his figure had been erect and proud; now he stood before him as if staggering under the burden of a terrible fate. Not yet thirty-five, his hair was as gray as that of a man of fifty; once his smile had been so confident and compelling that no one could resist it; today it was sad and painful when he saw how little Auban could conceal his fright and his agitation in consequence of his changed looks.

Then, as if he feared the walls might hear him, Auban called him by his real name, that name once so popular, now almost forgotten.

"Yes, it is I," said the other, and the sad smile did not disappear from his lips. "You would not have known me again, Auban?"

Auban shook off his excitement with an effort.

"Where have you come from? Do you not know—"

"Yes, I know; they are everywhere at my heels, even here in England. In France they would extradite me, and in Germany bury me for life, if they had me. Here also I am not safe. But I had to come here once more before I disappear forever. You know why—"

Certainly, Auban knew. On this man lay the terrible suspicion of having betrayed a comrade. How much, how little truth there was in that suspicion, Auban could not determine. It had first been uttered by Social Democrats. But so many wilful lies concerning the Communists had originated from that source, that this one, too, might have been made of whole cloth. Then it had been repeated by a hostile faction in his own camp. The accused had now replied. But whether he would not or could not: in short, in spite of many words, the matter was never fully cleared up. But it was altogether impossible to do it in public; too many things had to be suppressed lest the enemy should hear them, too many names had to remain unmentioned, too many relations untouched which ought to have been thoroughly discussed, to allow the accused the hope of ever again rehabilitating himself in the eyes of all.

Such was the curse of the slavery with which a false policy bound one to the other, so that no one could turn and move as he liked.

Although he was attacked on all sides, he could still have continued his work among the old circle of comrades, if he had not himself become wavering. Then one day he burned all the bridges behind him and disappeared. His name was forgotten; what he had done was forgotten, after his great influence, which had been fascinating where it had made itself felt, had disappeared with his person.

Auban knew it, and said, therefore:—

"Your trip was useless?"

"Yes," was the reply, and his voice gloomy as his eyes, "it was useless."

Completely broken down, he dropped his head as he continued in a lower voice, as if he were ashamed alike of his return and his cowardice:—

"I could not stand it any longer. I was alone two years. Then I decided to return and make a last attempt to justify myself. They do not believe me. No one believes me...."

"Then believe in yourself!" said Auban, firmly.

"Today I thought of you. They spoke to me of you. They criticised you for going your own ways. And, indeed, you are the only one who has preserved his freedom in the confusion. 1 thank you for having come."

He looked exhausted, as if those few words had tired him. Three years ago he had been a brilliant speaker, who could talk for three hours without showing a sign of fatigue.

Auban was deeply agitated. He would gladly have told him that he believed him. But how could he without becoming dishonest? The whole affair had remained almost unknown to him, as much as he had heard of it. The other seemed to feel it.

"I should have to tell you the whole story to enable you to pass a judgment. But that would require hours, and perhaps it would be useless nevertheless. Only so much, and this you may believe: I made a mistake, but I am innocent of the crime with which I am charged. Besides, I neglected to do many things in my defence that I ought to have done immediately. Now it is too late."

He looked at his watch.

"Yes, it would require hours, and I have not half an hour to spare. I am going away today."

"Where?" asked Auban.

"First, up the Thames with a boat. And then,"—sadly smiling, he made a motion with his hand in space—"and then farther—anywhere—"

He took a little valise which lay packed beside him.

"I have nothing to do here; let us go, Auban. Accompany me to the bridge, if it is not out of your way."

They left the room and the house without anyone looking after them. They walked silently as far as London Bridge.

But as they were crossing the bridge, the pent-up anger of the outcast broke forth.

"I gave all I had to the cause: the whole of my youth and half my life. After taking everything from me, it left me nothing, not even the belief in itself."

"Half your life still remains in which to win back in its stead the belief in yourself, the only belief that has no disappointments."

But the other shook his head.

"Look at me; I am no longer what I was. I have defied all persecutions, hunger, hate, imprisonment, death; but to be driven away like a mad dog by those whom I loved more than myself, is more than I can endure. Ah, I am so weary!—so weary!—so weary!"

He entered one of the resting-places of the bridge, and dropped on a bench, while the human stream rushed on. Auban sat down beside him. The tone in which the unfortunate man repeated the last words agitated him anew to his very depths. And while the grandiose life behind them was sweeping over the bridge, he talked to him, in order to give him time to collect himself, of his own sad experiences and lessons, and how his strength was nevertheless unshaken and his courage undaunted since he had found himself again and—standing on his own feet—doing and letting as he pleased—not dependent on any party, any clique, any school—no longer allowed anyone to interfere with his own life.

But the other sat indifferent. He shook his head and looked before him.

Suddenly he sprang up, seized his baggage, pointed to the chaos of ships, and muttered a few incomprehensible words.

Then, before Auban could reply to him, he vehemently embraced him and hurried away, making a sign with his hand that he did not wish to be accompanied any further....

Auban looked after him a long time.

Sacrifice upon sacrifice, and all in vain, he thought. For a long time he saw before him the aged face and the gray hair of the persecuted man, who—a restless wanderer—was facing a strange world, without strength and without courage to continue a life that had deceived him.

THE EVENING BEGAN.

The sun went down.

Two immense human streams surged across London Bridge; back and forth rolled, rattling and resounding, two unbroken lines of vehicles.

The black waters of the Thames flowed lazily.

Auban stood against the railing of the bridge, and, facing the east, contemplated the grand picture which presented itself. Everywhere, on both sides of the stream, towers, pillars, chimney-stacks, church steeples rose above the sea of houses.... But beneath him a forest of masts, poles, sails.... On the left Billingsgate, the great, famous fish-market of London.... Farther, where the four towers rise, the dark, dismal structure of the Tower. With a reddish glare the setting sun, the pale, weary sun of London, lay on its windows a few minutes; then also its light was suddenly extinguished, and a gray twilight drew its streaks around the dark masses of the warehouses, the giant bodies of the ships, the pillars of the bridge....

By the clock on the Adelaide Buildings it was already seven, but still the task of unloading the great ocean steamer at Auban's feet was not yet completed. Long lines of strong men carried boxes and bales over wavering wooden bridges to the shore. Their foreheads, heads, and necks protected against the crushing pressure of their heavy burdens by strangely shaped cushions, they looked like oxen in the yoke as they staggered along under their weight....

A strange feeling crept over Auban. Such was London, immense London, which covers seven hundred miles with its five millions of human beings; such was London, where a man was born every fifth minute, where one died every eighth.... Such was London, which grew and grew, and already immeasurable, seemed to aspire to the infinite....

Immense city! Sphinx-like, it stretched on both sides of the river, and the clouds of smoke, vapor, noise it belched forth, lay like veils over its panting body....

Lights after lights began to flash and mingled the warmth of their glow with the dampness of the fog. Their reddish reflections trembled through the twilight.

London Bridge thundered and resounded under the burdens it bore.

Thus day after day, week after week, year after year, raged that mighty life which never grew tired. The beatings of its heart grew ever more feverish, the deeds of its arms ever mightier, the plans of its brain ever bolder.

When would it reach the summit of its aspirations? When would it rest?

Was it immortal?

Or was it also threatened by destruction?

And again Auban saw them approaching, the clouds of ruin which would send the lightning that would ignite this mass of inflammable material.

London, even you are not immortal.... You are great. But time is greater.... It grew darker and darker....

Then he turned towards the north, and as he was walking along with his heavy, long strides, supported by his cane, many a passer-by looked after the tall, thin, proud form, round which swung his loose cloak.

AND AS AUBAN CROSSED street after street, and came nearer and nearer to his dwelling, he had already overcome the agitation of the last hours, and once more the wings of his thoughts circled restlessly around the longed-for light of liberty.

What was still resting in the womb of time as a germ but just fructified—how would it develop, and what shape would it take?

Of one thing he was certain.

Without pain it was to take place, this birth of a new world, if it was to live.

The social question was an economic question.

So, and in no other way, it could be solved:

With the decline of State authority the individual becomes more and more self-reliant. Escaping from the leading-strings of paternalism, he acquires the independence of his own wishes and deeds. Claiming the right of self-determination without restriction, he aims first at making null and void all past privileges. Nothing was to be left of them but an enormous heap of mouldering paper. Land left vacant and no longer recognized as the property of those who do not live on it, is used by subsequent occupants. Hitherto uncultivated, it now bears fruit and grain and nourishes abundantly a free people. Capital, incapable of any longer fattening on the sweat of others, labor, is compelled to consume itself: although it still supports the father and the son without obligating them to turn a hand, the grandson is already confronted with the alternative of starving or disgracing the "glory of his fathers" by working. For the disappearance of all privileges entails on the individual the duty of responsibility. Will it be a heavier burden for him than the thousand duties towards others with which hitherto the State saddled its citizens, the Church its members, morality the righteous?

There was but one solution of the social question, but one: no longer to keep one's self in mutual dependence, to open for one's self and thereby for others the way to independence; no longer to make the ridiculous claim of the strong, "Become weak!" no, to exhort the weak at last, "Become strong!" no longer to trust in the help "from above," but at last to rely on one's own exertions.

The nineteenth century has deposed "our Father in Heaven." It no longer believes in a divine power to which it is subject.

But only the children of the twentieth century would be the real atheists: doubters of divine omnipotence, they had to begin to test the justification of all human authority by the relentless criticism of their reason.

They would be imbued with the consciousness of their own dignity. Instead of seeking their pride as hitherto in subjection, humility, devotion, they would regard command as presumption, obedience as sacrifice, and each as a dishonor which the free man despises....

The race, crippled in uniforms, might require a long time to regain its natural growth and the erect carriage of pride.

Auban was no dreamer. By raising the demands of liberty, he did not ask of time their immediate realization. The great changes of the social organs would probably require centuries before they would attain to the normal condition of equal opportunities for all.

The development towards liberty would last the longer, the more powerful and triumphant the great opposition current of authority would become.

Violence would everywhere retard the peaceable cause of development. It was inevitable. Hate, blindness, want of confidence, were too intense on both sides to make impossible collisions such as would make the earth tremble in terror.

The nature of things must have its course.

The logic of events neutralized the wish for the impossible.

Ever and ever the follies must pay their tribute to experience before it will rise to the surface.

Socialism was the last general stupidity of mankind. This last station of suffering on the way to liberty had to be passed.

Not until then could the God of illusion be nailed to the cross.

Not until all faith lay strangled on the ground and no longer lent wings to any hope—to scale the heavens—not until then had the time come for the true "kingdom on earth": the kingdom of happiness, of joy and exuberant life, which was liberty....

But liberty had also a powerful ally: the dissensions in the camp of its enemies.

Everywhere divisions; everywhere unrest; everywhere fear; and everywhere the cry for more authority! Authority, authority!—it was to cure all evils. And the armies sprang from the earth, the nations were armed to the teeth, and dread of the bloody future frightened sleep from the eyes of the seeing.

The rulers no longer knew what to do. Like that general of antiquity, they ordered the sea to be lashed which flooded the deck with its billows and threatened to drown all on board.

Wars in whose streams of blood the holders of power would attempt to extinguish the flames of popular revolt were inevitable, such as the world had never seen....

Crime and injustice had been piled too high, and terrible would be the revenge!

Then, after the chaos of the revolutions and the slaughter of the battles, when the desolated earth had crumbled together from exhaustion, when the bitterest experience had destroyed the last faith in authority, then, perhaps, would be understood who they were and what they wanted, they, the lone ones, who in the confusion round about them trusted in liberty, calm and composed, which they called by the name: Anarchy!

How it surged and roared, that London! How its pulses beat faster and faster with the approach of night! What signified those thousand-fold voices?

Farther and farther had Auban gone, till he reached his dwelling.

Now he was again in the secluded stillness of his room, which he had left only a few hours ago.

The fire still glowed in the fireplace.

But before he again took up his work, he moved up a chair and sat a short time, his hands stretched towards the warmth, and, bent forwards, gazing into the glow.

A great, almost overpowering joy, such as he had never felt before, filled him.

The walls of his room, the fogs of London, the darkness of the evening—everything disappeared before the picture which he saw:

A long night has passed.

Slowly the sun rises above the sleeping house-tops and the resting fields.

A solitary wanderer passes through the expanse.

The dew of the night still trembles on the grasses at the edge of the road. In the woods on the hillsides the first voices of the birds are heard. Above the summit of the mountains soars the first eagle.

The wanderer walks alone. But he does not feel lonely. The chaste freshness of nature communicates itself to him.

He feels: it is the morning of a new day.

Then he meets another wanderer. And another. And they understand each other by their looks as they pass each other.

The light rises and rises.

And the early morning walker opens wide his arms and salutes it with the liberating cry of joy....

So was Auban.

The early morning walker at the break of the new day was he.

After a long night of error and illusion, he walked through a morning of light.

The sun of truth had risen for him, and rose higher and higher.

Ages had to pass before the idea of Anarchy could arise.

All the forms of slavery had to be passed through. Ever seeking liberty only to find the same despotism in the changed forms, so had the people staggered.

Now was the truth found to condemn all forms which were force. Authority began to yield.

The wild chase was approaching its end.

But still it was necessary to battle, to battle, to battle—not to grow tired and never to despair!

The issue was not one of transitory aims. The happiness of liberty which was to be conquered was imperishable.

Like the wanderer was Auban.

And like the early morning walker he also opened his arms, saluted the future with the cry of joy, and called it by the immortal name: Anarchy!

Then he took up his work.

Upon his thin, hard features lay a calm, magnanimous, confident smile.

It was the smile of invincibility.

Appendix

John Henry Mackay

AMONG THE MODERN POETS with a marked personality, John Henry Mackay undoubtedly occupies a conspicuous place. Surely the task of tracing the development of this poet-individuality is not without charm. The personal life, which in all cases reacts powerfully on a man's works, can here indeed hardly be touched upon, and I can consequently offer no plastic, but only a reflex, picture.

With a few exceptions, Mackay's poems so far have been so entirely lyrical, so entirely the expression of an inner mood, and so little addressed to the public, that they can be understood and appreciated only in their ensemble. To be delighted by rare beauty, surprised by original and saving ideas, one must allow his thought and soul-life to absorb him seriously and without prejudice. This is especially true of Mackay's latest and, for the general reading public, most incomprehensible book *Das starke Jahr* (*The Strong Year*). The following study is chiefly meant to serve as an introduction to the spirit of this remarkable collection of poems.

John Henry Mackay was born on the 6th of February 1864, at Greenock, in Scotland. After the death of his father, his mother, a Hamburg lady, returned to Germany with her three-year-old boy. He was given a German collegiate education, which inflamed his inherited British and Hamburgian spirit of independence to such angry rebellion that it gave rise to the precious series of songs, "*Moderne Jugend*" ("*Modern Youth*").

Studies in Leipzig, a sojourn in Berlin, travels in Scotland, England, Spain, and France, gave the young man a general idea of the contemporary state of European civilization. Now Mackay lives mostly in Zurich.

It is characteristic of the poet that birth and conditions made a cosmopolitan of him long before he declared himself one on principle. On what country, indeed, should he bestow his patriotic sentiments? He belongs to that class of men who are foreigners everywhere. Notwithstanding his extraction and his name, he cannot be classed with the English singers. Despite his perfect mastery of our language, he is in a certain sense also not a German poet. To explain this statement, it is sufficient to point, in contrast to him, to Bleibtreu and Wildenbruch. In their excellence and failings these are genuine Germans; with all their differences they are one in their enthusiasm for the spirit of nationalism. This element is wholly foreign to Mackay; yes, he is directly hostile to it. At a time when the spirit of patriotism dominates public opinion, we shall have to look to this circumstance for one of the reasons that will, for a long time to come, prevent the recognition of Mackay among the better class of people.

That the poet, however, is not without a great measure of warm love for his native land, for the soil on which the child first enjoyed the sun, the air, and worldly beauty, he has demonstrated by his first work, "*Die Kinder des Hochlands, eine Geschichte aus Schottlands Bergen*" ("*The Children of the Highlands; a Story of the Mountains of Scotland*"). Mackay also paid a delicate tribute of youthful gratitude to our classics for the fructification of his poetical genius in a small volume of "*Thüringer Lieder*" ("*Thuringian Songs*").

In Ilmenau he finds a melodious echo of the immortal strain: "*Ueber allen Gipfeln ist Ruh.*" And with a sense of power native to him also, he leaves the places dedicated to the memory of past greatness with the exclamation:—

> ...Doch ich trage voll von Hoffen
> Eine Welt in mir mit fort.

All honor to the enthusiasm for Goethe and Schiller; to English poets—Byron, Shelley, Swinburne—Mackay seems to be still more indebted for the form of expression.

His own world is first opened to us in the *Dichtungen* (*Poems*), published in 1886.

A charming, youthful world!

Aside from a number of pictures of life seized with the intuition of the genuine poet ("*Unschuldig verurteilt,*" ["Innocently Condemned",] "Martha," and "*Einsames Sterben,*" ["Lonely Dying"]), the book depicts the natural feelings of a youth just past boyhood. The love-songs bear the unmistakable stamp of the alike visionary and transitory inclinations of the young student. The poem "*Glückliche Fahrt*" ("Happy Journey") describes the pain of the mother on the departure of her son into the world. The feelings of a mother's heart in this heavy hour are expressed with such tender truth that one is led to infer a specially intimate relation existing between mother and son. Is it the unconsciously exhaled, the unconsciously inhaled influence of a filially loved woman which later gave the man the power of noble form, the pure feeling which Mackay always manifests when he treats of the most difficult themes with free inspiration?

In the *Dichtungen* all the qualities of his individuality are already to be found: the inclination to the crass, the weird, the passionately fanatical hatred of all tyrannical power, and coupled with it a deep soul-life, a love for nature which tracks its most hidden beauties, a power which knows how to reflect the finest shades of that indefinable something which we call mood. Above all, Mackay possesses feeling and language for human suffering which give him a place beside the greatest singers of the world's woe.

But all this is so far only indicated, just as one recognizes the features of the grown-up man in an old photograph of a child.

The *Dichtungen* do not yet contain anything that good fathers and mothers, cultured aunts, and loyal citizens could not pardon to a fiery and aspiring young talent. The lightnings play in it, but the storm may yet turn into a gentle, beneficent country rain.

The mutterings of the thunder become more ominous in the social poem, "*Arma parata fero*," which appeared in 1887. It is quite likely that it cost Mackay many a friend and patron. There indeed flames a kindling force in the melodious verses which far surpasses anything that the poet has hitherto accomplished; but for that very reason they are also doubly dangerous.

With this song he takes up the weapons, not again to lay them down; he becomes a clear-headed champion of the rights of the oppressed; he calls himself the spokesman of liberty.

Between the works reviewed, to which are to be added an attempt at a tragedy, "Anna Hermadorf," and the novelistic studies "*Schatten*" ("Shadows"), and Mackay's later works lies an important period. Evidently we are here in the presence of one of those mysterious turning-points which occur in the development of every superior mind, and in which such abrupt changes seem to take place within it as in the verdure of the earth after certain moist, warm spring nights. Indeed, if everything becomes suddenly green, it is because the buds were ready to burst. In the year 1888 Mackay published, through Baumert and Ronge, in Grossenhain and Leipzig, a collection of novels, *Moderne Stoffe* (*Modern Themes*), and a second volume of poems. The latter he called *Fortgang*. At the same time two books appeared at Schabelitz's in Zurich, anonymously, *Helene* and *Sturm* (*Storm*). John Henry Mackay very soon confessed himself the author.

Here we see an astonishingly rich harvest, which seems impossible to have ripened in a single year. Those must have been high-water marks of life, of creative power!

The four books belong together, although each one is in form an independent whole.

The promise, *Arma parata fero!* is kept.

What confusedly dawns on others from distant realms, stands before the clairvoyant eye of the prophet in clear, proximate reality. And he measures the present by the ideal of a liberty-illumined future. He dares see that which men must live, and is stronger than the Schillerian youth before the picture of Sais. The sight of truth has not paralyzed him. He finds powerful words to proclaim to all the world that one-half of mankind must suffer that the rest may enjoy, in order to arouse from lazy indulgence and dull resignation, to terrify and to encourage.

Characteristic of this epoch is the epilogue with which "Fortgang" closes:

"Freudig kämpfend bis zum Ziele!"
Freund, das sind ja Worte nur.
Nicht mit leeren Tönen spiele,
Willst do folgen klarer Spur.

Wann hat je ein Ziel ein Streben,
Wenn es schrankenlos die Welt
Seinem eignen kurzen Leben
Kühn und kräftig unterstellt?

Und wozo ein Kampf auf Erden
Wenn er nicht *ein* Ziel gewinnt:
Dass wir Alle froher werden,
Als wir waren, als wir sind?

"Freudig"—kämpft der Wahnbethörte
Und der Knecht auf blinder Spur.
Wer des Mitleids Stimmen hörte
Kämpft in herben Schmerzen nur.

Ueber Sterbende und Leichen
Wird vielleicht sein Wünschen gehn,
Und sein Ziel—er wird es welchen
Weit und immer weiter sehn.

The description of the fates of women, as illustrated in the characters contained in *Moderne Stoff* and *Helene*, is born of an infinite compassion.

These girls have nothing of dæmonic sensuality, nothing of the sentimentality of "fallen innocence" with which most writers love to invest such figures. They are poor, troubled, trembling, despairing slaves of the sin of others. It seems to me it might do many a young lady of the *bourgeoisie* a great deal of good to read the story of his Hedi, this Maxl', and the dance-hall singer Helene, in order to put aside her haughty scorn of such poor, dust-covered creatures.

Mackay has the gift of drawing the girls of the common people very attractively with the simplest means. The story of the brave little waitress Maxl' and her tragic defeat is a gem of modern narrative art. The cold scorn with which the well-bred hero Hans Grützmeier is described leads us to expect still more of the author in the domain of satire.

Larger in conception, more valuable by its form, and more overpowering by its glowing passion is the epic poem "Helene," written in blank verse.

It treats of the love of a young man of the upper classes for a girl who disappears after a chance acquaintance. And then he finds her again in the sad calling referred to above, which she took up not by choice, but into which deplorable conditions drove her.

Love, love, nothing but love! The exultation of young joy, sighs of languishing desire, wrestling with despair and newly-awakening pain of hope to the rage of the wildest passion! And then separation and her downfall—worse than death—and a curse shrieked into the air by the man who sees her drifting down the dark stream—ever farther and farther—and who stands on the shore and cannot help her.

What shall I say of the beauty of its lines, of its glow of passion, of its changing moods, of its climax? Whoever has lived through the heights and the depths of a great passion, will feel by the revival of all painful memories how true this book is;

and whoever does not know them—let him not read "Helene," for its contents will appear as madness to him.

The exception might be taken that the object of such a grand feeling is little worthy of it—but when did love ever go by the rule of middle-class respectability? Presumably the Levites and other distinguished personages of the people of Israel in their time also did not consider the shepherdess, to whom the royal singer, Solomon, dedicated his song, worthy of him. And yet it was the song of songs, and Shulamite became the symbol of the heavenly bride: every age has its typical heroine. The Middle Ages, where feudalism flourished, sang of queens; Beatrice and Laura were at least noble ladies.

When the *bourgeoisie* recalled its rights, and the clouds of the revolution of 1789 rose on the horizon, Lotte, the pure middle-class maiden, inflamed all hearts with emotion. Helene, the filth-covered, innocently ruined *proletaire* girl—will she not be the heroine of the threatening future?

That the heart of a son of the ruling caste, the caste which contributed no small part in causing her ruin, breaks for her, gives the poem the effect of deep tragedy.

"I have died, but I will live!" Mackay lets his hero say, after he has resigned youth and happiness. These words are fraught with a far-reaching significance.

A number of the men who are today undermining the *bourgeoisie* with their pencil and their pen, with their word and their brush, who are bringing to honor the rights of the fourth estate, be it through the artistic representation of its life, be it through unequivocal battle cries, are the defiant, spirited children of the fat and hoary bourgeoisie itself. Such is the Nemesis of universal history. Caesar died by the hand of Brutus—the absolutism of the Catholic Church was overthrown by a monk—and Mirabeau was a descendant of the French aristocracy. Almost always the insurgents have been nourished and equipped for their work with the best forces of the declining ruling classes.

The naturalistic, social artists and writers of the present time, too, have inherited from the bourgeoisie the results of science and the refined spirit which enables them, now that the age has opened their eyes, to feel the sufferings of their brothers so keenly and to depict them so powerfully.

A poet who with a creative imagination and the heart of a lover of mankind has made the studies that flowered in *Moderne Stoffe* and in *Helene* must be carried away to mad rebellion.

After Mackay could write *Helene*, he *must* write *Sturm*. And the poems of *Fortgang* are only the quieter intervals between the hurricane, the dying-away of it.

Mackay has broken with his past and with the old world. In Titanic wrath he shakes at the foundations on which society imagines that it lives securely. With sublime courage he hurls mighty war songs against a hated order of the world.

Of course the book was forbidden.

It is the right of civil society to defend itself by all means against an enemy who preaches the overthrow of all existing things in such magnificent language.

The melancholy gloom which broods over the songs of the *Fortgang*, the lamentations on the frigid loneliness in which the truth-seekers dwell, are only now comprehensible. We understand that, with this poet who is too deep, and with all his pity too proud to give himself over to the quickly changing favors of the masses, and who has forever broken with the applause of his own caste, they are no mere poetical figure, but bitter reality.

Fortgang is a serious, rich book, a treasure for uncommon people. The solitary observer acquires a keen glance for the events about him, in which he no longer takes an active part. The results of such observations are turned into bright, psychologically interesting little sketches by the poet of the *Fortgang*. Of these I enumerate the best: "*Ehe*" ("Marriage"), "*Die Knechtin*" ("The Hired Girl"), "*Der Wahre*" ("The True Man"), "*Fruhlingswind*" ("Spring Breezes"), "*Liebe*" ("Love"), "*In der Gesellschaft*" ("In Society").

There is in Mackay a peculiar blending of a clear, sceptical reason with an imagination soaring into the realms of the unknowable. His phantasies sometimes border on the morbid. Nevertheless, when he tries to banish them, the poet shows himself perhaps at his best.

A year after the four books just reviewed, Mackay published a small volume of translations from English and American poets. It contains much that is beautiful and successfully done; nevertheless—with the exception of Joaquin Miller's "Arizonian"—I cannot rate them as highly as Mackay's own poetical productions.

In the meantime Mackay made an acquaintance which had the greatest influence on him. The new edition of *Sturm* of 1890, which remained unmolested by the police, is dedicated to the memory of Max Stirner.

The highly significant, now almost forgotten book of this philosopher, *Der Einzige und sein Eigenthum*, must exert a saving influence on natures who are sick with an excess of the love of humanity and who yet understand that the sacrifice of their own personality not only does no good to anyone, but leads to deception and hypocrisy. Who has ever quite overcome his own self?

At bottom every largely endowed character with artistic talent is an individualist. If he wishes to be unusually true to himself and others, he will openly say so; and if he is at the same a thinker, he will try to put it into a system. Stirner, with his luminous demonstration of the right of egoism, could only offer to Mackay in a connected way what the latter had long ago experienced and even already expressed in his writings here and there.

The enthusiastic gratitude with which he recognized the master only shows that much-abused egoism does not necessarily make its disciples incapable of every so-called noble emotion.

Mackay says in the preface to the second edition of *Sturm*:—

Und langsam fand ich mich. Ein Jahr zerann
In letzten Kämpfen, bis ich mich gewann,
vom Nebel-Schleier war ich dicht umhüllt,
Von Rufen aus der Tiefe wild umbrüllt,
Höhen und Tiefen habe ich bezwungen.

It is very probable that the poet of *Sturm* was approached by the temptation of taking an active part in the social movement of our day.

But Mackay no longer believes in Utopias. As long as men do not make themselves inwardly free of illusions and prejudices of all kinds, outward liberty will be of little use to them.

Wenn Ihr die Stärkren geworden seid,
So seid Ihr in Eurem Rechte,

he exclaims to the dreamers.

The idea that Socialists and Communists might prepare a happy state for the people he opposes in the strongest terms in the following verses:—

—Wo ist dann Freiheit noch und wo Entfaltung,
Wenn Keiner sich mehr an dem Andren misst?

Was Staat jetzt heisst, wird dann Gemeinde heissen,
Der Einzelne wird mehr und mehr umengt,
Ihm ist versagt, sich los- und freizureissen,
Er ist in—Rosen-Ketten eingezwängt!

Die "Liebe" breitet ihres Mitleids Schwingen
Ueber der Tage unentschiedene Schlacht!
Sie lähmt dein Leben, meines Geistes Ringen;
Mein Lachen und dein weinen sind bewacht.

Und bleigrau-öde, trübe Langeweile
Sinkt auf die Welt herab ein Leichentuch,
Erfüllung hemmt des letzten Wunsches Eile
Und schliesst des Lebens unverstandnes Buch.

These words will hardly be pardoned to Mackay by the people whom they hit.

Thus he is separated from all parties, and it will be his fate to be much hated and little understood. He stands alone, as is his will, single and strong.

The last work with which John Henry Mackay has presented us bears the name *Das starke Jahr*. (Schabelitz, Zurich, 1890.)

The dedication of the poem reads:—

Dem gehassten Gefährten gehöre sein Werk.

Sturm gives us the answer thereto:—

Das ist der kampf, den allnächtlich
sevor das Dunkel zerrinnt,
Einsam und gramvoll auskämpft
Des Jahrhunderts verlorenes Kind.

Or is it that gloomy friend to whom the poet speaks:—

Reich mir die Hand, meiner Jugend Genosse, gewaltiger Schmerz!

The book consists of brilliant variations of the theme, "*Der Einige und sein Eigenthum.*" Stirner would be pleased with the fruits of his teachings. But the harvest is no longer his; it has become Mackay's own.

Only he alone—an idealist of materialism—could write such deep fancies on the right of the individual. It requires Mackay's courage of the truth to draw the last conclusions of one's philosophy with such a weirdly grand humor as is found in the poem "*Krähengekrächz*" ("The Cawing of the Crows")—to illustrate its dark side by a picture like "*Der Trinker*" ("The Drinker").

Some songs in which the wrestling with the unspeakable is not yet crowned by success, or which refer directly to experiences which the reader does not know, and which for this reason, despite his best efforts, remain obscure to him, might have better been omitted by the author. The fertile loneliness of the poet, the changing moods of the creative spirit, are sung with wonderful melody. Mackay finds touching expression, also for wild pleasure and the eternally wakeful longing after happiness.

How beautiful is the song, "*Frühlingsnacht*" ("Spring Night")! But little space is accorded to lore. It is the mature man who is talking here—the wise man, who introduces us like his pupil Walther to life's opulent feast, and whose "final perception" of the world is—

Einst wähnte ich sie zu verachten—
Ich verachte sie nicht mehr—
Ich kann nur noch betrachten—
Ich schaue um mich her—

Ich betrachte das Sein wie ein Haben,
Von dem kein Teil ich bin—
Ich bin mein—ich kann mich geben
Nicht mehr den Andern hin.

To what purpose any further quotations?

Whoever has recognized how rotten the pillars are which we commonly call "ideals" when the experiences of reality brutally rise against them—and who at the same time carries within him the unquenchable thirst for pondering on the riddles of human being, the great fate of the world—will find much in this book to move him and lead him by a rare perfection of form into a realm of serious, true beauty. "Das starke Jahr" will not capture the masses, but whoever has mastered it will find in it a true friend, and its influence will grow in the course of time.

On the last page of *Das starke Jahr* the publisher announces the early appearance of the novel, *Die Anarchisten*, by John Henry Mackay. With it the poet appears for the first time before the public with a prose work of this kind. One is curious to know how such an independent, courageous, and conscientious thinker will treat the question of the Anarchistic movement. And it will be interesting to see whether the lyric poet, the novelist, has grown into the mastery of the great picture of civilization.

John Henry Mackay the Writer:
Reflections on Characterization in His Novels and Tales[1]

Edward Mornin

John Henry Mackay's political, social, and philosophical views and their relationship to the ideas of Max Stirner and of Benjamin R. Tucker and other American anarchists have been summarized and discussed at length in the biographies of Thomas A. Riley[2] and K.H.Z. Solneman.[3] There would be little point, then, in my reiterating Mackay's ideas at length here. Instead, I would like to summarize briefly only the main features of his views as a background against which to discuss his novels and tales. For Mackay was not only an anarchist thinker and propagandist, but a creative writer (the author of five full-length prose works and of numerous tales and volumes of verse); and while these two functions, of propagandist and artist, do not contradict each other, they do often complement each other in an instructive fashion in his writings. Mackay philosophized on "the Individual" in general, but the characters in his works frequently deviate from what might be called "ideal models." An examination of his characters should tell us something about how he saw his ideas working in the real world around him. This in turn should serve as a commentary on his political-social ideas and throw light on his abilities as a writer, thus illuminating the interrelationship between propaganda and literature in his works.

Mackay's mature ideas are developed in their most programmatic form in *Die Anarchisten* (*The Anarchists*) (1891) and its companion work *Der Freiheitsucher* (*The Freedomseeker*) (1921), in passages of the novels *Fenny Skaller* (1913) and *Der Puppenjunge* (*The Hustler*) (1926), and in his autobiography *Abrechnung* (*Reckoning*) (1932). In these works, Mackay totally rejects the authority of the laws of State and Church over the individual. He also repudiates any claims that social custom or conventional morality might make upon him. Following Max Stirner of *The Ego and His Own* (1845), he asserts the fundamental egoism of all individuals and their absolute right to pursue egoistic goals, to seek happiness and develop as they please according to their own natures. And yet he does not see the social tyranny of the strong arising from this. According to Mackay, even the most powerful individuals will voluntarily restrict their own freedom-not because of duty, religion, or law (which are denied all validity), but because it is in their own interest. They will avoid offending or harming their fellows because they will not wish to provoke their anger or retaliation; and they will freely co-operate with others because it will be to their material advantage to do so. Stressing individualism and egoism, Mackay is at pains, particularly in *The Anarchists*, to distinguish between collectivist anarchistic communism on the one hand and anarchism pure and simple on the other (which he sometimes qualifies with the epithet "individualistic").

Now, it is obvious that the terms individualism, egoism, and anarchism do not coincide exactly. The individualist believes in the primacy of his person and of his personal desires and will. The egoist (in the Mackay-Stirnerian sense) believes that, like himself, all human beings are egoists motivated solely by selfish pleasure, whatever their claims to the contrary. The anarchist attempts to carry over into society what the individualist or egoist may be content to practice in private. Mackay himself was an anarchist, as are some of his most important characters. Many of his characters, however, are more specifically individualists or egoists. However, in so far as any person acting consistently out of self-interest must influence at least those members of society around him, he is an anarchist *avant le mot*. Consequently, what is said here about individualists and egoists as well as anarchists should contribute to a discussion of Mackay's individualist anarchist views in this broader sense.

Those characters who most completely embody Mackay's individualist anarchist ideas are Carrard Auban and Ernst Förster, the main figures in *The Anarchists* and *The Freedomseeker* respectively. Precisely because they are mainly embodiments, however, they are of little interest as characters or human beings. Mackay realized this, and that is why he insisted that these works should be judged as propaganda and not as "novels,"[4] *i.e.*, not as works of art. Nevertheless, *The Anarchists* and *Der Freiheitsucher* do employ techniques of the novel, including characterization, and contribute at least in part to an anarchist understanding of people as individuals responding differently to specific and changing problems. Auban and Förster are "model anarchists"; yet they have undergone personal experiences and possess character traits making them unique beings. Through this uniqueness, Mackay wished to emphasize that all people should not be forced into one mould, but should develop freely in accordance with their own natures.

The closest link between uniqueness of character and anarchist views occurs in *Fenny Skaller* and *The Hustler*, two very early examples of the homosexual novel in German. Fenny Skaller and Hermann Graff (the hero of *The Hustler*) find in anarchistic individualism the justification for feelings and behaviour which seem natural to them, yet are condemned by custom and the law. Like Auban and Förster, however, Skaller and Graff are largely idealized figures. They are intended as "models" and lack the conviction of real life.

The same might be said for the cold-blooded (and nameless) anarchist hero of the short tale *Ein glattes Geschäft, Eine anarchische Geschichte* (*A Simple Transaction: An Anarchist Story*) (1920). Here, in self defence, the hero kills a thief who is about to assault him with a murderous weapon, hides the body in the woods, and simply regards the case as closed. Through the portrayal of this kind of extreme situation, Mackay wished to demonstrate that neither law nor conventional ethics have any bearing on private matters between individuals.

Other tales by Mackay are important for the creative tension that they exhibit between the author's conception of how life could or should be and his realization of how it actually is. It is notable, for instance, that his individualists are not always appealing characters. Typical in this regard is Paul Jordans of *Existenzen* (*Empty Lives*) (1888). Jordans is an out-and-out individualist. He has been brought up in a ruthless love of truth; he is conscious of all people's fundamental egoism and of the hypocrisy with which they mask their selfish deeds; he accepts no guide to behaviour other than his own will; and he can see no ultimate purpose in life. Though he lacks neither intelligence nor education, he has sunk into a state of isolation and lethargy, becoming a pianist in a squalid Berlin night club, whose patrons, like everything and everyone else in his world, he despises and hates. Jordans tells the tale's narrator the story of his life, which culminates with his meeting Hedi, a night-club singer. Though believing he could never be permanently happy, Jordans had fallen in love with Hedi. Then, however, she was seduced by a degenerate night-club patron, a happening which Jordans might have prevented if he had felt that anything really mattered. Jordans had then expressed his contempt for the fallen Hedi, whereupon she left him forever. Jordans now realizes-too late-that he has destroyed his chances even of short-lived happiness through condemning Hedi in accordance with the bourgeois moral values he despises. His loathing and self-loathing reach new depths, and after telling the narrator his story, he disappears and is never seen again.

Jordans' tale may at first appear to illustrate the dangers of isolation and of a life lived without goals or love. This is how the narrator first understands it, though he also admires Jordans' loyalty to his own nature: "He had developed in such total freedom, had followed his innermost nature, as only few people can and may today." Being true to one's nature is the hallmark of the Mackay individualist from this, one of his earliest stories, to his last published tale, *Der Unschuldige* (*Innocent of Wrongdoing*) (1931). The narrator of *Existenzen*, who corresponds in part to Mackay in his pre-Stirner phase (the story was written in 1887 before he read Stirner), at first disapproves of Jordans' attitude. Then, after hearing Jordans' tale, he alters his standpoint. He learns to see "the monstrosity and vulgarity of all life," a new insight that is assessed wholly positively. Jordans has pointed the way to truth and to freedom from other people and their opinions, and the narrator resolves to follow this path. In the words of Jordans, "my life's happiness never resided in fun and merriment. I was happy when I was free. Any barrier to my freedom-that was unhappiness for me!" At the end, the narrator voices a similar view: "Some people strive only upward to the peaks of life, others strive only downward. But it is these who deepen their spiritual lives—who are driven relentlessly not to happiness, but to truth."

We can see in this early tale how Mackay (in the figure of the narrator) is on the way to developing the attitudes of his mature life. Yet how are we to interpret these attitudes? Must a life of truth and freedom necessarily lead to hatred, contempt and bitterness? Are truth and happiness forever incompatible? Mackay suggested as much when he chose as a motto for his autobiography the words: "To speak the truth does not bring happiness and fortune." Because his anarchist characters frequently reflect this view, they have probably contributed in part to the lack of success and popularity of Mackay's ideas.

It is important to realize, however, that Mackay was aware of the human shortcomings in characters who represent the individualist anarchist standpoint in his works. To be sure, he nowhere states this, but there are elements of irony in his works that suggest it. When we consider Franz Grach in *Menschen der Ehe* (*Married People*) (1892), for example, it is difficult not to feel that Mackay saw his anarchist hero fall short of being a wholly admirable person. I cannot agree with Riley, who sees Grach as a "glittering example of what a man can be."[5] Grach has returned to his hometown after years of absence during which he has developed anarchist views. Observing the absurdities of provincial life around him, he is moved to laughter. Yet his laughter is not good-humoured, but bitter. Like Paul Jordans, Grach speaks in a "pitilessly clear and cutting voice." The author's awareness of the undesirability of this is given through his accounting for it: "He had been so long accustomed to speaking as he really thought that he had forgotten how to mould his thoughts to the ear of his listeners." Grach's frankness, of which he is so proud, expresses itself too in impoliteness to his step-sister's servant. Such impoliteness receives no commentary, but Mackay cannot have approved of it, as we realize when we recall the warm and generous treatment accorded to his servant by the appealing individualist hero of the story *Der Sybarit* (*The Sybarite*) (1896). The author's awareness of the price that might be exacted for an anarchist's life of independence and revolt is suggested also through Dora Syk, who becomes Grach's companion at the end of this tale. When Grach meets Dora she is still a beautiful woman, but, we read: "This beautiful mouth was beginning to close in bitterness and pride. These deep eyes were already sunken and dark." Mackay, then, saw the difference between the theory of anarchism, based on our search for happiness, and its practice, which may (but need not) bring bitterness and loneliness.

Mackay put much of himself into his characters. Their isolation, bitterness, and even their hatreds, were part of his own experience, as is clear to any reader of *Reckoning*. His was not the sort of temperament that would allow him to take life lightly, and his homosexuality was a constant source of conflict between him and society. His misanthropic tendencies, his individualism, and his anarchism reinforced each other. Yet it would be wrong to regard him or his characters as only morose and resentful. Life and the enjoyment of life were of prime importance for him, too. Mackay struggled against despair, and perhaps more important than the achievement of happiness was his ability to accept life in its totality, the suffering with the joy.

Affirmation of life is not absent from Mackay's writings, and indeed he has consciously attempted to come to terms with his recurrent pessimism in what is perhaps his most delightful and optimistic tale, *The Sybarite*. In this story the narrator meets an old man by the name of Germann, whose first words are "What a pleasure!-What a pleasure!" and whose life is devoted to giving himself and others joy. He has a home furnished with great comfort and taste; he eats and drinks well, but in moderation; and he loves to travel. In the physical circumstances of life, and in his habit of swimming daily, he resembles Mackay himself. The narrator of the story, though a very different type, also resembles Mackay. Germann calls him "my bitter friend," and he knows him as a writer of books—"what sad books!" Germann reproaches him with making himself unhappy: "And you, who are a poet, how rich you are, and yet you delude yourself into thinking that you are poor and that the world is empty!" The narrator is involved in the political and social struggles of the age, as Mackay had been, and witnessing the old man's happiness he is filled with sorrow that his own life knows so much frustration. Germann is an egoist and he expounds Stirner's philosophy, though without naming him. He has achieved happiness through following his own desires and refusing to impose his will on others. In order to pursue his own interests he has abandoned his work (he had been a successful businessman) and left his wife and children after dividing his wealth among them and himself. The story is largely in dialogue form, and since Mackay has put himself into both the narrator and Germann, the effect is of a dialogue between Mackay the optimist and Mackay the pessimist. It is little wonder that this was Mackay's favourite among his stories, and its ending expresses more clearly than anything else he wrote that happiness for him implied not the pursuit of an epicurean life, but a life devoted to work, which for him meant the dissemination of anarchist ideas. In the words of the narrator: "I pondered and pondered and slowly I found my way back out of this stranger's life into my own life again. And when I was in possession of myself again, I had grown calmer, for I knew again, as I know today, that for me life is my work and that I have to torture myself with it until my end and that this torture is my happiness and my only happiness."

"*Herkulische Tändeleien*" (*Herculean Triflings*) (1904) is another story whose characterization shows Mackay's awareness of the compatibility of individualist freedom and joy. The central figure, Karl Ettermann, is a nonconformist. Like an anarchist (though not a conscious one), he has introduced mutualism and self-government into the factory that he owns, and he mixes with all social classes in the little German town where he settles for a time. Having grown tired of his wife, he arranges for his secret disappearance. Pretending to have drowned in Lake Constance, he actually makes off with his own share of the family fortune that he had helped to amass. Ettermann is not as brutally frank as Mackay's model anarchists Auban or Förster can be. He does not, for instance, tell his wife that he is leaving her. Yet he does not play-act out of fear or hypocrisy, but because it is in his nature to be mysterious and adventurous. Despite certain melodramatic features in the tale, Ettermann is an engaging character, and important because he combines Stirnerian egoism with a superabundant lust for life.

In some other tales Mackay even goes so far in his affirmation of life as to portray characters who, far from exemplary anarchists, actually flout values that he was prepared to affirm. This is the case in the three tales *Der Stärkere* (*The Victor*) (1904), *Samuel Goteswilens letzter Gang* (*Samuel Goteswilen's Last Journey*) (1910), and *Der große Coup* (*The Big Job*) (1924). The central figure of *The Victor*, who is presented in a positive light, obtains 8,000 francs from the management of the Monte Carlo Casino simply by threatening to commit suicide in a public room if his demands are not met. Mackay of course is not defending or recommending blackmail or any other kind of crime here as a means of achieving life's goals. Indeed, he speaks explicitly against crime in *The Anarchists* and *The Freedomseeker*. Non-violent crime of this sort may, however, have exercised something of a fascination over him. Mackay was not so naïve as to believe anarchism would bring about heaven and earth, and he seems to be experimenting here with ideas on the fringe of his philosophy.

The Big Job shows a similar fascination with an amoral character. The hero of this tale is an egoist in the Mackay-Stirnerian mould, acting on the conviction that all people are basically egoists like himself. He is a lone wolf who makes a living by burglary on a grand scale, usually in exclusive hotels where he also spends his gains, for he possesses impeccable taste. What is interesting about this thief is that he plays the game of life according to rules. There is an unwritten agreement between himself and society that he will rob only the wealthy and will not complain if he ever gets caught. Hardly the sort of egoist likely to gain acceptance for Mackay's ideas! And yet this character shows that Mackay was more than a theorist. He saw how egoistic ideas might be put into practice in a variety of ways, and *not* always for the benefit of society. And, strangely enough, the egoist as thief here possesses a candor and vitality, and indeed a certain charm, that make him much more appealing than his law-abiding victims.

Mackay is seen in a positive mood also in *Samuel Goteswilen's Last Journey*, a tale whose hero is an old Jewish pedlar, a man of independence and (above all) individuality. Samuel is something of a sharpster and gives an example of his trickery when he wheedles a mark out of a tourist in a railway station. He obtains the mark ostensibly to pay for his train fare, though he intends to continue on foot, and he is highly amused at the tourist's silly face when he departs leaving Samuel behind on the platform. This character, with the little deceits that he employs to make a living, is portrayed sympathetically and humorously, and in such a way as to amount to an affirmation of an individualistic life even in its somewhat dubious aspects.

Being true to one's nature has been stated above to be *the* hallmark of moral authenticity in a Mackay character. As has been seen, this does not necessarily lead to happiness in the usual sense. *Innocent of Wrongdoing* shows how far short of conventional fulfillment loyalty to one's nature might bring one. Heinz von Solden, the central figure in this tale, is a handsome young student of moral and artistic refinement who aspires to becoming a great art historian. By chance he witnesses a murder, but rather than risk involvement with the police, which he considers sordid, he runs away. His landlady, who thinks him guilty of the murder, then forces him into a degrading sexual relationship with her, from which he escapes only once the actual culprit has been arrested. Through this experience von Solden comes to realize the limitations of his refinement and moral courage, and decides to live within these limits. Instead of marrying the girl he loves, he remains a bachelor, lonely and withdrawn, and never writes the epoch-making book on art that he had planned. The story possesses particular interest because von Solden's life is seen through the eyes of two narrators. Narrator 1 first censures von Solden as a weakling, but is made to change his mind by Narrator 2, who actually tells him von Solden's story:

> No, he wasn't a weakling. He was courageous, courageous and clever. He possessed a higher kind of courage—namely, the courage to acknowledge his self, his self as it simply was. He possessed the courage to run away, instead of staying and letting himself be butchered.... He possessed this courage...to withdraw from the judgement of others by not recognizing it and to live his own life.

Perhaps one could take Narrator 2's response to Narrator 1's question as to whether von Solden was unhappy as Mackay's assessment of his own life's happiness: "Unhappy?—No, he wasn't unhappy.... But what's the point of the question anyway? Happy or not happy—he had sought the limits of his own nature and lived within them."

As a writer, Mackay was concerned not only to show individualists or anarchists who had fought their way to a clear understanding of their situation and to a position of freedom. His works also portrays failures, like Franz Felder in *Der Schwimmer* (*The Swimmer*) (1901) or Albert Schnell in *Die letzte Pflicht* (*Last Respects*) (1893) and *Albert Schnells Untergang* (*Albert Schnell's Downfall*) (1895). My discussion will conclude with a few remarks on these two characters.

Franz Felder, the son of a poor family in Berlin's east end, is a born swimmer. He is recruited into an exclusive swim club, which accepts even working-class lads if they promise enough for the club and the cause of swimming. The club moulds Franz, not only by training him, but by finding him work, teaching him manners, giving him friends, etc. Franz becomes club champion, then with great rapidity the champion of Berlin, Germany, Europe, and the world. Once he has reached the pinnacle of success, however, he abandons his original modesty and humility and begins to assert himself in his club. Yet he does so in such a graceless manner that he alienates himself from the other members. Resigning his membership, he continues to compete, first with another club and later as an unattached swimmer, but he longs to be accepted by his own club-mates again. They reject him, however, for succeeding on his own. Franz is financially dependent and is neither especially intelligent nor especially charming. He aspires to independence and self-assertion, but is too weak to survive on his own. In despair at being rejected by his club, he commits suicide in the end. Franz is a failed individualist, really, and serves as yet another comment by Mackay on the problematical situation of the individual in society. If they lack the courage or ability to survive alone, individuals may find desolation or death through asserting themselves by overstepping the limits of their nature.

Unlike Franz Felder, Albert Schnell never aspires to any sort of independence or individuality. Schnell is a schoolteacher in provincial Prussia, husband and father, a Christian, dutiful, compassionate, and self-effacing. He possesses the slave mentality against which Mackay constantly set himself. At the beginning of *Last Respects* Schnell visits Berlin in order to assist an old university friend, Karl Bergmann, but is on time only to arrange for his funeral. This Bergmann is an individualist, a scorner of religion, law, and convention who has sunk into the mire of Berlin and is on the point of committing suicide when he is accidentally run over by a carriage. He represents the opposite extreme from Schnell, who is virtually dominated by the memory of his dead friend. In *Albert Schnell's Downfall*, a sequel to *Last Respects*, Schnell moves from the provinces to Berlin, partly because of the memory of Bergmann, and partly to be close to a Dr. Hertwig, a strong-willed, individualistic friend of Bergmann's. Schnell's position quickly becomes intolerable in its isolation, an isolation relieved only through his (rather lukewarm) acceptance by the late Bergmann's friends. Estrangement from his relatives and from his own self-respect comes when he falls into the power of a prostitute who moves into his apartment and refuses to leave. Humiliated and powerless, and believing he is being summoned by the dead Bergmann, Schnell attempts suicide by drowning, but, inept to the last, fails in his attempt, though he dies of the after-effects. Now, one might think that Mackay's depiction of these characters would accord with the extent to which they conform to an egoistic philosophy, but this is only partly so. Bergmann, to be sure, has every right to follow the path of self-destruction if he so wishes; but he cannot serve as a positive model for the reader. Dr. Hertwig plays only a peripheral role in the story, and though he is respected and successful, he lacks (rather like Franz Grach) the human warmth which might recommend his philosophy to us. Schnell, for all his weakness, and despite the occasional sarcasm with which Mackay treats him, is a sympathetically portrayed figure. It seems to me that Riley over-interprets and underestimates Schnell in the light of Mackay's more theoretical anarchist works, when he writes: "Schnell is...in Mackay's eyes contemptible. The egoist, Dr. Hertwig, master of life, is twice the man Schnell is; Bergmann, terribly battered by life, but laughing in scorn to the very end, is three times the man Schnell is.... We must take everything that Schnell does and says as weak and despicable."[6] The actual characterization of Schnell will not stand up to such harsh evaluation; and this is because Mackay is not only a propagandist, but an artist. There is in this tale tension and contrast between the philosophy of anarchistic individualism (enunciated by Bergmann) and Mackay's actual characterization of Schnell, Bergmann, and Hertwig. These characters are not embodied ideas; they act like real persons. Except for Auban, Förster, Skaller, Graff, and the hero of *A Simple Transaction*, Mackay's characters cannot be satisfactorily understood exclusively in relation to his political and social convictions. His works present highly differentiated human beings: heroes, villains, and victims, certainly; but also philosophically sound characters with human failings and philosophically dubious characters with human warmth. If one approaches Mackay's literary works either too exclusively as documents of anarchism or as strictly peripheral to his propagandistic work, one may overlook this fact. Solneman underrates the philosophical implications of Mackay's creative works when he speaks against the "emphasis on his creativity, which constitutes only one side of his being."[7] Certainly, our understanding of Mackay's art is and should be enriched by a knowledge of his philosophy; but the humanity and depth of his philosophy will be missed if we fail to see how it is tempered by his art and in particular by his art of characterization in his novels and tales.

Notes

1. I am indebted to *Seminar: A Journal of Germanic Studies* for permission to republish here some material that first appeared in *Seminar* in 1982.
2. Thomas A. Riley, *Germany's Poet-Anarchist John Henry Mackay*. New York: Revisionist Press, 1972.
3. K. H. Z. Solneman, *Der Bahnbrecher John Henry Mackay*. Freiburg/Br.: Mackay-Gesell., 1979.
4. John Henry Mackay, *Abrechnung. Randbemerkunger zu Leben und Arbeit*, 3rd edn. (Freiburg/Br.: Mackay-Gesellchaft, 1978), p. 74.
5. Riley, *Germany's Poet-Anarchist*, p. 89.
6. Riley, *Germany's Poet-Anarchist*, pp. 91-2.
7. Solneman, p. 88.

THE EDITIONS OF *THE ANARCHISTS*

HUBERT KENNEDY

IN AN APPENDIX TO HIS *Werke in einem Band* (1928), Mackay numbered the German editions of *Die Anarchisten* and reported the number of copies printed in each edition; this information is given below. He also wrote: "*Die Anarchisten* has been translated into seven languages; there have appeared: an American edition (as first), two French, one each of Dutch and Italian, two Russian, a Swedish and a Czech-altogether, nine non-German editions." Of these, I have seen only the American, the first French, and the two Russian editions. I have been unable to find any information on a second French edition; information on the editions I have not seen is taken from national book catalogs. Curiously, Mackay failed to mention the translation into Yiddish, which I have seen.

In German:
Die Anarchisten. Kulturgemälde aus dem Ende des XIX. Jahrhunderts.
1st ed. Zurich: Verlags-Magazin (J. Schabelitz), 1891. (xi+370 pp.) (1,500)

2nd ed. [People's Edition]. Berlin: Magazin für Volkslitteratur (F. Harnisch), 1893 and 1895. (5,000)

This edition has a new preface and, as noted in it, a couple of lines were added to the text for clarification.

3rd ed. [Definitive Edition]. Berlin: Schuster und Loeffler, 1903. (2000)

4th ed. *Gesammelte Werke*, vol. 8. Berlin: B. Zack, 1911. (1,000)

[Separate Edition]. Berlin: B. Zack, 1912. (1,000)
Prepared simultaneously with that in *Gesammelte Werke* and identical to it.

5th ed. Berlin-Fichtenau: Verlag der Neuen Gesellschaft, 1924. (2,000)

6th ed. In *Werke in einem Band.* Berlin: Stirner Verlag, 1928. (5,000)

In an appendix to this volume Mackay wrote that the text of this edition "presents the result of a new, comprehensive revision." The changes are many-in comparing the first ten pages with the Definitive Edition I count over a dozen changes-but appear to be only stylistic, not affecting the translation into English.

7th ed. Freiburg/Br.: Verlag der Mackay-Gesellschaft, 1976. Also later editions.

In Translation:

The Anarchists: A Picture of Civilization at the Close of the Nineteenth Century. Translated by George Schumm. Boston: Benj. R. Tucker, 1891.

Anarchistes; moeurs du jour. Translated by Louis de Hessem. Paris: Tresse & Stock, 1892. (ix+420 pp.) (French).

In an autobiographical sketch in the Definitive Edition Mackay wrote that his work was translated into French "not without forbearance of great errors and under a mutilated translation of the title." (The subtitle "moeurs du jour" is literally "customs of the day.")

De anarchisten. Een tafereel uit het eind van de 19e eeuw. Amsterdam: J. Sterringa, 1896. (Dutch).

Anarchisté. Kulturni obrazy z konce XIX. století. Translated by V. Skruzny. Prague: Bibliotéka Vzdˇelavaci, (1896?). (369 pp.) (Czech).

Obshchestvennyya techeniya zapada-kontsa XIX v. Osuzhdennye ba Chikago. Translated from the French by O. Oblomievskoi and S. Shteinberg. St. Petersburg: N. P. Karbasnikov, 1901. (99 pp.) (Russian)

A translation of parts of the French edition above.

Anarkhisty; kartiny nravov kontsa XIX veka. St. Petersburg: S. E. Korenev, 1906. (285 pp.) (Russian).

Di anarkhisten. Kultur bilder fun suf 19-ten yahrhundert. Translated by Abraham Frumkin. With a foreword by Rudolf Rocker. London: "Arbeter Fraint," 1908-1910. (449 pp.) (Yiddish).

The Arbeter Fraint was a Yiddish paper published for workers in the East End of London. Mackay described it on page 183 of The Anarchists where, already in the German edition, he gave it the English name "The Worker's Friend." Rudolf Rocker was editor of the paper at the time this translation was published. Abraham Frumkin was a prolific translator of both the European classics and radical literature into Yiddish.

Anarkisterna; kulturskildrin fran slutet av XIX jarhundradet. Stockholm: Axel Holmström, 1910-1911. (407 pp.) (Swedish).

Gli anarchici, quadro della fine del XIX secolo. Translated by P. Flori. Milano: Casa editrice sociale (A. Ghio), 1921. (331 pp.) (Italian).

Mackay wrote (in English) to Benjamin Tucker on 22 May 1921 from Riva, Italy: "At Milan I visited a man, who wanted to translate three of my books in the Italian. He was sick then, but he came to Florence to see me. He is an extremely nice and clever young fellow, with name Marnoni; he paid me at once 1000 lire for one edition of 2000 copies of *The Anarchists.*" But this translation appears to be the only result of their meeting.

De anarchisten. (Holland). Bibliotheek voor Ontspanning en Ontwikkling (Gerhard Rijnders), 1927. (Pirate edition, Dutch).

Mackay Society

Books for Freedomseekers

These books and booklets are from various publishers, some are in short supply, and some are old and rare.

Books by John Henry Mackay

The Anarchists $12
The Freedomseeker $12
The Hustler $15
Fenny Skaller $25

Other Items

The Storm! A Journal for Free Spirits #16/17
John Henry Mackay Festschrift, $6

Anarchist of Love: The Secret Life of John Henry Mackay
by Hubert Kennedy.
Booklet, $4

John Henry Mackay: The Unique
by K.H.Z. Solneman.
Booklet, $2

Manifesto of Peace and Freedom
by K.H.Z. Solneman.
Paperback, $10

Slaves to Duty
by John Badcock, Jr.
Rare 1938 Laurance Labadie edition
booklet, $15

Benjamin R. Tucker and the Champions of Liberty
edited by Michael E. Coughlin, Charles H. Hamilton, and Mark A. Sullivan.
Paperback, $15; hardcover, $20

Liberty: Not the Daughter but the Mother of Order.
Original copies of Tucker's famous journal, published from 1881 to 1908.
Assortment of 10 issues, $25
Assortment of 20 issues, $40
Final issue added to selection, $10

Set of Three German Translations of Tucker Essays by Mackay
Booklets, $10

Prices and availability subject to change; please contact Autonomedia for availability
Please make checks out to Autonomedia

Mackay Society c/o Autonomedia
PO Box 568, Williamsburgh Station
Brooklyn, NY 11211-0568
phone/fax (718) 963-2603
www.autonomedia.org